"A rogue homicide detective is assigned to a grisly murder case, and through the investigation discovers core life values that overturn his world. Bertrand's first novel is an astonishing and powerful mystery. Extremely well-crafted."

—**Davis Bunn,** bestselling author of *Lion of Babylon*

"Bertrand's got a pitch-perfect ear for dialogue. The cop-talk, for fans of the tough guy genre, hits the right note every time. . . . Each sentence builds anticipation; each scene leads deeper into the distinct but converging crimes."

—*Comment*

"In comparison to many crime series protagonists, Roland March is cast on a refreshingly human scale."

—*Books & Culture*

"The first paragraph makes you feel like an astronomer discovering a growing brightness in an unmapped area of the sky, and as you continue you get the excitement of realizing you're the first to witness a supernova, and there's no way you're going to take your eyes off it until it's finished. The story and writing is that good. Give me more."

—**Sigmund Brouwer**, author of *Broken Angel*

"With exquisite prose and poetic style, Mark Bertrand has captured the surreal world of homicide detectives with a realism and power rarely seen in fiction."

—**Mark Mynheir**, homicide detective, author of *The Night Watchman*

"One of the strengths of this excellent novel is the credibility of this rogue detective's voice."

—*CBA Retailers and Resources*

For my parents,
David and Judy.
So much love, so much support.

PART 1

BYSTANDER

SATURDAY, DECEMBER 5 — TUESDAY, DECEMBER 8

. . . the shadow was there already.

—GRAHAM GREENE, *OUR MAN IN HAVANA*

CHAPTER 1

A uniform named Nguyen is on the tape tonight. The flashing lights bounce off the reflective strips on his slicker. He cocks his head at my ID and gives me a sideways smile.

"Detective March," he says, adding my name to his log.

"I know you, don't I? You worked the Thomson scene last year."

"That was me."

"Good work, if I remember. You got a line on this one yet?"

"I haven't even been inside." He nods at the house over his shoulder. A faux Tuscan villa on Brompton in West University, just a couple of blocks away from the Rice Village. "Nice, huh? Not the first place I'd expect to be called out to."

"You think death cares where you live?"

"I guess not. Answer me one thing: why the monkey suit?"

My hand-me-down tux, now speckled with light rain, stretches the definition of plainclothes. "It's a busy night, Nguyen, so they're pulling from off duty. They caught me at the wife's office Christmas gig. That snow yesterday drove the city a little crazy."

"Snow in Houston. Who woulda thought? But still—"

"I have a feeling the vic's not gonna mind."

"It's not the vic I'm thinking of."

He lifts the tape and I slip under, traipsing across the wet lawn.

The past ten years or so, deluxe mansions like this have proliferated. Stone and stucco. Tile roofing. Driveways of textured concrete. They're cropping up in the Heights, too. My neighborhood. At least they were before the market nosedived. Now the only thing proliferating are the foreclosure signs.

I pause inside the wood-and-glass double doors to shake the rain off my jacket, staring out at a sea of travertine newly muddied by a trail of HPD boot prints. All the lights are on. Wrought-iron chandeliers. Antique-looking lamps on side tables tucked in between an island of oversized couches. Through an arched partition I see more furniture and a floor-to-ceiling bookcase packed to the limit. What I don't see are any police.

"Hello?"

A familiar voice calls: "Come on back, March."

Passing through nested living rooms and a modern steel-and-marble kitchen, I find a cluster of patrol officers facing a set of sliding glass doors. One of them is my old mentor, Sergeant Nixon, long in the tooth but canny as ever.

"Look who's here," he says, motioning me over. "They must've run out of detectives and sent us the Phantom of the Opera."

I glance down at my tux. "That bad?"

"What were you shooting for, dressed like that? James Bond?"

"Now you're just hurting my feelings, Nix. What's the situation here? Get me up to speed already."

He taps the glass door. "Out there's the scene. Body's half in the water. We're still waiting on everything—CSU, ME, you name it—but supposedly they're on the way. I kept my people inside, figuring you'd be happier that way. And it saves us from getting wet."

I squint through the rain-streaked pane. A long, narrow swimming pool glows aqua in the darkness, an inky cloud floating near one side, transected by a pair of pale, bare legs. The rest of the body, the part out of the water, is hard to make out.

"I'll get the lights," Nix says.

He flips a wall switch, activating a hedge of lamps planted around the edge of the yard. Some Christmas lights draped around a pergola start blinking, too.

I can see her now, facedown on the gray slate, her arms stretched out like she's reaching for something. Her skin shines bone white apart from the pattern of wounds flaying her back.

"I'm gonna take a look."

I deposit my battered leather briefcase on the kitchen island, then slide the door open to slip outside. Nixon follows me.

"Watch where you step."

He sighs. "Will do."

From inside, she looked naked, but as we edge closer I make out a pair of white shorts soaked through and tinted pink with blood. The waistband tepees out at the small of her back. Puncture wounds, long and thin, run up and down her spine and across the shoulders, too many to count. The kind a kitchen knife might make. Neat, too. In and out. Inflicted postmortem, probably, or they wouldn't be so uniform.

We crouch a few feet away.

Her brown hair is still damp, the tangled locks arranged to leave her face clear. One cheek pressed to the slate, the other waxy and pearlescent with rain. Her eyelids gently shut like they might blink open at any time. Like she might notice us suddenly and cover herself in embarrassment.

"She's young," I say.

"Twenty-four. Her name is Simone Walker. She was sort of a live-in houseguest here, helped out with the rent. The owner called in the body. Says she came home and found the girl like this. I've got her upstairs waiting to talk with you."

"Do me a favor, Nix. Cut the Christmas lights."

The swimming pool is special, not the square slab of chlorinated blue you see out in the suburbs. This one's long and thin, hedged with gray slate, concealed from the neighbors by the height of the house and a perimeter of tall fences lined with taller vegetation. At the back of the yard, a door leads into a cottage-sized garage. This isn't a crime scene. It's the cover of an architectural magazine. Like Nguyen said, not the kind of place you expect to be called to. Maybe death doesn't care where you live, but murder does. A lot.

I bend down, breaking the surface of the water with my fingertips. It's forty degrees outside in Houston, just a day after our unprecedented, seemingly impossible snowfall. But the water is warm to the touch. Of course it is. A heated pool.

Something under the water catches my eye. Beneath the ripple of light rain, at the shimmering bottom of the pool, one of the chairs from the set under the pergola lies on its side. An expensive sort of chair, metal framed with hardwood slats, the kind my wife would buy in a heartbeat if her old-money ancestors hadn't also passed down the miserly gene.

The Christmas lights cut off and Nix returns.

"What do you make of *that?*" I ask, pointing into the pool.

"Got me. Don't they tell people to put the lawn furniture in the pool when a hurricane's coming? To keep it from flying around or something."

"You think they were expecting a hurricane?"

He shrugs. "You're the detective."

The glass doors slide open and a uniform sticks his head out. "Crime scene van just rolled up, Sarge."

"I'm coming."

"Listen, Nix," I say, touching his arm. "It's bad enough I've got an outdoor scene, and rain on top of that. But people are gonna start showing up, and they'll all want a look at the body—"

"Say no more. Necessary personnel only."

He goes inside, leaving me alone. The glass door closes and for a moment the world is quiet. I glance around. As far as I can tell, everything looks right. The body's been posed, the scene has been arranged, but even that isn't so unusual. Apart from the chair, it's all what I'd expect to see. But it doesn't feel right and I don't know why.

★

Upstairs a female officer baby-sits the homeowner, a tall, thin woman in her mid-fifties dressed in a clingy black sweater and dark jeans. She stands at the window in the corner of a paper-strewn home office, peering down at the street outside, arms crossed, a pair of glasses dangling from one hand. The uniform looks relieved at my presence.

"Dr. Hill," she says, "this is the detective."

The woman turns, inspecting me through narrow eyes. Her lined face is scrubbed of makeup and framed by a severe black bob, the sharp fringe cutting across her eyebrows.

"I'm Roland March."

I hand her one of my cards, pausing to write my mobile number on the back. A ritual of introduction, performed by rote a dozen times a day. She studies the writing, then motions me into a nearby chair currently occupied by a tower of reference books.

"You can move those," she says.

I get the books sorted and prop my briefcase against the chair leg, its worn sides drooping miserably, the leather spotted with dried water. A gift from my wife years ago. The key long since missing, the lock broken, the flap held down by wraparound straps. Digging inside, I retrieve my equally battered Filofax, another of Charlotte's gifts.

"Do people still use these things?" the woman says. She reaches forward and snatches it away. "It was such a Yuppie affectation." She thumbs the snap open to look inside. "I thought everything was digital these days."

"Excuse me, ma'am." I hold my hand out politely.

"Sorry," she says, closing the binder and snapping it shut. "That's a bad idea, isn't it? Grabbing things from the police. But it's not like I took your gun or anything."

She speaks in a low, gravelly tone I've always found strangely attractive, one of those scotch-and-cigarettes voices, minus the foreign accent.

"It's okay," I say, opening the Filofax flat on my lap, turning to a fresh page. I take my digital recorder out, too, proving I'm not such a dinosaur. Frankly the Filofax is an affectation, something I found in an old box and decided to put back into service, handier than the usual notepads when it comes to arranging and rearranging pages. Unlike the recorder, it never needs recharging, either.

"Just have a seat for me, ma'am. I need to ask you some questions about the victim."

"I don't think I can sit. I can't stop moving. I've been pacing a hole in the carpet. I'll go crazy if you make me sit still."

"Suit yourself."

She eyes the female officer with uncertainty, then lets out a long breath. "I'm sorry, Detective. I'm making a mess of this. Can we start over, please? I don't want you to get the wrong idea. I'm Joy Hill."

She extends her hand, then pulls it back, uncertain of the etiquette where policemen are concerned.

"What's the wrong idea you don't want me to get?"

"I'm making the wrong impression, that's all I mean. You're thinking I should be distraught and instead here I am running at the mouth. I can't help it. I was raised not to show people how I feel. I keep it bottled up until—is it all right if I smoke?"

"If it'll help."

She retrieves a pack of Dunhills from the desk, along with a glass ashtray, bringing both to a chair just across from me, finally sitting. She flicks a fresh filter half out of the pack, then pulls it free with her teeth. The lighter's in the ashtray. A metallic ping, a flash of fire, and then she exhales a column of smoke. A smile comes to her lips.

"What's funny?"

"I don't let anyone smoke in the house," she says.

And yet she keeps a pack handy all the same. "All right, let's get started. It's *Dr.* Joy Hill, right? And you're a doctor of what?"

"Literature."

"Hence all the books. You teach where?"

"At UH," she says. Then, catching my reaction: "It's a good school, Detective. A good department. People think we're handing out fast-food diplomas to a commuter population, but it's not like that at all."

"You don't have to convince me. I went there."

"And studied what? Criminal Justice."

"Worse," I say. "History. The victim, Simone Walker, she rented a room from you?"

"Rooms," she says. "Basically, we drew a line down the middle of the upstairs. I kept the master and my office, and gave her the other bathroom and the guest bedrooms. You probably know about my husband already. No? He met his soul mate a year ago and started fathering her children, but he left me the house."

"So you knew Ms. Walker from where?"

She glances at the ceiling. "A friend introduced us, I think. This was maybe seven or eight months ago. I was looking for a roommate and Simone wanted to move out on her own. She had marriage trouble, too."

"Divorced?"

"Not as far as I know. She pretty much operated like a single girl, though, if that's what you're wondering. I assume they were legally separated, but it's not something we ever talked about."

"What's her husband's name?" I ask, my pen poised.

Again she looks at the ceiling. "Jason Young. Walker was her maiden name. She moved her things in around the end of last semester—during finals, actually."

"Where did she work?"

"Ah," she says, templing her fingers. "That's a good question. Simone changed jobs pretty frequently, and for the last month or two I don't think she had one. I suspected something was going on, but then she confirmed it by asking for money. The whole point of having her here was to make money, not hand it out. Anyway, I said I couldn't help her. She found other sources eventually."

"We'll come back to that," I say, glancing at my watch. "But I need to know what happened today, the events leading up to your discovery of the body."

She pauses to think. "I saw her this morning around ten. I was leaving and she'd just rolled out of bed. She told me she was having lunch with a girlfriend, then spending the rest of the day in the pool. I said she was crazy. I mean, it was *snowing* yesterday. But she's, like, so what? The pool's heated."

"Did she say who she was meeting?"

Dr. Hill stubs her cigarette out, then sets the ashtray on the floor. "She didn't say, and I didn't ask. I had an appointment on campus, so I was a bit rushed. Anyway, this was her crash pad, Detective. She liked to play music, she liked to watch TV, and she liked to swim. When she went shopping—which she did a lot—this is where she'd dump her stuff. But mostly she went out. I told her she could have friends over, but she didn't. I don't know why."

I can think of a few reasons. "So you came home at what time?"

"After dark, maybe seven? I parked in the garage and used the door into the backyard. The pool light was on, and then I saw her. I froze." Her eyes get an unfocused, faraway look. "I kept willing her to *move*. But she was dead, I could see that. So I went back the way I came and I called 9-1-1."

"From the garage?"

"No," she says. "I went all the way around to the front door, let myself in, and then went to the kitchen where I could see her. I don't know why, but that's where I called from. To keep an eye on her, I guess."

"All right, ma'am." I tuck my pen away and drop the Filofax into my briefcase. "I'm going to ask you to show me where Ms. Walker's bedroom is, and then we'll have you wait with the officer awhile. I'm sure we'll have more questions in a little bit."

She beats me to the door, only too happy to be up and moving again. We pass the grand stairway and I get an earful of chatter from downstairs, signifying the arrival of more personnel. I recognize one of the voices: Lieutenant Bascombe, my boss. Dr. Hill continues down a white-paneled hallway, pausing at an open door.

"This is her bedroom."

Inside is a double bed, the covers hanging off the side, two tall dressers, and an overflowing laundry hamper. A stack of cardboard boxes in one corner. A vanity with stickers around the mirror, a blow drier and curling iron with their cords intertwined.

"Her mother lives in town," she says. "Somewhere around Piney Point, I think. Someone will have to call her. Is that something you'll do?"

"We can do that."

In the closet, a score of tightly packed clothing bags hang in disarray. The floor is lined with rope-handled shopping bags of every size and color. On the shelf over the rod, shoe boxes are packed three or four high.

"It might be better coming from you," she says. "I only met the woman once, but we didn't get on too well. I'd say she's a hard woman to like, which is probably why she and Simone weren't very close."

The room smells of perfume. On the vanity I see half a dozen designer scents to choose from. I bend down to inspect a low bookcase, empty apart from some grocery store paperbacks. There's a framed photo on the top shelf.

"Is this Simone?"

Dr. Hill peers at the photo and nods. Her eyes cloud and she clamps a hand over her mouth. Her shoulders shake. "She was sweet. She really was. I felt very . . . fond of her. I can't believe this is happening."

She retreats into the hallway, leaving me alone to study the photo.

Simone Walker is pretty in the snapshot, with high cheekbones and a toothy smile, her complexion washed out by the flash. She's dressed in a tank top and jeans, holding a red plastic cup in one hand, and the darkness behind her seems to conceal a party, though no faces are visible, just limbs. She gazes at the camera in a coy way, making me wonder who was taking the picture. It's an innocent look. A young woman enjoying herself. At ease in her surroundings. The expression pensive, but not melancholy.

This is who I'm here for. This is her. The body out there, whatever was done to her—

I'm going to make it right. Not that I can save her. I'm too late for that.

I'm always too late for that.

Dr. Hill reappears, wiping her eyes with the back of her hand. "There's something I should tell you. About her husband, Jason.

Something happened you need to hear about. Remember the money she asked for? The loan? Well, she asked him and he said yes. On one condition. She had to go to bed with him first."

"And did she?"

She nods. "The next morning there was some kind of argument and she left empty-handed. He kept calling her cell phone, and she'd send it to voicemail. When I asked her what was going on, she told me about the deal. Pretty sick. Whether it had anything to do with this, I don't know."

"Thanks," I say. "We'll check it out."

José Aguilar waits for me at the bottom of the stairs, hands buried in the pockets of his whiskered jeans, his muscled bulk hidden under a leather bomber. His impassive, pockmarked face is so red he looks freshly boiled, but that's normal for Aguilar.

"I heard you got pulled in," he says. "Figured you could use a hand."

"Nice jeans," I say.

"You're one to talk. What's with the getup? Prom night?"

"Charlotte's firm hosted a party and she dragged me along."

"Lawyers and liquor. And you're missing all the fun." He nods toward the kitchen. "The lieutenant's out there having a look at the scene, by the way."

"I heard his voice."

"So what do you want me to do?"

"Go upstairs and see if you can get anything more out of the woman who found the body. She's giving me an odd vibe."

"I'm on it," he says, slipping past me.

In the kitchen, Sergeant Nixon's not on the door, but I spot him outside shadowing my supervisor, Lt. Marcus Bascombe. Black. Six foot four. A glare that could put a hole in the ozone layer, assuming there wasn't one already. The lieutenant is my kind of police apart from the fact he doesn't like me. He tried to get me booted from the squad once, but that didn't work out. Now he treats me with grudging respect. All it would take to get back on his bad side is for me to stop closing cases. I'm not planning to start now.

I plant my briefcase on the island again, throwing the flap open and digging around for my flashlight, a little Fenix that puts out plenty of light. I grab my camera, too, then head through the door. Under the pergola, the crime scene technicians are just getting started running extensions and setting up lights. Bascombe crouches near the corpse, studying the wounds to her back, while Nixon whispers some commentary.

One of the crime scene techs motions me to the table, pointing to a cloud of black dust on the metal edge. "We've got some prints here, a few different sets it looks like."

"Good. Keep dusting."

As I approach, Nix heaves a sigh and detaches himself from the lieutenant's orbit, grateful to get away. We exchange a glance in passing.

"I've talked to the witness who found the body," I tell Bascombe. "According to her, the victim was meeting a friend for lunch, but didn't say who. I need to get a canvass started, and it wouldn't hurt if the ME would show up and give me an approximate time of death."

He straightens and steps away from the body. "I'll make a call and see what the holdup is. Not that I can't guess. That shooting on Antoine dropped three bodies, and I just came from South Central where a man drowned his seventy-three-year-old father in a bathtub and called it in as an accident." He shakes his head. "You could see the handprints on the old man's back where he was held down."

"Everybody's gone crazy," I say.

"Just like always."

I give him everything I have so far about Simone Walker, including Dr. Hill's story about the sex-for-money trade with her estranged husband. Then I flick on the flashlight and do a closer exam of the body. The way she's placed is so precise and unnatural: right-angled to the pool, bent at the waist, arms fully extended and perfectly parallel, hands resting side by side. Clean hands, too, nothing visible under the nails.

"It's almost like . . ."

"Almost like what?" Bascombe says.

I line myself up with her hands, then pantomime the motions. "Like he held her by the wrists. Like he dipped her into the water after he killed her."

"Or fished her out."

The big lights switch on, bathing the yard in white, glazing the mist overhead. The surrounding houses are mostly obscured by the tall fence and the screen of vegetation, reinforcing the sense of privacy. A few rooflines, a few attic windows. The lieutenant heads toward the edge of the slate, making room as the crime scene techs close in. I check the bushes for any sign of entry. Nobody scaling the fence could get down without breaking a branch. But there's nothing.

"You see the chair down at the bottom?" I ask him. "What do you make of that?"

He goes to the end of the pool opposite the house, taking a knee next to the water.

"Okay," he says, rising to the challenge. "How about this? She's over by the table when he attacks. She's sitting in the chair. He kills her, then drags the chair over with her in it, dumping them both into the pool. After she's been in the water awhile, he pulls her out and poses her. But he leaves the chair where it fell, 'cause he doesn't want to go in after it."

I nod. The scenario makes sense as far as the chair goes. If it was dragged from the table to the pool and chucked in, where it's lying is exactly what I'd expect. But what's the point?

"Why not drag the body and leave the chair?"

"I don't know," he says. "Find the guy and ask him. How's that for a plan? If I was you, I'd get the canvass going, and then I'd find out where this girl's husband lives and reel him in. The quicker you get him in an interview room, the less time he'll have to start believing he got away with it."

The glass door slides open and Sheila Green from the ME's office steps through, another charter member of my fan club. Dr. Green's boss, Alan Bridger, married my wife's sister a few years back. They have a house in West U. Considering this scene is practically in his backyard, I'd hoped to see Bridger here. No luck.

Gazing down the length of the pool, a tingle creeps up my spine. A ping of recognition. Something's been bothering me. And now I know what.

With the lieutenant looking on, Dr. Green takes one of the victim's wrists, lifting the arm, carefully turning the body to expose a breast and another network of punctures and a jagged, seeping gash in the chest.

I throw out my hand. "Wait."

The medical examiner freezes. After a pause, she lowers the body back. Bascombe stares at me, palms raised. Without explaining I switch my camera on and snap a photo. The preview on the LCD screen isn't exactly right. I realign the camera and take another shot.

"Everybody go inside," I say. "Except for you, Lieutenant. I need you over here."

The work stops, but nobody moves. Bascombe makes the call, signaling the crime scene techs to indulge my whim. He comes over, bringing Dr. Green with him. With the scene clear I take another shot.

I hand him the camera, displaying the photo. "Does that remind you of anything?"

"Yeah," he says, "it reminds me of what I can see with my own eyes." He squints at the screen, then shows it to the ME. "You gonna tell me or what?"

"The Fauk scene."

He looks again.

"Why does that name ring a bell?" Dr. Green says. "Wasn't that your big case, March? The one they wrote the book about?"

I ignore her. "You were there, Lieutenant, I wasn't. I inherited that case, if you remember. But ever since I got to the scene tonight, I've had this weird feeling. I couldn't put my finger on it until now."

He hands the camera back. "You've lost me, March."

"You were *there*."

"It's similar, I guess. But the Fauk woman had her clothes on and she was only stabbed once. She was floating in the swimming pool, too, not halfway out. Not to mention the guy who did it is doing time in Huntsville thanks to the confession *you* wrung out of him—"

"I'm not saying the crimes are the same. But look at that picture. I studied the Fauk photos so hard they're burned into my memory, and I swear there's one that looks exactly the same. The pool, the way the body's located off to the side, even the placement of the furniture. It's all the same."

"A lot of crime scene photos are gonna look alike," Dr. Green says. "They all have dead people in them for one thing."

Her voice trails off and it all comes back to me, that ten-year-old case, all the frustrations and roadblocks, all the drama. Donald Fauk murdered his wife and thought he'd gotten away with it. He had, as far as the investigation was concerned. But I was new on the squad, trying to prove myself, and the case was high profile enough to pass along once the lead detective retired. My old partner and I had gone to Florida, arresting Fauk as he planned his next wedding.

We flew him back on the morning of September 11, 2001, and after the Towers were hit in New York, our flight was grounded in New Orleans. After spending a few hours as guests of NOPD, we gave up on another flight out and rented a car. Somewhere along the Atchafalaya River Basin, Donald Fauk started talking and never stopped.

"The book," I say. "*The Kingwood Killing*. There are pictures in the middle, including this one." I point to the camera screen. "If you read that book and got inspired, *this* is what you'd do."

"March," Bascombe says, "this case here, it has nothing to do with the Fauk murder."

"When you see the picture in the book, you'll change your mind."

Dr. Green shakes her head. The lieutenant catches her gesture and frowns. Then he turns that high wattage glare of his on me, and just like that, all the respect I've won back over the last year is gone. All he sees is the screw-up he was trying to bounce out of Homicide twelve months back. I start to say something, but he cuts me off.

"Listen to me, you tuxedo-wearing dimwit," he says, moving closer so I get the full effect of his height. "I want you to get that canvass going, and then you find this girl's husband and bring him downtown.

If I have to hold your hand on this, March, I will. But believe me, you don't want that. Are we clear?"

I can feel my cheeks burning, my body starting to squirm. He outstares me and suddenly I'm looking away and nodding obediently. Behind him, Dr. Green is nodding, too, a faint smile of triumph on her lips.

"Everything's fine here," he tells her. "We're on top of this thing. Now, what we could use from you is an approximate time of death. . . ."

They circle back to the corpse, leaving me to stew. The crime scene techs file back to resume their work. Bascombe calls one over and starts explaining about his chair theory, pointing out the probable path they should fluoresce for signs of blood.

After a moment I collect myself and get busy. There are doors to knock, interviews to conduct, and still a chance that some physical evidence will be found. And there's a suspect to run down: Jason Young.

And when I find him, whatever else happens and no matter what Bascombe does in response, there is one question I am going to ask. Does he have a copy of *The Kingwood Killing?* Because whoever murdered Simone Walker had a picture in his head, and he rearranged his crime to fit the fantasy. I'm convinced of that.

Find the book and I'll find the killer.

CHAPTER 2

As I pull up the driveway, the dashboard clock reads half past six and gray light is already breaking through the corners of the sky. I push through the back door, dropping my briefcase just inside and my keys on the breakfast table, and try to make as little noise as possible on the creaky stairs. In the bedroom, Charlotte sleeps under the slowly revolving fan, her gray satin dress over a chair, the newly bought lingerie from La Mode discarded in a sad heap at the foot of the bed, a symbol of the wreck of our evening.

I sit at the edge of the bed, inhaling the scent of the room. She's turned during the night, letting the sheets pull away to expose her back. Her skin is warm to the touch. The angle is different, but I think of Simone Walker anyway and shudder.

"You're home," she says, rolling toward me without opening her eyes, the hint of a smile on her pale lips.

"Not for long. I've got to change clothes and go back in."

"Already? And when are you supposed to sleep?"

"You can sleep for both of us. I've got Aguilar sitting on a suspect's front door, but I need to get back over there before the guy comes home."

"A suspect already." She sits up reluctantly, stifling a yawn. "You work fast."

"We'll see."

Her eyes focus on my rumpled tuxedo. "You look nice, too."

"Yeah. This was a real hit with the boys. I think everybody's gonna start wearing them from now on."

She rolls out of bed and puts on one of my old T-shirts, heading downstairs to brew some coffee. In the bathroom I run the tap until the mirror fogs, then strip out of the tux, careful to put it back on the hanger. Charlotte might toss her dress over a chair, but if I show the same disregard, she won't be happy. This tux along with the contents of a dozen more garment bags stuffed into my overcrowded closet used to belong to her father, a beloved eccentric who kept his tall, trim figure well into his seventies. Apparently neither of the sons could fit into them—they'd tried, taking turns in his Austin mansion the week after he died—so Charlotte came back with the lot. The ways of the rich never cease to amaze me. With money like theirs, I'd just buy new clothes.

There's more of it, too, still at her Galleria alterations tailor waiting for my return visit.

After shaving I pull one of my old suits out of the closet, a plain navy one that means business, perfect for the interview I'm planning for sometime today, and a stiff white shirt fresh from the cleaners. Downstairs, Charlotte frowns at my choice while handing me a mug of steaming coffee.

"You should wear one of your new ones, Roland."

"It feels strange wearing somebody else's clothes."

She ignores me. "Say what you want about my dad, but the man had classic taste. Those suits will never go out of style, and they probably cost a fortune to make."

"I'm sure. What does it mean, though, psychologically, that you're dressing me in his clothes? Does it mean you have issues?"

"Oh, I have issues." She pulls her unruly slept-on hair into a pony-tail, then climbs onto a barstool to nurse her coffee. "But not *those* kinds of issues."

Leaving my cup on the island next to her, I go into the living room and dig behind the books on the shelf next to the television until my hand grazes a dusty paperback. I bring it into the kitchen, wiping the cover on a dishrag.

"What's that?" she asks.

I tilt the front toward her. Brad Templeton's *The Kingwood Killing*, the mass market edition with the shiny lurid cover featuring the Houston skyline—though the murder of Nicole Fauk didn't happen downtown—and a kitchen knife dripping with blood, even though the actual weapon was never found. The insert halfway through the book features eight pages of black-and-white photography: Nicole with Donald on their wedding day, Donald posing in front of the Enron building sometime in the mid-1990s, the house in Kingwood they shared. There's a photo of me, as well, looking grave but eager as I perch on the edge of my newly assigned cubicle in the Homicide Division with the Fauk case file under my arm.

She takes the book from my hands. "You looked good. You still do."

"I looked young then. Now I look my age. I feel it, too."

"You're very handsome and you know it. I would've shown you just how much last night, but you stood me up. I had to hitch a ride with some unsavory BigLaw types." She smiles as she says it, letting me know she was just fine. My sudden exits are part of the job, something she's learned to take in stride. "Anyway, why the trip down memory lane?"

"See this one?"

I flip the page and show her the crime scene shot, taken from the far side of the Fauks' swimming pool. Unlike the lap pool from last night, the Fauks had an expansive swath of blue complete with a decorative rock-walled alcove doubling as a waterfall. In the background, the redbrick house looms, the outdoor furniture roughly centered. Nicole's body floated facedown just under the left-hand lip of the pool, in the same vicinity as where Simone Walker was pulled up over the rim.

Charlotte frowns. "What about it?"

"I took this one at the scene last night." I grab my camera and pull up the fresh photo. "Maybe you don't want to see this, though."

She sighs. "Give it here."

Charlotte inspects the two pictures minutely, giving no sign that she finds the sight distressing, though of course she must. She has the gift of appearing untouched by shocks, even when they touch her deeply. The things I push to the surface, the things that weather and mark me, she somehow conceals deep down, showing the world a radiant mask, never conceding that it has any power to wound her. I love this about my wife—I envy it—but her control worries me, too. Because sometimes she loses it.

"They look the same, don't they?" I ask.

"Similar, yes."

"Not just similar. The scene last night was arranged. The guy who did it, he wanted to make an impression, wanted everything to look a certain way. This is what he was after." I tap the photo in the book. "He's seen it. He's read the book. That picture's part of his sick fantasy. I'm convinced of it."

Sighing, she hands the camera back. "A copycat, you mean?"

"I'm not saying he copied the crime, just that it somehow inspired him."

"I don't know," she says. "Isn't it a stretch?"

Now it's my turn to sigh. "If you ever get tired of corporate law, you'd make a great homicide lieutenant."

"Ah, it's like that."

"Yes it is. Bascombe blew a fuse when I brought it up. Right in front of Sheila Green, who just lapped it up. He's been testy recently. Butting in where he never used to. I had to keep my mouth zipped the rest of the night, even after he left the scene. But now I look at them and it's obvious I'm right—"

"Is it?" She rests a hand on my shoulder. "I think you're forgetting you had the Fauk case on your brain last night. As soon as we got to the party, you disappeared on me, and then I saw you in the corner with Charlie Bodeen. He was the ADA who prosecuted Fauk, wasn't he? Before he went into private practice?"

She's right and wrong at the same time. I did hole up with Bodeen, grateful to see a familiar face in that sea of reptiles. He'd been happy to see me, too. Over the past few years he might have gained a lot of weight and lost a lot of hair, but he was the same wisecracking cynic who had put a bruise between my shoulder blades after the Fauk jury came back with its verdict, saying this could be the start of a beautiful friendship. Him and me, putting the bad guys behind bars. Only it didn't turn out like that. Our first case together was also our last.

"We weren't reliving the past. In fact, we were actually talking about you."

Her eyebrows rise. "What about me?"

"I forgot all about it until just now. According to him, your firm is in some kind of financial trouble. It's common knowledge, he said. There are even people blogging about it." As I speak, she takes a sudden interest in her coffee. "I told him that couldn't be right or I'd have heard about it."

She winces. "You said that?"

"Not really, no. I *thought* it, though. But I acted like I knew what he was talking about. It would have been embarrassing otherwise."

"Oh, Roland, I'm sorry," she says, taking my hand. "The only reason I haven't said anything is that I didn't want you to worry."

"So things must be pretty bad."

"Bad enough. I'm glad I left when I did."

"But what about your contract work? Is that in danger now? I mean, I guess you don't need the money, but still—"

"Nothing's in danger. And don't talk like that about money. I love what I do. It's not about the money."

"It's always about the money," I say.

"You don't believe in my idealism, is that it? Then why don't we both chuck the jobs and sell the house. That's what I've been trying to get you to do for forever. We could retire. We could live on what we have and we could travel. Enjoy ourselves."

"Our twilight years? No, thanks. I'm not ready for the scrap heap yet."

"Like you said, we don't need the money."

That's not what I said. I said she doesn't. I never think of her money as mine and probably never will.

"It's not . . ." My voice trails off.

She jabs a finger into my arm, laughing triumphantly. "Exactly! It's not about the money. That's what you were going to say. You don't work like you do for the money, and neither do I."

"It's different, though."

"Why?"

"What I do," I say, "it doesn't require an idealist. This job won't let you be one."

"Don't kid yourself, baby. You *are* one." She hops off the stool and kisses my neck, slipping past me toward the stairs. "I've gotta get ready, too. Don't think I haven't noticed you're breaking *all* our plans for the weekend."

"All our plans?"

"It's Sunday," she calls from the landing. "You promised you'd go with me to church."

"Oh," I say under my breath. "That."

The shower starts upstairs and I toss my camera and *The Kingwood Killing* into my briefcase. According to the microwave clock, it's already ten after seven. I need to get back to Aguilar. I don't want him bringing Jason Young in without me.

I find Aguilar in Meyerland sitting in the Wal-Mart parking lot across from Jason Young's apartment, a bag from New York Bagels open in his lap. He's positioned with a view down Dunlap, and as soon as I'm in the passenger seat he points out a red pickup parked on the road.

"That's him," he says. "Rolled up maybe five minutes ago and went inside."

"You should have called me."

"Why, weren't you coming? Anyway, I was going to once I finished breakfast. Here, I got you something."

He passes the bag across. Before I can decline, the smell of warm, fresh bagels gets the better of me and I reach inside.

"We'll get him in a second."

"I been thinking," Aguilar says. "When he went inside, he kinda looked like he was in a hurry. I got the impression he'd be coming back out."

"And?"

"And if he does, maybe we should follow him, see where he's in such a hurry to get to."

"All right," I say, taking a bite.

We have to wait another fifteen minutes, but then Aguilar sits up straight, calling attention to a dark-haired, compact man heading for the pickup. He wears a cotton field jacket, jeans, and a pair of tan work boots, casual but neat. Even from down the street I can see something's wrong with his face.

"Does that look like bruising to you?" I ask.

Aguilar grunts. "Maybe she did fight back."

"The ME says no to that. Not that Green would commit before the autopsy, but I could tell what she was thinking. The stab wound to the heart was the fatal one, and probably the first to be delivered. He came up from behind, probably cupped a hand over her mouth, and stabbed her in the chest, holding the knife in an ice-pick grip."

"Makes sense," he says. "But somebody laid into the man."

"We'll have to ask him about that."

Young pulls the truck door shut and gets going. He drives up Dunlap and puts his right blinker on to turn at Queensloch. Once he reaches Hillcroft, tapping the brakes, Aguilar starts after him. We keep a few car lengths between us, but there's not much traffic around at a quarter to nine on a Sunday morning. If he's jumpy, there's not much we can do to prevent him from spotting us, but that's always the case with a one-car tail. To do it right, you need a team—or better yet, an eye in the sky. I tell myself not to worry, though, because nine times

I jab my thumb at the church. "I'm sure nobody will bother it here. Now, is there anything you need to get?"

He moves like he's in a trance, pulling open the driver's door, looking inside like he's never seen the truck's interior before. I glance over his shoulder. Simone Walker's clothes were missing from the scene, and so were her laptop and cell phone. According to Dr. Hill, she often took them out with her when she smoked, sitting at the outside table to answer email and update her Facebook page. No sign of any of that in the truck cabin, though.

Aguilar pops open the passenger door. "Anything I can help you with?"

"No," Young says. "No, thanks."

He takes nothing from the truck, only deposits the Bible on the dash. When he locks up, he has to use the key. Either there's no automatic opener or it doesn't work.

"Okay," he says.

I open the back door for him. He starts to get in, then pauses, conscious of the churchgoers watching on the periphery. His pale cheeks redden and he hurries into the car, pulling the door shut himself. Aguilar and I exchange a look over the roof. We're taking a chance not putting him under arrest or even patting him down. But it's a calculated risk. He knows what he did, but he doesn't know whether we know. He doesn't know how much we know. As long as he believes there's a shot at getting out of this, he's still liable to talk. Technically he's just a witness, a person of interest helping with our investigation. If we read him his rights and treat him like a suspect, he's not going to give us a thing.

We get inside and close the doors.

"You all right back there?" I ask.

"I'm fine," he says, nodding for emphasis.

I trade another look with Aguilar. Young hasn't asked why we want to talk to him. Either he's very trusting or he already knows.

The man who drowned his own father in the bathtub last night is sitting in Interview Room 1 with Jerry Lorenz, one of the greenhorns on our shift. So I install Young in Interview 2 with promises of coffee and breakfast muffins on my return. Down the hallway I find Lt. Bascombe in front of the monitors. He sends Aguilar off to his cubicle for a much-needed nap and beckons me into the room.

"And shut the door behind you."

He's set on interfering, I can tell.

On one screen, Young has his elbows on the table, hands folded, gazing blandly at the four corners of the room. On the other, Lorenz paces back and forth while his suspect, a fragile-looking man in a stained guayabera, cradles his face in his hands.

"That looks like it's going well," I say.

"This is what I like, March. Fresh homicides on a Sunday morning. Overtime for everybody, suspects for everybody, closures for everybody. We even have a name for the shooter on Antoine. When we pick him up, we'll be three for three—assuming the glove fits for Mr. Jason Young."

"It fits," I say. "We tailed him before picking him up, and he just about led us back to the scene. Then he veers off and starts heading north, where he pulls into a parking lot and dumps his breakfast onto the pavement."

"And you got him going into a church? That sounds like a guilty conscience to me."

I nod. "It'll sound that way to the jury, too. He didn't even ask why we brought him in. He just came."

" 'Cause the boy knows he done wrong," Bascombe says, breaking into a smile. "Now, are you ready to have a go at him?"

"I think so. We got a look in his truck and didn't see anything, but I'd like to get a warrant to search his apartment."

"I thought he didn't get home until this morning, and Aguilar saw him go inside. There's nothing in there."

"He could have come and gone anytime yesterday. I still don't have a firm time of death."

"Go look on your desk," he says. "The autopsy's this afternoon, but Dr. Green gave me some preliminary info over the phone."

"She did?"

"When you need something special from the ME, you just call your brother-in-law. When I need something special, I use my charm."

"Charm. I'll have to try that."

"There's something else on your desk, too," Bascombe says. "You left a message with your victim's mother? Well, she called back. I spared you the hassle of doing the notification, but she's coming down here to give a statement. She brought your suspect's name up and said she's positive he's the one."

"Really? So maybe I need to hold off on talking to him and see what she can give me first. The more information I have, the better."

"It's your call." He glances back at the monitor and his smile fades. "Listen, March. That penguin suit last night, what was that all about?"

"Charlotte's firm hosted a Christmas thing and she promised conjugal relations in exchange for my attendance. So thanks for ruining that."

"Don't blame me," he says, pointing at the monitor. "Take it out on him. But the question I wanted to ask is, did you see the captain at this party?"

"Hedges? No, why?"

He shakes his head. "No reason."

"Come on, Lieutenant. You asked for a reason."

"Let it drop."

"He never showed last night at the scene," I say. "That was a little odd."

"We had our hands full last night. Don't make a big thing out of it. I was just wondering if you two ran in the same circles is all."

But that's not all. I can tell. He dismisses me and I go straight to the captain's office, which is dark and locked tight. Of course it is. If he's not going to show on a Saturday night, don't expect him bright and bushy come Sunday morning. I go to my desk and read over the notes from the medical examiner's office, but the whole time the lieutenant's question eats away at me. Why would he think Hedges was at the party? Why would he shut down so quick when I asked him about it? One minute I think we have a good relationship finally, and the next he's bawling me out in front of outsiders.

I'm still thinking it over when my phone lights up.

"Detective March? There's a visitor in reception for you—Candace Walker?"

The victim's mother. "I'll be right down."

"I want to see her, please," she says.

"Your daughter's not here, Mrs. Walker. We can arrange for you to see her, though. That won't be a problem. You can see her when she's ready."

When she's ready. The woman swallows the euphemism down and I can see her mind chewing on it, working out what it must mean for Simone not to be ready now. She sucks in her hollow cheeks, her eyes fluttering.

If Joy Hill had a sister, a shrunken, shriveled sibling who'd gotten none of the breaks, who lived badly and suffered and made all the wrong choices, she would be a dead ringer for Simone's mother. The resemblance between the two women is striking enough to make me wonder about Simone, what her motives were for living under Dr. Hill's roof. Where Hill comes off as rather attractively dissipated, aged by the good life, lanky and at ease in her skin, Candace Walker is hard and grating, her mouth twisted into an involuntary frown.

Of course, she just learned in the past ninety minutes or so that her only daughter was brutally murdered, probably after having been sexually assaulted. Under the circumstances, maybe she looks just right.

"It's all right, ma'am," I say, my hand on her elbow to guide her. "We'll take this elevator right here."

She's quiet on the way up to the sixth floor. I let her through the Homicide Division door, leading her away from the interview rooms toward the lieutenant's office, since he's volunteered to sit in. She trails behind me, not paying much attention to her surroundings, still preoccupied with her grief. If she knew about Young's presence, her demeanor might change.

Bascombe stands at the door, leaning forward to take her hand. She withers before him and draws her hand back, not paying attention to what he's saying. I see the hardness in her mouth and know why. It's because he's black. He sees it, too, but doesn't take any notice, ushering her inside and onto the soft couch near the door.

"I'll leave you with Detective March," he says.

After he's gone, she lets out a breath. I try to think of a question to ask, but for the moment I'm stumped.

"He's the person I talked to over the phone?"

I nod.

"He seems real nice."

"He is," I say. "Let me begin by expressing my condolences, ma'am. I know how shocking this is, and you have my deepest sympathy."

The words sound hollow but I mean them. She does have my deepest sympathy, even though I took against her at first sight. She has it despite her reaction to my lieutenant. And I have nothing but the old clichés to communicate with, condolences and deep sympathy, even though what I want to tell her isn't boilerplate at all. I understand what she is going through. Oh, I know what it is to lose a daughter. I'd like to tell her that, only I can't. I'd like to tell her that above all others, I am the right man for the job.

It would mean nothing to her, though, and I don't have the words.

"It is shocking," she says. "That's exactly what it is. But let me tell you something right now: I am not shocked. I'm not surprised, I mean, that this would happen. It's just . . . For this to happen to *her*. After all she's been through. It's not right, it's just not."

She scrubs a hand over her face, dragging her eyes down, her nose, her lips.

"My girl had every right in this world to be happy. If anybody deserved it, she did—and trust me, nobody wanted it more. She *loved* being alive, my little Mona." She goes to her purse for a tissue, then balls it in her fist. "And *he* seemed so good for her at first."

"Jason Young?"

She nods. "Early on, she took after me. She was a wildcat of a girl, always going with the exact wrong men. She liked them bad." A wan smile. "And Jason, he brought some stability to her life, you know?"

"When did they meet?"

"I don't know exactly. She had *issues* with me." She makes quotes in the air. "And she was right to, I admit it. But one day I get a call from her and she says she has a good job and she's not in trouble and there's a man in her life, too. The first time I met him, I remember thinking, My baby's safe now. I could stop worrying." She shakes her head. "That didn't last. From the beginning he didn't care for me. That was fine, though, 'cause I understood why. She'd told him, you know. About . . . *everything*."

I raise my eyebrows. "Everything?"

"You don't know, then." She lets out a little moan. "I thought you could look on the computer or something and find everything out."

"What did she tell him?" I ask.

"I have to say it out loud?" She takes a deep breath. "It was my ex-husband, Simone's stepfather. He used to do it when I was at work and they were alone together. Starting when she was eleven or twelve."

The pulse in my temple starts to pound.

"They said I was wrong not to believe her, and maybe I was. The school counselor ended up reporting it, and they took him away to jail. After that, though, whenever there was a man in my life, I was always afraid, you know? That something might happen or she might say that something did. She could be very manipulative. She was always very mature for her age."

"And this went on for how long?" I ask, my voice dry.

"She was fourteen, I think, when they arrested him. She moved out when she was sixteen, into a foster home out in the suburbs. Those people had a lot of trouble with her. After high school, we kind of lost touch for a while. I used to have a substance abuse problem, but I got that sorted out."

"Were you arrested?"

"For the drugs?" She shakes her head. "I fell in love is what happened. I met somebody and we were together awhile, and we both ended up going to rehab." She starts counting on her fingers. "That was eight and a half years ago. The relationship didn't work out, but once I was clean, I stayed that way. Got myself some work, a place to live, and I never looked back."

"Okay. So Simone told Jason about all this, and as a result he wasn't your biggest fan. But you said he was good for her?"

"At first he was. They were so happy before. They had them a nice house, he bought her a new car. I remember on Saturdays, after they were out shopping, they would pull up in my driveway and she'd come in and show me all the things she got. It was sweet, like she was my little girl again. He would wait in the car, listening to the radio or something, but that was fine. I didn't have a problem with it."

"What changed then?"

"He got so strict with her. So controlling. She would call me on the phone because he said I was a bad influence. She couldn't visit me no more. Then he started taking things away from her. He took her credit cards. He even sold her car, and she loved that car. But I would tell her maybe he was right. She was raised without any discipline, so whenever there was discipline, she always bucked."

"Your daughter had separated from Jason, is that right? Was it a legal separation?"

"She just left, that's all I know. It was after a big fight. The other thing, in addition to how controlling he got, was he started getting religious, too. He started telling her how she had to dress and who she could be friends with. She couldn't have any men friends. It was getting scary. Every time she called, I kept expecting her to say he'd hit her."

"Did she say that?"

"No. She never said it to me, anyway. But she wouldn't have, because one of her things was that she always wanted to look successful in my eyes."

"To make you proud," I say.

"It was more like a competition. Since I failed in life, she was showing me that's not how she was gonna end up." Her face goes dead a moment; then she forces a smile. "But like I said, I could understand that. I wasn't a perfect mother."

"She never told you what the fight was about, then."

"All she said was, 'I outgrew him.' That was it. She changed jobs and moved in with that professor woman—and that was a terrible decision, too. That woman, Joy is her name, she was just as bad, just as controlling. That's what Simone said. Always wanting to know her comings and goings, always trying to squeeze more money out of her. I told her she could come live with me if she wanted. But she didn't. It was habit by then, being used by people. That's what they all did; they used her. He did, that woman did, everyone did. I was the only one . . . She should have come to me, shouldn't she? This would never have happened."

There's clearly no love lost between Candace and Joy Hill. Through the window I can see Bascombe leaning over Aguilar's cubicle to confer. I need to get into that interview with Jason Young, but first I need something I can use, a lever to pry him open.

"Mrs. Walker," I say. "According to Dr. Hill, your daughter recently had a falling out with Jason over a loan he promised to make—"

"Oh, *that*." She pounces on the subject, eyes brightening. "What a scheme that was. It was all the professor lady's fault because of the rent being behind. She wanted money from Simone or else. So she put the thumbscrews on her, and what could she do? Jason has lots of money—he works three different jobs, did you know that?—so of course she goes to him. And he says fine, I'll give you the money, but there's something you have to give me first. She had to sleep with him again. So he was paying for it, basically, like she was some kind of street hooker."

"And when was this exactly?"

"That was maybe two, maybe three weeks ago? It was before Thanksgiving, I know that." She shrugs. "Simone told me about it afterward. She was very upset. She didn't know what to do without that money, and she couldn't get him to pay up."

"Did he come around after that? To Dr. Hill's house?"

She pauses awhile, thinking the question over. "He's the one."

"Did she ever tell you that he'd been to the house? Maybe she saw him outside on the street? Maybe he came to the door?"

"Yes."

"She told you that?"

"Yes, she told me. He would go to the house and try to come in, but she wouldn't let him. She told him to go away. Go away or she'd call the police."

"You're sure about this? You'd testify in court?"

A pause. "Yes, I will. So help me God, I will."

I get up and go to the door, signaling the lieutenant.

"Detective," she says. "It's not right this happening to her. My girl wanted one thing in life, and that was to be happy. She at least deserved that."

CHAPTER 3

Jason Young watches me from across the table, the familiar hunted look creeping into his eyes as I unpack one stack of papers after another: my notes from the scene, the preliminaries from the ME, transcripts of the statements Dr. Hill made last night to Aguilar and Mrs. Walker just completed with me, the photos from the scene, facedown on the table. And a lot of unrelated paperwork to pad it all out. I'm sending a message through this bit of theater. We have everything. We know everything. Tell me a lie and I'll see through it because the facts are spelled out right here.

I square up a fresh legal pad in front of me, pen poised. "Now. Mr. Young. Why don't we start with some basics? Where you live, where you work, that kind of thing."

He glances from me to Bascombe, who sits to my left a few feet back, arms crossed. The wheels are turning. He's trying to work out how much we really know. All I'm after for now is to get him talking, though. I need a baseline read on the man, to see what he's like when he tells the truth. That way it will be easier to spot the deception later on.

"Don't you already know that stuff?" he asks.

"These are just preliminaries we have to get out of the way."

He sits back in his chair. "What was the question again?"

"Let's start with your address."

He gives me the street address of the apartment where Aguilar and I first spotted him. I write it down like it's new information.

"And where do you work?"

"I'm an assistant manager at the Luggage Outlet on Richmond."

"Okay." I make another note. "And that's your only employer?"

His eyes narrow. "No."

I've caught him by surprise with the question. He scans the stacks of paper in front of me, probably wondering what else I have in there. Good. I want him to wonder.

"You have three jobs, isn't that right?"

He nods slowly. "But only the Luggage Outlet is full time. I work nights and some weekends for Blunt Ministries, packing orders and duplicating DVDs, and there's a friend of mine with a landscaping business who hires me on big jobs maybe once, twice a month."

"Doing all that," Bascombe says, "you must not have a lot of free time, Jason."

"Not really."

"So what's your typical day look like? Take yesterday for instance. Walk us through that."

"Yesterday wasn't typical."

"Just for instance," I say. "Did you go into the Luggage Outlet at all?"

He shakes his head. "On Saturdays I go into the Blunt warehouse around ten—that's off of Twenty-sixth Street—and I'm there pretty much all day, until maybe six or seven, depending on the volume of orders from the week. People order DVDs and over the weekend I do the duplicating and packaging; then the reverend will take them to the post office Monday morning."

"The reverend?"

"Reverend Blunt. You know . . . Curtis Blunt? He's on the local radio."

"Is that his church you were going to this morning?" I ask.

"He doesn't really have a church. It's more like a ministry. He has his show, and he makes videos of his teaching."

"And he was with you yesterday?"

He shakes his head. "Not the whole day. He came by in the morning, but mostly I work alone. I get more done that way. The reverend's really talkative when he's there, so it's hard to keep going."

"What about lunch?" I ask. "You took a break, right? Where'd you go?"

"I'm not working three jobs so I can go out for lunch, man. I brought my lunch with me. That's what I do."

"All right, then. Why *are* you working three jobs?"

He shrugs. "Stupidity."

Bascombe chuckles. "You wanna elaborate on that for us?"

"I'm working three jobs because, until about a year ago, I was spending money I didn't have on a lifestyle I didn't need. I had a mortgage and two car notes and about forty grand in credit card debt, which I was rolling from one card to the other. It kept growing and growing and I was barely making forty a year before taxes. So I said enough is enough."

"Meaning?"

"Meaning I cut up the cards, sold the house, got rid of the cars, bought a junky used truck and started working sixty hours a week or more to put a dent in the debt. I'm getting out from under all that."

"And what about your wife?" I ask. "You are married. I notice you're wearing a ring."

He lifts his hand and stares at the ring, like he's only just noticed it.

"Yeah," he says. "I am."

"What did she think about all this?"

Young starts shaking his head in slow motion, a hard smile on his lips. "That's what all this is about, isn't it? You've got me here because of Simone."

I give nothing away. "That's her name? Simone Young."

He snorts. "She doesn't call herself that anymore, but yeah. Simone Young. And all this"—he waves his arm over my stacked papers—"it's for nothing, because whatever story she told you isn't true, okay? It's not even her fault, though. It's Candace, isn't it? I saw her out there when the other detective brought in the coffee. Listen, that woman is a bad influence on Simone, and if you separate the two of them and just ask Simone what happened, she'll eventually tell you the truth. But not with her mother in the room."

"The truth about what?" I ask.

"Come on. I'm not stupid, man. I see what all this is. But you know what? It's he said/she said, because nobody else was there."

"What's he said/she said?"

"You *know* what."

Bascombe chuckles again, acting like he's impressed with the performance. "You gotta spell it out for us, though. For the record."

"What you brought me here for," Young says. "I didn't do it. I mean, that's not what it was."

"What's not?" I say, raising my voice just a bit.

"Rape," he says. "Okay? It wasn't rape. I didn't rape my wife."

"All right. So tell us what did happen. Give us your side."

"It's not gonna make any difference."

"Telling the truth makes a difference," I say. "It always does."

I risk a glance at the lieutenant, who's on the edge of his chair. He raises an eyebrow ever so slightly and I answer with an imperceptible nod. This is going great. Better than expected. We've got him talking, and even though he's being careful to speak of Simone in the present tense, the more he says, the tighter we lock him into a version of events.

And once he's committed, every time we poke a hole in the story, he'll be forced to change it, forced to improvise on the spot. The worst case scenario is that we can go to trial with clear evidence of deception. The best case scenario is that we run him back and forth through the inconsistencies so many times that he sees it's hopeless and decides to come clean. We're going for the best case scenario, needless to say.

"Seriously, Jason," I say. "This is your opportunity to set things straight. We're here to listen, and like you said, it's her story versus yours. Only we don't have your story."

"Okay, fine. Here's what really happened. Simone left me and moved in with a UH professor named Joy Hill. The idea was, she'd pay rent and that way Joy wouldn't have to sell the house, because her husband had left her. But when I found out about this, I was like, 'How are you gonna swing that?' Because Simone was hardly making anything. She had some hours at a bookstore, but quit to take a job at this nonprofit center. Well, I looked that position up online and they listed the salary as eighteen grand a year. So I know this arrangement's not gonna work."

"You told her that? The two of you had a conversation."

"We had a fight over the phone. I tried to explain the numbers to her, and she said I was treating her like a child—which is true, but she was acting like one. She knew I didn't want a divorce and assumed that if it came down to it, I would hand over the money."

As he talks, he leans forward, elbows on the table, staring into his cupped hands.

"I knew she'd have to come to me eventually, so when she did, I was ready. At least I thought I was. She still managed to surprise me, though: the amount she wanted was ten thousand. Ten! I told her there was no way, but we could meet and talk about it. That's all I wanted, to talk. For the last six months, she'd barely acknowledged my existence. She wouldn't take my calls. If I went over there, she wouldn't answer the door. Now suddenly all that changes."

He admits he went over there. Knew the lay of the land.

"So you met up in person. When was that?"

He pauses. "It was Veteran's Day, whenever that was. We went to a restaurant and I remember on the TVs they were showing a lot of military stuff."

I reach into my briefcase under the table, consulting the Filofax. "November eleven was Veteran's Day. That was a Wednesday."

"Right," he says. "Anyway, she wanted a lot of money. A loan, she said, but we both knew there was no way she'd ever pay it back—and besides that, she's my wife, okay? If I was going to give her money, I'd *give* it, not loan it. But I told her the money wouldn't solve her problems. The solution was obvious, but it wasn't that."

"And the solution was what?"

"To move back in," he says, wide-eyed. "Obviously. And I could tell she was listening, too, in a way she hadn't before. We got married too quick, that's the problem. We weren't on the same page about a lot of stuff. But now she'd been on her own a little and she'd seen how hard it could be. She softened up some. I was like, 'You just need to come home.' But she said I sold her home. We couldn't afford it, I told her, but my new place, that was her home now."

"Did she go home with you?"

"You know she did. But I thought it was for real."

Bascombe nods. "You thought she was moving back in with you. Things were getting back on track."

"Exactly. She spent the night."

"You had intercourse."

He nods. "I remember waking up and thinking, Everything's gonna be fine now. But in the morning she's already made breakfast, and on the table there's my checkbook and she's already filling out the amount. It's just sitting there, waiting for my signature. I got what I wanted, she said, and now it was her turn."

"Those were her exact words?"

"Pretty much." He shakes his head. "I couldn't believe it."

"And what happened then?"

"We got into it then. She called me some names and I called her some, too. She said I was trying to cheat her. She said we had a deal. I was incredulous. I said if she thought I was paying her ten grand for last night, she had too high an opinion of herself. But it's her mother that puts these ideas in her head. Before she let Candace back in her life, things were different. Her new landlord didn't help things, either. She was filling Simone's head with all this girl power stupidity, be an independent woman, stand up for yourself. The thing is, Simone did have some things in her past, and people assume if that's the case, that you're gonna instinctively choose abusive men. So in her eyes, the professor's, the fact that Simone chose to marry me meant I was like that."

"But you're not like that," Bascombe says.

"Of course not."

The lieutenant gets up. "Look, Jason, this is really helpful. We need to take a quick break, all right, and confer on some of this. Can I bring you anything while you're waiting?"

The interruption surprises me, but I take it in stride and start gathering my papers. Bascombe puts a hand on my shoulder.

"Don't worry about that, March. Let me talk to you outside a minute."

It goes against the grain, leaving everything out, but I follow him anyway, pulling the door shut after us.

"All the paperwork's in there," I say. "I don't want him looking through it."

"Come with me."

We head down to the monitoring room, where Aguilar is on observation duty. On-screen, Young sits frozen, eyes fixed on the stacks of paper across the table. But he makes no move toward them.

"I want to see what he does," Bascombe says. "He's putting on a pretty good show in there, don't you think? Question is, if you leave an innocent man alone with all that paper, does he let it be or does he take a peek? I say he looks, because more than anything he's curious what's going on."

"If he's guilty, he'll look to see how much we've got on him."

"Yeah, but if he's guilty, he'll also know we're watching him."

My patience for interview room tricks runs out fast, but I know it's the lieutenant's thing. In a situation like this, he's looking at physiology and behavior, none of which is admissible in court, though if you're a good reader of signs, it might lead you toward some truth. Personally I believe in the story. You lock them in, then you trip them up. That takes time, though, and attention to detail.

"We need to lock him into a timeline for yesterday," I say. "According to Sheila Green, the killing went down sometime between four in the afternoon and when the call came in at quarter to nine. I want an explanation for the injuries to his face, too."

"And his movements this morning," Aguilar adds. "Was he on his way to the scene or not?"

"It's interesting, though, isn't it?" Bascombe says, ignoring us both. "Is he concealing something or not? He hasn't tripped up yet as far as your victim is concerned. He hasn't even let on that he knows she's dead. When you brought him in here, he did see the sign on the door, right? He knows this is Homicide."

"It's not like I pointed it out to him or anything. But yeah, he'd have to be pretty self-absorbed not to realize."

"Or pretty convinced he knows what's going on."

"Meaning what, you're buying his story? He thinks he's in here on a rape charge?"

"Maybe," Bascombe says. "Or maybe he's really good. Maybe we're not dealing with your garden variety domestic here. You're assuming he killed her in a crime of passion scenario, then tried to make the scene look like something else, a sex murder. What if this guy's the real thing? He just happens to be starting in his own backyard."

"That's what you're getting off him?" I ask. It seems like a stretch to me.

"I'm not getting nothing off him, that's my point. Here's what we need to do. Go back in there and get what you need—an explanation for the injuries, a full timeline—but do something else first. He's sticking to this rape story, so let's run with that. Whatever happened between them, it was at his apartment. He gave us that. So tell him we want consent to search."

"He's not going to give it."

"Try him. I think he just might."

"Meanwhile," I say, "how about those other homicides? I can handle this if you want to catch yourself up on one of those."

He sees through me and answers with a knowing smile. "Am I cramping your style, Detective? I'm sorry about that. I just like to see the way you work." He turns to Aguilar. "Get this Reverend Blunt on the phone, too. Let's get started on Jason's alibi, such as it is."

If Jason Young is surprised that I've returned alone, he gives no clue. My papers remain untouched where I left them. When I sit, he slumps a little, like he's relieved the temptation to reach for them is at an end. I slip a hand inside my briefcase and place my trump card on the table, watching his expression the whole time.

He glances at the book just long enough to see what it is, then loses all interest. Either he's unfamiliar with *The Kingwood Killing* or he's a better actor than even Bascombe is giving him credit for. I flip through the book for good measure, trying to bait him.

"So is this still break time or have we started already?"

The flash of attitude makes me smile. I close the book but leave it out on the table. "Here's the problem, Jason. You said it yourself. We have two versions of the story, and I could see it playing out either way. No offense, I just don't know you. I can't tell which version to believe. But I'll tell you one thing: I can respect what you're doing. Holding down these jobs, getting your life straightened out. Taking responsibility."

"Thanks," he says in a grudging tone.

"If it was your story plus something else, you'd be all right. But the way the courts work, if it's you against her, I think you know who's going to win. In every other type of crime, the system is weighted toward the defendant, but here it works the opposite way. Basically all she has to do is say you're guilty, and then the burden's on you."

As I deliver this slanted take on the legal system, Young deflates more and more, until his forehead's practically touching the table and his hands clutch the back of his neck. I'm talking not to his face but to the top of his head.

"What do you mean, my story plus something else?"

"Well," I say. "One thing would be if we took a look at the scene and there was no evidence to support the other side."

"The scene?" He looks up. "You mean my bedroom?"

"The bedroom. The apartment."

"It's been weeks, though. I mean, if there was any evidence, I'm not so stupid that I wouldn't have tidied up."

A charge goes up my spine. In a different context, that could sound like an admission, considering whoever killed Simone certainly did tidy up.

"The point is, it would help corroborate. And if we *were* to drop this thing, the first question the judge is gonna ask is whether we checked the apartment. If the answer's no, then we're back to square one."

He sighs. "Do I have to sign something?"

"All you have to do is say you consent to the search."

"I consent to the search. Do whatever. But when you come back, can you bring me some water or something? All this talking is doing my voice in."

He expects me to get up and leave, but I ignore him and keep on writing. After a moment, Bascombe walks in and puts a couple of bottled waters on the table.

"Here you go, sport."

Once he's gone, I can feel Young's eyes on me.

"Somebody's watching all this," he says.

I nod. "There are a couple of questions I still have to ask. Starting with what happened to your face."

"This?" He touches the wound on his jaw. "It's nothing."

"I'm going to need a little more than that. Like: who did it, what did they hit you with, and when?"

"It was . . . a couple of days ago. Monday, actually."

"No, Jason," I say, raising my pen. "That's fresh. Trust me, I can tell."

"It was Monday. I was in back at the Luggage Outlet, trying to get to a box on top of the shelves, and one of them fell and caught me in the face."

"Were you hanging upside down?"

"What? No. I wasn't hanging upside down."

"Then you're making this up, Jason, because the blow that made those marks came from underneath, swinging like this." I pantomime the arc, clocking his jaw with an imaginary weapon. "Lying like that just makes you look guilty. You're better off leveling with me."

"It has nothing to do with this," he says. "And anyway, I told you what happened. If you don't believe me, I can't help that."

"Let's go over what happened yesterday, then. That's when I think you had your little accident."

"Wrong," he says.

"That's fine. Just walk me through what really happened."

"I went to work, like I said. Reverend Blunt came in sometime in the morning. He wanted to check on me because I hadn't been in earlier."

"Did he ask about your injury?"

"No."

"That's strange, don't you think?" I let it slide, but the inference is clear: he didn't ask because on Saturday morning it wasn't there. "What did the reverend ask about, then?"

"Orders," he says. "Work stuff."

"And then he left? How long were you at the warehouse after that?"

"Until seven."

"That's a long time. Do you punch a card or something?"

"I keep track of my hours."

"Okay. So you left at seven and went where?"

"Home."

"Straight home? And then what?"

"Then nothing," he says, his voice sharp. "I watched TV, went to bed, then got up in the morning for church."

"Where we found you. And from the time you got home to the time you left this morning, you never went out?"

"No."

"Not at all?"

He meets my gaze, probably sensing this is important. But he doesn't change his story: "Not at all."

I dig through my paperwork for Aguilar's notes from this morning, taking my time, letting him sweat a little.

"Mr. Young," I say. "When you arrived at your residence this morning at 8:32 a.m., where were you coming from?"

"That's not right. I *left* around then."

"You left sixteen minutes later at 8:48 a.m."

He stares at me. "What?"

"You just said you were home all night, but in fact you didn't come home at all last night, did you? We already know your movements, Mr. Young. Why are you lying to me?"

"Why are you asking me this? It has nothing to do with what happened."

"Tell me where you were last night."

"You already know."

"I need you to tell me."

He shakes his head. "I don't understand what's going on here."

"Mr. Young—"

"No, listen. I've tried to cooperate. I've told you everything I can about what really happened with Simone. You can search my apartment, fine. But I'm not going to talk about anything else. Whatever happened yesterday, it's nobody's business. You can tell her I said that, too. If you want the truth, I already gave it to you, but if you're just out to crucify me, then forget about it."

"If you'll just answer a few more—"

"I'm not answering anything," he says.

I can see what's coming, too. He's going to lawyer up. Before he gets there, I stand abruptly and start filling my briefcase. "No, you're right, Mr. Young. You've bent over backward to be helpful. There's a limit to what you can reasonably be expected to share. Just sit tight for a little while and we can wrap things up."

"How long? I've been here for hours."

"Not much longer," I say, heading for the door.

Aguilar is alone in the monitoring room, telling me Bascombe grabbed some help and went to the apartment on Dunlap the moment Young gave his consent. He stifles a yawn. I drop into an empty chair and yawn myself. My limbs are heavy as lead. I close my eyes and melt into the seat cushions.

"He's on the hook now," Aguilar says. "He can't account for himself after the reverend left—I checked on that, by the way. According to Blunt, they saw each other around eleven in the morning and he has no idea what happened after that. He said he would go to the warehouse, see what got done yesterday, and call back. I gave him your number."

"Young's lying about last night, obviously. We know that."

"You don't sound excited."

"There's one part that doesn't fit for me. When I showed him the book, he didn't flinch. Of everything I had in there, that should've cut him the deepest. That should've surprised him. But it didn't even register."

"Maybe you're wrong about that part."

According to my watch, it's half past twelve. My internal clock's so far off that my stomach hasn't rumbled. "I'd better get in on the tail end of that search. You mind baby-sitting for me?"

"If he gets antsy, I got your permission to arrest him? We've got enough, don't you think?"

"I guess so. How are the other cases coming along?"

"The drowning is down," he says. "They're still looking for the shooter on the other one."

"We're still in the running, then."

"But the clock's ticking."

The sleep deprivation starts catching up to me on the road. I stave it off with some drive-thru coffee, pulling up behind the lieutenant's car in record time. Inside the apartment, he's sitting on the couch with a laptop opened in front of him, scrolling through emails with a tap of the finger.

"Anything?" I ask.

"His fantasy football team's doing all right. Apart from that, nothing here."

Walking through the six-hundred-square-foot apartment doesn't take long. Young keeps it tidy, everything squared away. The furniture looks cheap but newly purchased, and the colors go together. It's not an unpleasant place, just a spartan one. The contrast with his dead wife's room full of consumer goods couldn't be more pronounced. Only one photo on the wall, a framed wedding shot. Apart from the fridge, the kitchen seems to be mainly for storage, what you'd expect in a bachelor pad, assuming your bachelor's meticulously neat. I look in vain for a block of kitchen knives with a telltale empty slot.

Mack Ordway is in the bedroom opening dresser drawers. Mack's the graybeard on our shift, always on the verge of retirement and at the same time always up for a jolt of overtime. I'm not surprised to see him working on Sunday. Sometimes I think he lives in the office.

"What's the story in here?"

"Bed's still made, probably hasn't been slept in. There's an old shotgun in the closet, but I didn't see any shells. If you look in that valet thing on the nightstand, there's a Tanto Folder with a serrated edge. Could be your weapon, but it looks clean to me."

"Let's bag it anyway and make sure," I say.

"Then there's this."

He bends down to open the dresser's bottom drawer. It's empty apart from glass shards and a half dozen busted picture frames, all of them facedown. Ordway uses a handkerchief from his pocket to pick one up by the edge. It's a photo of Simone Walker in a powder blue halter top and a floppy straw hat, her smile huge, her eyes hidden behind round sunglasses. He turns over another, showing Simone and Jason arm in arm in front of a Galveston crab joint. The next one is Simone by herself again, looking up from a glossy magazine, her hair spread out on the back of a flower-print couch.

"They're all her," Ordway says, "or the two of them together. Maybe he got angry with her for leaving and did all this."

"Or maybe he did it yesterday before he went to her place and killed her. Let me take a photo, then you can bag those, too."

I leave him to it and head down the hall. In the bathroom, there are wet towels on the floor and a can of shaving cream on its side by the sink, a puff of foam clinging to the cap. No prescription drugs behind the mirror, though. A slatted door down the hallway conceals a stacked washer and dryer. The dryer's empty. I pull the washer door open.

"Hello."

"What you got?" Bascombe calls.

"Take a look."

He and Ordway both appear over my shoulder. I step back so they can see what I've found. A pair of jeans twisted into a ball by the spin cycle, a knotted white shirt.

"How much you want to bet he was wearing these when he came home this morning? Aguilar can say for sure."

"Did we not check the washer?" Bascombe asks.

Ordway ignores him. "Let's see what we got here."

He tugs the shirt and spreads it open in the air between us. "That's the thing about bloodstains. You can't just throw something in the washer and get rid of them."

The dark rusty blots across the front of the shirt do have the look of blood, but not as much as I would have expected from holding Simone against his chest as he stabbed her. Still, blood is blood.

"If this comes back a match for her," I say, "then I guess we've got him."

"Put that in a bag," Bascombe tells Ordway.

I pull the jeans out myself, letting the heavy fabric uncoil, then work my hands into the front pockets, turning them inside out. Nothing but lint. From the back pocket, though, I remove a soggy rectangle of card stock about the size of a postcard.

"Someone's been a very naughty boy," Ordway says.

The showgirl on the card has been surgically enhanced, her face heavy with makeup, the lips parted suggestively. The words along the bottom read EXOTIC ENTERTAINMENT, with the club's name in thick cursive across her body: SILK CUT.

"Lieutenant," Ordway says, snatching the card from me. "I'd like to volunteer personally to follow up this lead."

Bascombe smiles. "So now we know why the boy was going to church this morning. There was more than one sin he had to confess."

While the two of them talk this new development over and try to figure out how to check the laptop's history for any Silk Cut searches, I go through the place one more time with increasing impatience. There's one thing missing. One thing I was certain to find. I look under the bed, in all the drawers, even digging through a couple of cardboard boxes in the closet.

"You notice something?"

Bascombe shuts the laptop with a frown. "There's nothing on here."

"Look around," I say. "There's not a single book in here."

"People don't read anymore."

"Can you remember the last time you did a house search and didn't find a single book? There's always something. And this guy doesn't have any."

"What did you expect?" he asks. "A copy of *The Kingwood Killing* with a little sticky note saying 'gotta try this sometime'? Get over it already. I'm all in favor of hunches, March, and your instincts have been good in the past. But trust me, no district attorney is going to hold those pictures up side by side and try to convince the jury there's a connection. It's not gonna happen."

He's right, but that doesn't make it any easier to let go.

"You got the autopsy to worry about now, March. Why don't you go home for a couple of hours, get your head down, and then go to the medical examiner's office. As of now, you don't have enough to charge him."

"I don't agree. He's lying about his movements last night."

"That's not enough. What this case needs is physical evidence. We'll get that shirt tested, and if the blood comes back a match, then great. If a witness comes forward to put him at the scene, great again. Maybe forensics will get something, you never know. In the meantime, we can't keep this guy sitting in an interview room indefinitely."

"I'll take another run at him," I say. "Confront him with the scene photos. Tell him we've matched the prints on the table to him."

"Have we?"

I shrug. "I'll follow up on it."

He ponders my suggestion, or at least pretends to, then shakes his head. "You look beat, March. For real. Take a break and let me handle this. I'll bring the clothes in, hit him with the photos, and if he talks, he talks. Meanwhile get some rest."

"Sir, I'd rather interview my suspect."

"I'm serious, March."

"What exactly is the problem with me continuing the interview?"

He rises from the couch and looms over me. "Can we not get into this right now? Can you just listen to me for once without giving me lip? Most guys would be grateful for the help, you know that? But you wouldn't know gratitude if it came up and bit you. Just back off and listen to me for two seconds, okay?"

"Fine."

"Maybe he'll roll over when he knows we've got the clothes."

"I said fine. I'll check back in after the autopsy."

"You do that."

Outside, the wind is bracing. Most days in Houston, you walk into a cloud of steam and want to retreat back inside. But the cold wakes me up, brings me to my senses a little. That's twice the lieutenant has flared up on me suddenly, and over nothing. Something's eating at him and I don't know what. But he was right about one thing: most guys would be grateful for the assist. Bascombe's a good cop. There are half a dozen detectives on my shift I wouldn't trust to handle an interview like this. He's not one of them.

But he was right about something else, too. My instincts are usually good, and what they tell me is that Jason Young is our man. He has books somewhere, maybe in storage, and when I find them, *The Kingwood Killing* will be there. The thing about instinct is, you follow without knowing where it'll take you. You can't explain why, and along the way nothing adds up, making you look like a fool. But working homicide, looking like a fool goes with the territory. That's the job: getting it wrong until you finally get it right.

Back in the car, I scroll through the saved contacts on my phone until I reach Brad Templeton's number. He picks up on the third ring.

"Roland March," he says. "You're finally returning my call."

"Have you been calling?"

He laughs. "You're so used to dodging me, you do it on autopilot now."

"I didn't catch you in church, did I?"

"Right. I hope you're calling to buy me lunch. It's your turn, if you remember."

"I don't, but lunch is fine."

"How about the Black Lab? You like that place."

I check my watch. "Fifteen minutes?"

"I'll be there."

CHAPTER 4

The prized spots up front are all taken, forcing me to park in the garage around back and walk through the breezeway past the closed bakery. Brad Templeton waits at an outdoor table, the only one occupied, bundled up in a corduroy sport coat and a tartan scarf. He spots me and raises a finger, like there's a chance I might miss him.

"We could go inside like normal people," I say.

"Are you normal? 'Cause I'm for sure not."

I drop into the chair opposite. The ten years I've known Templeton have been no kinder to him than to me. He's grown pudgy and soft, and his ginger hairline has receded far enough to expose a patch of freckled scalp. He clutches a plastic-coated menu with spotted, swollen fingers and makes a periodic sniffing sound.

"You have a cold or something? Or maybe swine flu?"

"You'd like that," he says. "The crazy thing is, most people would thank me for making them famous, but not you."

"Did you make me famous and I missed it?"

"I've written two books about you, anyway. But can I get you to return my calls? Not on your life. I swear it's easier to get through to the chief than it is to you. And no, I haven't been calling him, but if I did, he'd have the courtesy to pick up the phone."

"This is the second time today I've been accused of ingratitude."

He sniffs. "And yet you still don't get the message."

"Speaking of the chief," I say, "you know the rumor is, he's on the way out. He was Bill White's guy, and whichever way the runoff election turns out, the new mayor will bring in somebody else."

"That's not a rumor; it's a fact. The rumor is that the new chief will be promoted from within. This is the first time I've heard you talk politics, though, March. What's the deal? Are you hoping to get the job?"

I laugh. "Not likely."

"Anyway, I thought I'd bump into you last night, but I saw Charlotte and she said you'd ducked out early. I tuned into the news this morning and now I know why. Which call did you get?"

"West U."

"The stabbing? Is it a juicy one?"

"No comment."

One of the waitresses emerges from the Black Labrador's front entrance dressed in a short khaki skirt and black knee-socks. She doesn't look too happy with us for sitting outside. I order black coffee and Templeton gets the fish and chips. He cranes around to follow her with his eyes. All for show. He doesn't swing that way.

"I have a question for you," I say.

"Good." He turns back to face me. "I have one for you, too. Which of us gets to go first?"

"Mine's important."

"Then go right ahead."

I put my copy of *The Kingwood Killing* on the table. He snatches it up with a frown, inspecting the spine. "This doesn't even look like it's been read. Have you seen the reprints with the new cover? They did a much better job."

"There's a photo in there from the crime scene, remember? Here's what I want to know. Has anyone ever written to you about that? Fan mail from readers, for example. Have you ever gotten a letter that seemed a little strange?"

"They all seem a *little* strange," he says. "I was in the true crime section the other day, and there was this woman flipping through the latest book. At first I was kind of thrilled. I almost introduced myself. But then I actually looked at her, and March, this woman hadn't brushed her hair for days. I mean, she was scary. I thought, I'll be writing about you one of these days, sister, and I trucked on out of there."

"I'm talking specifically about letters. Or emails. Somebody who seemed really obsessed with the details of the Fauk case, or maybe mentioned that crime scene photo specifically."

He shakes his head.

"Are you sure?"

"I think I'd remember something like that." He gazes at one of the nearby trees as it shifts in the wind. "The only person who fits that description is Fauk himself. You know Donald still writes to me?"

"You're on a first name basis?"

"He sends me these long handwritten letters, trying to re-argue every aspect of the book. For a while, after he first read it, he wouldn't talk to me anymore. During the interviews he thought I was leaning toward his version of events—"

"His version is, he confessed."

He waves the book at me. "Hey, I wrote it. You don't have to tell me what happened. The point is, he's a self-justifying egomaniac with plenty of time on his hands. He writes a lot of letters. He's frustrated that there aren't any fan clubs on the outside trying to reverse his conviction. I actually have a letter where he says he's the white Mumia Abu-Jamal. I should send you a copy sometime."

"No thanks. But I'm serious about the question."

My tone gets his attention. He narrows his eyes. "Why are you asking?"

"Again, no comment."

"Is it the new case? There's some kind of connection?"

I must be transparent as glass. The way he locks on to the truth so fast catches me off guard. I take the book from him and open it up to the photo section.

"You see this? Hold that for me."

I shouldn't do this. I know I shouldn't. But I dig out my camera and scroll through the photos snapped at last night's scene, landing on the one.

"Now, look at those side by side and tell me what you think."

With the book in one hand and the camera in the other, he goes back and forth for a while, taking the comparison seriously. The waitress returns with my coffee and he doesn't spare her a glance. He puts them both down on the table.

"This is legit?"

"Yes," I say, leaning forward, not even trying to contain my excitement. "You see it, too."

He nods slowly. "It's a little creepy."

"But there is a resemblance."

"Definitely."

"If you were me, you'd have a hard time believing that the perpetrator of the one crime had never seen the photo from the other, right? He has to have seen it and fixated on it, too, incorporated it into his fantasy. Because this didn't happen by accident. He arranged everything to look a certain way. It's not an exact copy, but if you ask me"—I tap my finger on the book—"this had to be his inspiration."

His eyebrows wrinkle up. "And it just so happens you're assigned the case? The same detective who investigated the original?"

"That part's a coincidence," I say.

"Which you don't believe in, right? There's a quote from you about that in here. Everything's related. Nothing's coincidental."

The coffee tastes burnt, but I drink it anyway. Talking to Templeton can be frustrating, which is why I avoid doing it. He's been strangely possessive of me for a long time, confusing the real life person with the character in his book. It doesn't help that I've made liberal use of him, not just as a source of information but to do back-channel legwork. Thanks to his celebrated run at the now-defunct *Houston Post* and his voracious appetite for gossip, he knows everyone and knows everything about everyone.

"Listen to me, Brad. The woman who was murdered yesterday was young and carefree. Maybe irresponsible, but who wasn't at that age? She was full of life. Her mother said all she wanted was to be happy, and instead she's on a slab at the morgue waiting to be cut open some more. Now I need a way to link the man who did this to the scene. You can help with that, but you're going to have to take this seriously."

"I do take it seriously."

"What I'm saying is, I need you to go back through any letters or emails or any kind of communication you've gotten, and make sure there's nothing out of the ordinary."

"Give me a name," he says.

"What?"

"You have a suspect, so give me his name. That'll make it easy."

"I can't give you a name, you know that." I cut him off before he can object. "But I can tell you this. The victim's name is Simone Walker, but her married name was Young. Because the guy she married, his name is Jason Young."

"Jason Young," he says.

"That's the name of the husband."

"Ah." He reaches inside his jacket for a pen, then writes the name on a napkin, stuffing it away as the food arrives. "You're not eating?"

"I don't have the appetite. I'm heading to the ME's office after this."

"Better safe than sorry," he says, digging in.

Between bites, he catches me up on his latest project, a book about Dean Corll, the notorious Candy Man serial killer from the early seventies, who terrorized the Heights neighborhood where I grew up, not so far from where Charlotte and I live now. Back then it was just as diverse ethnically, but more working class. Corll's victims, mostly teenage boys, didn't go unnoticed, but the police were all too quick to write them off as runaways.

The city's seedy underbelly has always been one of Templeton's obsessions. His first book, which I've never read, was about a Houston real estate mogul from the late forties who was found hanging from the rafters in his stable. It would've passed for a suicide except that the man's mistress had been strung up, too. During the interviews he did for *The Kingwood Killing*, he talked a lot about Dean Corll, so I'm not surprised he'd gone back to the story. Recent events may have contributed.

"They've found another one of his victims," Templeton says, using his fork to punctuate. "One of the bodies, I mean."

"I'm aware of that."

"So I was thinking maybe it was time to revisit that case. Tell the story from a fresh perspective. I've always been interested in Corll, you know that."

"The serial killer thing leaves me cold," I say.

"What's that supposed to mean?"

"It just does. The whole cultural fixation. There are so many books written about these people that they're practically celebrities. They're the ones you're making famous, not me. It's no wonder you have imitators, the way the pathology's been glamorized."

"That's so naive," he says. "The next thing you're gonna tell me is that listening to gangsta rap turns good suburban kids into stone-cold thugs. It's ridiculous. You can't blame writers for turning people into serial killers—and anyway, I don't think it's possible to glamorize a man who tortured and murdered young boys."

"You're right," I say. "Maybe you should write about him. It'll keep you out of my hair, for one thing. I was just a kid when it all happened. Unless you're looking for some insight into what it was like in the Heights for an eleven-year-old."

"I actually would be interested in that," he says.

"It wasn't like anything. We had no idea what was going on. I certainly didn't. Compared to now, we were sheltered."

He puts his fork down and starts chuckling. "Sheltered in the seventies? Drugs and the Sexual Revolution? Disco? Where were you, man?"

"I was eleven. And disco came later, anyway."

His smile fades. "But you're not being honest with me, March. All the time we've known each other you've been holding back. You *knew* I was into the Corll thing, and you never said a word. I can hardly believe it—but then, it's you we're talking about."

"You know what? I've got to get going."

"Not so fast. I'm helping you with your investigation, so you have to help with mine."

"I don't have any help to give, remember? I didn't work that case."

"March," he says. "I've been talking to your cousin."

"My *cousin?*"

"Tammy Putnam. You know who I mean. She runs a website devoted to the victims of Dean Corll, including her brother Moody. Now, I knew about the site, but I didn't know until I actually interviewed her that the two of you are family. She says you and Moody were inseparable."

"Brad, listen to me—"

"She also says you've essentially kicked her out of your life, and this is why."

If I hadn't been up all night, if I wasn't operating on a diet of black coffee and the bagel Aguilar fed me four and a half hours ago, I could handle this bombshell a little better. But I have, and I am, so I handle it by slamming my mug on the table, sloshing the last of my coffee onto the last of his fish and chips. He scoots back in a rush, but his eyes alight with glee.

"A palpable hit," he says. "Now fair is fair. I want to know the truth about your cousin's theory. She says Moody knew Dean Corll's friends, was definitely taken by him, and that you know it too, but refuse to admit it."

"Tammy's a lonely woman with a lot of bitterness about how her life's turned out," I say. "She never even heard about Dean Corll until she saw a thing on TV about him, and then she became obsessed. Moody, her brother . . . his disappearance is to her what the Kennedy assassination was to Oliver Stone. The moment when everything turned bad."

"So she's making it up?"

I shake my head. "She believes it. It's just not true."

"Have you actually looked at her website, though? I did and it seems pretty convincing. I can tell you the Corll experts respect what she's doing—"

"Then they're not too bright. No disrespect, but a lot of these armchair theorists aren't. And no I haven't read it. I don't need to. I know for a fact Moody wasn't kidnapped by Dean Corll. Please."

"And you didn't become a cop in the first place because of his disappearance? That's what she seems to think."

The sneer on my face must speak volumes.

"You deny it," he says. "But if you're so sure your cousin wasn't a victim, then what did happen to him? Answer me that."

"Like I said, I was just eleven. Moody was fifteen and that's a world of difference. His sister wants a glamorous explanation for what happened to him, and in our sick and twisted society being the victim of a serial killer is glamorous. But that doesn't make it true."

"You haven't answered my question."

"And I'm not going to, Brad. All I'm going to say is this: don't spread around what Tammy tells you like it's holy writ. She doesn't know what she's talking about. There's a reason I don't return her calls—and if you want me to return yours, then drop it."

"You already don't return my calls."

"Exactly," I say. "And you wonder why."

I'm awake now and burning with anger, the same smoldering rage I feel every time Tammy Putnam's name comes up. Charlotte knows better now than to even mention her. The woman is certifiable, and has a knack for dragging other people into her insanity.

First she'd ruined her own marriage and poisoned her kids against her, then left alone had started chipping away at the rest of us. Before he died, she even had my uncle all turned around, the man who pretty much raised me, halfway convinced his flesh-and-blood son had been murdered by a psychopath—and I, his adopted son, was keeping the truth from him. She's never had any idea the kind of grief she's stirring up, and wouldn't care anyway. Everything she does is about herself. It's always been that way, even in the spring of 1973.

I run a couple of lights on my way to the medical examiner's office, and screech to a halt in the mostly empty parking lot. Inside, I follow a path of bright corridors to my brother-in-law's lab, but Bridger isn't in. The shades are drawn and the door locked tight. I continue down the hall to Dr. Green's lair, wishing I'd gone home to sleep like Bascombe told me instead of wasting my time on Brad Templeton.

"You're early," Sheila Green says.

"Fine," I snap. "I can come back later."

"Who put the burr under your saddle, huh? Is that any way to talk to a lady?"

"I retract my statement."

"Good boy. Now let's go downstairs and get started. I'm looking forward to this."

In the elevator she takes out her cell phone and shows me the pictures she snapped on Friday, the day of the snow. Her Mercedes in the ME's parking lot, blanketed with an inch of white powder. A five- or six-year-old kid standing next to a stunted snowman in the front yard of a hulking brick two-story. Dr. Green and a distinguished-looking gray-haired man I assume is the other Dr. Green, the cardiologist, each of them palming snowballs like they're about to start a fight.

"What about you, March? You take any?"

"I was working." I rub my eyes. The snow seems like ages ago, but it's been less than forty-eight hours since it came and went.

"You were working," she says. "So was everybody else, but that didn't stop us from going outside and enjoying ourselves. I mean, when was the last time it snowed like that in this town? Oh, right: never. All people do around here is whine and complain about the weather, how hot it is, how miserable, all the mosquitoes flying around. I get sick of hearing it. Then something like this happens and you don't even take a moment to experience it?"

"Hey, I'm *from* Houston. Where were you born?"

She frowns. "I didn't know that about you. It explains some things."

"I don't complain about the weather. I like the heat. It's what separates the men from the boys. Only a certain kind of person can live in this town."

"Now, that I can agree with. You know what my husband says? This city is a cocktail of everything wrong in the country—suburban sprawl, consumerism, religious fanatics—with a little olive of sanity floating in the middle."

"Your husband sounds like an Inner Looper. Where's he from?"

She smirks. "Virginia. But like the bumper sticker says, we weren't born here, but we got here as fast as we could."

"You and half the population of Louisiana."

Her mouth twists. As Templeton would say, a palpable hit. "You know I went to Tulane, don't you?"

"I'm just saying. If you come here from Louisiana and complain about the heat . . . well, what were you expecting?"

Small talk with Sheila Green. I've definitely stepped through the looking glass. She seems to realize this, too.

"While I've got you in such an obliging mood," she says, "let me ask you one thing. Your lieutenant, that beautiful Denzel-looking man?"

"You mean Bascombe? I don't see the resemblance."

"You don't have the right kind of eyes. Anyway, did you pick something up from him last night, something a little off?"

"That tongue-lashing he gave me? Standard operating procedure."

The temperature drops as we enter the autopsy theater, where an assistant in scrubs is already busy arranging instruments. Simone Walker's body lies on a stainless steel table, translucently white under the bright lamps. Green goes straight over, but I hang back.

People say sometimes that you never grow accustomed to death, that something about a murder victim will always get to you, no matter how many you've seen before. But you do get used to it and it happens all too quickly. Perhaps the only profession that acclimatizes you quicker is war. Looking at the body on the slab, I feel nothing but curiosity. With the doctor's help, it might speak to me. It might assist me in my work. Whatever a person really is—a consciousness, even a soul—is long gone at this point. Simone, to the extent she exists for me at all, isn't lying on the table. She's in the air, ever present and not at all.

I approach slowly, taking in the cold, clinical details that only here can be revealed. From the rib cage down the long line of her body, the skin remains untouched, almost pristine. The fatal wound is just over the breast, and it looks like the blade was buried to the hilt and seesawed back and forth, opening the gash ever wider.

"What I think," Green says, "is that he killed her first with this one blow." She leans over the wound with a gleaming pair of tweezers, clamping onto something within the opening, then holding it up for inspection. "See that? Some kind of fiber. If you had the top she was wearing, I would bet this thread would match up. But the clothes weren't at the scene, were they?"

"Just the shorts she was wearing," I say.

"The other puncture wounds are very different. See how uniform they are?" She points to six thin punctures in a row, arcing in a crescent across Simone's chest. "He took her clothes off afterward, and probably straddled her, and started stabbing like this." She reverses a scalpel in her fist and pummels the air. "I don't know the significance of that, but it's interesting." The assistant hands her an instrument and she measures the depth of the wounds. "They're shallower than the first stab."

"Like he used a second knife?"

"Ah, I wouldn't say that. It looks to me like the same blade; he's just using the tip for the postmortem mutilation."

While I process this, she and the assistant turn the body. Once again, the skin is unmarked until halfway up her back, then suddenly destroyed by a chaotic flurry of puncture marks.

"Look at this," she says.

"He went crazy on her."

"No, he didn't. See this?" She uses the scalpel again to trace crescents over Simone's back. "There it is. One. Two. Three. Four. Five. Six. And there, too. Over and over again, but it's that same pattern. Six in a row, all with the same arch."

"Like the shape of a frown," the assistant says.

Green shrugs. "Maybe."

I stare at the diced stretch of skin, the same shallow gashes that mark the front of the body, only repeated over and over, one series on top of another. I study the shape, visualizing Green's arm moving up and down like the bloodless knife in *Psycho*.

One, two, three, four, five, six, again and again—but for what?

I take a few steps back, then turn, closing my eyes to concentrate. There's something coming, echoing up from the recesses of my mind, but it's not an image so much as a sound. A dull reverberation on wood.

"Hand me that," I say, reaching for the scalpel, but Dr. Green doesn't oblige. I go to the empty table a few feet away, slipping out my pocketknife, snicking open the blade. Green and the assistant both follow me with their eyes.

I spread my hand on the stainless surface, moving my fingers wider, then slowly—very slowly—I tap the point of the blade against the table. To the left of my pinkie. *One.* Between the pinkie and ring finger. *Two.* Between the ring and middle finger. *Three.* Between the middle and index finger. *Four.* Between the index and thumb. *Five.* To the right of the thumb. *Six.*

"You see what it is?"

I start to repeat the pattern, but Green raises her hand.

"I see."

"It's like a game," I say. "A dare. You start slow and you go faster and faster to prove just how good you really are, and how cold-blooded."

She sets the scalpel down and holds her open hand just above Simone's back, checking the pattern and nodding. "I think you're right."

Everything's related. Nothing's coincidental. A seemingly random frenzy isn't random at all once you break it down. The logic emerges as all the brutality is reverse engineered, peeling back the layers until the first blow has yet to fall, then running it forward to confirm that your conjecture is right on target.

The man who killed Simone Walker stripped her to the waist and sat on top of her. He pressed his hand against her skin, spreading the fingers out, and then he tested himself. The shallow wounds weren't meant to kill or even to cause her pain. She was only the canvas. No, not even that. She was the tabletop, existing only for one thing: to help her killer prove something to himself. He would have started slowly at first, just like I did. And once that initial practice was complete, he would have rolled her over to start fresh, going faster and faster.

"This changes things," I say. "It's not what I was expecting."

"We're not done yet."

"I realize that. But I better make a call."

I go into the hallway to use my phone, but all I get is Bascombe's voicemail. I try Aguilar with the same result, and then Ordway, who picks up on the fifth ring and sounds winded. He listens to my news with mild interest, then informs me that after confronting Jason Young with his wife's murder and his bloody clothes, the suspect responded as you'd expect.

"He lawyered up."

"Is he still there?"

"Not anymore. Everyone's packed it up for the day, in fact. I'm just heading out."

"We'll need samples from Young," I say. "There's no way he did this without cutting himself—did you check his hands for cuts? I remember seeing some on his knuckles."

"Chief," he says, "this'll keep. The L.T. took his shot and came up with nothing."

"And prints? You did print him before cutting him loose, right?"

"Beats me. Take it up with the man first thing in the morning."

Back inside, Green looks at me expectantly and then not at all, catching from my body language all she needs to know. She gives the wall clock a reflexive glance.

"That Denzel-looking man just struck out," I say.

"There's something up with him, March. And it's not just you."

When she starts the Y-incision, I tune her out. The rest is merely confirmation of what we already know. Still, organs must be removed and weighed, the results spoken aloud for the benefit of the recording.

My wave of excitement crests under the wet monotony of it all, my eyes growing heavy. I prop my back against the wall for support.

"I've had people cry in here, and I've had them throw up. I've had them run out in disgust. But I've never had anybody fall asleep, March, and it better not happen today."

"Don't worry. I've got plenty to keep my mind occupied."

"Here's something else." She wipes a gloved hand on her apron and takes a step toward me. "I don't see any signs of sexual assault. If you were thinking along lust murder lines, I've got nothing for you. This is about the strangest thing I've ever seen."

"That's saying something."

"Not the most horrific, maybe. But the strangest."

I can't argue with that.

Outside, I strip my scrubs off and retreat to the back door where the cracked slab and sand-filled ashtrays serve as a smoker's lounge. This is where Bridger always comes to decompress, but now I have it all to myself.

Simone Walker didn't have much in life, as far as I can tell, and what she did have she might not have valued. What she'd endured as a child, maybe that had made it impossible for her to ever find what she really wanted, or keep wanting it once she did. But the people in her life, they all used her. Her mother used her silence, and then her very existence, for her own validation. Her husband rewrote the rules on her, and finally just used her for sex. Her landlord, Dr. Hill, who'd admitted after all that self-absorbed chatter that Simone was "sweet," was just using that sweet girl to keep up with the bills.

And the man who killed her—maybe it was Young, maybe it wasn't—what he did to her was worst of all. He used her, too. As nothing more than a backstop. A convenient surface. A warm body inserted into the nightmare he'd been nurturing for his own excitement. So it's only right that when I find him, when I can prove his guilt conclusively, at least to myself if no one else, that I make sure of one thing: that he too suffers the indignity of being used.

Call this revenge if you want.

But to me, it's only a question of balancing the scales.

CHAPTER 5

I know this place. I've been here. With a few changes I might have grown up on this street. The sidewalk breaks under my feet, new fissures pushing toward the storm drains on one side and the sun-browned grass on the other. I stretch my hands and no matter how far they reach, the rolling chain-link fence is a little bit farther, barely restraining the Aranda dog as it jumps and barks at me, making no sound.

I remember when that dog was run over, the summer of the bicentennial.

Strange that I can't hear it, strange that the roiling ground makes no noise and neither do the trees swaying in the empty park across the road.

The one thing I can hear, coming from somewhere behind me that remains invisible when I turn to look, is the clicking of a bicycle chain, the hum of tires coasting over concrete. But the bike isn't here, I know that. It's somewhere safe, wedged in the gap between two corrugated storage sheds, blocks and blocks away, out past the school.

It's the car making that sound, a gleaming green Ford circling the block. I follow the flash of sunlight on the glass, the heads silhouetted inside, three or four of them. Only the driver's window is down, a brown and thin-wristed forearm jutting out with a hand-rolled cigarette clutched in the fingers. The sidewalk moves under my feet, but I get no farther. It's like a swaying, fragmented treadmill keeping pace with my every move.

—*You can go here and you can go there, but you can't go away.*

There's another sound, a metallic pop, and slowly the fact dawns on me that it's the thumb break on my old duty rig. My old pistol slides up into my hand, the one I carried as a rookie and only fired once in anger. I look at my arm and it's blue. All of me is. My old uniform fits again, like a suit of polyester-blend armor.

The ground settles and up through my legs a sense of calm takes hold, the rootedness of an ancient tree. More heads appear in the car, too many to count, all pressing against the glass as the Ford bears down. Chrome glistens and blinds me, then my pistol answers it—one, two, three. Four, five, six. The air moves, and my rounds carve tracer arcs around the fast-approaching green car. The misses baffle me.

—*Come to me, kid. Don't be scared.*

Brass tumbles at my feet while the Aranda dog silently wails. One, two, three. A cigarette bursts on the curb. Four, five, six. The brown hand tapping on the Ford's green door. The car sails past me, gliding over air, the driver's eyes behind gold-rimmed sunglasses. Under the long trunk, a thumping sound. And the metal quivers in circuits like rippling water.

"Roland, stop."

A cold touch sinks through my forehead.

"You're burning up."

I find her wrist in the dark and pull the hand away. "It's nothing."

"You were kicking me."

"Sorry." I throw the covers back, swing my legs onto the hardwood floor. "Just another bad dream."

Her laughter is soft and kind. "You and your dreams. You should see somebody."

"Go back to sleep."

A minute or two under the shower and I can't remember the details anymore. Just a handful of surreal and disconnected puzzle pieces from a moviemaker's idea of an acid trip. I run my uncle's old double-edged safety razor under the tap, shaving in the usual sleepy, imprecise way, then go to the closet. From bed, Charlotte's voice echoes.

"Wear one of your new outfits."

They're not new and I hate that word *outfits*. But I pick through the zippered bags anyway, still reluctant to admit that my father-in-law of all people had more style in his little finger than I'll ever possess. Or care to. I don't come from a world where clothes are chosen for how they look. Though we have a few peacocks in Homicide, a jacket's main function is to keep your side arm from showing.

My old partner Stephen Wilcox saw it differently, always dressing like a cut-rate English gentleman to the extent the weather allowed. If he knew, he'd burn with envy over this hand-tailored wardrobe and have no qualms about wearing a dead man's clothes. He doesn't know, however, because despite our recent truce we are not really on speaking terms.

"I like the brown checks," Charlotte calls.

The most old-geezer-looking option of the bunch, a tweedy sort of jacket with brown horn buttons. I put it on over a blue shirt and a pair of khakis, checking in the mirror to make sure the grip of my SIG Sauer doesn't poke out through the side vent.

It's just past six when I head down the stairs, leaving Charlotte to sleep awhile longer. The stairs out back leading up to the apartment over the garage are wet with dew, and the window next to the door glows gold, meaning our tenants are already up. Unlike Dr. Hill, we don't rent the apartment out from necessity. The original idea was that we'd live there while having the house updated, only that project never quite came to fruition. Once the apartment existed, Charlotte wouldn't let it go to waste.

As I gaze toward the door, Gina Robb comes out. She teaches at a private school out in Spring, commuting back and forth every day against the flow of traffic, while her husband, Carter, works at something called an outreach center in the Montrose area, where people hang out over coffee to talk about books and watch movies and have old-time religion subtly forced on them. Carter was a youth pastor at a suburban megachurch last year, a standard-bearer for the fanatics Sheila Green mentioned yesterday. Now he's in a kind of free fall, a feeling I can easily relate to.

"Good morning, Mr. March."

Gina's always so formal with me, despite the closeness that's grown between us all since the Robbs moved in. She dresses formal, too, in a high-necked, round-collared overcoat that looks too warm even for our cold snap, and a velvet thrift-store beret, just in case the French Resistance needs some backup. When she comes down the stairs, her eyes light up in a way that makes me cringe with anticipation.

"I like your blazer," she says. She *would* like it. "Is that what you call it, a blazer?"

"You got me," I say. "It's one of the ones Charlotte brought back from her father's. She's trying to make me look more distinguished."

"She's doing a good job."

"Thanks."

When I first met her, I didn't see the appeal of this rather plain and eccentric girl, and certainly couldn't understand what it was Carter, with his more athletic, unreflective cast of mind, would find appealing. Now I do. She's constant and bright, an optimist grounded in reality, an eccentric with breathtaking disregard for how other people perceive her.

"Your husband's a lucky man, you know that?"

She bunches her lips the way she always does when I say something silly. "I'm sorry we missed you yesterday, but I know they work you so hard."

"I guess we're both the early risers in our families."

"Carter's up," she says quickly, almost defensively. "I can get him if you want to—"

"No, no. I'm just on my way out, like you."

"He does want to talk to you about something, Mr. March. It wouldn't take long."

"Right now, you mean?"

"We just weren't sure when we'd see you, and here you are." She pleads with her whole body hunched forward, hands together in a prayerful gesture. "Let me go get him real fast, okay? It'll take, like, two minutes."

Set loose by my nod, she bounds halfway up the stairs before stopping herself, ascending the rest of the way at a calmer pace. When she returns, Carter is with her, his hair still matted from sleep, looking ridiculous in shorts and an unzipped hoodie.

"I do have to go," Gina says, getting on tiptoes to kiss his stubbly cheek.

Once she's reversing down the driveway, leaving us alone together, Carter wipes the traces of a sheepish grin from his lips, signaling that whatever he wants to tell me must be important. In his mid-twenties and no stranger to tragedy, he still has a boyish way of steeling himself for serious talk, like he's afraid of not being taken as an adult.

"Roland," he says. "There was something I wanted to talk to you about."

"So I gathered."

"It's . . . really, I don't know if it's awkward or not. But we thought we should say something to you first—in case it might be, you know?"

The hoodie falls open. I scan the words on his wrinkled T-shirt. MY SAVIOR CAN BEAT UP YOUR HONOR STUDENT.

Nice.

"Gina," he says. "We just found out that she's pregnant."

My chest tightens, like somebody just inflated a balloon under the ribs.

"You're having a kid?" The words sound hollow in my ears. "That's great, Carter. Congratulations. That's . . . wonderful news."

"It's just . . ." His shoulders rise and his head starts shaking, physically disowning his own thoughts. "We were worried, you know? About how to tell Charlotte." Not able to look me in the eyes. "You know," he says. "Because of Jessica."

"Oh."

I'm not prepared to hear her name on his lips, not ready to talk like this about something I hold deep inside, cherishing it like a cancer.

My mouth twists and I feel my whole body tensing up, which Carter sees and goes wide-eyed over, the way he would if he'd inadvertently knocked over a vase.

"I didn't mean to upset you," he says. "I know we've never really talked about it. Theresa Cavallo said something, and then . . ." His voice trails off. "I wouldn't bring it up at all except that Charlotte said something about her in church. About Jessica."

"Let's . . ." I begin, but my throat tightens. "She said something at *church*?"

"During prayer time, she shared how she still struggles with what happened. How God could let it happen, you know—and also the way she misses her daughter, misses just having a daughter. It was really honest of her . . . and it just made us worry that maybe we shouldn't say anything yet."

I'm moving my head. I'm clamping my hand over my mouth. Trying to look thoughtful while buying time. Trying to get control of what's happening in my head.

She talked. She told these people. She shared.

The way she misses her daughter.

Even having a daughter.

Words I couldn't bring myself to think, let alone broadcast, words I couldn't whisper to Charlotte in the dark. She *shared* them. She was *really honest.*

"Tell her," I say. "She'll be fine. Or if you want, I'll do it. But I know it would mean more coming from you two. Congratulations again—"

"I know you've gotta go." He reaches for my arm but stops short of contact. "But I thought we should talk about this other thing, too. Charlotte and church, I mean. We'd really like to see you there, too, but I'm sensing that's not gonna happen anytime soon. Is it a problem for you, her coming with us?"

I throw my briefcase into the car and slump behind the wheel. "Carter, it's a free country. She can do whatever she wants—" Pulling the door shut. "Obviously. She does what she wants already."

He has more to say, but the engine drowns him out. I reverse down the driveway, smiling my heartfelt and skin-deep good wishes, leaving behind a household I've increasingly lost the ability to understand.

I know how Simone Walker must have felt, having a spouse turn religious on her. There's not much chance of Charlotte cutting me open—not literally—but otherwise I can relate. The rules change in the middle of the game, and it's not enough for you to stand by and let it happen, to pretend you're okay with it. No, you have to bend with the rules. You have to go along. At first they'll accept lip service and platitudes, but before long it's sincerity or nothing. The line will be drawn and if you ignore that line it will be pointed out to you. Cross here, but do it with both feet and never think of crossing back.

As I drive, the memory comes to me, Charlotte apprehensive on the bedroom threshold, saying it was only polite to go to church since they'd asked her. Saying it would be interesting to go back.

"Do it if you want," I'd said. "If it makes you happy."

"I think it would make *them* happy."

And I'd said: "Some people find comfort in the ritual," or words to that effect, which earned a quizzical smile from her, like she was amused and surprised all at once that a thing so obvious would be inaccessible to me. We'd once laughed together about the cross-wearing Theresa Cavallo, a missing persons detective I'd worked with and grown to respect, who'd psychoanalyzed my professional faults as the result of my anger toward God.

Only Charlotte wasn't laughing anymore and isn't laughing now. Every Sunday she goes with the Robbs to their newfound church just inside the Loop, cloistered in the shell of a defunct electronics super-store. And every Sunday I find a reason not to go with them, excuses of a secondary order to keep me from having to address the real one, the obvious one.

I've been telling myself I'm fine with this, that I can live with it. There was a time not too long ago when Charlotte popped pills to sleep at night and we were at each other's throats, and I am relieved finally to be through it—her low-wattage religiosity seemed like a small price to pay for peace on the home front. And I like Carter and Gina. Having them in our lives has been good for us, and I'd like to think the reverse is true, as well.

The thought of Charlotte opening up like that, though, baring her soul to these people. Not just her soul but ours, throwing out our shared tragedy like it's nothing more than an issue in scare quotes that needs working out in therapy. That I can't bear. We were three once and now we're two, and if there's anyone she needs to talk to, it should be me, the only person who shares the loss.

Giving it to them, not just Carter and Gina but whoever else was present for the spectacle, handing it over to strangers is like betrayal.

No, it is betrayal.

Everything's public, of course, and always has been. Every reader of *The Kingwood Killing* reaches the part of the story where March, the intrepid detective, learns of the car crash that put his wife and daughter in the emergency room, on the very same day the Towers fell and his plane was grounded in New Orleans. Wilcox and March driving the wife-murderer Donald Fauk across the Atchafalaya River, capturing his confession on a handheld recorder.

There's a reason my copy of the book appears unread. At least I've never had to sit there before as someone read the passage, never had to endure the reader's prurient sympathy.

Fingerprints are old school, a technology I understand completely. I lifted my first set at age thirteen using a kit jury-rigged from instructions found in a library book, then eyeballed a match with the only subject who'd submit to ink, my long-suffering uncle. Without the aid of computer databases or trained crime scene technicians, I can still develop prints from a variety of challenging surfaces, and if push comes to shove make side-by-side comparisons with the aid of an honest-to-goodness magnifying glass.

"Which is why," I tell Lt. Bascombe, "I cannot understand how the Houston Police Department, which the last time I checked does have computer databases and does have trained crime scene analysts, still can't tell me after thirty-six hours whether the prints on that table are a match with my suspect or not."

He glances up from a stack of overtime forms he's been autographing, acting surprised to find me still in the room.

"What do you want me to do? I'm sure they can tell you if there's a match. They just haven't yet." From a wad of newspaper on the credenza behind him, he withdraws a creased copy of the *Chronicle* from sometime last week. "You realize, don't you—and I'm quoting here—that 'a criminal investigation is under way into alleged wrongdoing at HPD's fingerprinting comparison unit,' end quote."

"Yes, I know," I say, snatching the paper from him. I skim the article and give up halfway through, slumping into a chair. "Can I just say one thing? Throughout all the closings and openings and re-closings of the DNA section, all the inquiries and panels and reshufflings, you know what I did? I did like the poster says: kept calm and carried on."

Entertained, Bascombe allows himself a faint smile.

"When I had to, I pulled some strings and got my DNA work done through back channels, and when I couldn't, I'd grin and bear it. Was it frustrating to farm out lab work? Check. Was it humiliating to work for the fourth largest city in America and be reduced to that? You bet. But I told myself this DNA thing was newfangled stuff. I told myself they were overwhelmed, they were still working out the kinks. Hey, listen, I don't understand how it all works, but then I'm not a scientist. But you know what? I *can* dust for prints—"

"That's what you said. Thirteen years old."

"And I can hold two prints next to each other and tell you if they look the same or not. That at least is not rocket science." I ball the *Chronicle* up in my fist. "That's basic. I mean, Sherlock Holmes could process fingerprints, right? And that was the eighteen hundreds. So why all the sudden can the Houston Police not do it?"

"Amen, man, but you're complaining to the wrong person."

Disgusted, I shoot the newspaper off the rim of Bascombe's trash can. "Don't just leave that there," he says.

I scoop it up and make the dunk.

"I'm gonna go watch the tapes of your interview yesterday."

"You do that," he says.

"And if I don't hear back on those prints, heads are gonna roll."

"Let 'em have it."

Outside my cubicle, I run into Captain Drew Hedges, a file folder under one arm and an HPD mug in the opposite hand, his usual plain gabardine suit traded in for an expensive-looking pinstripe model. He still has the weather-beaten leathery appearance of an old-time Texas lawman, still the same piercing gaze, but the hair is different, too. The gunmetal salt-and-pepper is gone, replaced by an even patrician white.

"Morning, sir."

"Oh, March," he says, making it sound like we've just been talking and he's remembered something he wanted to add before I left. "I just wanted to say . . ." Then his voice trails off. He reaches with his free hand and pinches the lapel of my sport coat, rubbing the fabric back and forth. "Where did you get that?"

"What, this old thing?"

Aguilar's head pops above a nearby cubicle wall and doesn't retract when he sees I've spotted him. Clearly anticipating some kind of show.

Hedges drops my lapel thoughtfully, his eyes still lingering on the fabric. "I just wanted to say, good work this weekend. I knew you were fast, but that was something else."

A fishhook of a smile digs into Aguilar's poker face.

"I haven't closed mine, sir. Not yet. In fact, I'm having a hard time getting all the forensics back from the scene."

"Ah," he says. "I must have heard wrong." He gives my shoulder a pat. "Keep your nose to it, March, and get that thing cleared."

The thing I've always liked about Hedges is that he stays on top of cases. The higher up you go in the food chain, the harder it is for a sworn officer to stay true to the calling. The pressure to manage, to be an armed administrator, comes at you from all sides. For as long as he's run the Homicide Division, his sights have been set on what's happening underneath him, not up on high. To see him with his head in the clouds all the sudden, confusing one case with another and not being bothered about it, really throws me.

Not Aguilar, though. He wanders over with a glint in his eye.

"Is he gonna help you with your fingerprint conundrum?"

"He didn't even offer."

"So what's up with Hedges, anyway?"

"Maybe Bascombe knows."

"Ask him if you want, but I wouldn't. All you gotta do these days to get the lieutenant sideways with you is bring up the captain's name. Used to not be that way."

"Right, I know."

A glance behind me confirms what the tingling along my neck already suggested, that Bascombe is staring at me right now through his open door. I raise my eyebrows in his direction, then retreat into my cubicle to make another futile round of phone calls in search of reports that haven't arrived. Once I'm done, I lay everything out before me—the photos, the paperwork, the notes—doing my best to work out what happened.

What I know so far is that on the afternoon or early evening of Saturday, December 5, Simone Walker went outside to have a smoke. She brought her laptop and phone outside with her, and I have a request in for phone records. Either she was sitting facing the house or the pool—I don't know which, but if I did, it would help figure out which direction the killer came from. He might have entered through the house, but he might also have come through the garage or over the fence, even though there are no signs of forced entry or the inevitable broken foliage if he'd landed in the bushes.

Simone was wearing white shorts and some kind of top. The fiber recovered from the wound appears to be a light blue cotton. According to Dr. Hill, Simone often wore a baby blue Lacoste pullover that now is missing from her room. She might also have been wearing sweats on top of the shorts because of the cold.

The killer entered somehow, came up behind Simone while she was seated, covering her mouth and plunging the knife in. He worked it around in the wound, holding her tight until she bled out. There would have been blood all over her and most likely all over him. He must have stripped her while she was seated, then tilted the chair back to the ground before getting on top of her. Then he did the mutilation game, first in front and then on her back, probably rolling her away from the chair.

I think Bascombe was wrong when he suggested she was dragged to the pool's edge while seated. That would explain how the chair ended up at the bottom, but I can't make sense of the action. He probably threw the chair in after her because it was filthy with blood. The crime scene techs did fish it out and check for prints, but there was nothing.

Once he'd finished his game and thrown her body and the chair into the lap pool, he used towels and possibly Simone's clothing to wipe up the blood, rinsing everything in the water. When he left, he took all of it with him, along with her laptop and phone. He left the ashtray on the table with her cigarette inserted into a notch. All the butts in the ashtray were bagged for testing, but the results will no doubt be long in coming.

His second-to-last gesture, I think, was to pull her out of the water and pose the body. By the time he departed, he'd done a thorough job cleaning up after himself. Thanks to Luminol, recreating the spatter at the scene proved straightforward—the report, neatly wrapped in a binder by a tech named Edgar Castro, sits proudly on my desk, a reproach to the missing fingerprint results—so there's not much doubt that the attack took place under the pergola.

According to Dr. Hill, the furniture had been rearranged slightly. That's because of what his final move must have been. With everything he was taking packed away, probably in a bag brought to the scene for that purpose, he went to the far end of the pool and crouched down, just where Bascombe and I perched ourselves, and made sure that the image he was leaving behind matched the one in his mind.

Only one thing troubles me. With this much planning and this much method behind the killing, there's no way it happened on impulse. The killer I'm looking for is organized, a details man, a mechanically inclined problem solver. There was a rage driving him, sure, a dark mania, but on top of it was a ruling and rational template.

Is that Jason Young? So many things point to him, but I just don't know. Like Bascombe said yesterday, what I need is physical evidence. The blood from Young's shirt. The results of the fingerprint analysis. None of which I'm likely to get fast.

Aguilar comes into my cubicle, nudging my chair. "The lieutenant said you were gonna look at the video from yesterday. Mind if I sit in?"

I shake my head. "I need some coffee first. Get it cued up and I'll be there in a second. Want me to bring you anything?"

"I'm good."

In the break room, as I'm searching the drawers for something other than nondairy creamer, afraid that the unadulterated brew might prove toxic, my phone starts buzzing. I dig it out of my pocket and see Templeton's name on the screen. I'm tempted to let him go to voicemail, but it's always possible he checked his correspondence and found a letter from Jason Young.

"Hello?"

"I've got something for you." The delight in his voice is unmistakable, which gets my hopes up. "First thing this morning I read the news stories about your case. There was something you forgot to mention, wasn't there?"

"I told you what I could."

"But you didn't tell me that your murder victim was living with Joy Hill."

"You seemed to know already."

"I knew it was in West U., but not that the dead girl was found in Joy's house. That is too much of a coincidence, don't you think?"

"In what way, Brad?"

"Dr. Joy Hill," he says.

"And?"

"You don't know about her? A couple of years ago, the parents of one of her female students brought a civil suit. For sexual harassment."

He chuckles over the line. "It was withdrawn, probably settled out of court, but at the time there was some talk about her tenure being in jeopardy."

"In this day and age? Professors and students hooking up isn't exactly a new phenomenon."

"Well, her husband obviously thought it was a big deal. He said sayonara tout suite, even though it cost him. She got the house and a nice chunk of change."

"According to her, she took in a tenant to help make ends meet."

Templeton laughs. "You might want to check her bank balance just in case. I can think of other reasons why she'd want to have a pretty young girl at her beck and call. And if that girl wasn't so amenable, well, people get killed over things like that."

"Is that all you've got for me?"

"Isn't it enough?"

"Go back through your correspondence file and make sure you haven't gotten any crank letters that fit the profile I gave you."

"What about Joy Hill? Did you go through her bookshelves?"

"Brad, has she ever written you a letter?"

"Not that I know of."

"Then why don't you check. Goodbye."

I gulp some coffee down without any creamer, which only gives me something else to worry about. My first conversation with Joy Hill replays in my mind, from the time she snatched my Filofax to her last-minute tribute to Simone. Self-absorbed, calculating, condescending—all characteristics of methodical killers, though the qualities are not exclusive to them. Unless she's stronger than she looked, it is hard to imagine Dr. Hill committing such a physical crime. But then, I hardly know anything about her. If she was lying about her relationship with Simone, that's something I need to find out. A liaison between them would give her a motive.

And if he discovered something like this, given his religious convictions, how would Jason Young have reacted? If what Templeton says is true, it might give him a very compelling reason to lash out.

When I get to the monitoring room, Aguilar isn't alone. Mack Ord-way leans against a filing cabinet with a plastic evidence bag dangling from his hand. Inside is the promotional card from the strip club we found in Young's back pocket.

"You boys are gonna watch a video?" he says. "That sounds nice. But I'm thinking we ought to run out to this place and take a look around."

I pluck the envelope out of his hand, then drop into the chair next to Aguilar.

"Hit play."

After a lingering glance at the card, during which Ordway exits in a huff, he leans forward and mashes the button.

CHAPTER 6

Driving south from Bush Intercontinental Airport, half the billboards on I-45 advertise places like the Silk Cut, the upscale establishments catering to the affluent business set. Unlike the seedy roadside joints with neon signs and gravel parking lots full of dusty pickups, these gentlemen's clubs offer up their vice in a polished, sanitized form complete with a buffet.

The Silk Cut is screened from the surrounding chain restaurants and hotels by a line of sickly brown palm trees. A pink stucco building. A circular drive leading up to the covered entrance with a tail of asphalt wrapping around back. Rectangular brickwork to suggest the outline of absent windows. The landscaping up front is in worse shape than the trees, and the walls could use a good power wash. Business must be down.

Inside, the place is empty. Ordway would have been disappointed. The manager greets me and Aguilar at the front door, ushering us past an empty bar and an unlit stage into a back office where stored boxes of liquor compete with a cramped desk and a bank of video monitors. He's a clean-cut kid in his late twenties in designer denim and a tight-fitting

T-shirt with a chain hooked to the fat wallet stuffed in his hip pocket. He gives us the two available chairs and sits on the edge of the desk.

I produce a photo of Jason Young. "Can you tell me whether this guy was in here recently?"

"This guy?" He flicks the photo with his finger. "I had a feeling when you called that's what it was about. We came this close to calling y'all in the first place. I kept the video, too, just in case."

"You have video?" I ask.

"Give me a second and I'll pull it up."

He goes to the computer linked into the video system and mouse-clicks his way through the software. I leave my chair to peer over his shoulder.

"He'd already had plenty to drink when he came in here, but at first he didn't make any trouble. Just sat at the bar and watched the girls from there. Next thing I know, he's going at it with these other customers—here, look."

For the second time this morning, I find myself staring at Jason Young's image on-screen. The interview footage with Bascombe, crystal clear in vivid color, is a sharp contrast to this pixelized black-and-white view, and Young's demeanor is entirely at odds, too. Where he'd been shocked and tearful in Interview Room 2, giving a convincing performance of a man who's just learned of his wife's death, at the Silk Cut bar he holds himself with the tense, aggressive posture of a compressed spring. Facing the distant stage with his elbow propped behind him on the bar, he keeps turning his head sharply at the circle of customers to his right, a mix of men and women straining to order drinks.

The time stamp on the video reads half past eleven, well after Simone's body was discovered. The action at the Silk Cut was unfolding simultaneously with my investigation of the scene, which means it doesn't give him an alibi.

"He was making rude comments to the ladies."

"Are those girls strippers or something?" Aguilar asks.

The kid shakes his head. "They came in together, that whole group. I think they're all servers at one of the restaurants down the street. One of the men with them finally got in his face—see that?—and then *wham*, it all breaks loose."

The man accosting Young gets a word or two out before the fist shuts him up. When he stumbles, Young charges forward into the group, swinging at the others, and then I lose sight of him in the press of bodies until a couple of black-shirted security men start pulling everyone apart.

"Our guys didn't know what exactly went down, but if you have ten against one, guess who gets tossed to the curb? That's me." He points to his own silhouette on-screen, following security as they frog-march Young out of frame. "Here's the front door camera. We chuck him outside, and as soon as my back is turned, two of the guys he went after stream out after him. See, right there. He turns and *bam*, they clock him with something—maybe a belt buckle?—and he doesn't go down. He just takes it and goes right after them. Our guys had to break it up again." He taps the monitor. "There we are."

One of the security men gets Young in a bear hug and hustles him out into the parking lot off-screen. The other men stand and argue with the manager, then leave in the opposite direction.

"That's it."

I keep a USB hard drive on my keychain for moments like this. "Can you copy this stuff over for me?"

Once the transfer is made, we find our way back through the building quietly, saving the debrief for the privacy of the car. Light rain dimples the windshield.

"So what do you think?" I ask.

"I'd say it cuts in his favor. If we're looking for a calculating, methodical planner, this behavior doesn't really fit. Why would he go through all the trouble of orchestrating that scene if his next play was to tie one on and pick fights in a strip club?"

"Well, he could have been blowing off steam. After so much controlled activity, he needed some kind of break."

"But the killing is the release, right? After that, how's a stupid punch-up gonna give him a high? It don't make sense to me."

"No," I say. "Me, either. But he was lying to us."

"Everybody lies to the police, but that doesn't make them murderers. If a guy like Young, who makes himself out to be so upstanding, saving money and going to church and even working for that reverend, is at the same time getting drunk and blowing money on strippers, maybe he's not gonna come clean about it without some pushing."

"All right, then. I guess we'd better push."

Before he'll talk to us, Reverend Curtis Blunt insists on a guided tour through his facility, an uninsulated steel-framed warehouse with corrugated walls and a warren of nicely appointed offices in back. His silver mane sits high on his head, shellacked in place and rendered stiff by a large volume of hair spray, and he dresses all in black—black Justin boots, black jeans, a black shirt open at the throat, a black leather sport coat—except for the shiny Western buckle at his waist.

Of the four businesses he's successfully founded in his life, he tells us he sold two and passed the other two on to his sons, freeing himself up for full-time ministry. Then he shows us where this ministry occurs: an elaborate movie set made to appear like a book-lined study with a clear plastic lectern standing in the middle.

"We're doing a two-camera shoot these days," he says, indicating the tripods set up at opposite edges of the stage, "and we're doing the cuts in real time back there behind that glass." A window at the rear of the room reveals a darkened control center, much more elaborate than the bank of monitors at the Silk Cut.

Next, he takes us to the duplicating room, where stacks of DVD cases are lined up along a row of folding tables. On the wall hang a series of artful portraits showing Blunt in action against the blurred backdrop of the set we've just witnessed. Blunt with a raised finger in the air, an open Bible clutched in his other hand. Blunt with eyes closed, hands folded in prayer. Blunt waving the Bible above him, almost as if he's a quarterback cocking his arm for a pass. He sees me looking at the photos and smiles.

"Take a couple of these," he says, pulling some videos off the stack. "Just so you get a feel for what it is we do here."

In his office, place of pride is reserved for a pair of massive Frederic Remington bronzes: a cowboy straddling a bucking bronco and a stampede of bison. Again, Blunt smiles as I take note of them, though he stops short of offering me one.

"As a man of God, I have an obligation to cooperate with your investigation, but I'll tell you this right now: you've got the wrong end of this thing. A man of my experience doesn't get where he is in life without being a good judge of character, so I can say this with absolute certainty. Jason Young did not harm his wife."

"You can't actually vouch for his whereabouts after you left here Saturday morning, is that correct? That would have been before noon."

"Before noon, that's right. I'm not saying I was with him, Officer, just that I know him. Believe me, I have looked into that young man's heart on many an occasion, and what I've found there is a great deal of confusion and a great deal of misery but a complete absence of guile."

Aguilar gives one of his impassive nods, which Blunt takes as encouragement.

"There were problems in that marriage, I can tell you. When a couple is unequally yoked like that, strife is inevitable, and naturally I've been called upon to counsel many young people in that predicament. In Jason's case, though, the difficulties were particularly acute on account of the girl's background and temperament."

"How well did you know Simone Walker?" I ask.

"I only met Simone Young," he says, emphasizing the last name, "a handful of times, and spiritually speaking she was very closed off, very hostile. Although Jason had his heart set on reconciliation, if I can be perfectly frank with you, there didn't seem much hope of that, short of a miracle. I counseled him to reconsider divorce, since in my view there were biblical grounds." Seeing another of Aguilar's nods, his voice raises an octave. "I'm not one of those old-fashioned Bible thumpers who believes there are no biblical grounds, Officer. Maybe that surprises you."

"What grounds are you talking about?" I ask.

"There's infidelity, there's abandonment." He ticks them off with his fingers. "I believe both criteria were met in this case."

"She was seeing someone else?" Templeton's remarks about Dr. Hill spring to mind again. "You know that for a fact?"

"I don't *know* it," he says. "But I did discern it."

"I see."

"When I spoke to Jason, he told me you already knew about the seduction. That's what it was, a seduction. She thought she could lure him back into her power—and frankly, the boy was weak. Who wouldn't be, under the circumstances? He believed what he wanted to until she made her mercenary motives too obvious for him to ignore."

"The woman you're talking about is the victim of a vicious murder," I say. "Isn't there something in the Bible about not speaking ill of the dead?"

"Is there?" he says. "I don't think so. And I'm not speaking ill, Officer, I'm speaking the truth. That's what you want, isn't it? The truth is, Jason was struggling to put back together something that was already rent asunder, and that's enough to drag any of us down. It is not, however, a motive for murder. He truly loved her."

"As far as you're aware," Aguilar says, "does Jason Young have a drinking problem? 'Cause when we picked him up at church yesterday morning, he looked like he'd spent the night with a bottle, if you know what I mean."

The question checks Blunt for a moment. He moves behind his heavy mahogany desk, behind the red leather chair, nervously fingering the line of brass tacks along the seat back.

"Consuming alcohol is prohibited by his employment covenant."

"So you're not aware—?"

"Listen," he says. "None of us is perfect. And while I do not condone such behavior, it's not my place to interrogate the people who work for me about their practices outside these walls."

"So you have kind of a 'don't ask, don't tell' policy in place?"

Blunt recoils at the term. "I wouldn't say that at all. If Jason does partake, I'm not aware of it, and frankly, I would be surprised. But as I said, we are sinful by nature, meaning that when we are tempted, we sometimes succumb. I won't get on a high horse and pretend otherwise."

"What about violence?" I ask. "Did Jason ever confide in you about any abuse in the relationship?"

"There was some abuse in her past, I understand."

"I'm talking about now. Did he ever hit her?"

"Absolutely not."

In the silence that follows, Aguilar signals with a tilt of the head. We're getting nowhere and it's pointless to continue. Blunt can't give us anything but a character reference. I'm half tempted to mention the Silk Cut to him, but I can't help feeling it would give the reverend more satisfaction than it would me.

The Rice Village swarms with shoppers flitting back and forth across University Boulevard, forcing me to ride the brake as Aguilar eyes them with suspicion. Charlotte could spend a whole day weaving through the cluster of boutiques and restaurants, which have also played host to most every impromptu rendezvous in the course of our marriage. But my colleague's downturned lip prevents me from letting on that I have a history with the shopper's mecca.

"Do these people not have jobs?" he asks.

I answer with a noncommittal grunt.

The seclusion of Dr. Hill's house just a few blocks away is all the more surprising when you consider how many people are in close proximity. I can understand the location's appeal—in the heart of everything, and yet strangely remote. Despite the reputation West U. has for maintaining its neighborhood feel while having long since been swallowed by the city, the canvass of surrounding houses turned up next to nothing. Not only did the neighbors claim not to have witnessed anything, half of them didn't know who Dr. Joy Hill was or that a woman named Simone

Walker lived in her house. The professor keeps to herself, apparently, and Simone followed the same example.

"It never hurts to knock on doors again," I say. "Assuming you're up to it."

Aguilar answers with a shrug. "It wouldn't hurt to take another look at the scene, either."

"Great minds think alike."

After pounding on the door for a few minutes and deciding no one's home, I try to reach Dr. Hill on the three numbers I have for her—home, office, and cell—leaving the same message each time. Then we duck under the tape near the garage and effect an entrance by climbing the fence, which leaves an indentation in the professor's shrubbery and a needlelike wood splinter in my palm. I linger too long over the injury, prompting Aguilar to ask if I'm planning to retire on disability.

Again, I'm struck by how intimate and enclosed the yard feels. As distant as the surrounding block is from the bustling Rice Village, the backyard seems more distant still from the surrounding block. Apart from the tops of the neighboring houses, an upper floor window here and there, and a second floor veranda just visible over the back fence, the pool and its outbuildings give the impression of absolute privacy. It's not hard to believe the neighbors saw nothing. From the street outside, a passerby would be oblivious to anything going on back here.

I take a slow walk along the length of the pool, ending up at the far side, confirming yet again the uncanny resemblance of Saturday night's scene with the photo from Nicole Fauk's murder.

Aguilar comes up alongside, hands in pockets. "You really aren't letting go of the Fauk connection, are you?"

"It fits with everything else. Simone's death was meticulously planned, and part of that included the way the scene was arranged."

"Was there a chair at the bottom of the pool back then?"

"No," I say, "but the chair wasn't visible from the angle of the photo. It didn't matter."

He crouches down. "You have the old picture on you?"

I do, tucked in my pocket along with the snap of Jason Young. I hand it over for examination, then make my way around to the pergola, checking the ground in daylight in case we missed some telltale sign before. Glancing back, I see Aguilar holding the photo in front of him, closing one eye and then the other like an optometrist's patient trying to bring the chart across the wall into focus.

"Are the chairs over there exactly how they were before?"

Glancing at the furniture underneath the pergola, I'm not exactly sure whether the crime scene techs moved them or not.

"It looked like in the Fauk picture," I say. "He edged them around just the same."

He nods and walks over, gazing down at the picture the whole time.

"Here," he says, handing it to me. "How many chairs?"

"Three."

"And there's four there now. But one was in the pool. You were wondering the other night why he threw one in, and you just answered your own question. From the angle of the photo, the chair in the water wouldn't be visible. He wasn't dragging her body in the chair or throwing it down there to wash it off. He just couldn't think of an easy way to get rid of it."

"To match the picture."

The simplest explanation. And it never even dawned on me. I tuck the photo back into my pocket without meeting Aguilar's gaze, embarrassed he had to walk me through the answer.

"Sometimes you can't see the forest—"

"Thanks," I say. "That makes me feel a lot better."

"The point is, maybe there's something to this Fauk angle, after all."

Instead of retracing our route, we slip out through the garage. Aguilar heads toward Brompton to canvass while I take the doors on Wakeforest, using the notes from the patrol officers who did the work Saturday night to prioritize houses where we found no one home. Signs spiked into half the yards remind me of the impending mayoral runoff election. A cleaning woman answers my first knock, resulting in an oblique conversation in pidgin Spanish to the effect that, no, she'd seen nothing and knew nothing. At the home behind Dr. Hill's, a plump and cheerful housewife named Kim Bayard invites me inside and tells me how shocked she was to hear of the crime. Just when I start to get excited, though, and think she has information for me, Mrs. Bayard explains she heard about the murder late last night when she got back from a weekend in Colorado.

"Maybe your husband witnessed something?"

She smiles. "He's in Nigeria. Consulting for an oil company. But you know who you should talk to? Emmet Mainz. He knows everything that goes on around here. He's a sweet old man, and I'm sure he'd be happy to help."

Emmet Mainz turns out to be a wealthy widower in his late sixties. From the housewife's description I'd expected an elderly busybody, but Emmet is nothing of the sort. He leads me across glossy parquet floors, graceful in a sweater and loose wool trousers, into a room he refers to as the conservatory. The corridor outside is decorated with a series of double frames, each containing a typewritten letter on one side and a newspaper clipping on the other.

"My letters to the editor," he says with a smile. "Now that I'm at leisure, I have to do something to keep busy, so I fire off these letters. Whenever one of them is published, it goes up on the wall. You'd be surprised how satisfying it can be."

I scan the letters quickly. Most of them seem to be factual corrections or quibbles with the opinions expressed in book reviews. Once I've had a look, Emmet guides me into the conservatory, resuming his seat at a black piano, shuffling through the jumble of sheet music on the stand. He knows everything that goes on, he says, thanks to the fact that he sits on just about every neighborhood committee in existence and regularly hosts musical evenings.

"All I can tell you about that poor girl is that she had no ear for music," Emmet says. "Joy brought her over once, sometime during the summer, and she banged out one of the worst performances of 'Chopsticks' I've ever heard in my life—and that's saying something."

To prove his point, he pounds a few discordant measures on the keyboard, smiling wickedly at the conclusion, eyes alight with mischief.

"You never met her husband?" I ask. "Or observed anyone visiting the house."

His fingers move over the keys again, wringing out a few elegiac notes with the slightest pressure, letting them hang on the air. Gray light pours through the drawn curtains, etching faint shadows across the floor.

"What you must think of me," he says, "asking questions like that. I'm not a peeping Tom. I'm afraid I can't help you. I wouldn't even have remembered her name if it hadn't been in the paper."

I thank him for his time and turn to go.

"Now, if you'd asked about Joy's husband, I could have told you a thing or two. The girl he ran off with, she lived with them. I used to call her the *au pair*, but that was just my little joke. They didn't have children, you see."

"Dr. Hill's husband left her for a girl who lived in their house?"

His fingers dance lightly over the keys. "The Polish girl . . . Agnieszka. Now she was a beauty and very musical. A former student of Joy's, too."

"And Mr. Hill married her?"

"Oh, no." He laughs at the thought. "She was only having her fun. He did marry another girl eventually, but no, Agnieszka dropped him, I'm afraid. She doesn't visit anymore, but I know she used to work in a dress shop in the Village. She's the sort of girl you'd want standing around in a dress shop, though she did more than stand around. Her dream was to be a designer."

"Does she have a last name?"

Emmet nods. "And it's full of consonants, too, but if you're asking whether I remember it, again, I'm afraid I can't help you. Ask Joy, though, she'll know."

"She might be sensitive about that subject."

"Not her," he says. "I think you'll find that Joy was relieved more than anything else. I know what it's like to be trapped in a loveless marriage. For my wife and I, though, there were the children to consider. I'm sure Joy would have divorced him ages ago if she hadn't been so consumed with work. She's a very driven woman, but sometimes it's the driven ones who are most complacent."

"It sounds like you're fond of her."

"Does it?" He smiles and plays me another enigmatic tune. "The human situation has always fascinated me, which I suppose is just a fancy way of saying I like people, and the best sort of people in terms of entertainment value are the characters, the eccentrics. You must run into all sorts of eccentrics in your profession."

"Not just the criminals, either."

"You might just be one yourself—an eccentric, I mean, not a criminal. I don't imagine normal policemen dress that way."

"My wife's father was the eccentric in this case," I say, skimming my hand over the brown check jacket. "He was an attorney in Austin who had all his clothes made for him in England and shipped over. When he'd had too many gimlets, he used to tell me he could make my career by revealing where all the bodies in Texas politics were buried."

He gives me the opening of Beethoven's Fifth, the first thing since "Chopsticks" I've recognized.

"That sounds like Lyndon Pellier," he says. "Did you marry Charlotte or Ann?"

My stunned expression draws a melodious laugh. "Don't be so surprised. After all, I do know a lot of people around here. I should have realized. He always was a snazzy dresser. So which girl was it?"

"Charlotte."

He wags a finger at me. "The pretty one. I should've guessed."

For the next ten minutes he regales me with stories of Lyndon Pellier, each punctuated by a tune on the piano, by which time I'm convinced that while he got the name right, he has confused the man. Either that or Charlotte has concealed from me some of the family's juiciest gossip. Strangely enough, it's hard to make excuses and leave when a chance personal connection like this crops up. My ringing phone eventually extricates me.

"I'm looking at the forensics report from your scene," Bascombe says. "You want the summary, or are you coming back in?"

"Hold on just a second."

I make my apologies to Emmet and head for the sidewalk. He follows me out, waving as I walk down the street.

"Sorry about that. Go ahead."

"You've got nothing on the prints. Some belong to your victim, some belong to Dr. Hill, and there's another set that doesn't match anything in the system. We do have Young's prints on file, by the way. He was arrested on a misdemeanor battery in 2004 after a brawl outside a nightclub. Pled no contest and did community service. That would have been before he married your victim in '07."

"Thanks, I did the math." I fill him in on the story the Silk Cut manager gave us, which suggests a pattern. "Anything else?"

"We've got her cell phone records, so you can start working your way through. Just skimming through them I can see some recurring numbers." He shuffles papers on the other end of the line. "And how about you, March? You got anything for me?"

Now that I have Aguilar's confirmation on the photo from the Fauk scene, I'm half tempted to bring the subject up. But I decide to wait on that one for fear of setting him off again. "There is one thing." I repeat the story Emmet Mainz told me about Joy Hill's husband running off with a former student who lived in the house. "I have reason to believe she's in much better financial shape than she let on—meaning she didn't need a tenant for the money—and there's also this: apparently she was named in some kind of sexual harassment suit a while back. I don't have the details, but I'm thinking I should follow up."

"A female student?" he asks. "March, I can't see a woman doing this. I doubt she'd even have the strength."

"Maybe not. But if she's lying to us, I should at least check it out."

"That's your call. My advice would be to tread softly, though. If your new theory is that the professor butchered this woman in some kind of lesbian breakup, you might want to keep it low-key. I'm thinking specifically of the captain."

"What does Hedges care? He's barely tuned in on this one."

Bascombe sighs over the line. "I'm glad I can't reach out and touch you right now, or next they'd be puttin' a charge on me."

CHAPTER 7

Always follow up. On everything. *No exceptions.* Good advice from the lips of Buddy Fitzpatrick, Irish Catholic cowboy and all around burnout, a self-proclaimed legend in HPD Homicide who actually had cleared more than his share of cases, though he didn't exactly shine his last time out.

It was Fitzpatrick who ran the original investigation of Nicole Fauk's murder into the ground, who infamously carried the case file over to the FBI field office and tried to sell her as yet another victim of the recently apprehended Railroad Killer. It was Fitzpatrick who had to come clean to then-Lieutenant Hedges about the fact he'd misplaced the file on his way back.

When I inherited that case a few hours before his retirement party, Fitzpatrick repeated the mantra in my ear, his breath thick with fumes: *"Always follow up. On everything. No exceptions."*

If Buddy had lived by those words, he might have gone out under a brighter cloud.

With his slurry voice in my head, I work my way through Simone Walker's phone records, matching numbers to names, breaking the news of her death to a few out-of-town friends she'd recently chatted with. There's a cluster of calls to Young over two weeks' time in November, corresponding to their night together. The only suspect number is a mobile phone with an 832 area code. When I dial it, a computerized voice repeats the number back. I leave my details and ask for a return call.

I work through the postmortem and the other forensics reports waiting on my desk. The only new information is Dr. Green's speculative description of the murder weapon: a wide, single-edged blade approximately eight inches in length and quite sharp. Probably with a clip point. Perhaps a bowie or survival knife. Not something the killer would have found at the scene. He brought it with him, reinforcing the impression that this was a carefully planned crime.

Bad news on the Jason Young front, too. The nicks on his hands are consistent with the Silk Cut fight, and the blood on the shirt recovered in the washer isn't Simone's. Which means we have nothing tying him to the scene.

In the break room, Ordway gives me a sullen look. "You went without me."

"You didn't miss anything," I say.

He shakes an inch of nondairy creamer into his mug, then adds a little coffee on top. When he's finished, I do the same.

"Forensics isn't putting any wind in my sails, and I just re-canvassed with Aguilar and got next to nothing. I hate to say it, but I'm running out of juice on this one."

"What about your professor? I heard you had some questions about her."

"I'll do another interview, but it's hard to believe she'd be up for something like this."

He replies with a snort. "Because she's a woman? That's a very sexist attitude."

"She doesn't strike me as the praying mantis type. I'm gonna follow up, though, don't worry. Always follow up on everything."

"No exceptions," he says.

We clink our mugs and go back to work.

★

The news reports on the sexual harassment case against Joy Hill make for interesting reading, though the juicy details were sealed as part of an out-of-court settlement. According to the plaintiff, Dr. Hill attempted to initiate "inappropriate relations" with twenty-year-old Shayna Zachariassen, a female undergraduate enrolled in one of her seminars. When Zachariassen rebuffed her, Hill accused the student of plagiarism on a term paper. To back up the charge, Hill supposedly substituted a doctored paper for the one the student actually turned in.

The story sounds bogus to me, a charade cooked up by a student caught cheating. To explain away the evidence—the plagiarized paper—she had to concoct a ridiculous scenario.

After the plagiarism accusation went public, Zachariassen disappeared. Her roommates contacted her parents, who initiated a police investigation. Twenty-four hours later, the girl reappeared unharmed.

Zachariassen claimed she was abducted in the University of Houston parking lot. A man came up behind her, putting a black hood over her head, and forced her inside the trunk of her own car. She was driven to what she believed was a motel, her wrists tied together and lashed to a chair. The whole time, her abductor never spoke. He turned up the television volume. She listened to news reports of her own disappearance. After a day in captivity, the phone rang and her abductor held a muffled conversation with the caller.

"Like he was getting instructions," she said.

He put her back in her car and started driving. Afraid for her life, she begged him to let her go. Then the car stopped and the man got out. After a long silence, she got up the courage to remove the hood and her abductor was gone. She was sitting in the same part of the lot where she'd originally been kidnapped.

The *Chronicle*'s original coverage of the incident includes a quote from one of the detectives working the case, Theresa Cavallo, who offered boilerplate assurances that the girl's story was being taken seriously.

When the civil case made headlines a year later, no one from HPD was available for comment.

I haven't talked to Cavallo in a while. I reach for my phone and dial her direct line.

"I'm looking at reports of an old case of yours," I say. "What are you doing right now?"

She sighs. "Paperwork."

"Perfect. How about a field trip?"

A pause. "Are you driving or am I?"

That's what I like about Cavallo. Ready to drop everything at a moment's notice, no explanation needed. My last ride in the passenger seat with Cavallo aged me ten years, so I volunteer as wheelman, telling her to meet me downstairs in ten minutes.

She's waiting for me when I step off the elevator, looking sharp in a tailored pea coat. Curly tendrils of hair snake out in every direction. She greats me with a knowing smirk.

"Married life suits you, Cavallo."

"Thanks," she says. "I think."

When we worked together on the Mayhew case, she was engaged to a soldier deployed in Iraq. He'd come back, tied the knot, and headed out for another hitch, this time in Afghanistan. That had to be hard, but we've never talked about it. That's not the kind of relationship we have.

"Where are we going, anyway?" she asks.

"My alma mater. The University of Houston."

In the car, I tell her about my homicide and the connection to Joy Hill, whose alibi for the time of the murder is that she was on campus all day. Then I share what I've gleaned about the sexual harassment suit. My skepticism about Zachariassen's claims comes through loud and clear.

"Something *did* happen to her," Cavallo says. "She took a lie detector test and passed."

"Fair enough. But if you put her on the box, you must have had your doubts."

"Bizarre as the story was, we all assumed she'd made it up. There was a history of emotional problems, depression. The plagiarism charge brought it all to a head. When she disappeared, the family feared suicide. So when she turned up, everybody was relieved, and yeah, the story sounded fishy, like she was trying to save face. But she insisted on it, March. And she had the hood."

"Was there any physical evidence in her car?"

She shakes her head. "We collected some fibers, but never matched them to anything. No prints, nothing like that."

"And later on, when you heard about the sexual harassment case, what did you think about that?"

"I'd interviewed the professor and there was definitely something weird about her."

"Why'd you interview her?"

"Ah," she says. "Part of the story that didn't make it into the papers: Shayna accused her teacher of putting out a hit on her."

"You're kidding me."

"When the police got involved, the professor was spooked and decided to call it off. That's what the call Shayna overheard was about. Why are you laughing? Crazier things have happened. Like I said, she did pass the lie detector."

"Maybe she was crazy, though. You said she had problems."

Cavallo nods stiffly. I can't tell if she's irritated with me or not. "According to the professor, Shayna had formed an unhealthy attachment to her. Dr. Hill saw herself as the victim in all this. All she'd done was turn in a cheater, and people were acting like she was responsible for this girl's mental breakdown. I guess the lawsuit made her feel even more victimized . . . but it was dropped, right?"

"Settled out of court."

"And now you're looking at the professor as a suspect in your homicide?"

"Honestly?" I give her a noncommittal shrug. "I'm just hoping to check her off my list."

Rising from a sea of blacktop lots, the stadium at the University of Houston is surrounded by glistening commuter cars that mostly clear out by late afternoon. On a map of the city's crime stats, this area is ground zero, colored bright red, the highest rating on the chart. At one point the campus briefing for incoming freshmen included advice on what to do when being chased through the parking lot—*Pull a security phone off the hook and keep running!*—but the ratings have more to do with the surrounding neighborhoods than the campus itself.

Cavallo guides me behind the stadium to a line of trees marking the transition from pavement to deeply rutted grass and gravel. Since classes ended last week and final exams are coming up, there aren't many cars this far back. The muddy ground is crosshatched with tire tracks, pools of stagnant water standing in the potholes.

"This is where Shayna was abducted," Cavallo says. "After a night class, she had to walk back here alone."

"But there were no witnesses, right? Nobody saw her being taken, nobody saw her being returned."

"No, but UH security did several sweeps after she was reported missing and didn't locate her car. So we at least know it wasn't here."

"She could have driven anywhere, though."

We get out of the car and walk around a bit, but there's nothing to see. Cavallo checks her watch a couple of times as I work things out in my head. At the same time Dr. Hill was having trouble with Zachariassen, a former student of hers from Poland named Agnieszka was living in her home, carrying on with her husband. After the harassment suit, he and the girl moved out and eventually split up, leaving Hill on her own. And she turns around and invites another girl, Simone Walker, to move in. Six months later, Simone is dead.

"Where's Shayna Zachariassen now?" I ask.

Cavallo shrugs. "Do you keep up with people after a case is closed?"

"Only the dead ones."

I motion her back into the car and we drive around the stadium, crossing Cullen to enter the campus proper at University Park. I snag a metered space near the Agnes Arnold Building. Since Cavallo doesn't know the territory, I have to guide her now, taking the cut-through behind the Science building past the placid waters of the man-made lake where, in sunnier weather, students are prone to congregate by the hundreds.

It's been a while since I was on campus. The squared concrete buildings, the aging modernist landscape, used to remind me of fascist architecture—an ironic association for a university. Now it seems almost futuristic. A vision of the future from the late sixties, anyway.

We climb the steps to the Roy Cullen Building, home of the English Department, ascending to the second floor. Dr. Hill's office is tucked at the end of a short corridor. The door is shut. I knock, but there's no reply.

"The department office is just down there," I say, pointing to the far end of the main hallway. A glass wall partitions administrators and their secretaries from the rest of the building. "The problem is, I'm supposed to keep my inquiry low-key. If I go in, flash my badge, and start asking a bunch of questions, that'll get back to the professor. You, on the other hand, could walk right in without raising suspicion."

"And do what?" she asks.

"Do nothing. Just grab some forms to fill out and sit in the waiting area. See what the secretaries are talking about."

She shakes her head at the idea.

"Give them some time," I say. "Let them get used to you being in there. Once you've got all you're going to get, ask them if Dr. Hill is around. Say you had an appointment Saturday, but she wasn't here. See how they answer."

"Is this why you brought me? To do your legwork? All the sudden I'm remembering what it was like to work with you. And the memories aren't pleasant."

"You loved it, Cavallo. It was pure excitement."

"Right. Getting shot was exciting."

Getting shot. Last time around, we traded gunfire with a rogue officer named Tony Salazar and his accomplice. I put the sidekick down and wounded Salazar mortally. Cavallo and I came out unscathed, or so it seemed. Afterward, though, Bascombe dug a spent round out of

Cavallo's ballistic vest. It was a scary moment. No wonder she didn't jump at the opportunity to transfer to Homicide.

"Don't remind me," I say. "Look, nobody's gonna shoot at you in there. The worst that can happen is that they'll use a thesaurus on you. You're a tough cop. You can handle that."

"And what will you be doing?"

"I'll be outside by the fountain, soaking up some rays."

Twenty minutes later, she comes outside with a stack of papers in her hand, striding toward the concrete bench where I've set up camp. Cavallo's got a stride to her, a long-legged, intimidating walk that says she'd just as soon trample obstacles as cut around them. The same kind of confidence Charlotte had when I first met her, only with Cavallo being a cop, it's more a physical than an intellectual thing. She stands over me, hands on hips, triumphant and challenging at the same time.

"How'd it go?"

She jabs the papers at me. "I signed up for a full load next semester."

"Anything else?"

"Quite a bit, actually." She sits next to me on the bench. "I did what you said and hung around for a bit. They picked up the conversation and sure enough, they were talking about the girl who got murdered at Dr. Joy's house. That's what they call her: Dr. Joy." She smirks. "It sounds like there was some kind of job opening in the office, and Dr. Joy tried to get your victim the position, only she missed the interview. And apparently there was a scene earlier today."

"What kind of scene?"

"Dr. Joy bawled out one of the secretaries, that's all I know. I got the impression the departmental staff doesn't like the professor all that much. I also got the impression she doesn't usually keep office hours on Saturdays. When I asked, they looked surprised. They didn't see her . . . but that doesn't mean she wasn't there."

I nod slowly. "She could get into her office without them noticing. Still, that's great work. Maybe it's time to interview Dr. Hill again. What do you think about tagging along? I'd like a second opinion."

"Don't you have a partner, March?"

"Aguilar's not the most talkative man, in case you don't remember. Plus, you have some background with her. If she remembers you, that might shake her up."

"I do actually have work of my own."

"Tell you what," I say. "Come with me to see Dr. Hill, and afterward we'll grab some dinner with Charlotte. She'd love to see you again, and it'll save you having to order pizza and veg out in front of the television."

"That's your idea of how I spend my off-hours?"

"Isn't it?"

She ignores the question. "How's Carter doing? Are they still living in that garage apartment of yours?"

"You've just reminded me. Now you really do need to come home with me. I talked to Carter this morning, and guess what he said? He and Gina are having a baby."

She breaks out in a smile. "That's great."

"So you're in? I'll call Charlotte right now."

"Fine. I'm in."

It takes a few minutes to get my wife on the phone. I tell her Cavallo was asking about them all and I suggested dinner so we could all catch up. Surprised, she agrees to book a table somewhere and make sure Carter and Gina are onboard. We settle on seven o'clock, which will give us time to swing by Dr. Hill's house again and try to catch her at home.

As we walk back to the car, my phone rings.

It's Joy Hill.

"I'm sorry I didn't return your message sooner," she says, "but I've only just gotten home."

"I'd like to swing by, if you don't mind."

"Detective," she says. "Something strange just happened. A man I've never seen before came to the door. I thought he might be one of you people—that's the only reason I answered the knock. But he asked for Simone. He said he'd been trying to call her, but she wasn't answering."

"Did you get his name?"

"Oh," she says. "I didn't think to ask. It happened so fast. When I told him what happened to her, he pushed inside the house. He was calling her name up the stairs, like he didn't believe me, and then he broke down and started crying."

"He cried?"

"He was sobbing. He said she was going to have his baby, Detective."

"A baby?"

Cavallo raises an eyebrow at me.

"Over and over he kept saying it. Then all the sudden he got up and left. It was very disturbing."

"He's gone now? How long ago did he leave?"

"He just left. I called you immediately."

"I'm coming right over."

I toss the keys to Cavallo, who'll get us there quicker, and drop into the passenger seat. I dial the medical examiner's office. The switchboard puts me through to Dr. Green's voicemail. I dial back and she does it again.

"Do you have Sheila Green's direct number?" I ask Cavallo. Unlike me, she has a good relationship with the doctor. She tosses her phone over, telling me to scroll through the saved numbers. Seconds later, Dr. Green picks up the line.

"Hey, girl, what's going on?"

"It's Roland March," I say. "I have an urgent question for you."

"What are you doing with Terry's phone?"

"She's sitting right here. Now listen, is it possible that when you did the postmortem on Simone Walker, you missed something?"

"Anything's possible," she says. "What kind of something do you have in mind?"

"Was she pregnant?"

A longish pause. "March. Are you asking me if I did an autopsy on a pregnant woman and somehow missed the fact she was pregnant?"

"She couldn't have been far along," I say.

"March. For real?"

"There's no chance of that?"

"Put Terry on the phone. I'm gonna tell her to whack you upside the head."

"Okay," I say. "Is it possible she had an abortion?"

Green exhales into the phone. "Is it possible she had an abortion. Depending on when, that's not necessarily something I could tell. If there was scarring or something, if the procedure went sideways, then maybe there would be a sign. But there was nothing like that."

"Could you check again?"

"I don't need to check—"

"Because a man just turned up on her doorstep claiming she was pregnant with his kid."

Another sigh. "You want me to wheel her back in here and take a second look? I'm telling you, if there was any sign, I would have noticed. Your new baby daddy is either lying, or she had a termination sometime back."

I want to argue, but Cavallo grabs the phone out of my hand and hangs it up.

"You wonder why people don't like you, March."

We cruise silently down the road, not looking at each other. She pulls up to a red light and flips the blinker on, drumming her nails on the steering wheel.

"Theresa," I say. "Seriously. People don't like me?"

CHAPTER 8

The door opens before I get a chance to knock. Joy Hill leads Cavallo and me into the cavernous living room, pointing out the very sofa where her mysterious visitor sat and wept. She describes him in her low, husky voice: a dark-complected Caucasian male in his late twenties, athletic build, black hair combed back from his forehead, dressed in nice jeans and a cream-colored turtleneck sweater, his cologne evident from several feet away, and his speech tinged with an East Texas drawl.

"Did he touch anything?"

"He touched *me*," she says. "Took me by the shoulders and moved me out of the way."

"Anything we can get prints from, I mean."

"He sank down on the couch right here." She shows me the indentation on the leather cushion. "I think his hands were like this . . ." She cups her face in her hands, leaving only her hooded eyes visible.

"What about his car? Did you happen to see what he was driving?"

A slump of the shoulders. "I didn't think to look. The whole experience was so—" she struggles for the right word—"*disorienting*."

So convenient, too. An unidentified man appears on her doorstep, tells a story that can't be verified, raising all kinds of questions about who killed Simone Walker and why, and then disappears without a trace. Like Zachariassen's abduction story, it's a little hard to take seriously, despite the professor's vivid description.

While I squeeze more details out of her, Cavallo trails along the built-in bookcases, a picture of distraction, scanning the spines along each shelf. Another of my little assignments: checking the library for a well-read copy of *The Kingwood Killing*, hidden in plain sight. Though she's given no sign of remembering Cavallo from their interview several years ago, Dr. Hill keeps stealing glances at her as we talk.

"Excuse me, but Dr. Hill . . ."

"Please," she says with a wave of the hand. "Call me Joy."

"Joy, then. It's come to my attention that Simone wasn't your first tenant. There was a woman living here before, one of your former students."

"You mean Agnieszka Oliszewski. She wasn't a tenant so much as a houseguest. There were complications with her immigration status vis-à-vis employment, and until she could sort that out and get a job, she couldn't really afford a place of her own."

"So you did a favor for Ms. Oliszewski," I say, stumbling over the name. "And she repaid it by running off with your husband."

Her face hardens. Then she gives me a broad, indulgent smile. "You're trying to get a reaction out of me. But no, I'm not resentful. Agnieszka wasn't the first woman he brought into the picture, just the last. Having it going on right under my nose . . . I guess that's what I needed to finally take action. They didn't run off together, as you put it. They were pushed."

"By you?"

She lifts her palms as if to say, *Who else?*

Cavallo touches a book and the professor's head snaps toward her. Cavallo's hand drops and she relaxes.

"Their departure coincided with your legal problems, isn't that right? The Zachariassens brought their sexual harassment suit—"

"Which was thrown out."

"Thrown out? Or was it settled?"

Her shrug implies the two outcomes amount to the same thing. "You know why people agree to settle? Because what they were looking for in the first place was a payoff. Say somebody does to your daughter what those people accused me of doing: would you take a check and move on, or would you want to see justice done?"

"Justice," I say.

"Exactly. If there's any substance to the claim, you don't settle. You don't take your money and slink off into the darkness. That girl was hysterical—and I use the word advisedly, well aware of the negative connotations. I caught her cheating, and she responded by trying to destroy me." She gets a faraway look. "Their claims had no basis in fact. None of them do."

"None of what?"

"The claims," she says. "The rumors about me."

"What kind of rumors?"

She laughs the question to scorn. "I have never been involved with any of my students. Oh, I could give you a list of colleagues who have—but I'm *not* one of them. I don't know how stories like that get started, but once they do, you're branded for life."

"What about Simone? She wasn't one of your students."

"Was I involved with her, is that what you're asking?"

I hold her stare without repeating the question.

"There are reasons other than money to want to have someone under the same roof. And at my age, sex isn't one of them."

"You're not so old," I say.

"For me it was never—" She stops herself, conscious of Cavallo moving in the background. "Never mind what it was. I've answered your question, Detective."

"Why did you invite Simone to live with you?"

"I just wanted someone to *be* here. Is that so hard to understand? I never had children, never wanted them, and I was happy to see my husband go. And yet, once he was gone I felt alone. You may find this hard to believe, but people don't naturally gravitate toward me. I've never had the gift of attraction. But having a tenant made it easy."

"Only she wasn't paying the rent."

She concedes with a tilt of the head. "It didn't take Simone long to figure out that the money wasn't a big concern for me. What I really wanted was . . . companionship."

"And when she didn't give you that?"

Silence.

"How did you feel when you realized she was taking advantage?"

"I pitied her. Simone could be selfish and manipulative, but after all, she was just a single-cell organism repeating her basic programming over and over again. Once you've realized that about someone, it's very hard for them ever to hurt you."

Cavallo returns from the bookshelves, shaking her head at my raised eyebrows. No sign of the book. She sits on the sofa next to Dr. Hill.

"Do you remember me, Professor?"

Hill leans back, like she can't focus without some distance between them. "I do now."

"Only it's strange," Cavallo says. "The way you're describing Simone Walker sounds a lot like the way you described Shayna Zachariassen the last time we met. Maybe you do attract a certain type."

The professor says nothing, letting the words hang in the air.

"You must be quite a reader," I say. "So many books on the shelf. You haven't read all of them, have you? People must ask that a lot."

She blinks in slow motion, making her contempt for my banter unmistakable.

"There's a particular title I'm wondering about, a true crime book about a case here in Houston from ten years back. It's called *The Kingwood Killing*. Have you ever come across that particular book, Joy?"

"I don't read that sort of book," she says. "I find them sordid. And that goes for the people who read them, too."

★

Charlotte and the Robbs hold down a table for us at Hungry's Café, rising in unison to take turns giving Cavallo a hug. They say the usual things about not seeing her often enough. I smile and nod through it all like I'm paying attention, like my mind isn't still on the job.

I'm as far away as ever from Simone's killer. As far away as ever from her, too. Everyone in that girl's life was using her. And she was using them, too.

Beside me Charlotte slips her hand into mine. Her face is radiant in the gold artificial light. To anyone but me, she would appear happy. But it's a frantic sort of joy, a smile that never reaches the eyes.

"You okay?" I ask under my breath.

She ignores the question.

Carter and Gina wear the same awkward, excited expressions they always do when they're taken out to dinner, anxious to please and be pleased. Carter must have raided the laundry basket. Instead of the usual ironic T-shirt, he's found a tight-fitting plaid cowboy shirt with pearl snaps.

"So are you two working together again?" Gina asks Cavallo.

"Not really. March here hijacked me from the office, that's all. He was having trouble getting any of his Homicide buddies to do the heavy lifting for him."

"Well, it's good to see you," Charlotte says. "How is your husband doing? You get to talk to him, don't you?"

"I worry a lot more about him than he worries about himself. But the good news is, when he finishes this tour, that's it. He's finally had enough. He's not going to re-up again. I'm not going to let him."

"He was crazy to go back in the first place after you two got hitched," Carter says. "Not to be critical or anything."

"You can be critical." Cavallo smiles. "He was crazy, and now maybe he realizes it. I'm not getting any younger, so if we're gonna start having babies, it's time. Speaking of which . . . congratulations."

She raises her glass, getting nothing but Cheshire cat grins out of the Robbs.

"Congratulations about what?" Charlotte asks. She looks back and forth between Cavallo and Gina, pulling her hand out of mine, a quizzical smile on her lips. "Is there something I don't know? What's the big secret?"

Gina's cheeks flush with embarrassment.

"Are you—?"

As the truth dawns, Charlotte pushes her chair back. She reaches toward Gina but clips the side of a water glass by accident. A slurry of ice slides over the table. Carter scoots back to avoid getting wet. Gina stays frozen. I grab the glass, setting it upright.

"Oh," Charlotte says, covering her mouth with both hands. "I'm such a—"

"It's okay," I'm saying, while Carter gives an awkward laugh.

Cavallo: "Did I spoil the surprise?"

It takes a moment, but Charlotte recovers. She gets up and goes to Gina, throwing her arms around the still-seated girl, hugging her from behind.

"That's wonderful," she says. "I'm so happy for you."

A waiter comes by and helps me mop up the mess. Before I know it, the seating arrangements have changed. Carter takes Charlotte's place beside me while the two older women close in around his wife, showering her with attention.

"Get used to it," I say. "For now on, you've officially dropped off the radar screen."

The specter of looming fatherhood doesn't seem to faze Carter, though it should. He didn't make much working at the church and makes even less from the outreach center, and I know for a fact they don't have health insurance. The rent they pay for the garage apartment is next to nothing—but that's no place to raise a kid.

No, they'll have to move out.

Out of the apartment and out of our lives.

The thought leaves me empty inside, suddenly nostalgic for the present. Looking at the smiling faces around the table, hearing the lilting voices, I now realize this will all come to an end. It will end, it will end, and tonight we celebrate the high tide.

Charlotte catches my eye. "Hey, we're supposed to be celebrating."

"I was just thinking about Carter changing his first pair of diapers."

He laughs. "I'm trying *not* to think about that."

"I'm so jealous," Cavallo says. "By the time she was my age, my mama already had three girls. So when you need a baby-sitter, you call Aunt Terry, you hear me?"

"Have you thought about names yet?" Charlotte asks.

Gina shares a smile with Carter, then shakes her head. "And we're not going to find out if it's a boy or girl. We want it to be a surprise."

Once we've ordered and the food arrives, there's an awkward moment when Charlotte asks Carter to pray. The rest of them link hands. I stare at Carter's proffered palm until he rests it on the table.

As he thanks God in heaven for his goodness and blessings, I think of the man crying on Dr. Hill's leather couch at the loss of a child who probably never existed. Maybe the man is pure invention, too. Part of me would like to believe so, but then I remember that 832 number on Simone's call log. Perhaps it was my voicemail message that prompted his appearance on the professor's doorstep.

The reverend was right. Curtis Blunt said he had "discerned" Simone's infidelity, whatever that means. My guess is he merely assumed the worst, knowing that when you do that, your future predictions are bound to come true. A prophet predicting doom will never be starved for an audience.

When the prayer ends and the others dig in, Charlotte smiles wanly in my direction, the way she does when I've intentionally excluded myself and she wants me to know I'm always welcome to reconsider. That smile only heightens my desire to be apart, but since I organized this get-together, I have to stick it out. In this company I've grown accustomed to being the odd man out.

After dinner, Charlotte volunteers to run Cavallo back downtown, taking Gina along so the three of them can continue their conversation about parents and children. That leaves me and Carter on our own.

He's silent as we drive through town, so silent I remember that our talk early this morning was interrupted before he could tell me the second thing on his mind. I remember why it was interrupted, too.

Afraid he'll take the opportunity to open up, that he's bracing for it even now, I flip on the radio and skip through a couple of stations, landing on a local call-in show where everyone's still going on about the runoff election and Friday's snow.

"Charlotte wants me to talk to you," Carter says.

I study the lights in my rearview mirror. I shift lanes and the car behind me does, too. Carter shifts in his chair, pulling the seat belt away from his chest.

"You know it's not my style," he says, "to come on strong with the God-talk, right? But she's worried and she wants me to say something. She feels like maybe, because of the stuff we've gone through, you'll hear me out. She feels like you might not listen to her." He pauses and waits for some kind of reply.

"Go on," I say, adjusting the mirror.

"With the kind of work you do, the kind of things you see, there has to be a corrosive effect. You're always in the presence of evil. When we met, I got a firsthand taste, so I think I have an idea what it must be like."

I smile. "You think I'm corroding?"

"It comes off you in waves. When you look at people, it's like you're sizing them up for the casket."

"Are you trying to hurt my feelings or something?"

"I'm being serious."

"About what?"

"I just think . . ." He grasps for the words. "You carry a burden, and I'm just saying, if you ever feel like you need to talk—"

"About what?" I repeat.

"The job. Life. Spiritual things."

"I talked to a guy this morning, a reverend. He said he often had to 'counsel' people. Is that what you're talking about, counseling?"

A defensive note creeps into his voice. "I think it might help. Charlotte feels like it might, too. She worries about you, Roland. She's afraid that if you keep doing what you do, you're going to lose yourself."

"Lose myself," I say.

Of all the people I know, I'm the least likely to do that.

"The thing about this job is, it opens your eyes to reality. There are certain truths I have to own up to, certain lies I can't tell myself. Like Malcolm McDowell in *Clockwork Orange*, there's no looking away. Everybody else, they can afford to deceive themselves about human nature and the way the world works. But not me, Carter."

"I don't think I'm deceiving myself."

"People don't. That's the whole point. But they go on believing what they've been told, they keep voting and buying and praying, they live good lives surrounded by good people in a good world where everything is good. And they think when it's *not* good, that's the aberration. That's the exception to the rule. But underneath, Carter, if you could turn this city upside down, you'd see it's all rot down there, all corruption."

"Of course it is," he says. "Because of sin—"

"Carter, listen to me. You mean well, I realize that. But there's no magic formula or platitude they taught you in seminary that's going to turn me into one of you. It's not gonna happen. You have no idea what I've seen and what I've done. Trust me, if you did, you'd be like me, and we wouldn't be having this conversation."

"I know it's all rot and corruption," he says, "and with what I've been through, you can't sit there and say I've got rose-tinted glasses on."

"That's not what I mean." I start to go on, then stop. What's the point? "Why don't we just drop this, okay?"

"How am I supposed to do that, exactly? This is my job, what we're doing right now."

"Maybe *you're* the one who needs the counseling, then."

"Probably so," he says. "But it's precisely because of the evil and rot that I have faith. Knowing that on top of all that, there's someone loving and all-powerful who can bring good out of evil—that's what keeps me going. Otherwise, I *would* be like you and we *wouldn't* be having this conversation."

The worm in my domestic apple starts to turn, and I imagine the conversations they must have had about me, the intimacies Charlotte unthinkingly revealed, and I find I do want to cut him down to size just a bit.

"Carter," I say, "if there really was some loving, all-powerful force out there, I wouldn't be hunting a man down for plunging a bowie knife in a woman's chest and then stripping her and using her dead body as a pincushion. That's what he did. He spread his fingers out on her skin and stabbed in between them over and over. One, two, three, four, five, six—just like that. And when he was done with her, he dumped her in the swimming pool and he posed her like she was nothing but a stage prop."

He's quiet now, but I can't shut myself up.

"Now, what you're saying is that, seeing something like that, I should be comforted. I should feel good knowing that as bad as it looks, it was all for the best. God was up in heaven watching it go down, and even though he didn't lift a finger, he sure wishes us well. I'm sorry, Carter, but that doesn't do it for me. If I believed that, I think I'd be miserable."

"You are miserable," he says.

"My point is, you're out of your league."

"Have you ever considered *why* God lets things like that happen?"

"No, Carter. I don't believe I have."

"It's not that he doesn't have the power to stop it, man. It's just . . . God wants us to choose what's right. He could force us—he has the power to—but he also loves us and you can't force love."

"If you were taking a knife to someone," I say, "believe me, I'd force you to stop."

"You don't get what I'm saying—"

"This isn't new to me. My aunt was dragging me to church and force-feeding me the catechism before you were born, Carter. You think God could come down if he wanted to and make things right, but he doesn't because he wants us to choose right of our own free will—is that it?"

"Only we don't because of our sin."

"Let me tell you a story," I say.

We're on Heights Boulevard not very far from home, so I pull into a convenience store parking lot, idling on the far edge next to the air machine, determined to get this over with before we pull up the driveway.

"A long time ago, we got this call. My old partner Wilcox and me. All we knew was that this woman had been talking on the phone to her daughter, and then there were screams and the line went dead. Patrol got to the scene and called it in, saying a guy had bludgeoned his wife to death in the kitchen, and they'd caught him out in the driveway siphoning gasoline out of his truck. You know what he was gonna do with that gas? Burn the place down. And he confessed to everything, right then and there. We arrived on scene and he was ready to give it up.

" 'Why'd you do it?' Wilcox asks the guy.

" 'Because of the baby,' he says.

"Sure enough, we go into the bedroom and find the body there in the crib. Suffocation."

"That's horrible," Carter says.

"You never want to see something like that. And for me it was extra hard. This was maybe a year after Jessica, so I mean . . . I could understand why he did what he did. Not the murder, but the rage. Because that's what you *want* in a situation like that. You want to kill someone."

"I don't understand what this has to do with what we were talking about," he says. "I already admitted there's evil in the world."

"So we do the canvass," I say, ignoring him. "That's what it's called, knocking on people's doors, asking if they saw anything. In this case, it's just a formality, but for detectives it's force of habit. Something bad happens and you start asking everybody what they saw. I walk next-door and the garage door's open; there's this set of free weights, and this guy is pumping iron, doing fifty-rep sets, that's how intense he is.

"When I ask what he observed, he goes into a rant about the people next-door, how they're always fighting and screaming, how he's not surprised what happened. Did he hear them going at it that night? Oh yes. He heard them shouting, he heard her shrieks, he heard furniture crashing—which was the man beating his wife to death—he heard all that. And he did nothing.

"Now, this guy, he was built like a Greek god. The sweat's dripping off of him and I'm standing there thinking, This is not somebody I'd want to face down. I mean, witnesses standing by and doing nothing, that's par for the course. They're afraid, they don't know what's happening, it's all just too much to process. But *this* guy, he could have stopped it. He knew there was a history there, and he knew whatever was going down had to be serious.

"He could've done something, Carter, but he didn't, and he had his reasons." My throat feels dry and I realize I've been talking too fast, too loud, letting the memory take over. "Whatever you think about his reasons, they made sense to him. He was busy. He couldn't be bothered. He did not want to get involved. It was no business of his. But, Carter, here's the point: If *I'd* been there, I would have done something. And I'll never feel anything for that man but contempt. So the last thing you want to tell me is, God could do something but doesn't, and he has his reasons. 'Cause I'm not much, but I'm better than that. And you are, too."

I put the car in drive and roll out. As we hit the pavement, a car veers around us, forcing me to brake. Next to me, Carter props his elbow on the windowsill, his hand covering his mouth. His jaw tenses and releases like he's forcing himself not to speak. And I can see the wheels turning in his head, trying to fit back together the thousand pieces I've shattered him into. Or maybe he wasn't listening, I don't know.

There's more I could tell, but that would mean bringing Carter deeper into a part of myself I don't much want to share.

That body builder wasn't my first.

I started with a bartender at the Paragon, the guy who'd served drinks to the woman who later T-boned Charlotte's car and mortally injured our daughter. Finding dirt on him wasn't hard. He was selling more than liquor under the bar. All I had to do was make sure my friends in Narcotics visited just after he'd topped off his stash. He only did a year, but if I'd let him off, he'd have done nothing.

The driver herself would've gotten worse, only she helped herself to a bottle of pills before I could get any leverage on her.

Wilcox caught on. He thought I'd planted the drugs—he probably still does—but the fact is, you can find dirt on most anyone if you're motivated and very patient. I was both. In the end, he decided to let it slide.

Before long, I became obsessed with spotting people on the periphery of an investigation, the ones who'd otherwise slip the net. Settling scores on behalf of Lady Justice, though never in a big way, and never targeting anyone who didn't have it coming. I framed no one, despite Wilcox's suspicions. I just made sure the law was enforced in a few instances where it otherwise would not have been.

I don't apologize for any of this, but there were consequences. My job performance suffered. I cut corners I shouldn't have, fudging reports, missing court dates. My partner covered for me the way partners do, but he wasn't happy about it. I was pulling a Fitzpatrick, he told me, and he was right.

With the body builder, everything changed. The guy was squeaky clean, as much a bystander in the rest of life as he'd been for our homicide. I had to get creative on this one: a sting of some kind, opening a door to some criminal enterprise that my subject was sure to walk through. To help flesh out the plan, I made the mistake of bouncing some things off an informant, and my informant went straight to Wilcox.

That was the end of our partnership. He wouldn't grass on me, but he wouldn't cover for me, either. I put him in a tight spot, and he extricated himself in the most unexpected way, sacrificing a promising career to make the jump into Internal Affairs. Even now, he's half convinced I'd stoop to anything, utterly missing the point of my windmill tilting, which had to do with bringing more justice, not less.

Carter would understand none of this, or he'd chide me for trying to play God.

But what was I supposed to do? If the Almighty was gonna sit back and let it all happen, somebody had to step up.

There's no such thing in my book as an innocent bystander.

CHAPTER 9

In Homicide the detectives are suiting up, strapping Kevlar over their white dress shirts and patterned silk ties, slipping their arms through the sleeves of reflective POLICE jackets, shifting the paddle holsters tucked into their waistbands with martial anticipation. Aguilar walks over to me with a spare vest.

"You wanna get in on this just for fun?"

I strip off my suit jacket and pull the vest on like a life preserver, battening down the side straps until they're nice and tight.

"What's the occasion?" I ask.

"Lorenz found his shooter from Friday. According to the tip, he's holed up in an apartment right off Antoine, not more than a hundred yards from the scene. The tactical team will take the door, but the captain wants everybody out there for a show of strength."

"Where is the captain?"

"In his office, probably. Working on the press release."

"Funny," I say, knowing that's not the captain's style.

While the boys load up on caffeine and testosterone, I bring the recurring 832 phone number from Simone's records over to one of our non-sworn computer jockeys with instructions to find the matching name. On my way back I come face-to-face with Hedges, who's wrapped in body armor of his own with a badge dangling from his neck.

"You're rolling out on this, sir?"

He ignores the question. "How's your case coming, March?"

"It's a stone-cold whodunit."

"I have confidence in you," he says, patting my shoulder. "Get me that clearance, you hear? If Lorenz is bringing them in, anybody can."

I give him a halfhearted smile. "True that."

We head down en masse and I tuck myself into the backseat of an unmarked car with Aguilar, Ordway, and a tense-looking Lt. Bascombe at the wheel. The caravan snakes through downtown and onto the highway, winding around to the Northwest Freeway. The atmosphere in the car doesn't lend itself to conversation, but I don't let that stop me.

"We're certainly gonna make our presence felt. It's kind of strange, though, the captain charging in like this."

"March," Bascombe says, catching my eye in the rearview mirror. "You wanna zip it?"

Ordway rotates his bulk in the passenger seat, giving me a pair of raised eyebrows and some pursed lips.

"I'm just saying—"

"I know what you're saying, and if you don't zip it, you're gonna be saying it on the curb." With that, Bascombe flips on the radio and cranks up some commercial Nashville bubblegum, only to switch it off when his walkie starts squawking.

There's an audience already when we arrive on scene, hooking up with the tail end of a stack of armed officers counting down the push. The lead man swings the ram, crunching open the cardboard door, and it's *Go! Go! Go!* along the line. By the time my group is in the apartment, everybody's re-holstering and there's a skinny little perp in boxer shorts lying facedown on the carpet in cuffs, an upended cereal bowl spilled out next to his head. On the side table by the TV remote is a Glock 9mm that might as well be wrapped in gift paper with a pretty red ribbon.

Jerry Lorenz goes down the line high-fiving everybody, and as much as I don't like the man, I don't have the heart not to give him his due. Maybe we'll make something out of him, after all. The captain snatches him by the arm and heads outside. I follow them as far as the door. Over by the curb, the local news cameras are already setting up, framing their shots of the apartment complex. Hedges advances toward them with his big hand clamped on Lorenz's shoulder, a proud father introducing his boy to the world.

"What is this?" I say.

Bascombe curses under his breath, the word coming out like a gob of spit. He pushes past me and heads outside, taking a route well clear of the cameras.

The drive back downtown is even more tense than before. I spend most of my time thinking of what I'll do to the clerical help if there's not a name waiting on my desk when I get back, though my options are limited to adulterating the break room coffee, which could only be improved by the addition of kerosene or rat poison.

Instead of results, though, I get back to my cubicle only to find it occupied by a familiar-looking stranger with a Fu Manchu mustache and a nickel-plated barbecue gun on his hip.

"You March?" he says.

"In the flesh." I toss my Kevlar on the desk and retrieve my jacket. "And you are?"

"Roger Lauterbach, Harris County Sheriff's Department. You and me seem to be working opposite ends of the same case."

"How so?"

"You've got an open homicide with a victim stabbed to death and left in a swimming pool, right? Well, I've got one, too."

That *well* comes out like *whelp*, and the news hits me hard. On top of that, I know I've seen this guy before, though I'm having a hard time placing him. He's having the same trouble, too, eyes narrowing.

"You're . . ." His voice trails off and he shakes his head. "I seen you somewheres."

Then it comes to me. I remember the nickel Government Model more than the man. "You were on the Hannah Mayhew task force, right? I think we stood next to each other at the back of a briefing."

A shrewd smile: "You were on that thing, too, huh? That must be it. What a fiasco."

"I wasn't just on it," I say, "I put that case down."

"Good for you." His smile persists, letting me know how unimpressed he is. I don't blame him, though. A county detective coming downtown needs some ego the same way a space shuttle entering orbit needs heat shields. "Then I guess you've got your stabbing all squared away, too. That'll sure make my job a heck of a lot easier."

Touché.

"Who gave you the connection?" I ask.

"Doc Green down at the medical examiner's office. There's the swimming pool in common, but she says your killer used a bowie knife. Whelp, so did mine."

"And your case is from when?"

He glances sideways. "Happened back in April."

"That'll sure as heck make my job easier," I say. "You have a suspect by any chance?"

"What I have is this." He grabs an unfamiliar folder from off my desk and hands it to me. Inside, a stack of reports and a bunch of glossies from his scene. "Same deal as yours, from what I gather. She was out on her back porch sunbathing when it happened. The suspect must have seen her through the gaps in the fence, climbs over, rapes her, then uses the knife. Cut her up real good and left her in the water."

"My victim wasn't raped," I say. "You have DNA from your scene?"

He does that sideways thing again. "There were some preservation issues."

"Someone screwed up."

"Pretty much, but it wasn't me."

I flip through the photos. Blood in the water, all around the reclined plastic-covered chair she'd been lying in, her torso slashed up in a terrible frenzy. There are a couple of shots of the body on the mortuary slab, showing the wounds in bright clinical light. There's no rhyme or reason that I can see, just a jagged and random flay job. I pick out the most illustrative angle and hand it to Lauterbach, along with a similar shot from Simone Walker's postmortem.

"You think that's the work of the same man?" I ask.

"A killer don't always work the same way. They change things up over time to keep it interesting. The similarities are pretty strong otherwise."

Just a hint of a plea enters his voice, and I realize what this visit must mean to him. He's been sitting under a cold one for months now, and suddenly sees the chance to unload it on another agency. He's doing the same thing Fitzpatrick was trying when he walked his case file over to the FBI. Anything to get it off his plate, no matter how desperate.

I decide to let him off easy. I flip through his scene photos again, finding the closest thing to my own snap from the far side of the pool. Then I line the two pictures up side by side on the desk. Everything's off. His victim floats on the wrong side of the pool and there's blood where there shouldn't be. Even the outdoor furniture doesn't match.

"Do those scenes look the same to you?"

He rubs the back of his neck in confusion. "Say what?"

"They're not the same. Clearly."

"Whelp, I guess not, but what's that got to do with anything?"

I dig my copy of *The Kingwood Killing* out of my briefcase, flipping to the photo insert. "Now, these two"—I give the book a tap, then the Walker photo—"these two *are* the same, you see? The placement of the body, the way the furniture's arranged, everything."

"Let me take a look at that." He grabs the book and spends a few seconds going back and forth. "I guess there's some similarity," he concedes, "but I'm not seeing the connection." He turns the book around to examine the cover, then fans through the pages. "What is this, anyway?"

His eyes flare with recognition.

"That's a book about the Nicole Fauk murder back in '99," I say. "I put that one down, too."

"Hey now," he says, "I'm not trying to lock horns with you, brother. You see my situation. I've got a girl sliced up with a bowie knife and so do you. I got a girl floating dead in the water and so do you. All I'm asking for here is a look-see. If it's nothing but a coincidence, I'll be on my way and there's no harm done."

"You want to look at the case file, be my guest. All I'm saying is, there's a lot of swimming pools in this town and a lot of bowie knives, too. It'll take more than that to connect the dots on this one."

"If you're willing to let me look, what more could I ask?"

"Go ahead, then. Have a seat. I've gotta follow up on some things, so I'll be back in a bit. In the meantime, the coffee's through that door and I recommend it highly."

I go straight to Bascombe and bring him into the picture, though he's too preoccupied to do more than stare at Lauterbach through the blinds and shake his head.

"That's your problem," he says. "I've got headaches of my own."

He ducks over to the captain's office, so I avail myself of the phone on his desk, dialing Sheila Green on the number Cavallo gave me.

"Thanks a lot," I tell her. "You sent that hayseed over to torment me?"

Green's laughter echoes over the line. "Shoot, March. I thought you and Lauterbach would hit it off like old buddies. He is the Roland March of the Sheriff's Department, you know, and causes just about as much trouble."

"Now he's trying to unload his case on me. It's painfully obvious there's no connection between the two."

"Not to me it isn't."

"You're just messing with me, aren't you?"

"Tell the hayseed I said hello."

Bascombe returns as I hang up, frowning at the intrusion. "Did they not put a phone in at your desk? I can call somebody and have it done."

Leaving him to it, I drop in on my civilian researcher, who lights up the moment she sees me, an unusual occurrence. She hands me subscriber info on the phone, but that's not all. The number belongs to a certain Sean Epps, age thirty, who has a DUI on file from eight months back. He's a real estate agent with a Porsche Cayenne and a wife in Bellaire.

"I found all his contact info online," she says. "And here's an extra little nugget: the number you've got is billed to the office, not home—but it's *not* the mobile number listed on his agency page."

"Maybe he only gives it out to the women he sees on the side."

She nods in agreement. "Anything else you need?"

"This is more than enough. Thanks for the help."

With Lauterbach still thumbing through the Walker case file, I set up shop in Aguilar's cubicle, dialing the office number for Sean Epps. The real estate agency receptionist answers with false cheer and a country twang, then tells me Epps is out at a showing and offers me his mobile number, the official one. I dial him up and he answers the line.

"Mr. Epps," I say. "I'm Detective Roland March with the Houston Police Department. I left a message for you on your other phone, but I never heard back."

"Ah," he says. "I'm, uh . . ."

"We need to have a face-to-face talk in my office. You know where police headquarters is downtown?"

"Can I ask what this is about?"

"It's about your visit to Simone Walker's house last night."

Silence. In the background I hear road noise and the sound of an announcer's voice on the radio.

"Mr. Epps?"

"When do you want to do this?" he asks.

"We need to do it right now. How long is it going to take you to get downtown?"

"Now? I don't think I can—"

"Let me explain something, sir. If you'd called me back yesterday, we would've made an appointment at your convenience, but since you didn't, it's in your best interest to show some willingness to cooperate. Do you see what I'm saying?"

"Yes," he says. "Of course. I've just been really busy. I can be there in, like, fifteen minutes?"

"Make it ten."

There's always the risk of spooking someone, coming on strong like this, but my instinct tells me how to play the hand. His reaction to the news of Simone's death was emotional, but given his marital status, I can understand why he'd want to conceal the relationship if he could. Now he'll be wondering how to do damage control, trying to trade cooperation for my assurance that his extracurricular activities won't get back to his wife.

I lean over the cubicle partition. "I've got a witness to interview. How much longer you think this will take you?"

Lauterbach looks up from the case file. "You really don't see the connection? Boy, it's staring me right in the face."

"Good try. But if you don't mind packing up . . ."

"All right, all right. I can take a hint." He puts his own file into an old-fashioned hard-sided attaché with combination locks on either side of the handle, then scans around to make sure he's not forgetting anything. As he leaves, he tips an imaginary hat. "Just don't be surprised if this one comes back to bite you."

Sean Epps unzips a close-fitting, tab-collared leather jacket and perches lightly on the chair across the table from me, like he might be called away any second and doesn't want to make himself too comfortable. He unclips a BlackBerry from his belt and sets it in front of him.

"That's not the phone Simone Walker would call you on," I say.

He glances down at it and shakes his head.

"You want to explain why you have two cellular phones?"

He shrugs. "One for business and one for personal."

"Your wife know about the personal phone?"

He shrugs again.

"So tell me everything you know about Simone Walker."

"Everything I know," he says. "No problem. But before I do that, you have to promise me something. Can we agree up front that this is off the record? I want to be helpful, but at the same time I don't want to hurt anyone, if you see what I mean."

"I see what you mean."

"Okay, then. That's cool?"

"I'm a homicide detective, Mr. Epps, which is why I'm investigating Simone's murder and not your marriage. So if you don't mind, let's get on with it."

A wave of relief washes over him, followed by an ingratiating smile. He scoots his chair forward and leans over the table.

"Thanks," he says. "The thing is, I have a great marriage. You can believe what you want, but that's the truth. There's other women, but they're never serious. Simone was the same: it was no big deal. I met her at a cooking class I signed my wife up for. She worked at the store—for all of a week, I think—and we got to talking. It was my wife's birthday coming up, and I thought she'd like this. But I'm talking to this girl, and she's pretty cute and she seems up for it, and . . . anyway, you know how it goes."

"You asked her out?"

"Something like that. It wasn't exactly a relationship. It's not like we were dating. It was just convenient, you know. Easygoing. We hooked up a couple of times, no big deal."

"If you didn't date her, where did you go?"

An impish grin. "There are a lot of properties sitting on the market these days."

"You took her to houses you were listing?"

"Good, huh? The thing is, for me, I like to keep a firewall between this kind of thing and my real life. I like to keep things in their place. So I never went to her house and, obviously, I never took her to mine. And when we were together, well, we didn't do a lot of talking."

"So what changed?"

His smile fades. "The thing with the baby." He says the word and his lip trembles. "You gotta understand, me and my wife, that's something we haven't managed to do. We went to a specialist even, and he said my sperm count was low, that was the problem. Which I had a hard time accepting. All the things they can do now, the artificial stuff . . . it's not the same, is it? So Simone calls me and I'm thinking she's just looking to hook up. But no, she's pregnant. We didn't use any protection—I mean, hey, I didn't think it was necessary, according to the doctor."

"When did you have this conversation, the one where she revealed her pregnancy?"

"The exact date, you mean?"

I stare at him.

"It would have been a few weeks ago. Middle of November, maybe?"

Around the time of her attempt to get money out of Jason Young. I check the date against the phone records and find several calls back and forth on Tuesday, November 17. He shrugs when I mention the date, but concedes that could be right.

"Me, I was kind of thrilled to hear the news. She was acting like it was some kind of tragedy, and if I'd just give her the money she'd take care of it. But I'm like, hey, this is a good thing. I'm gonna have a kid." His eyes cloud and he wipes them with the heel of his hand. "She was saying she'd need five grand, and I'm like, it doesn't cost that kind of money to get rid of a pregnancy. And anyway, I told her I was gonna pay support, that was no problem."

"Did you give her any money?"

"What do *you* think? Of course I did. We met up and I gave her some cash, but she needed more so we went to the ATM. I gave her five hundred that day. Then I got a call over the weekend and she said she needed the other forty-five hundred."

"Did she say why?"

"She wanted to move out of the house where she was staying. She said the old lady who lived there was crowding her."

The old lady. Dr. Hill would be pleased to hear that.

"And did you give her the additional cash?"

"I pulled two grand out of the bank and said I'd have some more for her when I could. It's not like I'm totally liquid, but I have an account where I keep some fun money. Bonuses, that kind of thing."

In my stack of paperwork, I have the bank balances for Simone Walker's checking account, retrieved along with the bills she kept in one of her dresser drawers. There are no big deposits from the last couple of weeks, and during the search of her rooms, we recovered no large sums of cash. Her purse was in the bedroom, the wallet inside containing less than a hundred dollars. The money went somewhere. I can't help remembering all those bags in the closet, all those names of expensive boutiques.

"Did Simone ever talk to you about her husband?" I ask.

"I didn't know she had one until the old lady told me. She said it was him that killed her, is that right?"

"Simone never said anything to you about him? What about her past?"

He laughs. "Like I said, we didn't talk all that much. When she quit her job at the kitchen store, we talked about that. She would tell these funny stories about people, imitating the way they talked and everything. She cracked me up with that stuff. But she wasn't real serious. She was all about having a good time. Even when she was making fun of people, it wasn't spiteful or anything. She was just being entertaining, you know? Eager to please. Although . . ."

"Although what?"

"She was fun on the surface," he says thoughtfully, like he's only just working this out, "but underneath she had that damaged-goods, self-destructive thing, you know? And it's no good hooking up with someone who's only with you to punish herself."

"Mr. Epps," I say, "where were you on Saturday from noon until midnight?"

"Me?"

I wait him out again.

"I was . . . My wife and me, we went to Herman Park on Saturday morning. Rode our bikes and everything. I stopped and threw the Frisbee around with some kids. Around two, I had to go into work. I had an open house from two to six. A few people showed up, but no offers. When I got home, she made us dinner and we watched a movie I recorded off the cable."

"You didn't see Simone Walker at all?"

He shakes his head. "I tried calling her earlier in the week, but she didn't answer. To be honest, the last time I saw her was when I pulled the money out of the bank. She met me in the parking lot and didn't even get out of the car. I passed the money through and leaned in to kiss her, then she was gone."

"And you're saying that the only person who can verify your where-abouts on Saturday is your wife?"

He starts to nod, then stops himself. "No, that's not what I'm say-ing. You don't need her to verify anything. Like I said, from two to six I was at the open house. I can give you the sign-up list if you want, and you can ask everybody on it."

"But after that?"

"After that I went home. I can't help that, can I? And anyway, what does it matter where I was? I didn't do this. It was the husband, right? Me, I was just in the wrong place at the wrong time. I've suffered enough just losing the baby."

I could tell him there was no baby. I could tell him it was a story Simone manufactured so that he'd cough up the money. Either she'd intuited his weakness somehow, or made a lucky guess. Regardless, she'd gotten what she wanted from him and then stopped returning his calls. Maybe it would comfort him a little to know this. Maybe it would wound him to realize his fertility doctor was right. But it's not my place to comfort or wound. I get his statement typed up and have him sign it before cutting him loose, leaving Sean Epps none the wiser as he walks out the door.

CHAPTER 10

After flipping his way through my report, his reading glasses low on his nose, Hedges gives me a steely-eyed, penetrating once-over. Bascombe perches on the credenza behind him, arms crossed, glaring for once not at me but the back of the captain's head.

"I'm a little surprised," Hedges says.

I shift my weight in one of his cantilevered guest chairs, wishing I was positioned a little more securely—in the case, not the seat.

"There are three possible suspects in there," I say, nodding toward the report. "The case on Young was shaping up pretty good, but we just don't have enough. And he's pretty convincing in the interviews, too. The other guy, Epps, is relying on his wife for an alibi, but I'm guessing she'll back him up. There's no physical evidence tying him to the scene, and from what Dr. Hill says, he seemed genuinely shocked to learn of the victim's death, just like Young was."

"Maybe you're giving up too easily on Young," he says. "The strip club fight puts him somewhere later in the evening, but he doesn't have an alibi for the murder itself."

Bascombe's lip curls downward, but he doesn't speak.

"There are some lines I can follow up," I say. "For one thing, I still think it's strange there were no books in that apartment. Maybe he has a storage unit from when he moved out of the house—?"

"Can I be honest with you?" Hedges says. "I think you're straining with the Fauk connection, reading too much into the similarities. Maybe if you'd focus more on the concrete facts of the investigation."

"The facts." I shift again. "I'll make a note of that, sir. Thank you very much."

"Don't be smart with me, March. If you could charge a suspect on this, I wouldn't have to sit here and spoon-feed you advice. What I'm particularly concerned about is your third possible suspect."

"You mean Dr. Hill."

He adjusts his glasses. "That's right. I'm a little worried about what we might call the political aspects. If you let the press get hold of the idea that we're looking at Dr. Hill as a murder suspect, that's going to look a little dubious, don't you think?"

"How so?"

He turns to Bascombe, expecting him to weigh in, but the lieutenant keeps his counsel. With a sigh, Hedges struggles for a compassionate tone. "Look, March. This is sensitive stuff at the moment. With the runoff election this coming weekend, you need to be reasonable. We've got a candidate in the race who's positioned to become the city's first, ah, lesbian mayor." He glances at Bascombe again like he's worried he got the term wrong. "And the other side is really playing up that angle in a negative way."

"I see."

"You're looking at me like a deer in the headlights. Marcus, help me out here."

Bascombe clears his throat. "Here's the concern, March. The captain doesn't want a headline in the papers saying 'HPD Names Prominent Lesbian as Homicide Suspect.' That would look political."

"I don't plan on going to the *Chronicle* with anything." The words come slowly, which is how you talk when picking your way through a minefield. "And I'm not naming Dr. Hill as a suspect, not at this point. We have her prints outside, but it would be stranger if we didn't. There's no indication that a sexual relationship existed between Dr. Hill and the victim, and for that matter, Dr. Hill says the rumors about her orientation are groundless. So even if we found the bloody knife hidden in her nightstand, I would hardly call her a 'prominent lesbian.' "

"*That's not the point*," Hedges snaps.

"It's what the media would call it, March. Not you." Bascombe stares at the drawn blinds, looking as disgusted with the conversation as I feel. "I think what the captain is asking is for any inquiry into Dr. Hill's involvement to wait. After the election, she'll be fair game."

Hedges sits back in his chair. "Exactly."

"So I'll be free next Monday to investigate one of my suspects?"

"You said yourself she didn't rise to that level."

"In the meantime, is it all right if I take another look at Young?"

The captain slides my report across the table. "Be my guest. It wouldn't hurt if you'd take a page out of Lorenz's book and close this thing."

"Assuming the prominent lesbian didn't do it."

"You said yourself she wasn't that, either," he says. "Now get out of here and show me some police work for a change."

"Yes, sir."

I rise to go, but Hedges motions me back into my chair.

"One more thing," the captain says. "You might have handled that Sheriff's Department detective a little better."

"I thought I handled him pretty good."

"You don't read the paper at all, do you?" He takes a rolled section of the *Chronicle* off the credenza and hands it over. "Read the underlined part."

My eye goes to the headline: SHERIFF'S DEPARTMENT HUNTS SERIAL KILLER. According to the article, the murder of a young woman in northwest Harris County in April was the work of a serial killer known to have struck at least once more in the area. I scan the piece for any mention of Simone Walker, but thankfully Lauterbach at least had the good grace not to link the cases publicly. But the implication is clear.

A killer's been operating with impunity in the Houston area with HPD none the wiser, and if he hadn't made the mistake of striking on Sheriff's Department turf, law enforcement wouldn't be on his trail.

"This takes the cake," I say. "Not that they haven't pulled this kind of thing before. Seriously, I saw the guy's case. There's no connection."

"That's not what the ME is saying."

"You're kidding, right? Since when does the ME saying so make something true? When they send back your accidentals as homicides, you don't roll over and take it, so why would this be any different?"

Hedges frowns deeply, shaking his head just enough to suggest pity. "Here's what I want you to do, March. Listen carefully. I want you to go back to your desk and take a good, long look at this case. I want you to be absolutely sure you're not missing something here—"

"I am absolutely sure. Lauterbach's either desperate to unload his case or he's delusional. Maybe he thinks a cock-and-bull serial killer story will make his name."

"March, you're not listening. That's a problem with you. If it keeps up, I have ways of making myself heard."

"Fine."

I reach for the report and head out, sensing Bascombe on my heels. I'm tempted to shut the door on him, but petty little things like that get petty little guys like me in all kinds of trouble. Back in my cubicle, I ball the *Chronicle* section up and dunk it into the trash bin. Bascombe rests his hands on each side of the gap in the cubicle wall, effectively bottling me up.

"Take it easy," he says. "I don't care what some peckerwood from out in the sticks thinks about your case. That's all coming from the captain, and you're missing the real issue."

"What's the real issue?"

He glances around, then lowers his voice. "The issue is, there are rumors going around about the new mayor promoting from within. And they are more than just rumors. There's been some back-channel talk, and one of the possibilities floating out there is that if she wins, she might reach deeper than the assistant chiefs to find new leadership."

"But not . . . I mean, she's not gonna reach that deep."

"Do you want to tell him or should I?"

"You can't be serious. Hedges chasing after rank? That's not him."

"It's more than rank," he says. "But you're right: it's not him. At least it wasn't until now. I don't know who exactly, but somebody poured the poison in his ear. The campaign maybe, or somebody with connections to it. And now he's going out of his way to make a fool of himself, which is what that charade yesterday was all about. He thinks he needs to give them a pretext, so they can justify his jump to the front of the line."

"Are you sure about this?" I say. "We're talking about Hedges here."

"He's making a mistake not keeping ambition like this to himself. People are noticing, March, and that's gonna cost him. It's gonna cost us. 'Cause I'll tell you one thing right now. Homicide can't do any better than Drew Hedges, but we could do a lot worse."

I don't know what to say, so all I do is nod.

"This conversation is between the two of us, understood? I wouldn't be telling you this in the first place except that if I don't, you're gonna keep running afoul of him and I'm not running interference for you anymore."

He heads back to his office leaving me dazed, feeling the same way I did the first time I realized my mother wasn't coming home anymore. One of life's supposedly unshakable foundations breaking open just under my feet.

A phone rings and after a while I realize it's mine.

"This is March."

"We need to talk." The voice is vaguely familiar. "Something big is about to break, and if we don't get out in front of it, you and me both are gonna get fried."

"Who is this?"

"March, my feelings are hurt. It's Charlie Bodeen. Make whatever excuses you have to and get over here. Now would be nice."

At the party Saturday night, all Bodeen could talk about was the impending doom of Charlotte's firm. She resigned her partnership years ago, after Jessica was born, and took on contract work for a variety of legal types, but the majority of her hours are still billed to the old firm. According to Bodeen, they've lost some bread-and-butter clients during the recession and are now facing serious cutbacks.

"But the cutbacks won't be enough," he confided. "That thing's headed for implosion and you better make sure Charlotte's aware of that fact."

Since my mention Sunday morning, when Charlotte dismissed the subject out of hand, it hasn't come up. I've had my hands full, after all.

I decide to humor the man with a visit. Not because I'm overly worried about Charlotte's employment prospects, but the fact is, I could use the break. Bodeen's office is in a glass mid-rise on San Felipe not far outside the 610 Loop, and all I can think about during the drive is the change in Hedges over the past few weeks, coming to a head during this case. The lieutenant's edginess starts making sense. He's known all along what the captain's up to, and he's been doing his best to screen it from everyone on the shift, picking up the slack.

Inside, I consult the board between the elevator doors, finding Bodeen's practice listed on the fourth. It turns out to be a small suite of offices, just a reception area, a conference room, and three private offices. The secretary tells me I'm expected and leads me straight to the door at the end of the hall.

"Have a seat," Bodeen says. And then to the secretary: "Close that door behind you."

One of the walls is glass and the other three are bare apart from some framed degrees and a shelf overflowing with matched legal volumes. The room still has the bare unfurnished feel of his bolt hole in the district attorney's office.

"I said something to Charlotte," I tell him, "but she didn't seem too concerned."

He stares at me, then blinks. "That's not what I called you about. I just got wind of something big and what I need from you right now is some reassurance. Because frankly, I'm blindsided by this thing and what I'm hearing makes absolutely no sense."

"Are you going to fill me in or what?"

"It's about Donald Fauk. Remember him? The guy we put away for butchering his wife and running to Florida with his new girlfriend?"

"I remember, Charlie."

"What do you know about Donald Fauk filing an appeal?"

My mental gears make a grinding sound. Did I wake up this morning in an alternate universe? First my homicide is reclassified as the work of a serial killer by some boondock detective who can't say *well* without putting a *p* at the end. And now Donald Fauk, who dictated a free and uncoerced confession of his crimes into my recorder, is filing an appeal?

"Is this some kind of joke?" I ask.

"Not in the slightest. It'll be officially filed this afternoon. Now, tell me everything you know about the case. New developments, everything."

"What new developments? There's nothing. What could there be? Over the weekend I had lunch with Brad Templeton and he had a few things to say about Fauk. They've kept in contact apparently, and he claims Fauk is trying to start some kind of fan club on the outside." The pulse in my temple starts to throb. "Look, I'm no lawyer, but you're gonna have to explain to me how a guy who confesses on tape to the crime in excruciating detail turns around and appeals. On what grounds?"

He consults a legal pad on the desk in front of him, where a page of illegible notes has been scribbled down. "Number one, there's some evidence that's gone missing. They wanted to retest the DNA samples from the scene, saying your match came out of the same crime lab that self-destructed a couple of years later. They requested the samples, and according to HPD that evidence is no longer available."

"DNA testing can be destructive—"

"No," he says. "There were samples left, only now nobody can find them. Defense theory? You guys destroyed the evidence to make sure it couldn't be retested."

"That's not true, and it's also not enough for an appeal—is it?"

"Here's the second thing. Apparently, Nicole Fauk's murder is being looked at as part of a serial killer investigation."

Lauterbach. I showed him *The Kingwood Killing* to dissuade him from making an impossible leap, and all he did was insert another link into his serial killer theory. But the story in the *Chronicle* said nothing about the Walker case, let alone Nicole Fauk. Where would Donald Fauk's attorneys have gotten hold of this?

"Since when?" I ask.

He shrugs. "I found out ten minutes before I called you. All I know is, they had paper down at the courthouse and it's about to be filed."

"There's this detective, this Sheriff's Department guy," I say, and then I tell him about my visit from Lauterbach, which requires an explanation of the Walker case and how it supposedly links up with the killing back in April.

"So you gave him the Fauk connection."

"I gave him nothing," I say. "And besides, this guy may be an idiot and a snake, but I don't see him getting on the phone to Fauk's lawyers and letting them in on the good news. He's still a cop at the end of the day."

"All I know is, they're alleging Nicole Fauk's murder is part of a larger series and that they have a list of open homicides with identical *modus operandi*. Since Fauk was in jail when some of these were committed—including the one you're working on now—he couldn't have committed them, which means—"

"Which means absolutely nothing because the man confessed. Besides, my open homicide wasn't committed by the same person who killed Nicole Fauk. The killer imitated the crime scene photo reprinted in Templeton's book."

"It *does* mean something . . . because of Number Three."

"Go ahead," I say. "Lay it on me."

"March, that confession you keep talking about?" He looks me square in the eye. "They're saying they have solid evidence that the confession you obtained was coerced."

PART 2

A MIRROR BLINDING

This night has opened my eyes
and I will never sleep again.

—THE SMITHS

CHAPTER 11

The district attorney and an entourage of pinstriped ADAs anchor one end of the conference table with an extra rung of associates lined like gargoyles along the window ledge, obscuring the glass-and-steel view of downtown. On the other end of the table, the HPD contingent consisting of myself, Bascombe, Wilcox, and a newly appointed crime lab supervisor crowds one side, elbows touching, leaving plenty of room opposite for Roger Lauterbach and his boss from the Harris County Sheriff's Department to spread out. Just inside the door, Charlie Bodeen, the last to arrive, sits in a chair he dragged in with him, a wheeled accordion case at his feet. There are no water glasses on the table, and the thermal pitchers of coffee down the middle remain untouched. Most of us are keeping our heads down, pretending to reread bits from the Fauk appeal, even though the details should all be familiar by now.

The DA clears his throat. "Does anyone in this room have something to say?"

Oh, I have something to say, but a preemptive glare from Bascombe shuts me down. *You're not here to talk,* he told me. *You're here to listen. Open your mouth once and see if I don't shove something down your throat.*

"Anybody?"

"The conviction is solid," Bodeen says, waving his copy of the appeal. "And they're not going to get a hearing based on this."

"You don't think so? I wouldn't be so sure about that. Not having the DNA available for retesting looks bad, but it's par for the course. If that's all they had, you'd be right."

"That is all they have. The rest is speculation."

The DA turns to one of the lawyers blocking the window, a round-faced woman clutching a stack of papers to her chest, signaling her to commence with some prearranged briefing. She starts talking without looking up from her notes.

"An attempted homicide case went to Orleans Parish Criminal Court twelve weeks ago with the defense arguing that the investigating officer, Detective Eugene Fontenot, had extracted a false confession from the accused. During testimony, several past complaints about Fontenot's interrogation techniques were entered into evidence, and the jury came back with a not-guilty verdict. I've been in touch already with the Orleans DA and NOPD's Public Integrity Bureau, and there is definitely an ongoing investigation of Fontenot. They're taking this very seriously."

Bodeen interrupts with a sarcastic laugh. "So what you're saying is, if a detective who had nothing to do with my case is accused—not convicted, just accused—of applying the thumbscrews in the here and now, the fact that eight years ago he helped with prisoner transport calls my conviction into question?"

"*I'm* not saying it," the DA replies. "Fauk's counsel is. And it's no use arguing your case to me, Charlie. If it was my call, I'd obviously deny the appeal. When we argue this thing, though, my people need to be ready. Either we take this seriously or Donald Fauk will get his shot at overturning the verdict."

Across the table from me, Lauterbach strokes his mustache. His boss—older, fatter, and grayer than him, but cut from the same cloth—throws his hands up in theatrical exasperation.

"Don't y'all think maybe we're jumping the gun here a little? Don't you want to hear what my people have come up with before going on the warpath? 'Cause I'll tell you one thing right now: this conviction ain't worth defending, not from where I'm sittin'. I know y'all got your pride invested in this, but I've been through the whole case backwards and forwards and the one thing this isn't is an isolated incident. This Fauk killing, it's just one of a whole series of homicides, and if we don't wake up to that fact, if we start going on TV saying otherwise, then the egg'll be all over our faces."

His outburst is greeted by cold silence. Bascombe keeps flexing his hands, like he's trying to prevent a fist from forming, while on the other side of me Wilcox fiddles nervously with his ballpoint pen.

"With respect—" the DA begins.

"Just hear my detective out, that's all I'm asking for. Let him talk, and if you still wanna go down with the sinkin' ship, it's your call."

As much as I dislike the man, I have to admit I'm a little jealous of the way Lauterbach's chief is backing his play. I can't imagine Hedges or Bascombe doing the same for me, not in a roomful of prosecutors with the DA himself holding court. By the door, Bodeen raises his eyebrows at me, keeping up his smartest-man-in-the-vicinity act, but even he seems a little surprised at how committed the Sheriff's Department supervisor comes off. In the lead up to this round-table, he'd led me to expect a dressing down for Lauterbach and company, not a fair hearing on equal footing.

"I really have to object to this," Bascombe says.

The DA silences him with a raised finger. "Hold on a sec. With all that preamble, I think we might as well hear what the man has to say. I mean, I've already read what the detective shared with the *Chronicle*, but if there's anything else he'd like to add . . ."

Lauterbach bristles at the criticism, even though he had to know it was coming. Past convictions are like precedents in law. In theory you can always go against them, they can always be overturned, but in practice they benefit from extreme deference. Even stronger than the presumption of innocence is the presumption that, if a jury sided with the prosecution, the verdict was sound. By suggesting otherwise, Lauterbach threatens not just me and my reputation but HPD and the Harris County District Attorney's Office, too. It feels nice for once to be sitting on this side of the table.

"Mr. District Attorney," he says with icy formality. "You're mistaken if you think I've shared anything with the media. I don't know where they got their information, but it didn't come from me. If it had, they'd be having a field day with this story. You'll see why in just a minute."

He opens a black laptop on the table and starts untangling wires, hitching the computer via a VGA cable to the projector on the table.

"There's a PowerPoint?" I ask, rolling my eyes.

Wilcox crosses his arms and sinks back, the ballpoint clicking in my ear.

Nobody lifts a finger to help Lauterbach. Eventually his boss goes to the light switches, fumbling through the row until the projection screen whirs down from the suspended ceiling. After a moment, Lauterbach's computer display appears on-screen. The cursor glides over a series of desktop icons, double-clicking on the presentation file. But not before I notice the title on one of his folders: TEMPLETON.

Bascombe scratches a note out and slides it in front of me: *You need to have a talk with your writer friend.* I nod in agreement, trying to work the timing out in my head. At the beginning of the week, Lauterbach seemed never to have heard of *The Kingwood Killing*, and now there's a file on his desktop with Templeton's name on it? Either the man works fast, or he knew more than he was letting on.

Don't be surprised if this one comes back to bite you.

The screen displays a map of Texas zoomed in so that San Antonio and Houston form the base of a triangle with Dallas at the apex. Interstate 10 runs along the bottom with I-35 and I-45 forming the triangle's sides. The map is labeled 2009.

"During the course of an ongoing investigation," Lauterbach says, "I noticed similarities to an unsolved case I worked back in 2005. Digging deeper, I became aware of a number of open homicides with strong similarities. While the details changed from case to case, some things remained constant: female victims discovered in or around water, usually in their own homes, stabbed to death and frequently mutilated afterwards. Including the case Detective March here is working on, there are three this year."

He touches a button on the laptop's keyboard and three red circles appear on the map, two in the greater Houston area and one in Dallas.

"The further I went back and the wider I spread my net, the more I found. One in 2008, two more in '07 . . ." More dots appear as the years change, each series coded with a different color. "None in '06, but then there are three again in '05. This goes all the way back to '99, and there's a total here of twenty-one homicides. And this is not counting deaths with similar circumstances where a suspect was charged and convicted. There are four more if you include those . . ." The additional dots appear, including one in the Kingwood area color-coded for 1999. "What that means is, we could be talking about as many as twenty-five homicides, and as you can see, there's a pattern at work."

The colored dots are clustered around the three cities: fourteen in the Houston area, eight around San Antonio, and three in Dallas.

"As I'm sure everyone in this room knows, Donald Fauk sold his house here and moved to Florida after his wife's death. That was in 2000. From then until he was extradited in September of 2001, there were two homicides here that fit the pattern, and of course most of these took place once he was behind bars."

The map dissolves, replaced by a lineup of photos, twenty-four victims arranged in rows of eight, the only one absent being Simone Walker. Dates and case numbers are affixed to most.

"After reviewing Detective March's case file, I came to the conclusion that Simone Walker fits the profile, too."

He taps the keyboard and the photo of Simone at the party materializes, the one I first saw on her shelf when Dr. Hill took me to her room. Seeing it again, a strange sensation comes over me, a mix of disappointment and shame. As if she's looking down on me, her smile faked, trying to hide her sense that I've failed her.

Bascombe passes me another note: *How are we not on top of this?*

"When you say there are similarities," the DA asks, "what exactly do you mean? Are these killings all the work of one individual, or do they just happen to have a few things in common? I mean, there's a lot of women in Texas and a lot of knives and a lot of swimming pools. That doesn't mean every time you find those three things together that it's Colonel Mustard with the knife in the swimming pool, if you see what I mean."

The ADAs crack a collective smile, letting their boss know they get the joke. Lauterbach takes it in stride.

"Some of these cases I've reviewed in more detail than others," he says, "so I'm not standing here telling you each and every one belongs to the series. But if you look at those numbers, the reality of the situation has to sink in."

"The reality?"

"Whelp, we've got a serial killer at work here. He's active in our backyard and in several other jurisdictions on top of that. Based on the way the numbers are weighted, I think he lives here in Houston and travels often to San Antonio and occasionally to Dallas. When he's on the road, he has enough time to identify victims and plan the murders. The question is, are we gonna put all our effort into defending past convictions, letting this guy continue to operate with impunity, or are we gonna wake up and start going after him?"

A pause during which all eyes move to the DA's side of the table. "This is legit? We're not talking smoke and mirrors here?"

Lauterbach advances the screen again, revealing the mug shot of a hollow-cheeked Hispanic male. "This is Raúl Guzman. In 1999, Detective Fitzpatrick identified him as a suspect in Nicole Fauk's murder. Guzman was seen leaving a convenience store shortly after she did, and he had a sexual assault charge in his jacket. When his DNA was checked against samples from the scene, they came back negative.

"Of course, I had no idea about this when I interviewed Guzman in 2005 on my earlier case. He'd overseen some construction work on the victim's house, and I had a witness who saw a pickup in the neighborhood the evening of the crime and gave a description that more or less matched Guzman's truck. But he was drinking cervezas at a taquería while my victim was getting herself killed and he had half a dozen men who'd back his story, all of them employees. I didn't like it, but what could I do?"

He taps the keyboard again, showing a copy of a Louisiana police report.

"Here's the clincher. In 2006, the year we had none of these homicides, Raúl Guzman took a truckload of construction workers to Lake Charles, Louisiana, and made a bundle doing cut-rate repairs after Hurricane Rita blew all the roofs off. The local police talked to Guzman and two of his men for trespassing. They confronted a sunbathing teenage girl in her own backyard and a neighbor called police. Guzman said they'd been talking to the girl about fixing her roof, but that's not what she said."

"Did this go to court?" the DA asks.

Lauterbach shakes his head. "At the time, the officers accepted Guzman's story that it was all a misunderstanding. They chalked it up to the language barrier. But knowing what we know, it looks like something else entirely."

"So the theory is what?" Bascombe asks. "That Guzman and his crew are responsible for all of these homicides, that they're working together? There's no evidence of more than one suspect in the Walker case."

"It's too early for me to say exactly," Lauterbach replies. "I've had as much trouble liaising with other agencies as I had with you. But it's certainly a possibility. Where there are differences in the individual homicides, that could be the result of different workers being with him." He glances over his shoulder at Bodeen. "But that really is speculation. Maybe Guzman is working alone. Maybe he's not even the right guy. That's something that needs investigating. So long as we're wasting time on the one guy we know *ain't* responsible, that's not gonna happen, is it?"

"Let's get the lights back on," the DA says. "When we break up here, I want to review all this in more detail, Detective Lauterbach. In the meantime, I'm going to ask Lt. Bascombe to ensure that his people widen their investigation to accommodate the possibility of a serial killer. That does not mean that Donald Fauk didn't murder his wife. At least for now, these are two separate issues. But if it turns out Fauk is innocent, I do not want to hold a press conference saying so unless I can name Guzman or whoever is responsible at the same time. Am I making myself clear, everybody?"

Perfectly clear. Lauterbach packs his laptop away with a smile on his lips, realizing what a huge concession he's won. Bascombe isn't looking at me, and Wilcox has a hand over his brow, looking like an actor in an aspirin commercial. The crime scene supervisor is still inspecting his copy of the appeal, trying to will himself into invisibility. The DNA evidence has only come up obliquely, and he couldn't have relished the task of defending HPD's disastrous track record on that score.

As the meeting breaks up, I can feel it starting already: the random whispers, the sighs of relief, and cutting through all that, a new energy, a new sense of purpose. The gathered prosecutors are feeling their way toward galvanization. Evil has a face now. There's a target to hunt down. They entered the room afraid of one homicide opening up again, and now they're leaving with the dream of closing twenty-five. Who wouldn't make a trade like that?

Wilcox slips toward the door. Since Bascombe seems to be angling for some one-on-one time with the DA, I follow my ex-partner out, hoping to get his take on what's transpired. Bodeen frowns as I pass, but he doesn't say anything. The slide show seems to have dampened his enthusiasm for me.

"This is classic *you*," Wilcox says.

We have the elevator all to ourselves, ticking off the floors.

"What is that supposed to mean?"

"Dragging me into it, expecting me to cover for you—"

"You don't have to cover for anything, Stephen. You were there, remember? You know the confession is good."

"Here's what I know," he says. "I know I wanted to stay with Fauk when you went to pick up that rental, and you left him with Fontenot instead. I know I tried to stop you from doing the interview in the car, and you went ahead and did it anyway."

"But listen—"

"No, *you* listen. If you did anything, anything at all . . . I'm not in Internal Affairs for nothing. I will come down on you like a ton of bricks, March. I promise you that. I already know you'll sacrifice your own career, but you're not dragging me down with you, understand?"

The elevator stops on the ground floor and the doors slide open. He bolts, leaving me undecided about whether to follow. What's the point? He will believe whatever he wants, regardless of the facts. Wilcox is like Lauterbach in that sense, letting his preconceived idea rearrange the world around him, only Wilcox is obsessed with corruption instead of serial killers. Either way, we see what we want to see, making connections where there are none, ignoring obvious links when they become inconvenient.

I'll say this for each of them. At least their ruling passions make them popular. There will always be ears ready to listen. Police corruption is an explanation you can get your head around, just like a serial-killing psychopath. The cops are bent because they're cops. The killers kill because they're killers. And all you have to do to end the corruption or the killing is put the person responsible behind bars. It's an easy cause to rally round. And of course there are bent cops and serial killers, though not as many as people seem to think.

As I'm standing there, Charlie Bodeen breezes past, his shoulder dipped by the weight of his accordion case.

"You got taken," he says.

Brad Templeton has a little place on Peden Street, a one-story in gray brick with white trim and a red Mitsubishi SUV under the carport.

Instead of a yard, there's a layer of fist-sized rock, an artificial riverbed accented with an ironic cactus here and there. He writes at a large table in the living room, where a wall of glass looks out over the equally rock-strewn backyard. Attached to the worn fence, a bright red bird feeder, and underneath it a stone birdbath.

Instead of knocking, I cut through the carport and let myself into the back, my leather soles making a crunching sound against the rock. Through the window I see him bent over his computer keyboard, fingers rapid as a piece of machinery, a chewed pencil between his teeth. When I pound against glass, Templeton jumps.

"You lied to me," I say.

He sits there frozen.

"Open up, Brad. It's your day of reckoning."

"What do you want?"

My fist sends vibrations through the windowpane. *One, two, three.* "Open up." *Four, five, six.* "Don't make me break it, Brad. And don't think I won't."

He circles the table and unhitches the lock, dragging the door open to release a rush of warm air. That's a strange feeling in Houston, heat blasting from inside instead of out. Without a word, he retraces his steps, dropping back into his chair with a groan.

"Roger Lauterbach," I say. "Tell me everything."

Templeton rubs his eyes. "He's a detective."

"Keep going."

"He works for the Sheriff's Department."

"And?"

"He's an expert on Dean Corll, which is how I met him. He gave a talk about Corll for a local group, focusing on the police response or lack thereof. He told me he wanted to write a book someday—who doesn't, right?—and we compared notes. A couple of weeks later, I got a call from him. He'd read all my books in the meantime and wanted to talk."

He's holding back on me. I can tell.

"About what?" I ask.

"I thought it would be about writing," he says, "but instead he had a lot of questions about the Fauk case."

He's holding back all right.

"And this was when?"

"A couple of months ago. I can check if you want." He opens a web browser on the computer and starts typing an address, which the software finishes for him. A lurid banner loads first: FOR THE VICTIMS, in red lettering, with a hack-job montage of black-and-white photos underneath, teenage boys from more than thirty years ago, some with buzz cuts, some with long hair. Underneath, in white on a black background, a column of text headed with THE HOUSTON CANDY MAN TERRORIZES THE YOUTH, a grainy photo of Dean Corll floating in the middle.

"What is this?" I ask, already knowing the answer.

Templeton scrolls down, revealing my cousin Moody's school photo circa 1972. He looks like such a kid, even though I remember him as much older, practically grown-up. The text is littered with blue hyperlinks, so much information packed onto the page, so many old pictures, giving the material an almost psychotic intensity. Conspiracy theory sites always look like this, the form itself a stinging refutation.

At the bottom of the page is a contemporary photo of Tammy, Moody's older sister, and a schedule of events listing bimonthly meetings at the public library branch in Katy. The meetings are news to me.

"There," he says, clicking on the link for September's meeting.

A photo of Lauterbach, innocuously smiling, pops up along with a blurb about a multimedia presentation titled *Catching Corll: Lessons for Law Enforcement.* According to his bio, Lauterbach has "a special certification in the investigation of serial crimes," which probably means he sat through an in-service training with a bunch of other bored cops.

"This morning I endured one of his multimedia presentations, and let me tell you, I did not enjoy it. For one thing, I couldn't help thinking you've been keeping things from me."

"It's not like that," he says.

"I showed him your book, Brad. I gave him the link between Fauk and the case I'm working on. And I find he knew about it all along.

You could've warned me what this guy was up to—and don't tell me you didn't know."

"You're right, I did. And I would have said something, but . . . you're hard to talk to, you know that? You don't listen."

"I'm listening now."

"Roger was working on a case," he says, "and the details reminded him of another murder from a couple of years ago. When he read *The Kingwood Killing*, there were some similarities there, too. But obviously Donald Fauk had already been convicted, so how could there be a connection? I put some questions to Fauk—"

"You what?"

"In a letter. I asked him to clarify some things. He sent me back some newspaper clippings from the trial in New Orleans, the one where Gene Fontenot is supposed to have threatened that kid into confessing. He said that's what happened to him, too. There was no point in telling anyone because they wouldn't have believed him."

"So how come I didn't hear about Fontenot until today?" I ask. "That was three months ago, right? And you never said a word to me. You didn't mention it Sunday, either. I asked you to check for strange correspondence and you didn't say a word."

His face reddens and he rotates his chair away from me.

"You have no idea what you've done," I say.

"I did some checking, March, and there were more cases. A lot more. Women stabbed to death, their bodies left in swimming pools, bathtubs . . . One of them, this girl in San Antonio, she was decapitated, March. Her head was left floating in a fish tank." His voice trembles with emotion. "Always the same pattern: the woman alone, the knife, the water. And I started to realize what it meant. I started to realize the mistake I'd made."

"You made a mistake all right—"

"No, *you* made it. You made it and you sucked me in. You used me, March. You told me your stories and I believed them."

His wet eyes bore into me, the accusation sharp enough to cut. I take a step back. I can't help it. The pure rage of an idealist betrayed.

I hadn't realized until now what a façade Templeton's world-weary act really is.

"Brad," I say, softening my voice. "You don't understand. There's no connection between these murders. The DA said it himself. There's a lot of women, a lot of knives, and a lot of water in this state, and having the three of them together . . . it's a coincidence."

"There aren't any, though, March. You said it yourself. Everything's connected. And anyway, one or two or three of these cases, that could be coincidence. Four, five, whatever, but twenty? Twenty-five? That's straining credibility, don't you think?"

"You don't know what you're talking about. Trust me. The guy who killed Simone Walker, he has a certain signature, a certain style, that is worlds away from cutting heads off and putting them in aquariums." Just saying it, I'm tempted to laugh. "Lauterbach is obsessed, so he sees the links he wants to see. You've given him a gift, you know that? I'm guessing before he met you, he spent a lot of time daydreaming about a case like this, wishing he was hunting the great white whale instead of one sad domestic call after another. Now he's giving PowerPoints to the district attorney and his boss is seeing nothing but dollar signs and headlines."

He listens with sullen resignation, crossing his arms almost like he's hugging himself. I can tell I'm not getting through, but I can't stop arguing. Until now, I had no idea the scale of the disaster. This isn't one rogue deputy throwing a roadblock into my path. Templeton did all the legwork, making Lauterbach's serial killer fantasy come true, and he handed everything over to Fauk's legal counsel, too. Which can only mean one thing.

"Brad," I say. "You do know Fauk's guilty?"

"*How can you even say that?*" he shouts, coming right out of his chair. "Did you hear a word I just said to you? Fauk was in jail when most of these murders were committed. You put him there, and I made you a hero for doing it."

"Calm down, Brad."

"Just get out of here, all right? I'm done with your questions."

"I still need more—"

"If you want more, make sure your *Texas Monthly* subscription is up-to-date. You can read about it with everybody else!"

"You said before I used you, but you got it wrong. Fauk's the one using you. So is Lauterbach. And you're letting them do it."

"Get. Out. *Now.*"

This time I use the front door, crossing through a pair of cacti and giving the rocks a good kick, sending one of them along the concrete and into my car door. Serves me right. I toss it back and get behind the wheel, conscious of Templeton's face in the front window. Part of me wants to go back inside and shake him until he sees reason. But if his raw show of unaccustomed emotion tells me anything, it's that he's a true believer.

He was stringing me along before, telling me what he thought I wanted to hear. Not leveling with me because, in his eyes, I'm tainted. He really thinks Fauk is innocent.

And that I'm responsible for putting away the wrong man.

CHAPTER 12

Back in October, the city clocked a streak of days without a single homicide. Every morning we'd sit hunkered by the phones waiting for the inevitable call, only to have it not come. Two, three days. Four. Five. We kept ourselves busy with open cases, knowing the respite wouldn't last.

It did, though, day after day.

Nobody could remember anything like it before. The shifts stacked up like a house of cards, and the higher they went the more afraid we were just to breathe.

We went from talking about the streak all the time to saying nothing, afraid of jinxing the run. Nine days and counting. I remember getting up on the morning of the tenth day, wondering what would happen if all the sudden people stopped murdering each other. Just like that, for some random reason, they finally stopped.

Lying in bed staring up at the fan, pretending I didn't have to go in that day because the city didn't need me anymore . . . on that day, the tenth day, I loved my job.

On day eleven we got a call: a body found in an empty house. On ten I was in love, and on eleven I hated it more than I ever had, and I'm still not sure I could explain why.

Staring at Jason Young across the table, I feel that way again. Maybe it's a reflection of the hate Templeton turned on me, making me loathe myself and what I do.

"I'm sorry to have to ask you this, Jason, but were you aware that Simone was involved in a relationship with another man?"

He rubs at the puffy flesh under his right eye, shakes his head.

"Can you answer out loud, please? For the recording."

"No," he says.

There are fresh cuts and bruises on his face and hands, livid against the backdrop of the fading injuries of a week ago. Another fight at another bar, though he is naturally reticent on the subject, deferring to his attorney, a young, fat counselor cinched too tightly into his suit at the waist and throat, his button-down collar flapping free on one side. Despite his slovenly demeanor, the lawyer is sharp, scrutinizing every word out of my mouth as if he can actually see them on the air. I've had enough of lawyers for one day.

"Did she ever say anything that would give you reason to suspect?"

He shakes his head again. "No."

"When she came to you for money," I ask, "did she mention anything about being pregnant?"

His eyes flash in surprise.

"Did she say anything about needing the money for an abortion?"

"A *what?*"

He tucks his head down, shoulders rolled forward, almost like he's trying to curl up into a ball. I take no pleasure in this line of questioning. If I'm going to eliminate him as a suspect, though, I have no choice. If he knew about Epps and the pregnancy ploy, that might be enough in a jury's eyes. But judging from the reaction, I doubt he knew a thing.

"There's something I've been wondering about," I ask finally. "When you gave us consent to search your apartment—" The lawyer interrupts with an audible huff, letting me know how much he thinks of that consent. "When we searched, there was something I found surprising, something missing. Do you know what I mean?"

"No."

"There weren't any books. I was looking for one in particular. I showed it to you, remember? You didn't recognize it, and there wasn't a copy in the apartment, but I started to wonder if maybe you had a storage unit or kept some things over at a friend's house. It's strange not to find any books at all."

"So what?"

"Where are the books? You do have some, don't you?"

He looks to the attorney, then back at me. "I sold them. Put 'em all in a couple of boxes and brought 'em to Half Price Books, the one on Westheimer."

"What kind of books were they?"

"The kind they don't give you much for," he says.

I place *The Kingwood Killing* on the table, drawing a raised eyebrow from the lawyer. He motions me to slide it over, which I do, his strategy being to glean as much information from my questions as possible without letting his client answer anything detrimental. Turning the pages, he glances up with recognition and I half expect him to say something. Instead, he slides the book back across the table and makes a note on his pad.

"You ever read this book?" I ask.

"It's a free country, Detective," the lawyer says. "People can't be prosecuted for what they read. I think this line of questioning has run its course."

"It's okay," Young says. "I never even *seen* that book before. That's not my kind of thing, anyway."

"What is your thing?" I ask, expecting him to say the Bible.

He rubs his eye again. "I don't have a thing. *This* is my thing." Pounding the table. "*This* is all I think about anymore, and I . . . I don't think I can stand it."

This is not my thing either, not anymore. We wrap the interview and I ask the attorney to meet with me for a second, leaving Young at the table. With another impatient huff, he accompanies me back to my cubicle, where I pull up the Silk Cut surveillance footage for him to watch. He asks to see it a second time.

"What is this?"

"You can see what it is."

"What I mean is, are you charging him with something related to the incident?"

"I'm not. But it looks to me like he's been in another fight, and that combined with what he said just now makes me wonder about his emotional state. Your client seems to have some kind of death wish."

"He loved his wife, and she's been brutally murdered, and now he has you telling him she was cheating on him and pregnant with someone else's kid. Maybe he's just upset."

Something Candace Walker said comes back to me. *"She liked them bad,"* she'd said, referring to the kind of men her daughter had once preferred. Now that she's dead, Jason Young seems well on his way to becoming one.

"You're right," I say. "Maybe it would be a good idea to see about getting him some help."

"I'm touched by your concern. I wish I'd seen more evidence of it in the interview room."

"My concern is genuine."

"And so is my skepticism. Now if that's all?"

He collects Young and leads him out, putting a paternal hand on his client's back despite the similarity in their ages. That hand makes me feel better, but not enough. I pick up the phone and dial Reverend Blunt, the only person in Young's life who might feel an obligation to help and have the means to do so. He doesn't pick up, and though I'm reluctant to leave a message, I do it anyway, warning him to keep an eye on Young.

When I hang up, Bascombe appears over the cubicle wall, the first time I've laid eyes on him since this morning's conference.

"How did that go in there?"

I shrug. "He's not looking like a suspect to me."

"I'm sorry to hear that 'cause you could sure use one about now. I had a look at Detective Lauterbach's case after you left, and if we don't close this thing quick, it might never get closed. For sheer insanity, that guy is brilliant. He's come up with a way to link all those different cases and left enough wiggle room so the inconsistencies can all be explained away."

"In other words, the cases *don't* connect."

A hard smile. "They do when it's him talking. There are some real similarities, too, enough to get you thinking. It wouldn't surprise me if some of these really are the work of the same person. Just not all of them."

I give another noncommittal shrug, not wanting to concede even a partial victory to Lauterbach.

"I think you're being sold a bill of goods," I say. "I talked to Templeton today, and it turns out he's the one behind all this. He met Lauterbach at a talk he gave, then they collected all these cases and concocted a theory for how they could fit together. And I helped them out, though I didn't mean to. I gave Templeton some details on Simone Walker—but even then, he already knew about the case—and he realized she could plug into their grouping just as easily. It was probably him that sent Lauterbach over here, all out of spite. He blames me for letting a serial killer run amok."

"So you think there's nothing to it at all?" he asks. "The district attorney isn't so sure. And frankly I'm not, either. There could be something to this, even if the Walker case doesn't connect. I want you to take a look at the cases—"

"*Even if?*"

"Don't hassle me on this, March. I'm trying to help."

"You've got a funny way of doing it."

"You know something, you are one piece of work. Some of us have been doing this longer than you, March, and maybe you should listen for a change." He throws his hands up in mock surrender and turns to go. "All I'm saying is, if you're determined to dig your own grave, it's only gotta be six feet down. You can stop shoveling anytime."

★

Over dinner, Charlotte listens as I run my mouth, decompressing after a day of insanity. The conference with the district attorney piques her interest, and she asks a lot of questions about who was in the room, which for the most part I can't answer. She even sits through my lecture on the problem with hyping the work of serial killers, the way it can blind ordinarily solid cops to the more mundane and far more likely explanations. It's a good lecture, well rehearsed, and she does everything but applaud at the end.

I've worked three legit serial killer cases in the ten years I've been on murder. I've seen plenty more shoehorned into the mold, usually by young and inexperienced investigators who think that when a bona fide serial killer wields the instrument, death has more meaning than it otherwise would.

"You take so much of this to heart," Charlotte says, running her fingers through my hair. "This will sound stupid, I'm sure, but it's almost like you—all of you, the police, I mean—it's like you're the victims, too. The things you have to deal with, the things you have to witness."

"Victim isn't the word," I say.

"That's why I could never have practiced criminal law. When you get that close to the darkness, even if you're there for the right reasons, it can't help but affect you, can it?"

"It hasn't affected me."

She laughs. "No, of course not."

"Other people can see what I see and call it what it is, but then they get to move on. They're not expected to do anything. The difference is, I am."

"Sometimes there's nothing you can do, either."

"Sometimes," I say.

After dinner she puts a rental movie in the player, a romantic comedy, and after half an hour I wander into my home office, flipping up the laptop screen. I can't remember the address Templeton entered to pull up my cousin's website, so I type in a few search terms until the right link pops up. Although I've known of the site's existence for a while, this is the first time I've actually gotten up the nerve to visit.

As the page loads I start to feel queasy, the way I always do when it comes to her: the Tammy Effect. With such a close-knit family, Charlotte has never understood the networks of estrangement in the March clan. My father, a widower in his early sixties, took up with his thirty-two-year-old secretary much to the consternation of his adult children, who only discovered the liaison when the secretary, my mother, turned up pregnant on my uncle's doorstep. I call him my uncle, but in fact he was my brother, which makes my cousins actually my nieces and nephews, but the relations were reclassified for public consumption and I've grown so accustomed to them I can't change.

It was left to my brother/uncle to sort out the mess. There was no question of my parents marrying. Neither of them was particularly keen on my arrival. In fact, if I'd been born a decade later, I probably wouldn't have been born at all. So my uncle took me, raising me alongside his five-year-old son, Moody. Tammy was nine, and in just a few years became our de facto baby-sitter when her mother got a job as a secretary, despite the choice words my aunt had for working women whenever the topic of my own mother came up.

A disapproving Presbyterian whose elegant outward appearance concealed a jumble of superstitions and prejudices, though not very well, my aunt drove us like cattle to church each week, making it clear that of us all, I was the one most in need of cleansing. She would catch me out at awkward moments, firing off questions from the catechism.

What is the chief end of man?

To glorify God and . . . something.

Man's chief end is to glorify God, and to enjoy him forever, she'd say, adding a swat sometimes to aid the memory. Because she was beautiful, and because making impossible sacrifices for the children in her care was part of her marrow, I grew up wanting to please this woman and never feeling like I had succeeded. Noting this, my uncle took a special interest in me.

All this talk about chiefs and their ends, he would say. *What about the braves and their ends? This is the land of the brave, ain't it?*

Who are the braves?

You and me, he'd say. *We're the braves. The ones put on this earth to get the job done.*

What job?

But he'd just smile. I knew the job he meant, though, because he had a gun and a badge. Later on, after retiring on disability, he would hobble on his cane between the glass cases full of revolvers and automatics, holding court among the band of brothers he'd served alongside, who uniformly held him in esteem. At least they did when I was there.

Her website includes a page dedicated to Daddy, as she calls him, with a photo of him in uniform and a much later one taken in the gun shop not long before he sold it, when he'd traded in his cane for a wheelchair. There's a juvenile poem, awkward in meter and rhyme, apparently written by Tammy herself, followed by the text of my uncle's obituary. At the bottom of the column, his headstone at the cemetery, decked with fresh flowers. According to the caption: A GRAVESTONE FOR DADDY, BUT NO MARKER TO REMEMBER HIS SON.

There's no tribute to her mother that I can find.

Tammy inherited all of her mother's bad qualities and none of the good. No, that's not fair. If I put on my psychoanalyst's hat, it's not so hard to come up with the formula that creates someone like her. Starved of attention, either through neglect or because she craved so much of it, Tammy found ways of standing out.

When I was in first grade, for example, she fed me laxatives wrapped in foil like chocolate, then skipped a day of school to take care of me during my "sickness." Then there was the time a few years later when she sent Moody and me on a trek through the neighborhood after school, then called her mother at work to say we'd both run away from home. She didn't do this to get us into trouble; she just wanted to be the focal point of the crisis. But often her plans had a way of producing unintended results, which often included an appointment with my uncle's belt—for me and Moody, not for her.

It's strange to think that the boy she did so much to torment early on is now her cause in life. Though of course Moody isn't the cause, only the means to an end. Once again she's using him to get attention.

When Moody disappeared in 1973, I was just eleven and he was fifteen, about to turn sixteen. Tammy had graduated high school and shown no interest either in college or getting a job. Her presence in the house kept me and Moody on the streets after school, though by then we were not often together. Tired of his prepubescent shadow, Moody had taken advantage of his new ten-speed to leave me in the dust.

The afternoon it happened, I came home to find Tammy alone on the couch watching television. My aunt drove my uncle home, arriving just before six, and there was an argument over who was supposed to set the table. When Moody missed dinner, my aunt fretted some, but it wasn't the first time. At nine, my uncle told me to go to bed. From behind my door I could hear the three of them talking, my aunt accusatory and Tammy shrill and defensive, my uncle trying to calm them both down. He made calls to the parents of some of Moody's friends—though of course he didn't know the identities of Moody's real friends—and then took my aunt out in the car to search, leaving Tammy with me.

I fell asleep waiting for their return.

Wake up, Tammy said.

She was on top of me, straddling my chest, her knees cinching the blanket over me in an inescapable cocoon. I thrashed a little, which only made her laugh. Then she leaned down very close to me in the dark, close enough that her hair brushed my cheek.

Now, she said. *You're gonna tell me where Moody went, do you understand? I know he tells you everything, so either you tell me or else.*

Or else what?

Or else this. She took a fistful of my hair and started to squeeze, pushing down into the pillow with all her strength. My head caught fire and I tried to kick free, but she was too heavy for me to move. I clenched my teeth, tried to take the pain, but the tears welled up regardless. *Don't cry, you little baby, just tell me.* If she'd known about waterboarding, I might have cracked, but that night I discovered a reserve inside me, a tank of fortitude lined with rage. Sensing this, she let go of my hair. She sat back, still trapping me, taking a moment to catch her breath. Then she grabbed the pillow, tore it out from under my head, and held it above me just an inch or two. *If you don't say something, I'm gonna smother you.*

I did say something, but it was not to her liking. She gave me a slap on the cheek and said, *You want me to tell Mama so she can wash your mouth out with soap?* If suffocation was my other option, then yes, I would have taken the soap. But I kept my mouth shut this time. *Okay, then. You're forcing me to do it.*

She didn't press hard enough at first. I turned my face to catch a pocket of air, and I remember thinking I could hold out forever, that nothing she could do would break me. Then she readjusted her grip, getting a good seal over my nose and mouth. After a few seconds I really panicked, bucking so hard that Tammy came off the bed and cracked her lip on the toy chest next to the dresser. I scrambled out of bed, but with her on the floor between me and the door, I didn't know where to go.

Tammy got to her feet and touched her fingers to her lip to check for blood. Then she saw me crouched for action in my underwear and started to laugh. *Never mind. We're even now. If you wanna take it out on anybody, it's Moody's fault for running away.* She came over and tried to ruffle my hair, pretending like she was one of the adults. I would have popped her right there, only the braves don't hurt women, and I was still scared of her, too.

None of this is on her website, of course. Her account of Moody's disappearance omits me entirely—not that I'd have it any other way. She writes in her best approximation of a journalistic tone, citing the time when her parents left, their return, the initial call to the police station. Teenage runaways not being a departmental priority at that time, my uncle rousted a sergeant he knew out of bed, which resulted in the arrival of a single squad car. Some men from the neighborhood organized a search, driving in two cars from our house all the way to Heights Boulevard, but no one spotted Moody. Maybe he'd run away, but more likely he was at a friend's house or even with a girl. That's what they told themselves to justify getting to bed.

Throughout her account, Tammy refers to other victims of Dean Corll, noting the similarities in police response. Like so many of their parents, it never occurred to Moody's that he'd been abducted for purposes of torture and murder by a local sex deviant and his teenage accomplices. Even my uncle, with his policeman's knowledge of the world, didn't imagine anything like that.

But Tammy says otherwise. In her version, she had heard rumors in the neighborhood. She had noted the strange epidemic of runaways, boys her brother's age and younger who were among us one day and gone the next. She knew from the beginning that her brother had been taken, and was tireless in searching for him. For the past thirty-six years she has thought of nothing else. Or so she claims.

In fact, the assumption was always that Moody had run off. He'd been working at the gun shop one day a week—a fact that made me as jealous as the ten-speed did—and after he left, so did a nickel-plated Smith & Wesson Model 66. The bike was never seen again, either, though I recall my uncle joking that he wouldn't get very far on that. I could have told him what happened to the bike, but I didn't, not for many years.

Why Moody had run off was a topic of speculation early on. Not knowing left each of his parents free to shoulder the blame. My aunt upped her intake of bourbon and lowered her Sunday attendance, letting the rest of us off the hook entirely. My uncle bottled up the frustration and didn't let it out until three years later when with my own eyes I saw him shoot a man down. A black man with an unloaded shotgun who'd walked into the gun store by mistake, not realizing the jewelry store was one door down. My uncle got the drop on him and could have let him run. But he didn't.

Only Tammy remained unscathed. The one true thing in her online account is this: I remember right away that she insisted on Moody's being dead. At dinner one night (before we stopped having dinner together as a family), she suggested that we have a big funeral for him, volunteering to organize everything and to sing during the ceremony. Her mother went pale and got up from the table. Her father dabbed his lips with a handkerchief, looking at us both with a hangdog expression, then followed after her to the bedroom.

"Roland," Charlotte says. "What are you doing?"

She stands in the doorway, silhouetted from behind, then moves closer when she sees what's on the screen. Leaning over my shoulder, her necklace gracing my skin, she scrolls down the page, making a clucking sound with her tongue.

"What in the world are you reading this for?"

"Research."

She kisses me on the temple. "Well, don't research too long."

She leaves a trace of scent on the air behind her, and I feel almost blessed to have this woman in my life. Almost as if in marrying her I've ducked a terrible destiny, though not entirely. Perhaps it's just that in Charlotte, despite our problems, I have someone to share the pain with, a partner in suffering.

Before closing the laptop, I skim through my email inbox, deleting the junk and the forwards and the solicitations for porn. My finger hits the key automatically, the messages disappearing as I read them. The name in one address catches my eye, then vanishes.

SIMONE_WALKER

I open the trash folder to make sure I read that right. The address is real. The message title sends a chill through me: THE RUMORS OF MY DEATH . . .

I open the message.

HI DETECTIVE,
    GUESS WHAT HAPPENED. IM DEAD THATS WHAT.
    THE RUMORS WERE NOT EXAGGERATED ONE BIT.
    DO YOU LIKE MY NAKED BODY. I CAUGHT YOU LOOKING.
    MAN THAT WAS COLD. SEE YOU SOON.
    LOVE, SIMONE

CHAPTER 13

The car pulls up on the curb outside and through the blinds I see two men getting out. Eric Castro, my go-to source when I want special favors from the crime scene unit, and a squat, curly-haired guy in an inside-out T-shirt who looks like he's about to wake up any minute. I open the door before Castro can knock.

"Shh," I say. "My wife's asleep upstairs."

After creeping into the office on tiptoes and shutting the French doors behind us, Castro introduces me to Quincy Hanford, dubbing him a computer genius. I shake hands with the genius and motion him into my chair. The email is still on-screen.

"I want to know two things," I say. "First, is this legit? Anybody can make up an email address, and the victim's name has been all over the papers. Second, if it is legit, I want to know if we can trace it back to the source."

Hanford skims his finger over the trackpad, pulling down a menu, and suddenly the email converts into code.

"Okay," he says. "Looking at the long header info gives us the IP address. That's the easy part. I'm going to forward this to myself, if that's all right."

"Fine. What's the hard part?"

"Castro says your vic's laptop was stolen from the scene, is that right? So what you really want to know is whether this email is from the offender. Is he now using her computer to initiate some kind of cat-and-mouse game with the investigating officer?"

Cat-and-mouse game. I query Castro with a raised eyebrow—*Is this guy for real?*—and he replies with a nod of reassurance.

"That's what I'm asking," I say.

"Do you know your victim's email address?"

"I can easily find out."

"You might want to do that, then. If she was using this address prior to her death, then your first question is pretty much answered. As far as where he sent it from, that's where things get tricky." He opens a new web browser, types in an address, then pastes the IP number into a field. "I can do this more easily from my own computer, but let's see what we can get for free." The web page refreshes with a location map of southeast Texas, a thumbtack marking Houston. "So that tells us something. The IP is local, and there's the provider. You have a good relationship with Comcast?"

"Does anyone?" I ask. "Don't get me started on Comcast."

Castro grins in sympathy. "They're unbelievable. I tried upgrading to HDTV—"

"I'm just kidding," Hanford says, without a trace of mirth. "What you need is a good relationship with a judge. I have some contacts over there, but I'm guessing they'll want to see a subpoena before letting anything go."

"What will they be able to tell us?"

Hanford seesaws his hand back and forth. "Sometimes they come back with a little, sometimes with a lot. Best case scenario would be that your killer sent this from his living room using his own network, and they come back with a name and address."

"That'll work."

"Don't hold your breath or anything. That's a best case scenario, like I said."

"Detective March understands all that, Quincy." From Castro's impatient tone, I can tell he's anxious for his friend to make a good impression. "If the killer really is using her laptop, that means he's mobile and time is of the essence."

I check my watch. "It's half past midnight, boys. Getting you two out of bed is one thing, but I'm not making any late night calls to a judge."

"Tell you what," Hanford says, rising from the chair. "Let me work on this and give you a call later on. Maybe I can make something happen through back channels."

"Music to my ears."

I usher them out with whispered promises to stay by the phone. As the door closes, Charlotte calls from the top of the stairs.

"Do I hear voices down there?"

"Just the TV," I say. "I'll be up in a little while."

I return to my office, pull up a saved file to use as a template, and start typing up a subpoena for the cable company and a search warrant just in case, leaving the location and specifications blank.

Two hours later, Hanford calls my cell number with news. When he said he had contacts, the man wasn't kidding. I can tell from the tautness in his voice that he's outdone himself.

"This gets pretty complicated," he says.

"We can cut to the chase."

"It's kind of impressive, though. They've got the email server set up to call a real-time blacklist service—a third-party spam blocker—and that communication actually gives us a snapshot in time. If you get a subpoena, you can have a look at that snapshot."

"Okay," I say, a little disappointed.

A tone of triumph enters his voice: "And when you do, here's what it's going to tell you. The static IP belongs to the router in the victim's house. Dr. Joy Hill is the cable customer, and this message came through her router."

"You really are a genius. I owe you one."

"So what you'll need to do is, get your judge to sign off on the subpoena and a search warrant for the premises. You can—"

"Thanks, Quincy. I can take it from here."

Now he's the disappointed one, but I don't have time to comfort him. I get him off the phone with profuse thanks and dial Bascombe, and when he doesn't answer I go for Hedges, whose home number is programmed into my phone. I get voicemail, redial, get voicemail again, and redial. When he answers, he doesn't sound happy to hear from me.

"This is important or I wouldn't have called."

The deeper I get into the story—the email, the forensic results, Dr. Hill's network—the more awake Hedges gets, and the more agitated.

"You're doing this intentionally," he says in a half whisper, half hiss.

"I don't know what you mean."

"What part of 'hold off on this' did you not understand? Come Monday morning, you can do your worst, but—"

"Sir, I didn't *do* anything. I received an email from my victim's missing computer, and when a judge signs off on the paperwork, I'll be able to prove it originated from Dr. Hill's house. How am I not supposed to act on that?"

I hear his feet pounding, a door shutting behind him, and then he's free to dispense with the whispers. "This is the story you want running on election day, March? Is that what you're telling me? If this is your way of taking a shot at me, you better get one thing straight: when I hit back you'll be down on the mat."

"Election day . . . I forgot about that."

"Of course you did. And now that I've reminded you, I'm guessing it makes no difference. Wait one day and I'll support you on this."

"I can't, sir. The longer I wait, the more time she has to dispose of the laptop."

"Does this have to be adversarial? Couldn't you just ask her for consent to search? You got the husband to consent without a warrant."

"And if she says no, then what? The last thing I want to do is get on your bad side, but if I don't follow this up immediately, I'm not doing my job. I promise you there won't be any leaks to the media. They'll have their hands full anyway staking out the polling places. This will not come back on you, sir. You have my word on that."

He lets out a long sigh. "It better not, March."

"Thank you, sir. I'll email the warrant—"

"Don't thank me yet. I'm gonna back you on this. I'm gonna make the necessary calls and if need be irritate some very important people. And if the end result is, you seize your missing laptop and charge a suspect, then fine. You rolled the dice and won. But, March, if you don't charge a suspect, if you don't close this case for good, then I'm gonna whip you like a dog until you beg for mercy. Understood?"

"Like a dog, sir. Understood."

I slip upstairs to grab my coat, kissing Charlotte on the forehead before I go. The night air is cool and wet enough for the streetlamps along the road to have golden haloes. From the car I call Aguilar and leave another message for Bascombe.

Ten minutes later, I pull up just in front of the neighbor's Maserati down the street from Joy Hill's house, waiting for a green light from the boss.

In the dawn's early light, I present a bleary-eyed and possibly hung-over Dr. Hill with the hastily printed and even more hastily signed warrant, hand-delivered a few minutes earlier by Lt. Bascombe himself. Aguilar is with us and so are Castro and Hanford, last-minute invites in case any technical challenges arise.

"You expect me to read this?" Hill says. "I'll need my glasses."

"You can read it while we execute the search."

She lets us inside, pulling a terry-cloth robe tighter around her frame. "Should I make some coffee?"

"If you like. Officer Castro here will keep you company in the kitchen."

Castro does a lousy job concealing his disappointment.

We start upstairs, working our way from one end of the house to the other, opening drawers and emptying the contents of boxes, sifting through clothing and papers and the unlocked metal filing cabinets in Dr. Hill's office. Bascombe stands around most of the time, arms crossed, smoldering in silence, leaving me to imagine the conversation he had with Hedges before arriving. Aguilar shines a flashlight under Hill's bed, dragging a couple of plastic storage boxes into the light.

While I busy myself with the bookshelves in the upstairs office, the lieutenant breathes down my neck. "You think there's a computer hidden in one of these books?"

"I just thought—"

"I know what you thought, but the search warrant I brought over doesn't say anything about *The Kingwood Killing*, so unless you have another one I don't know about . . ."

"Just making sure there's nothing hidden behind the books." I pull a few out at random and shine a light through the gap, eliciting a huff from Bascombe.

Hanford eyes the laptop on the desk, but it's the same one I remember from a week ago and doesn't match the description of Simone Walker's white plastic MacBook. He crouches under the desk and announces the router is down there.

"Can you use that somehow to locate the laptop?" I ask.

He looks at me like I'm a dinosaur fresh from prehistory, but then his eyes light up. "As a matter of fact . . ." Seating himself at Hill's computer despite Bascombe's grunt of protest, he starts clicking through preference settings with increasing intensity. "I'm checking to see who's currently logged into the network." More clicks, and then a sigh of disappointment. "Never mind. The only user on the network is this machine here. But let me check the router log."

The three of us gather behind him, waiting as he works.

"Yes, here it is." His finger runs down a column of data. "I'm betting that MAC address belongs to Simone Walker's laptop, and it was on the network for about twenty minutes last night, logging off just before twelve."

"So it's around here somewhere," I say. "Make a copy of that information."

"I can make a forensic image of the system."

"Sounds great. Now let's find that laptop."

The end of a case feels like the last moments of a race. You see the tape stretched across the finish line and you push yourself hard, knowing it will all be over before you know it. Mentally I'm already reading Dr. Hill her rights, already sweating her in an interview room. All my doubts about her disappear and the right questions come to me unbidden. I can already see the hooded eyes cutting sideways, unable to bear my gaze, and hear the nervous self-absorbed chatter. She'll think she's smarter than us, that she can talk her way out of anything, a conceit I will take advantage of in a thousand little ways, coaxing her to reveal more and more until her guilt is impossible to deny.

Aguilar works his way through a linen closet in the hall while I look over his shoulder.

"I didn't think it would be her," I say. "This isn't a woman's kind of crime. Or a professor's."

He sneers. "A person who'd force Shakespeare on kids will stoop to anything, man."

I start in Simone's room, retracing the ground I covered a week ago. Bascombe goes through the cabinets in the attached bath.

"This isn't looking too good for Lauterbach's serial killer theory," I say.

He looks at me. "Have you found anything? 'Cause I haven't."

"Keep looking."

After finishing upstairs we move to the ground floor. In the kitchen, Hill sits by the open glass doors, blowing cigarette smoke through the gap. When he sees me, Castro sets a coffee mug on the island and steps away from it, not wanting to look too cozy.

"It would be a lot easier," I say, "if you just told us where the laptop is."

She gives me a dry, reptilian smile. "For all I know it is here some-where. But I haven't seen it. I assumed you people had already checked."

"Castro, come with me. We're gonna have to pull all these books off the shelf."

Hill follows us into the book-lined living room but offers no protest as I follow through on the threat, dislodging the books four and five at a time, dropping them on the floor.

"I didn't have you pegged as a Philistine," she says. "Are you plan-ning to take them out front and burn them when you're done?"

Ignoring this, I continue the search while Aguilar pulls cushions off the couches, unzips the covers, and runs his hands inside. Castro leaves after a while to assist Hanford upstairs, passing the lieutenant on the landing. Bascombe pulls me aside and speaks softly into my ear.

"If this turns out the way it's looking, my advice is to make yourself scarce. Hedges says he's gonna use your skin as a rug in front of his fireplace."

The sun shines brightly outside before I'm ready to give up. The forensics techs are huddled on the curb along with Aguilar, and Bas-combe waits at the threshold. I'm the last one out, still dazed at the lack of a result. The laptop was here. The email originated from here. But we've gone through the place with a fine-tooth comb and come up with nothing.

Dr. Hill follows me out like I'm a late-staying guest.

"I'm sorry I couldn't be of more assistance," she says.

Bascombe heads straight for his car, and after a pause Aguilar fol-lows. I thank Castro and Hanford for their help.

"Look at this," Hanford says, turning the screen of his smartphone so I can see. "I'm on her wireless network. Meaning anyone out here on the street could access it. He didn't have to be inside the house. He could've pulled up in front, got the laptop out, and sent his message. Then he just drove away."

"That's great," I say. "Thanks for sharing. I wish that had occurred to you a little sooner."

"I'm sorry."

The two techs stand there speechless, Hanford overwhelmed by what he must consider to be his own failure, not mine. I don't have the heart to leave him writhing.

"No, don't be. You've done a great job. I'm the one who screwed up. Well, boys, enjoy your Saturday. If anybody needs me, I'll be lying in front of the fireplace."

Their puzzled looks give me only the slightest satisfaction.

CHAPTER 14

Stephen Wilcox emerges through the elementary school's glass double doors, the corduroy collar of his waxed cotton jacket turned up against the drizzle. He lopes along with his hands in his pockets, his chin jutting forward like a ship's prow, zigzagging through a cluster of campaign supporters stationed at the perimeter of the school's circular drive. He checks both ways before stepping into the street, making for the same Land Rover Discovery he'd bought used in 1999 around the time I first met him. He doesn't notice me leaning against the hood, my heel hitched on the bumper.

"Doing your civic duty?" I ask.

He walks right by, yanking the driver's door open and climbing in. I go around to the passenger side before he can activate the lock, hauling myself into the cracked leather seat.

"You look like the lord of the manor in this thing."

"I don't remember asking you to tag along."

"Don't kick me out just yet," I say. "At least let me tell you why I'm here."

He turns the key in the ignition, triggering a shake and a few squeals before the four-liter V8 rumbles to life.

"That doesn't sound good. You should get that checked."

His cheeks flush and he balls his sinewy hand into a fist. "Get out, March. I've had enough, okay? Whatever this is about—getting the fix in, making sure our stories are straight—I don't want any part of it. How much clearer do I have to be?"

"I thought we'd buried the hatchet after the Thomson thing. You thought I was dirty on that, and I proved you wrong. How much clearer do I have to be? Stick your head in the ground if you like, but the Fauk appeal isn't going away. What you saw yesterday is just the tip of the iceberg. The only way we're going to be vindicated on this is if we do the vindicating ourselves. Now, that's nothing new for me, but you're in for a rude awakening."

"It has nothing to do with me."

"Keep telling yourself that. But you were right yesterday in the elevator: this thing does have the power to drag you down. Donald Fauk was a career case for you and me both, and if that conviction is overturned, I don't think your buddies in Internal Affairs are going to be too keen on keeping you around."

He gives me a wicked smile. "Don't worry about me. If it is overturned, there won't be any doubt in people's minds who's to blame."

That's probably true. While he's kept quiet officially, I know for a fact that behind closed doors Wilcox has never been reticent about his suspicions concerning me. After teaming up to bring down Reg Keller, though, I'd let myself believe we had turned a page. Things would never be like they were, but at least some of the venom had been drained. But going by the look on his face—the raised vein in the forehead, the twisted mouth—perhaps I was wrong.

"How many times do I have to apologize?" I say. "If it'll help, I'll do it again. I dropped the ball when we were partners, and you picked it up way too many times. I cut corners, I screwed up, whatever you want me to eat, I will. But you're wrong about what I was doing. I never framed anyone. I never planted evidence. I was never what you think I am. You're determined to fit me into that mold, but that was never me."

"Then we'll just have to agree to disagree."

"Not good enough. Maybe I'm not making myself clear. The DA's not going to fight this thing like he ordinarily would. Lauterbach made too good an impression. He's even got Bascombe second-guessing. You were in the car with me when Fauk confessed, and you know he was ready to talk long before that. Nobody had to threaten him—in fact, you kept telling him to keep his mouth shut. If you can't trust me, Stephen, trust yourself."

He unclenches the fist and lets out a breath. After a pause, his body relaxes a little, sinking down into the seat. He hangs his left hand over the wheel, kneading the leather with his thumb. I give him time to calm down, time to let his brain work.

"That much I agree with," he says. "Fauk's confession was genuine. He didn't need any prodding to give it up."

"But you and me are the only people who know that for a fact."

Another pause. "This is against my better judgment, but . . . what exactly do you want, March?"

"I'm meeting Lauterbach this afternoon to look at his case in detail. Bascombe didn't give me any option. So blowing that apart is up to me. Your mission, if you choose to accept, is to find out what's happening with Fontenot. That lawyer yesterday morning said there was an investigation in progress. We need to find out how far back they're looking."

"You have the relationship with Fontenot, not me."

"And I can talk to him if it comes to that. First, though, we need to know exactly what he's facing. As far as I'm concerned, Gene's a good cop. Having said that . . . Look, I don't know how else to put this, so let me be blunt: if there's a full-blown investigation going on, getting in touch with him directly might not be such a great idea."

"It'll look like conspiracy," he says. "You've given this some thought."

I ignore the barb in that last remark. "I'm gonna take a drive up to Huntsville tomorrow."

"Turning yourself in?"

Shaking my head, I pop the passenger door open. "I have an informant up there who might be able to help with Fauk."

"Wait a second." He grabs my sleeve. "What kind of help do you mean?"

"Brad Templeton says he hasn't had any suspicious contacts, but I'm convinced there's a connection between the Fauk murder scene and the one I'm working—only not the connection Lauterbach has in mind. Maybe someone's been in touch with Fauk, though. If my guy can get close to him, I might be able to find out. You wanna let go of me?"

His hand trails down to the buttons on my jacket sleeve. His eyes narrow as he pulls at the fabric, working one of the buttons undone.

"Those are horn buttons," he says. "And they work."

I pull myself free. "Charlotte's dad inadvertently left me an inheritance."

"Lyndon Pellier?"

His mouth crumbles into an eloquent frown, the kind of frown a Roman senator might have worn contemplating the rise of the barbarians and the complex ways of fate, rewarding the undeserving with gifts beyond their comprehension while overlooking virtuous men like himself.

"I have a whole closet full," I say, slamming the door behind me.

His sad eyes follow me through the rain-dimpled glass.

Back at my car, I wait a few minutes for Wilcox to get going. The rain picks up, drumming across the roof and windshield. Everything is gray outside, even the brownish grass, but the sky seems unaccountably bright, like the effort of concealing the sun has just about exhausted the clouds overhead. I feel exhausted myself and thinking about Gene Fontenot doesn't help one bit.

After Hurricane Katrina, Gene endured his own dark night of the soul, running concurrently with the collapse of civilization all around. His house swept away by floodwater and out of contact with his ex-wife and their two kids, all he could do was roam the powerless, swarming city, teaming up with other overwhelmed officers in an effort to improvise law and order. Six months later, sitting on the stairs outside my garage apartment with a sweating beer bottle in his grasp, Gene told me stories that made the hair on the back of my neck stand up.

By then, thinking he'd had enough of the Big Easy, like a lot of his fellow New Orleanians he contemplated a permanent move. I offered to recommend him, for what that was worth, and it wasn't until the interview with HPD was arranged that he had second thoughts. The zydeco in his blood wouldn't let him stay. Or something sentimental like that.

Our late night talks had convinced me that Gene was a kindred spirit, another lawman out of step with the world around him. After I confided in him about the bartender at the Paragon and some of my other projects, he opened up with a few of his own extracurricular enforcement efforts. Mostly stories about standoffs in knee-deep water with angry citizens on one hand and panicked cops on the other: *I accomplished more in six days with a Remington pump gun than in the whole rest of my career put together.*

If he'd had a talk with Donald Fauk in that interview room while me and Wilcox jumped through hoops at the car rental agency, I believe he would have told me on one of those nights in late 2005. But he never said a word.

Though I'm half tempted to call him, what I told Wilcox is true. The last thing I want to do if Gene is caught up in an internal inquiry is mix my name up in the case—especially if the accusation in the Fauk appeal is being actively investigated. Even so, I can't help feeling I owe the man more. Leaving him in Wilcox's unsteady hands doesn't seem right. For now, that's all I can do. There's just too much on my plate.

Before Cavallo's husband went back to war, the newlyweds played house in a dilapidated Montrose cottage that must have seemed like a good investment at the time. A little sweat equity and they could flip it for a tidy profit. From the curb it looks like the sweat was invested elsewhere. Nothing has changed since my last visit apart from the wreath on the door and the jumble of unlit lights hanging from the rain gutters.

I step through the open door and call Theresa's name. She walks through from the kitchen dressed in sweats and a v-neck shirt, a laundry basket balanced on her hip.

"Give me two minutes," she says, disappearing down the hallway.

The nice thing about the cottage is that it's never been updated. The floors, the wood trim, and even the windowpanes look original. I shudder to think what state the wiring must be in. Cavallo's flat-packed furniture and rock band posters are an incongruous fit, and despite the passage of months, the place still feels like she's just moved in. I sit on the edge of a shiny black sofa to await her return.

Five minutes later, she reappears, now dressed in jeans and a baggy sweater, her curly hair tied back into a ponytail. She sits cross-legged in an overstuffed chair across from me, the only piece that's seen much use, and I fill her in on everything that's happened since our visit to Dr. Hill's place on Monday. When I finish, she shakes her head in amazement.

"You've had quite a week," she says. "But I still don't see what you want from me."

I look at my watch. "An hour from now, I've got to sit down with this guy Lauterbach and compare notes. I'd like you there as a fresh set of eyes."

"Wouldn't you be better off with a fellow homicide detective?"

"Not particularly. Look, I want someone I can trust, and you fit the bill. Plus, you have a connection with Brad Templeton, thanks to his book on the Mayhew case, and that could be useful now that Brad's got me in his crosshairs. Someone has to talk sense into him, and it might as well be someone young and pretty like you."

"I'm flattered," she says. "Though I don't think I'm Brad's type."

"You can turn on the charm if you have to."

"But what's the real reason you want my help? It's not like last time where I can go to Wanda and get her to sign off. You've gotta give me a good reason, March, or this isn't gonna happen."

"I'm asking you because you're not in Homicide and don't want to be. That means my bosses can't put a word in your ear and turn you against me."

"You don't trust your colleagues?"

"Aguilar's all right. Reliable. But he's not going to stick his neck out."

"But I will?"

"You won't have to," I say. "And it's not like I'm asking you to work the case with me. It's just this one meeting. All you have to do is sit there and take everything in, then afterward tell me what you honestly think."

"And if it's not what you want to hear?"

"When has that ever stopped you?"

We take my car downtown, parking on San Jacinto and walking the rest of the way. Cavallo tells me that the last time she spoke to Brad Templeton, he was agitated about his Hannah Mayhew book, *The Girl Who Forgave Her Killer*. Thanks to the case's nationwide profile, the market had been inundated with competing accounts, most of them hitting the market sooner. Though they were slapdash affairs riddled with errors, these books soaked up most of the demand, leaving only a hardcore audience for Templeton's definitive text. It's hard for me to believe that just a few months ago we were on good enough terms to have hosted a book party at our house.

"The night of the party," I say, "he must have already been working on this thing with Lauterbach. Did he drop any hints to you?"

She shakes her head.

We enter the six-story redbrick building and breeze through security, letting the first available elevator, half occupied, leave without us. The second one's empty, so we take that.

"If Brad is responsible," she says, "and he did all this behind your back, I can't help thinking he has a reason."

"He probably thinks it will make a great book."

"That's not fair. He believes in his work, March, just like you. I can't see him undoing it unless he was really convinced he'd made a mistake."

"You mean *I'd* made a mistake."

"That's the hard part for you. People thinking you were wrong."

"I don't know much," I say. "Right now, I'm not sure what direction to move in. But I do know that this hayseed we're about to sit down with is dead wrong."

"How could he not be, going up against you?"

"I'm serious, Cavallo."

"Oh, I know."

Lauterbach eyes Cavallo from the other side of the conference table, then rises to take her hand. His smile strikes me as almost sinister underneath the drooping mustache. His Western yoke jacket is over his chair, giving us a prize view of the tooled leather holster and the gleaming Government Model on his hip. The laptop is already projecting onto a screen, and there are six tall stacks of paperwork down the spine of the table. He offers us our pick from the cluster of bottled waters on the sideboard.

"What?" I say. "You didn't light any candles?"

"Have your fun," Lauterbach replies. "I laid everything out for you as a show of appreciation. I know you think I blindsided you on this thing, but that's not the case. Did I or did I not bring everything to you in advance?"

"You did not. One case, that's all I got from you—and you pretended like you'd never seen Templeton's book before, when the fact is he's the one who drew the map for you. It was a slick move, I'll give you that. But now you have my full attention."

"Don't mind him," Cavallo says, inserting herself between us. She takes one of the water bottles and twists off the cap. "And don't mind me, either. I'm just along for the ride."

"I remember you now," Lauterbach tells her, a twinkle in his eye. "You helped run the Hannah Mayhew task force."

"That was me." She gives a self-deprecating shrug. "Though it's March who deserves the credit on that case."

"That's what he told me."

Ignoring them, I start sifting through the reports on the table. All told, there are records on fifteen open homicides going back ten years. Scene photos, autopsy photos, an assortment of videos shot on-site by detectives and crime scene photographers. Out of curiosity and a deep-rooted morbid streak, I dig around for the macabre example Templeton cited to me, the severed head floating in the fish tank. There are things that strike a veteran homicide cop as darkly funny that would be horrific to anyone else. As far as I can tell, though, the beheading is not among these files.

Lauterbach goes for the light switch.

"Hold on a second," I say. "You're not gonna put me through another PowerPoint."

"Not another one, no." He flicks the light off. "Detective Cavallo hasn't seen the first one, so I figured I'd catch her up."

Sinking into a chair, I suppress my desire to moan. The Sheriff's Department detective will not allow his inner showman to be denied. Cavallo tucks herself into a seat across from me, smiling at my discomfort. Spectators at old-fashioned bear baitings no doubt wore very similar expressions, anticipating the blood sport to come.

CHAPTER 15

SATURDAY, DECEMBER 12 – 4:19 P.M.

Lauterbach reads aloud from a summary sheet while Cavallo and I follow along:

1999, Nicole Fauk, age 43
*Kingwood housewife discovered in swimming pool. Probable 6" blade,
not recovered at scene. [Suspect charged, convicted.]*

"We'll skip over that one for the time being," he says, flashing me a smile. "Once you've seen the rest, maybe you'll wanna come back to it of your own volition."

"I only count fifteen cases on this list. Yesterday there were more than twenty."

"Like I said, some of these I've looked at in greater detail than others. This is a work in progress, so as I'm able to, I rule them out. But the ones on this list are looking pretty solid, with one or two exceptions, which I'll point out. Now, if you don't mind . . ."

"Go right ahead."

2000, Maria Olivares, age 28
Houston prostitute, multiple stab wounds, single-edged blade (probably 4"), not recovered. Body dumped in reservoir. No suspect.

2000, Shelly Lloyd, age 17
Student found in flooded ditch, NE Harris County, drowned and multiple stab wounds. Ka-Bar knife recovered at scene, partial print. No suspect.

"At the time, the Olivares case doesn't seem to have gotten much attention. Just a hooker who got herself cut up. The body was in the water awhile. But the Shelly Lloyd murder was big news at the time. She was held down in the water and stabbed to death as she drowned. The murder weapon was an army surplus Ka-Bar knife—a clip-point 7-inch blade—but the partial print on the guard was never matched to a suspect."

"And you think these two cases are connected?" Cavallo asks.

"It looks that way, doesn't it?"

She gives a noncommittal shrug. "Right here, it says the knife that killed Olivares was probably four inches long, and you just said the other one was seven inches."

"That's the thing," he says. "This killer isn't attached to a particular weapon. He seems to use a variety of blades. Personally, I think he brings one with him as a backup but always makes a point of looking for available alternatives at the scene. Let me keep going and you'll see what I'm talking about."

He rattles off three cases from 2001—Kathy Ann Morrison, Tonya Stall, Mira Echeverría—before he gets to Amber Dawson from 2002, who was found in a ditch. He passes around a couple of crime scene photos. The young prostitute's body, displayed on a coroner's stainless autopsy table, is bloated from being in the water, her torso crosshatched with slashes.

"Those wounds could have easily been made by a Ka-Bar."

"And they look nothing like what was done to Simone Walker," I say.

"A killer's profile can change over time. His technique evolves and develops."

Next is a Jane Doe. Then a restaurant server. And then he gets to a familiar case, perking Cavallo up.

2004, Tegan McGill, age 29

Woodlands homemaker found in backyard swimming pool. Raped, stabbed, mutilated by kitchen knife, recovered at scene. Husband charged but found not guilty at trial. Alleged prosecutorial misconduct.

"But the husband did do it," Cavallo says.

"You know that for a fact?"

"It's common knowledge. The prosecution bungled the case, but that doesn't make him any less guilty."

"If you'd asked me six months ago, I would have said the same thing. Knowing what I know now, though, seeing the pattern here, the husband's story makes a lot of sense. He left her by the pool and went upstairs to shower, and when he came back she was dead. Sounds crazy, doesn't it? Unless you know there's a killer with this exact MO and stalking his victims is how he gets off. Trust me, I've gone over the case file and this one fits like a glove."

I suppress a sigh, but Lauterbach is undeterred. He opens the file on another prostitute, Janice Smith, summarizes the notes, then sets it aside for another vaguely familiar name.

2004, Dawn Nickerson, age 25

Houston paralegal found in bathtub, throat cut, similar circumstances to 2001 Tonya Stall homicide. Investigators theorized connection, but no suspect was charged. Mentally disturbed person confessed to both crimes after media coverage. Follow-up eliminated him from suspicion.

"It's not me saying there's a connection with Tonya Stall; it was the original HPD investigators. As a matter of fact, I have the documentation right here." He thumbs through the nearest stack of reports, withdrawing a thin folder he's marked in advance with a sticky note. Inside, a two-page report that I immediately recognize as one of my own. "You worked this case, didn't you?"

The case was Ordway's, but he had asked for help from Wilcox and me. While I was busy trying to dig up dirt on my bystander project, Wilcox came up with the connection to the 2001 case. Covering for my disengagement, he'd handed the find over to me. *Write this up and it'll look like you're pulling some weight around here.* So I'd knocked the report out and gotten on with my extracurricular work, forgetting all about the brutally murdered paralegal and the nurse from 2001. I feel a sickness radiating like heat through my chest. What had I told Wilcox this morning?

I cut some corners. I dropped the ball.

Clichés to hide behind. Both Lauterbach and Cavallo are looking at me, expecting some kind of response. I slide the report back without comment: "Keep talking."

A cell phone company manager from 2005.

Another restaurant worker in 2007.

A third grade teacher for HISD in 2008.

"If Guzman's your suspect," I say, "he's in the system. It was a DNA test that cleared him of killing Nicole Fauk. We have prints from the Walker scene, which don't connect to him."

"Those prints belong to the homeowner," he says. "I've read the file, remember?"

"The homeowner is looking like a suspect."

Lauterbach greets this news with a smile. "I don't think a fifty-something English teacher is the person behind all this."

"There's not one person behind all this," I say. "All these names, all these poor, dead women. Pile the paperwork up and I feel like we've been asleep on the job. And I'd love to be able to pin all this on some larger-than-life villain, so I can understand what's motivating you right now. Problem is, you're chasing the bogeyman. All this"—I sweep my hand over the spread of files—"it's the work of many hands."

"We shall see." He folds the page in his hand over, examining the last entry. "We're this far, so I might as well finish . . ."

2009, Ramona Sanchez, age 30

Harris County fitness trainer, body discovered in swimming pool at private gym. Multiple stab wounds, mutilation, sexual assault. Several clients interviewed, no suspects. Weapon believed to be an 8" "survival knife" as in 2005 Mary Sallier slaying. Strong similarities to Simone Walker homicide investigation led by HPD *Det. Roland March.*

"Back in April," he says, "I started off with the assumption that one of Ramona's male clients did this to her. She had quite a few, and it wasn't unusual for her to be at the gym after-hours. That hypothesis didn't pan out, and when the ME came back with the description of the weapon, this time I immediately thought of Mary Sallier."

I raise my eyebrows.

"The cell phone manager," Cavallo says.

Lauterbach nods. "We went over the details a couple of times, me and Dr. Green, so when your case came up and it looked like a similar knife was used, she gave me a call."

"Was this before or after Brad Templeton put your list of cases together for you?"

He glares. "You're confusing things. I don't make any apology for consulting Templeton. It's not like you haven't. When I first met him, I'd been working on Ramona Sanchez for months without getting very far. I suspected there was a serial killer, but I'm experienced enough to know that making that kind of claim before the facts are in can be risky. There are always small-minded people looking to cover themselves." He turns to Cavallo, stabbing a thumb at me. "Case in point."

"The problem," I say, "is that Brad Templeton isn't an expert on serial killers. He's a writer with a nose for sensationalism. He's also prone to hero worship, and I can see he's moved me off the pedestal and put you on it. You talked about water being essential to the fantasy, but the real fantasy here is the one you and Brad have cooked up. You're enabling each other."

Cavallo pauses me with a half-raised hand. "But, March, there *are* some connections here."

Et tu, Brute? When I told her I wanted an honest opinion, I never considered the possibility of her giving it while Lauterbach was on hand to smile and nod.

"If you gather enough material," I say, speaking slowly, choosing my words, "and you look at it from enough perspectives, you're inevitably going to find some commonality. You should know that, Cavallo. Remember that thing a few years back—the Bible Code? They put the text into a computer and discovered all these hidden messages by connecting the dots. The Bible predicted the Kennedy assassination, the Cold War, Adolf Hitler, pretty much everything. Only it turned out you can do the same thing with Dickens or whatever else you fed into the computer—probably even the phone book. You could find messages that really weren't there.

"There's no difference between that and this. If you strip a bunch of cases down to only the details that match, then hold them up side by side, they probably do look interrelated. But you could do the same thing with a hundred other cases, even if you had a hundred confessed murderers already behind bars. That's what's happening here. Donald Fauk confessed. He killed his wife. And all the similarities and parallels in the world don't cancel that out. And besides, all of this, it forgets one thing."

Lauterbach leans back in his chair. "What does all this forget?"

Instead of answering, I pluck the folding knife from my pocket, flipping open the blade. Slapping my hand onto the table, fully aware that what I'm about to do is deeply stupid, I stab the pattern into the wood: *One, two, three. Four, five, six. One, two, three. Four, five, six. One, two, three—*

"Stop it, March. Stop!"

Cavallo times her hand just right, clamping her fingers around my fist as it ascends, arresting the movement without spilling any blood. She looks at me like I'm crazy, and maybe she's right.

"*That*," I say, "is what the man who killed Simone did to her afterwards. Over and over. That's the one thing you could have shown me to change my mind about your theory. But you can't. Because it isn't there."

I close the knife and put it away. Both of them are stunned, both of them staring. The fresh gouges in the conference table are staring too, so I shift a stack of files to conceal them.

"I think we're done here," Cavallo says.

Lauterbach stands. "You are right about that."

He follows us all the way back to the elevator, making sure I don't have the opportunity to vandalize any more Sheriff's Department property. Overcome by a sense of my own immaturity, I keep my eyes on the ground, not looking up until I'm in the elevator and the doors are sliding shut. Cavallo shakes her head at me like I'm a naughty schoolboy. A disappearing Lauterbach raises his hand and delivers a one-fingered salute.

CHAPTER 16

"I feel like I'm baby-sitting a spoiled brat," Cavallo says.

Walking through drizzle under amber lights, she stays a few steps in front of me all the way down San Jacinto, throwing remarks like this over her shoulder as we go. I try closing the gap, but her anger proves to be a reservoir of strength, always keeping her a stride ahead.

"You accuse everybody else of operating with blinders on. Everybody else is twisting the evidence to fit some preconceived idea. Have you ever considered that maybe *you're* the one wearing the blinders?"

"Lauterbach doesn't have a case."

"Not yet—but with more time he just might. Then what are you going to do? If you were smart, you'd try to make an ally of the man, just in case he's really on to something. But your pride has to come first, doesn't it?"

"He thinks Fauk faked the confession. He's wrong."

She wheels on me. "Are you sure about that? Whatever you think about Brad Templeton, I highly doubt he'd do an about-face without good reason."

"Lauterbach is good at snowing people."

"Or maybe what he's saying makes sense, March. You wanted my honest opinion, so here it is. As of right now, the story he's telling would probably be laughed out of court. I'm with you on that. But every investigation I've ever worked would have been laughed out of court on day one. The further he gets, the tighter the case will be. The media is already sniffing around the edges, which means—"

"Which means they're as gullible as everyone else."

"March," she says with a sigh. "Talking to you is like driving nails with my bare hands. It takes too much out of me, and doesn't do much good."

"If you'd let me get a word in, I'll explain why he's wrong about everything."

She raises her hands in surrender. "What's the point? Convincing me won't do any good."

"I'd like to convince someone."

"Is that all you want? Someone to pat you on the back and say you're right about everything? I could do that, but then I wouldn't be much of a friend. Or much of a cop. I've worked all of one homicide, so it's not like I'm the expert. From what I know about Simone Walker's murder, though, it sure *looks* like a serial killing."

"Yes, but—"

"And you made the connection between her case and Nicole Fauk. You did. So are you gonna trust your instinct from ten years ago or trust your instinct today?"

The drive to her place consumes more silence than it does time. After she slams the door shut and dashes up the walkway to her front porch, I roll my window down for a parting wave. She disappears behind the door without turning.

Whatever I wanted from her, I didn't get it.

My car follows a path of its own, taking turns and shifting lanes, carrying me toward home without going the full distance. I pull to a stop in the empty parking lot of a half-abandoned chain of storefronts, parking near the darkened entrance of what used to be a bar called the

Paragon. On the radio they're tallying election results, declaring Captain Hedges's candidate the clear winner. A historic moment. I switch it off and listen to the rain.

On September 11, 2001, a woman sat at the bar inside the Paragon for hours, watching coverage of the terrorist attack on New York, downing one drink after another. When she finally left for home, she blew through a traffic light and struck the passenger side of Charlotte's car. Since October of that year, I've kept coming back.

This is the trickle, the mountain spring that eventually swelled into my river of numbing pain. Tracing it back to the source has never done me any good. I still seem compelled to do it, though, to repeat the futile routine of nighttime vigils. Now that the bar has closed, one more victim of the economic downturn, I find I prefer the company. Alone at last with a swirl of blackness and no pretenses to maintain.

My phone begins to buzz. On-screen, a stack of missed calls. My cousin Tammy and, strangely, Reverend Curtis Blunt. The incoming call is from Quincy Hanford, probably looking for absolution after this morning's disappointment, and I'm half inclined to ignore it. But I don't.

"I have an idea about your email," he says, almost panting over the line. "I could try explaining, but it might be easier just to show you."

"Now? It's eight o'clock at night."

"That didn't stop you before."

"Where do you want to meet?"

Hanford's condo in Midtown must have been acquired mid-renovation. Clearly he hasn't done anything with it since. The wood floors are half refinished, the kitchen island comes with a plywood top, and down a short hallway there's an unmade mattress sitting directly on the bedroom floor.

"Come on in," he says.

In the living room, arranged on several folding tables, there's a semi-circle of glowing computer screens. Behind them, several scavenged server racks house banks of computers tethered together with multicolored cables.

Hanford sits enthroned in an ergonomic Aeron chair, probably salvaged from a corporate bankruptcy auction. He wears the same inside-out T-shirt he had on earlier, but he's put on an extra layer of confidence. Home-court advantage.

"This might not work," he says, the glow in his eyes belying the words, "but according to some hacker friends of mine it should. Originally I was thinking we could do it through a link in the email, only he'd have to click on that for the program to work. This way, all he has to do is check for new mail."

I give him a blank stare. "Back up a little bit and explain it to me from the beginning."

"It's really simple. He sent the message from her MacBook, so maybe he's expecting some kind of reply. If we send one with some embedded HTML code that exploits a loophole in WebKit—that's the rendering engine in the Macintosh's Mail software—we can grab his current wireless network name and possibly zero in on his location. We could even activate the laptop's built-in camera and snap a picture of the guy that the software will mail back to us."

"You're serious? Is it really that easy?"

He smirks. "It's not easy, but based on what I've done so far, I think it might be possible."

"Might?"

"I've never tried it," he says. "And nobody I've talked to has, either. In theory it should be doable, assuming I can figure out the rendering engine issue. The point is, it's worth a try."

When it comes to information technology, I'm out of my depth. Having the killer open an email and send us a photo of himself seems like television, not reality. But in the brave new world of bits and bytes anything is possible. At least Hanford seems to think so.

"It's ironic," I say.

"What is?"

"I doubt he took her laptop just so he could send taunting emails. He must have had some contact with her, and he was afraid emails, pictures, something would lead us to him. He's been smart enough not to use the phone, knowing we can trace him when it pings the nearest tower, but he couldn't resist sending the email. It must give him a thrill, a sense of power. Without realizing it, he's left a trail of bread crumbs that lead right back to him."

"Assuming my plan actually works."

"How soon can we try it?"

Hanford cocks his head. "If I can get the help I need, there might be something to test by this time tomorrow. At the latest, we'll have something Monday. Obviously, we'll have to send the reply through your computer. Then it's a waiting game until he checks for mail. I can't guarantee we'll have a lot of information to work with, but I'll get as much as I can."

"Get me a picture, Quincy, and you'll become a crime-fighting legend. Then you can buy yourself a couch."

I delete Tammy's message within a second or two of hearing her voice. Force of habit. The one from Curtis Blunt leads me to the emergency room at Ben Taub, where I find the reverend in another all-black ensemble wedged into a row of molded plastic seats with his face resting in his hands. I pause over him, not wanting to interrupt any in-progress prayers. Sensing me, he gives a startled jump.

"Where is he?" I ask.

"Surgery. They beat him up pretty good. You know what an open skull fracture is? The doctor says they've gotta pick all the bones out of the brain before they can suture it up."

"Was he conscious when they brought him in?"

He shrugs.

I sit next to him, exhaling. "What happened?"

"All I know is somebody cracked his head open. I thought you'd want to be informed on account of that message you left yesterday. I take it you expected something like this might happen to him? You don't seem surprised."

"Jason seems to have a self-destructive streak. He goes out looking for a fight, and if he can't find one, he starts it. So yeah, I'm not surprised. It was a week ago today Simone was killed. He's just marking the anniversary."

"The way they made it sound, he'll be lucky to survive. And if there's no permanent brain damage, it will be a miracle."

"You believe in miracles."

"Yeah," he says, "but I'm not so sure the Lord will bless a thing like this with healing."

"Jason's not a bad kid."

He turns in his chair. "Last time the two of us spoke, you were telling me Jason filleted his wife, and now you think he's not a bad kid?"

"It's my job to think people are guilty," I say, "until I know otherwise. The presumption of innocence is for the jury."

Blunt gives my words more weight than I intend, chewing them over as he rubs his tired eyes. The fact that he's here at all surprises me. His concern for Jason Young must be genuine.

"You know something, Detective," he says. "The devil's name—Satan—it comes from an old Hebrew word that means 'the accuser.' *Ha-Satan.* The way you talk about your job has me wondering if there's a whole lot of difference between you and him. On the one hand, you act like you care about what happens to this boy, and on the other you drive him to it."

"Jason was on this path long before I showed up," I say, shaking my head. "Last weekend, while I was with his dead wife, he picked a fight in a strip club."

He winces. "At a what?"

"Never mind," I say. "Forget I said that."

"You just don't stop, do you? Jason's laying in there on the stretcher with his head in pieces, and here you are, kicking him when he's down."

"I wasn't going to say anything, but you—"

"So it's *my* fault now? Listen, Detective, I made a mistake calling you. I can see that now. You've done your duty, so why don't you get on out of here? Whether that boy lives or dies, it's got nothing to do with you."

"I'd like to see it through—"

"I absolve you of guilt," he says. "I'll handle this from here on out."

Since my daughter died, I haven't touched a drop of alcohol, but at times like this, standing outside the automatic doors as a fresh ambulance pulls up, feeling the glare of the jumped-up preacher right between my shoulder blades, I could drink myself into oblivion without regret.

But he's right, I tell myself. It's got nothing to do with me. I didn't push Jason Young into anything. He made those choices all on his own.

All I did was stand by and let him.

The lights are on in my kitchen, and when I push through the back door, a solemn conversation is in progress between Charlotte and Carter Robb. She leans in a crook in the counter, the right angle connecting the sink and the stove, with an oversized coffee mug in both hands. Carter perches on a stool by the island. Both of them stare, surprised by my sudden appearance.

I've had enough people staring at me for one day.

"I was beginning to think you weren't coming back," Charlotte says. "You left so early this morning, I didn't hear you go."

"I left last night about one. Something came up with the case."

"Have you made a breakthrough?" Carter asks.

I ignore this. "Tomorrow morning I'm driving up to Huntsville. I'd better get my head down for a few hours."

"We were just talking about Carter's job," she says. "If you have a few minutes to spare, maybe you could give us your opinion."

"My opinion on what?" I lay my damp jacket over the back of a breakfast table chair, then help myself to some of the newly brewed decaf. "If it's a life coach you're after, I'm not exactly your best option. Not tonight."

"Things with Murray are getting a little awkward," Carter says.

His boss, Murray Abernathy, is a wealthy benefactor in the mold of Curtis Blunt, only instead of minting DVDs of himself preaching to a studio audience, Murray bought an old brick building off of Westheimer and opened an outreach center for the community, a place where people can walk in off the street for a little social interaction, shoot the breeze about the great philosophical conundrums, and leave feeling better about themselves. When Carter was a suburban youth pastor, he'd taken a group of his teenage charges to the center to do volunteer work, and a couple of them met their future murderer, a man named Frank Rios. Personally, I would have razed the place to the ground before taking a job there, but I'm not Carter.

"Awkward in what way?" I ask. "Murray seems all right."

"It's not him exactly. It's just . . ." He glances toward Charlotte. "I assumed Murray was dipping into his own pocket to support the center, that it was a labor of love. And I found out today it's not exactly like that."

"What did you discover?"

"Usually Murray keeps me out of the support side of things, but I saw some paperwork I wasn't supposed to. Turns out the center wasn't Murray's idea. Some of the larger churches around here got together and they came up with this as a kind of experiment. They brought him in to run the center. I asked him point-blank and he admitted it. The center's a laboratory for new ideas. What we're doing today, he says, will be best practices for the church of tomorrow."

I smile at this. "In that case you should ask for a raise."

"It's not funny."

"I realize that, but what exactly is the problem?"

"When I made the move, I was looking for a more authentic ministry. I wanted to get clear of the corporate church and all the ordained CEOs. I wanted to do something real."

"And now you're out of the frying pan and into the fire."

"Pretty much. With a baby on the way, I feel like there's a decision I need to make. Do I keep up this charade, or do I move on?"

"What does Gina have to say?"

He gives me a pained look. "She'll support my decision either way, but she says it's up to me to decide."

"Oh."

"Exactly. As it is, she's already making more from her teaching job than I bring in, so what am I supposed to tell her? I want to quit again and look for something else?"

"Carter," Charlotte says, and by the tone of her voice I know what's coming.

She's going to swoop in and solve his financial anxiety: *If you need money, you just have to ask.* I stop her with a look. I'm not against helping the couple, but there are some problems the magic money wand can't wipe away.

"Gina is right," I tell him. "You do have to make this call on your own. If Murray's deal somehow violates your principles, then suck it up and walk out. If you can live with it, then stay there." Charlotte starts to interrupt, but I shake my head. "But if you're hoping to find the perfect scenario, you should give up now. You already know what I think. Everything's tainted, and this is no different. If you believe in the work, what does it matter who pays the bill?"

"It does matter on some level."

"If you say so. It's your choice to make. I've already been accused once tonight of being the devil, so maybe you shouldn't listen to what I have to say."

"The thing is, if I could just get clarity. On just one thing."

"Give it up," I say, patting him on the shoulder. "We always operate in a muddle. That's the human condition."

Charlotte comes over to me, loops an arm under mine, and leads me toward the stairs.

"Now you do sound like the devil," she says.

"It's the company I keep."

CHAPTER 17

Against a backdrop of tall pines, a statue of Sam Houston looms over I-45, marking my arrival in the prison town of Huntsville. He's made of concrete atop a granite base, but to me the lack of detail from the neck down makes him look like an oversized soap carving. This morning the great man is wreathed in fog, glowering down on the half-empty highway, bone white against the gray sky.

Across the highway from the penitentiary, there's a museum in the form of a miniature block house, complete with a half-sized guard tower. Inside, you can put your head and hands through the holes in a painted display and have your picture taken as a prisoner in old-fashioned black-and-white stripes. I've always wondered how many wives and kids visiting Daddy in jail actually stop by and take some souvenir snaps.

One day I'll grow up to be just like him.

The seventy-mile drive gave me plenty of time to think, and I get plenty more at an empty visitors' table, waiting for the correctional apparatus to deliver the requested prisoner, a repeat offender named Coleman who once helped put some of his colleagues behind bars.

Thanks to that cooperation, he spent his first few months back in prison waking up each day expecting a shank in the ribs. But I talked to some connected people inside, doing what I could for him. I even visited his grandmother a few times, a courtly old lady who walks every morning to Emancipation Park, finds herself a shady spot, and reads her daily psalm. Today I'll discover whether Coleman appreciates my effort.

The visitors' area is silent. On the other side of the door I hear the muffled hum of voices, the clang of metal, the squeal of rubber soles on linoleum floors.

It's always possible that Jason Young did murder his estranged wife, that afterward, consumed with guilt, he sought to punish himself in a series of provoked fights, until he finally found the darkness. If I could ignore the Fauk connection, ignore the oddly detached frenzy of the wounds to Simone Walker's body, then the textbook answer could be made to fit.

The only problem is that I don't believe it.

Whatever inner demons haunt that man, they aren't ones that would drive him to such a controlled and depraved execution.

Which leaves Joy Hill, an unlikely perpetrator to say the least. Middle-aged academics might be likely murderesses in an Agatha Christie yarn, but in real life not so much. The only scenario in which I can imagine Dr. Hill wielding the knife is a crime of passion, if she found herself over-whelmed by thwarted desire. But in that case, the scene would have looked very different, the deed stamped indelibly by the motive that drove it.

It sure looks like a serial killing.

Cavallo's words, and they happen to be right. Which means she is probably right about the rest, too. The blind man in this situation isn't Lauterbach. It's me. I need to turn the table on this thing, to look at it with fresh eyes.

The door at the far side of the room opens. Coleman is escorted in. When he sees me, he stops in his tracks. He's put on a few pounds since last time, lost some of his muscled definition. Maybe he hasn't been put-ting in as many hours on the prison yard weights. Maybe he's afraid to. A couple of corrections officers hang by the door, giving us plenty of space.

"Aw, come on, now." He makes a show of turning, but when the guards look ready to let him retreat, he pauses. "All right, all right. I'll talk to the man. I'll let *him* talk, anyway, just don't be expecting no replies."

"Lower your voice," I say. "Nobody can hear you. How you doing, anyway?"

He cracks a smile. "Just grinding time up here until I get out. You know, you can't just drag a man out of church. I got a right to worship, just like everybody."

"Did I interrupt? Accept my apologies. As much sin as you have to confess, I know the time must be precious. I'll make this as short as I can."

"All right, all right," he says. "You drove yourself all the way up here; least I can do is hear you out."

Coleman props his elbows on the table, clearly curious about my unexpected arrival, calculating how he might work whatever I want from him to his advantage. When I don't say anything, his smile fades.

"It ain't my grandmama, is it?"

I shake my head. "Far as I know she's fine. This is about something else. I need a set of eyes and ears back in the cages, all right? There's a fellow inmate of yours I'm interested in."

"Man," he says, "I ain't no snitch. I start acting like one now and somebody in here's gonna cut me a new orifice, feel me? Now, I'll be happy to barter back and forth on something *out there*." He waves a hand to indicate the outside world. "Up in here, though, you can't even be asking."

"Maybe you already have the information I want."

A pause. "All right, then. Shoot."

"Donald Fauk."

"Fauk?" He smiles. "What kind of name is that?"

"Do you know him?"

He sits back, arms crossed, casting a glance up at the ceiling. "Maybe I know of the man."

"What do you know of him?"

"Doing life, ain't he? Got him some juice inside, for an old white boy, on account of he's rich. Hear tell he's fixed some people up on the outside."

"Fixed them up?"

"In a financial way." He pauses again. "Speaking of fixing, how you gonna fix me? Ain't no milk until you buy yourself the cow."

"That's charming," I say. "Nicely put. How about I have a word with the warden and take you home with me today? You like the sound of that?"

He shakes his head. "You offering me *nothing*, is that it?"

"Coleman, you have to think of this relationship like an investment. You want a big return over time, and that means putting in something up front, and putting in a little bit more every so often. Now, can I offer you anything right this minute? Probably not. I can't move your next parole hearing forward. I can't even switch you to a nicer cell. Think about it: if I did, would you really want to go back into general circulation and try to explain?"

"So you want something for nothing."

"I want something today for nothing today. But a time's gonna come when I can help you in a big way."

"Man," he says, "you the one put me back in here."

I show him open palms. "My bad."

He laughs a little, waits, then laughs a little more. Getting used to the idea. "There is something I can give you, and I got half a mind to do it. Only you gotta give some assurances that when that day comes when you got the power to do me a good turn, I can count on you to pay up."

"Scout's honor."

"All right." He leans forward. "There's a story about this dude. I don't know if it's true or not, but I hear people talking—you know how they do. Anyways, this boy who was getting out, Mr. Donald Fauk, he gives him a job to do. And in return there's something waiting for him."

"What kind of job?"

Coleman shrugs. "A job out there. A favor, like. He gets paid to run an errand for the man. And there's more of them got that treatment, too. All white boys. I don't know what they gotta do, but when they done it, they get taken care of." He sees my expression and laughs. "Not taken care of like that. I mean, financial-like."

"So Donald Fauk pays inmates to do favors for him on the outside when they're released? And you don't know what kind of things they do?"

"Delivering messages? How should I know?"

"There have to be rumors. If guys are talking about this, what are they saying?"

"Man, I done told you I don't know."

I can think of a dozen reasons Fauk might want to recruit errand boys from the prison population, none of which include committing copycat murders. What I don't understand is why a man with his kind of fortune can't arrange anything he wants done in the outside world through his legal team. Presumably he's up to something the lawyers won't touch. Something he wants to keep from them.

"If you hear anything more," I say, "you know how to get in touch. I'm not asking you to risk your neck or anything. Just keep an ear to the ground."

As I start to rise, he motions me back.

"Hold up. There is one thing."

"What's that?" I ask.

"Is it true you done beat a confession outta this man? 'Cause I don't wanna mix myself up in nothing illegal."

Wait a second.

His broad smile tells me all I need to know.

Coleman saw me coming a mile away, and probably knows more about Donald Fauk than he's prepared to say. Maybe he'll leave here and report straight back, telling Fauk everything that's transpired across the table. Fauk can do more for him than I can, after all.

"Don't freak out," he says, reading my thoughts. "I'm just messing with you, man. Look here, I'll give you something. There's a New Orleans white boy, name of Bourgeois." He pronounces it *Boojwah*. "When he got out, Mr. Fauk give him one of these jobs. I knowed the boy, and while he wouldn't tell *me* what the job was, I bet he'd get one look at you and give it up."

"What's the Bourgeois boy's first name?"

"They call him Peeper in here. Don't know his real name."

★

I'm not sure I can trust what Coleman tells me, but by the time I pull out of the penitentiary heading back to I-45, there's a computer printout in my briefcase courtesy of an obliging corrections supervisor. Wayne "Peeper" Bourgeois, another post-Katrina immigrant, did a two-year stretch in Huntsville for beating up a hooker. His release date was back in August and he was supposed to report to an East Texas parole officer whose contact information is now scribbled in my Filofax.

After driving through a fast-food joint for lunch, I dial the parole officer's number. He picks up right away and, once he's satisfied with my credentials, confirms that Bourgeois checked in with him after his release.

"But I haven't seen the boy ever since. If you ask me, he hightailed it back to Louisiana. A lot of 'em do. They get sick of not living in the third world."

The obvious next step is to call Gene Fontenot for an assist. But under the circumstances I'm not sure that's the best idea. So I dial Wilcox instead to see what he's managed to find out about the NOPD investigation. With any luck he'll give Fontenot a clean bill of health and I can call in a favor on the Bourgeois thing. After the trouble he's stirred up, Gene owes me.

"Where are you?" Wilcox asks. "Your voice is breaking up."

I fill him in on my chat with Coleman, asking for the all clear so I can call Fontenot.

"So you really went up there? I wish you hadn't."

"Why not? I told you I was going to."

He ignores my question. "This thing with Fontenot . . . I think it would be best not to have any contact with him."

"What did you find out?"

"Well . . ."

"You did check around, right?"

"March," he says with an exasperated sigh. "Not everybody works the same hours as you. This might come as a surprise, but I can't just call somebody at NOPD on a Saturday night and get them to send over everything they've got."

"Did you do anything at all?"

A pause. "I really don't think you should get in touch with him."

"You said you were going to help out."

"And I will," he says. "But not on your timetable. Give me a chance to get the wheels in motion, then I'll call you."

"When will that be?"

"Whenever it happens, okay? That's the best I can do."

I'm not sure if he hangs up on me or I hang up on him. We both hit the button so fast it could have been a draw.

I pound the steering wheel a couple of times before pulling onto the shoulder. I should have known better than to trust Wilcox to hold up his end. How many times does a man have to let you down before you learn not to trust him? Of course it cuts both ways. I've given him plenty of reason to ask the same question of me.

I've driven back and forth between Houston and Huntsville so many times I can do the trip with my eyes closed. But for the idea I'm hatching, I need a map. I take the next exit and circle under the highway, heading back toward town. Passing under Sam Houston's gaze, I give the old man a wave.

At the next service station I buy an atlas and flip through the pages, working out the quickest route. From Huntsville I can take 190 east to Woodville, heading south on 69 until I connect with Interstate 10 at Beaumont. After that I'll travel east into Louisiana, hitting Lake Charles, Lafayette, and Baton Rouge in succession, reaching New Orleans sometime between seven and eight in the evening. Seven hours to work out how to find Wayne Bourgeois, and how to break him once I do. Seven hours to decide if what I'm doing is crazy. With luck I can conclude my business by midday tomorrow and get back to Houston early in the evening.

There's no point in cloak-and-dagger, but seeing the pay phone at the service station, I dig some change out anyway. I take my Filofax, open up to the page where I've written Gene Fontenot's address and phone numbers, dialing him at home.

"Hello?" he says.

"It's me."

A pause. "I wondered when I'd hear from you."

"You still have that spare bedroom?"

"What I have is a spare couch," he says. "And you're welcome to it."

"I'm on my way. And in the meantime, there's someone I need you to locate."

Charlotte sounds icy over the phone, indifferent.

"You didn't pack a bag," she says.

"I didn't anticipate making the trip. I'd come back through Houston, but that would add another hour to the drive."

"I've hardly seen you the past week."

"It's this case," I say. "Everything is unraveling on me and I'm not sure what to do."

"Bridger called the house looking for you."

"He has my cell number."

"I guess he thought you'd be home on a Sunday afternoon. He wants you to call him."

"I'll do that." The phone is warm against my ear. "Charlotte, I don't want you to be mad. I would have said something before, if I knew this would come up."

"I'm not mad," she says.

A pause.

"Look," I say. "It's this pregnancy thing, isn't it?" Silence. "It's been eating at you ever since you found out. I know it's . . ." My voice trails off. Still nothing. "Is it the thought of a baby in the house, or the fact that they'll probably move out—?"

This time there's no question who hangs up first.

I decide to give her time, calling Bridger instead. He picks up and I get a blast of wind noise over the line, immediately picturing him on a golf course green. He's just the sort to play in this weather. But no, he's in the car, smoking with the window down.

"You should give up," I say.

"Thanks for the advice. Now, what's this I hear about Donald Fauk appealing his conviction? There's no chance of the court entertaining this, is there?"

I start to explain the situation. He makes a series of affirming grunts, prodding the story along. Occasionally I hear him exhale loudly, and I imagine a cloud of smoke swirling around the pathologist's windblown head.

"I heard about the DNA samples going missing," he says. "What do you think about that?"

"Is it any wonder? Evidence gets lost even under the best conditions, and these days nobody's calling HPD's DNA section the best."

"You don't think it's convenient, though?"

"In what way?"

"This particular set of samples going missing."

"Fauk must be happy," I say, puzzled.

"But you think it's just a coincidence."

Now I'm really confused. "What are you getting at exactly?"

"Maybe it's nothing," he says. "But when the original tests were done, the results were verified by an independent lab. We send a lot of work to this particular lab, and I happened to be talking to one of their doctors earlier this week when the subject came up. He brought it up, by the way, and he had a strange story to tell.

"When the evidence couldn't be retrieved from HPD, Fauk's attorney queried the independent lab about whether they had samples in storage. My friend answered that they did—these guys keep everything—but the lawyer insisted on him physically checking to see whether they were there. And when he did, guess what?"

"No samples."

"Exactly. And it's not like somebody misplaced them. He checked every test they'd run the same month as the Fauk evidence, and all of it was there. The only thing missing were the Fauk DNA samples."

"Did he have a theory?"

"He told me they were still looking into it. But off the record he said the only explanation was that someone on staff removed them.

He doesn't know when, but at some point, a lab employee went into storage and took the evidence."

"So Fauk's counsel insisted on them checking because he knew already the evidence was no longer there."

"That's how it looks to me."

"If this is true," I say, "then what are the odds the same thing happened in the HPD crime lab?"

"Pretty good, if you ask me. A lot of heads rolled during that inquiry. Maybe somebody decided to make an extra buck. It might not have seemed too serious to them, knowing there was a confession and those backup samples at the other lab."

"You've given me something to think about. Thanks for passing it along."

"How are you doing, March? The whole Fauk thing coming back like this has to be taking its toll . . ."

"There's a lot going on," I say, brushing his concern aside. "If I can keep Fauk in jail, that'll be one thing I don't have to worry about at night."

After I hang up, I remember Carter Robb saying something similar to me last night.

If I could just get clarity. On just one thing.

And what had I told him? Something stupid about the human condition. Speeding through East Texas with New Orleans in my crosshairs, I keep repeating Carter's words to myself. *If I could just get clarity on just one thing.* A mantra doubles and redoubles in my head, syncopated by the roar of the road, by the rush of forced air, and the beat of raindrops on the windshield. I hear the *tap, tap, tap* of the knifepoint, first on the stainless surface of the autopsy slab and then chipping away at the sheriff's conference table. It all becomes white noise and then fades to silence, and in the silence a new sound, wet and whispering, fills my ears. It's the porous sucking hiss of a blade through flesh.

CHAPTER 18

When he returned to New Orleans a year after the hurricane, Gene Fontenot found himself a brick one-story in Westwego across the river from Audubon Park, an ugly house with a bare concrete patio, where he could grill steaks and drink beer after-hours, separated from the mud-colored Mississippi by a rusted shipyard. To mark my arrival, he carries a chair from the breakfast table out onto the slab. We sit and listen to the sizzle of cooking meat, and Gene pulls a couple of longnecks from the cooler.

"None for me," I say.

"Come on, now." He extends the bottle closer, then sets it aside with a suit-yourself smile. "I don't recall you being a teetotaler—but whatever. I checked up on that boy you were asking about, Wayne Bourgeois, and if you want, we can pay him a visit later on. He stays up at his stepsister's place on Desaix Boulevard, over by the fairgrounds. It wouldn't hurt to know why he's in your gunsights."

"Remember Donald Fauk?"

He lifts his hands. "How could I forget?"

"My information is, when Bourgeois got out of Huntsville, he had an errand to run for Fauk. I assume, based on the fact he came back here, that this task of his was local. Now, what would Fauk want done in New Orleans? The only thing I can come up with has to do with you."

"I've never heard of this boy before. What's his sheet look like?"

"He beat the living daylights out of a prostitute, but I don't think that's got anything to do with the situation. Apparently, Fauk's been paying off newly released cons to do odd jobs he can't run through his team of lawyers. For example, this trial that just fell apart on you, the one that sparked the internal investigation? Is it possible Bourgeois coached your suspect on what to say, maybe gave him a plausible story that would make the confession sound coerced?"

He laughs at the idea, takes a swig from his bottle, and sets it on the concrete. He wipes his mouth with the back of his hand.

"That doesn't sound too likely."

"Are you sure about that?"

"What that defense attorney said in the courtroom . . . Much as it pains me to concede anything to the man, that's pretty much what happened." The words come out light and sarcastic, like this admission is no big deal, only he can't look me in the eye.

"What are you saying, Gene?"

"The little dirtbag was guilty, make no mistake. But without any physical evidence tying him to the scene, and with my witness coming over with a sudden case of amnesia, there was no sticking it to him without a straight-up admission. Lucky for me when we picked him up he'd collected a few bruises, including a nice one right here on the biceps." He taps his arm to show me just where. "Before the interrogation, I conducted a little pre-interview, and whenever he lied to me I gave him a punch on the arm. This boy had just smoked a man in cold blood, two shots to the head, and I had him crying like a baby from a few taps." He chuckles at the memory, still avoiding eye contact. "And don't tell me you never do things like that in Houston, 'cause I wasn't born yesterday. In fact, I seem to recall a little talk we had once upon a time, a regular meeting of the minds . . ."

I shake my head.

"You've had your eyes opened, too," he says. "Don't deny it."

The steaks are too rare for my taste. I eat mine anyway, chewing in silence, listening for sounds of the river in the distance. The air is stagnant and wet, as thick or thicker than what we breathe in Houston, but not cold. He's comfortable in shirt-sleeves and I'm almost tempted to strip out of my jacket. Something makes me not want to get too comfortable in Gene's presence, though.

When we're done, he goes into the house to retrieve his side arm, wedging the paddle holster into his belt. Then he pulls on a black windbreaker and cocks his thumb at the door.

"Ready to roll?"

We take Gene's pickup, looping on Highway 90 to cross the river. The bridge takes us into downtown. Gene cuts over to I-10 and exits at St. Bernard Avenue, taking that all the way to Desaix. As he drives, I glance out the passenger window, entertaining a host of second thoughts. Meeting Gene again is like reconnecting with a buddy from high school, someone you had everything in common with at one point, and nothing in common with now. More than awkward, the reacquaintance calls into question all my earlier impressions of the man.

I glance over at him. He seems content, maybe a little excited by the prospect of bashing some heads together. Operating in his element. It dawns on me that Gene Fontenot is bent. He's the proverbial crooked cop, convinced what he's doing amounts to greasing the wheels of justice, helping the jammed machinery get itself moving again. In my time I've only met a few bad cops, and before now I've always worked against them, as committed to the fight in my own way as Wilcox is in his.

But Gene looks at me and sees another version of himself. Another cop who's had his eyes opened, as he put it. In other words, he sees in me the same thing my ex-partner does, the only difference being that he's delighted.

★

We pull up in front of a painted stick shamble overshadowed by a live oak. Small symmetrical windows on either side of the front door, a cracked concrete walk stretching from the door to the sidewalk. Tree roots run straight across the path. In lieu of a driveway, two paved ruts in the grass run alongside the house. An old-fashioned refrigerator lies upended in the yard with a kid's bicycle propped against the dented metal.

"The woman's got no husband," Gene says. "She lives in a dump like this raising her kid, and now she's got an ex-con half brother bringing the law to her doorstep. How's that for a life?"

He pushes the driver's door open and slides down, tucking his windbreaker behind his pistol the way a woman brushes a lock of hair behind her ear. Then he strides up the walkway with me a couple of paces behind, using his flashlight to inspect the surrounding ground.

"Maybe I should do the talking," I say.

Gene just smiles, rapping a knuckle on the door. "My patch, my lead."

A kid maybe five or six years old answers, looking up at us with big eyes, his skinny arms poking out of a wife-beater.

"Wha'*chall* want?" he asks in a surprisingly mature, even world-weary voice, like he's been manning the door all night and is tired of being disturbed.

"Your mama in there?" Gene asks.

"No, she ain't."

"How about your uncle, then?"

The kid looks over his shoulder, then back. "Who wants to know?"

"Who do you think?" Gene pushes the door wide, forcing the kid back and revealing a man frozen on the threshold of the hallway, still holding a finger over his lips. "Don't make a big deal out of this, son. We only want to talk to you."

Wayne Bourgeois scratches his chin in thought, eyes darting, and for half a second I expect him to run. But then he sighs and motions us inside, telling his nephew to beat it into a back bedroom. The kid starts to argue until Bourgeois raises the back of his hand.

"Go on," Gene says. "And *you* put your hand down before I break it off. Now grab yourself some chair and get your vocal cords ready, because we're gonna have ourselves a little chat—and by 'little' I mean as long as it takes."

Bourgeois lowers himself onto a plush recliner, the fabric all rubbed to a high shine. He's barefoot with only his toes sticking out from the hem of his ragged jeans. His body is hidden by an oversized Saints hoodie that leaves the prison tats on his neck in full view. Judging from the stubble on his chin, he hasn't shaved in days. And there's a smell coming off him, a bouquet of body odor and marijuana.

"Now, Mr. Bourgeois," Gene says, "it seems you've got yourself a problem. My colleague here is from the state of Texas, and you know how them folks get when us Louisiana boys start running roughshod over their rules."

"This about my parole?"

"It ain't about collecting for the Policeman's Ball."

He starts to rise. "Now, see, I got a paper somewheres—"

"Park it, brother, or I'll park it for you."

"It's all cool, man. Stay chill."

"You gotta let me finish. What I was saying was, you got a problem, and me, I'm the solution. I can't have these cowboys coming over the state line thinking they can snatch up my people without so much as a by-your-leave. Only to make 'em go away, there has to be something in it for them. Am I making myself clear? You answer the nice man's questions, and the nice man goes away. You don't answer, and the nice man goes away, but he leaves me here to continue the conversation." He smiles. "And I ain't nice."

Bourgeois glances toward the hallway where the kid disappeared. "I'm an open book, man. No secrets. You fire away and see if I'm lying."

I walk over to the side of his chair. "Tell me everything you know about Donald Fauk."

He looks up at me, confused, but all it takes is a shift of Gene's weight and the knit eyebrows smooth away.

"Oh," Bourgeois says, "you mean *that* guy." Like there'd been some doubt. "What you wanna know about him?"

"Everything," I say.

"Well, he's pretty rich, I can tell you that. Doing time for stabbing his wife to death. He's got a lot of muscle around him, too. You can't hardly get near the man unless he invites you."

"What did he want from you?"

"Me? He didn't want nothing"—another movement from Gene—"although, come to think of it, there *was* something. When I got out, he needed something done for him on the outside, and as a favor I volunteered."

"Were you compensated for this favor?" Gene asks.

"Compensated?" He turns the word over in his mind. "I guess you could say that. There was some money in it for me."

"What did you have to do?"

"Nothing much," he says. "He gimme some letters, is all. 'Go to the post office and mail these,' he told me, 'and when they arrive you'll get a letter of your own.' And I give him my sister's address to send it to. That's the only reason I had to come here. I wasn't breaking parole or anything. I just wasn't thinking when I give it to him, is all."

"Tell me more about the letters."

He shrugs. "There was four or five of 'em. All sealed up and the address written on. Two of 'em was real thick, filled up with papers, and the others seemed like there was just one or two pages inside."

"Where were they going to?"

"The thick ones went to people in Houston, I think. There was one in Florida. I'm not sure about the rest. All of them but the one were to places in Texas, though. I do remember that."

"And the letter you got, where is that?"

He smiles. "That one was filled with cash."

"That wasn't what the man asked," Gene says.

"Oh. You mean *where* is it? I done spent the money way back."

"What about the envelope?"

"One of those big ones," he says, drawing a box in the air. "Overnight."

"Which service? FedEx, UPS—"

"I can show you. I still got it somewheres."

"Well," Gene says, "that's more like it."

Bourgeois hops out of his chair to go and fetch the envelope. Right then I see something in his eyes. Gene sees it too, putting a hand out to stop him. The ex-con ducks under the arm, though, springing straight into Gene. Pushing him off-balance. They lock up, staggering backward. Toward the exit.

Gene topples onto the ground. Bourgeois scrambles over him, bolting out through the open door. I kick it into gear.

As I try to cross over him, Gene rolls. My foot catches on the crook of his knee, nearly forcing me face-first into the walkway. But I regain my balance in time to see Bourgeois hoofing it across the boulevard.

"Go get him!"

I run after him. Over my shoulder I hear Gene struggling back to his feet.

"I'll get the truck," he calls out, a note of pain in his voice.

Bourgeois has a head start. And twenty years on me at least. At first it looks like he's gonna leave me in the dust. I don't even know why the boy's running, but I run after him.

I can't remember my last foot pursuit. My legs can't, either.

Before long my chest is pounding and a wheezing sound is coming from my throat, and the distance between me and the ex-con keeps getting longer and longer. I expect the truck to roll up anytime, relieving me of the task, but I listen in vain for the roar of the engine.

Bourgeois pauses, then zigzags back across the boulevard, heading for the houses on the far side. He turns to see where I'm at. I pick up some speed. He loses his footing and sprawls onto the pavement.

I kick my legs harder, willing myself forward. As he gets up, I get a glimpse of his face under the streetlight, the features twisted with fear. *Why is he running?* He takes off down one of the driveways. As I reach the yard, I see him lifting himself over the back fence.

There's no telling where Gene is, but I yell as loud as I can, hoping he can hear me.

"Fontenot! We're going over the fence!"

It takes me two tries to grip the top of the fence. I hook my leg over and roll across, landing awkwardly on one foot. I hit the ground. When I pick myself up, my side is damp with mud. I keep running, then climb a second fence, cursing the fact that I didn't bring a change of clothes with me. And all for nothing. I can't even see him anymore.

I look around me and pause. I find myself standing at the end of a long row of aboveground sepulchers. The cemetery stretches out before me as far as the eye can see, pitted white marble crypts rising to eye level and higher, like an ancient city recessed into the mud.

Bourgeois lopes between them maybe fifty yards ahead, one hand clamped to his side. He's in some pain, too. That gives me satisfaction, anyway. I start after him, but my limbs turn to lead. My toe catches on the edge of a cobble and I'm on the ground again, this time for good.

I lie there a second, breathing hard, then get up on one skinned knee. Gene is nowhere to be seen. Off in the distance, Bourgeois gives a cry of mingled pain and exhaustion. I'd yell back, but I can't catch my breath.

The mausoleums crowd around, and the night grows quiet except for the sound of my breathing and the song of some far-off nocturnal bird.

I retrace my steps and find Gene leaning against the truck with one leg tucked against the other, his hand clutching his raised knee.

"I think I blew it out," he says, panting.

"Why'd he take off like that?"

"I forgot to ask him on his way out."

I start toward the house. "We should take a look inside."

"Without a warrant?" he says, sneering through the pain.

"I'm concerned about that minor in there."

"Yeah, right."

The nephew is watching TV in his shoebox of a bedroom, knees tucked under his chin. I mutter a few reassurances, asking where his mother is, but the boy gives no reply. I pull the door shut. In the next bedroom, there's a nude girl lying facedown on the bed, her outstretched wrist tied to the post with a knotted T-shirt. I crouch by her head, feeling her neck for a pulse. Her skin is feverishly warm to the touch.

"Are you okay?"

I switch on the bedside lamp, then lift her eyelid. Her pupil is just a pinprick. Her lips part and she whispers something.

"What did you say?"

"Is he gone?"

She's bleeding from one nostril. There's blood on her legs, too. At the doorway, the nephew makes a sound. He stares at the girl, then at me.

"Is this your mama?" I ask.

"My mama ain't no whore." He goes back to his room.

Gene hobbles in as I untie the girl's wrist. He pulls a blanket over her, then goes back into the hallway to call an ambulance. The girl rubs her hand. She sits up, pushing her legs over the edge of the bed. She looks no more than seventeen, eighteen.

"I gotta get going," she says. "I'm gonna be in trouble."

"Just sit still. There's an ambulance coming."

She tries to stand, but she can't. I brush a sweat-damp curl out of her eyes and she recoils.

"You gotta let me go, mister."

From the hallway, Gene snaps at her: "Don't make the man repeat himself."

The girls goes docile, tugging the blanket around her, and I feel like giving Gene's knee a kick. I step back from the bed, realizing that all this time I've been treading on the girl's torn clothes. I bend down and start to gather them, but there's no point. A couple of joints are stubbed out in the ashtray under the lamp, but there's something more powerful in the girl's system than weed.

"You're gonna be okay," I tell her.

"I am not."

The ambulance arrives, along with an NOPD patrol car. Gene stays put in the hallway, hiding his limp as he gives the uniforms a rundown. During the course of questioning, the suspect fled. Instead of pursuing, we secured the scene to ensure the minor's safety, and in the course of this discovered the girl. One of the uniforms recognizes her and goes over while the paramedic is taking her vitals.

"Remember me?" he asks. "I ran you off the corner last week." He looks at me, noting the state of my clothes. "She's got a couple of priors for solicitation, but she's all right."

"I'm gonna get in trouble," the girl says.

"Don't you worry about that, Cher. Just let the doctor have a look."

Gene motions me out of the room. In the yard, he checks his watch and gives me a gloomy look.

"You gonna write on this, or am I?"

"Your patch, your lead."

"I knew that was coming." He hobbles over toward the back of the ambulance. "Let's see if there's anything stronger than aspirin in here."

"Gene."

"Just kidding," he says, throwing up his hands. "Let's get going. Those boys can handle everything from here on out." He rustles in his pockets and tosses me the truck keys. "You're gonna have to drive, I'm afraid."

Back on his patio with a homemade ice pack resting on his knee, Gene slurps the dregs of his fourth or fifth beer, tossing the bottle into the yard with a sigh. Beside me the grill still radiates heat. I stretch out, legs crossed at the ankle, feeling childish in Gene's oversized sweat suit. My clothes are slowly revolving in his dryer, all except for my jacket, which hangs from a peg near the front door.

"Not bad for one day, huh?" he asks. "If you'd known when you got up this morning you'd interrupt a rape in progress—maybe worse—and chase some degenerate through the St. Louis cemetery, I bet that would have put a spring in your step."

"At least I know now why he ran."

"We'll pick him up soon enough." He reaches into the cooler for another bottle, finds there aren't any, and stares longingly toward the kitchen. "You gonna make me get up?"

"What do you make of those letters?"

"I think better with a cold one in hand."

"That's a lot of trouble for Fauk to go through, don't you think?"

"Some people don't like their mail being read. If there were five of those envelopes, at least one of them must've gone to his people, whoever arranges the payments. That's how they'd know the others were sent. I could check with the carriers and see who made a delivery to that address, and where it came from . . . if you'll do me a little favor and refill the cooler."

I ignore him. "I think I know where those fat envelopes were going: Brad Templeton."

"The writer?"

"He let slip that he'd been in contact with Fauk, and he's the one who primed the Sheriff's Department with all these supposed serial killer victims."

"And you think they came straight from Fauk."

"Maybe. Something did."

"Now will you get me a beer?"

"This appeal has been a long time coming. Somehow they managed to get the DNA evidence to disappear so it can't be retested. Then they planted the serial killer theory—or at least got the ball rolling, trusting Templeton's creative mind to connect the dots. Before tonight, I assumed they cooked up this false confession angle, too. Now I don't know."

He shifts in his chair. "What's that supposed to mean?"

"You admitted it, didn't you?"

"Now listen here, brother. You and me just turned in a sterling piece of police work, and in record time, too. Don't go ruining the moment."

"It was special, you're right. But did you not sit in that very chair a couple hours ago and confess to beating a confession out of someone?"

"A *guilty* someone."

"What about Donald Fauk? He was guilty."

"Are you for real, March? You're honestly gonna ask me if I forced a confession from that man? You and me both know he was dying to give it up. That guy was touched in the head, and he was only too happy to admit what he'd done."

"Did he admit it to you?"

He glances away.

"Gene, don't lie to me."

"Listen, while you and your partner were gone, you think I sat with the man and asked what he'd been up to? In case you don't remember, there were more pressing concerns at the moment. Does 9/11 ring any bells? Excuse me if I don't take a piece of wife-murdering scum like Fauk too seriously on the same day somebody flies jets into the Twin Towers. I guess I lost a little perspective."

"So he didn't say anything to you?"

"It's been ten years. I don't remember what was said."

"But something was?"

He throws the ice pack at my feet, sending half-melted cubes skittering across the concrete. The chair creaks under his weight as he rises.

"You're worse than fish," he says. "You stink from day one."

He goes inside, slamming the door behind him. A tiny slice of moon hovers in the sky overhead. In the far distance the lights on a jetliner twinkle red. I wait for him to come back, but he doesn't. I relax and let my eyes close.

There's no point in staying longer than I have to. First thing in the morning I'll make the drive back to Houston and try to forget this little episode ever occurred. Gene's confession. The cemetery. The prostitute on the bed. It takes a toll, seeing all that. Like Charlotte said. My legs are like rubber, my arms sore, my neck and shoulders tight from carrying unseen weight. I could sleep right here under the hiding moon if I didn't know Gene would be back any moment, flush with bottles, holding himself up to me like a mirror. A reflection of what I might have been, and what in the eyes of the people closest to me I am either becoming or already am.

"Last chance," he says, coming through the door and depositing a bottle in my lap. The cap is already off, sloshing amber fluid onto the sweats.

I lift the bottle, measuring its heft in my hand. Before he can stop me, I send it spinning across the yard, thumping to a halt at the base of the fence where the contents gurgle out into the grass.

CHAPTER 19

I wake up on the couch, sticky with sweat, the sound of Gene's snoring in my ears. He lies sprawled in a recliner surrounded by bottles, his leg elevated, a deflated rag still dripping across his swollen knee. The blanket, now coiled around my ankles, must have been kicked off during sleep, during my muddled recurring dreams. The girl on the bed was there, but she was dead now and her face didn't belong anymore to the teenage New Orleans prostitute. That one I saved, but the girl in the dream I didn't. As far as I know, the dream girl lies at the bottom of the Gulf, left there by two policemen, one of whom I killed.

The green Ford was there, too. Leaving the bedroom, I walked out onto the churning pavement, where the silent dog barked and the gleaming car from thirty years ago made its circuit around the park, a recurring *thump* buckling the metal trunk lid, like something wanted out.

My bones ache as I hoist myself up, padding across the carpet toward the bathroom, where I borrow Gene's cheap space-age-looking Gillette to hack at my face, then dress in my clothes from yesterday sitting cold and wrinkled in the dryer.

There's a can of chicory in Gene's pantry and an electric kettle on the counter, but instead of settling for a pot of instant, I gather my things and slip out the front door. Café du Monde, open twenty-four hours, beckons from across the river. Coffee and beignets, and then I'll start the seven-hour drive home. As I climb into my car, the horizon glows in anticipation of sunlight.

My grasp of the geography fails me. After a wrong turn, I end up cruising along River Road, feeling a deep kinship with the immobile rust-colored barges out on the Mississippi that, like me, could probably use a dry dock and refitting. But they still get the job done, regardless of looks.

The thought of me running through a graveyard, winded, while Gene clutches his blown knee brings a smile to my lips. Old men playing at what looks to be a young man's game.

With some effort I find the highway and cross the river into downtown, driving in the general direction of Jackson Square. My tourist's knowledge of the city is long out of date, forcing me to resort to a little trial and error until I find Decatur and take it all the way, pulling into one of many empty parking spots along a stately and semi-decayed building with a series of French doors on the ground floor and wrought-iron galleries decked with hanging plants on the two above.

As I cross the street to the porticoed café, my phone buzzes in my pocket. The screen reads CARTER ROBB.

"It's a little early for you to be up, isn't it?"

"Roland? It's Carter."

"Yeah, I know."

"Are you . . . I need to . . ." He lets out a sigh. "Listen, the first thing is, everybody's okay. There's no need to worry. But I have to tell you . . . Something bad happened."

Despite the preamble, my heart constricts.

"What happened?"

"Someone broke into the house."

"Was Charlotte there? Is she all right?"

"She's a little banged up," he says.

"Let me talk to her."

"They're with her now. She's the one who told me to call."

"Who's with her?"

"The police. They're here. Gina called 9-1-1."

My legs go weak. I lean against one of Café du Monde's pillars for support, clutching the phone with one hand and my forehead with the other. I tell him to go back to the beginning and talk slow, explaining everything that happened.

At four thirty in the morning, Carter woke up to the sound of his phone ringing. When he answered, Charlotte whispered to him that she'd heard a noise and there was somebody in the house. He roused his wife and told her to call for help, then descended the apartment stairs to the back door of my house, keeping the line to Charlotte open. He found the door ajar and went inside. There was a crashing sound from upstairs.

"I raced up two at a time," he says. "The noise was coming from the bedroom. Over the phone I could hear Charlotte screaming that he was trying to get in. I found him pushing against the bathroom door. She'd locked herself inside, and the crashing was him kicking the lock open. They were pushing back and forth on the door."

"Did you get a look at him?"

"It was dark," he says. "I yelled at him to stop. For a second, he just stood there, and then I saw something shiny in his hand. He rushed at me and shot his arm out. He sliced my forearm pretty good, but I got ahold of him and wouldn't let him do it again."

He tells me this in a boyishly calm voice.

"For a couple of seconds we kind of wrestled—it seemed like forever. I could smell the guy's breath, feel his spit on my face. Then Charlotte came out of the bathroom and threatened to shoot him."

In her nightstand I keep a loaded .38 revolver, an older all-steel model so she can manage the recoil, fitted with red-dot laser grips. The laser activates as soon as she picks the revolver up, and the bullets hit wherever the dot falls.

"I could see the red dot on the wall next to us, and he must have seen it, too. One second he's trying to gut me, and the next he goes slack. I misjudged it, though. I thought he was giving up. Instead he kneed me and took off through the door."

"Are *you* all right?"

"My arm is bandaged up, but they gave me something for the pain. I've had worse."

"You said Charlotte was hurt? Did he *do* anything to her?"

"The door hit her in the face when he kicked it, but she's okay. She was a real trouper. She probably saved my life."

"I want to talk to her," I say.

"Hold on."

In the background I can hear voices, some close and some far away. A portable radio squawks. The phone changes hands and a woman speaks. Not Charlotte.

"March, is that you?"

Theresa Cavallo. "What are you doing there?"

"Gina called me after it happened, so I figured I should come over. Charlotte's giving a statement, but I'll put her on when she's done. She's holding up well under the circumstances. She says her only regret is not shooting the guy."

"She's really okay?" I ask, hardly believing it.

"I promise. And you owe Carter a debt of gratitude."

"It sounds like I do."

"Not just for rushing over," she says. "Thanks to him, you might just have a break in your case."

"What are you talking about?"

"I'm holding it in my hot little hands." She rattles what sounds like an evidence bag over the line. "*The knife*," she says, her voice electric. "He dropped it on the floor."

I take a deep breath.

"There's Carter's blood on the blade, but they've lifted some good prints off the handle. They're gonna take the hilt apart and see if there's any other blood or trace evidence."

"You're saying the guy who broke into my house is the same one who killed Simone Walker? How would he even know where I live?"

"I don't know. The same way he knows your email address? Obviously I can't say for certain it's the same man, but I told the detective to make sure Dr. Green gets a look at the knife to see if it matches."

"No," I say. "Have Bridger do it."

"Whatever. That's your problem. The point is . . ." She pauses. "Never mind. Here's your wife."

"*Roland?*"

At the sound of Charlotte's voice, a wave of relief goes through me. My mouth twists into a painful smile.

"Are you okay, baby? Are you sure you're all right?"

"It was horrible," she says. "I had the gun and couldn't use it. He could've killed me, Roland, and I couldn't pull the trigger. I feel ashamed. Terry says it was probably him, the man you're after. I couldn't even give them a good description."

"Don't worry about any of that," I say. "None of it matters. You're safe and that's everything. You stood up for yourself and I'm proud of you." My throat catches. "I'm so sorry. I'm so terribly sorry."

"It's not your fault."

"I should have been there. I'm never there."

"Roland, no—"

"I shouldn't be here. It was pointless. And he could've hurt you without me there to stop him. I'm so, so sorry, baby."

She shushes me with a whisper. "Just come home."

"I will. I'll go to the airport and get a flight."

"No," she says. "There's no rush. I'm fine. Everyone's here. Just come home."

If everything is really connected and there are no coincidences, if that's more than just a platitude I've repeated over the years, then how do I explain a drive like this, the second in my life, both of them westward over the long swampy stretch of Interstate 10 that crosses the Atchafalaya? How do I account for such a repetition? Absent again when

I'm needed most, forced again to trace the seemingly endless road of shame, only this time alone.

Between them, Charlotte and Carter could only sketch the barest outline of a suspect. Caucasian, male. To obscure his face, he wore the kind of white germ mask that pinches shut over the bridge of the nose. Despite the prints on the knife handle, Carter thinks he wore latex gloves. The whole time he spent in the house, the man never uttered a word.

Around nine I reach Lafayette and decide to give Bascombe a call.

"You wanna tell me what you're doing in Louisiana in the first place?"

"No," I say, but I tell him anyway, starting with my trip to Huntsville. The deeper I get into the story, the quieter his breathing grows, to the point that I have to take it on faith that he's still at the other end of the line. "Lieutenant?"

"You're aware that Eugene Fontenot is under investigation, right? What am I saying, of course you are. You were sitting right there in the same briefing as me. I'm glad you don't let details like that prevent you from doing whatever you want and going wherever you want."

"The lead about Fauk is solid." Even I'm not convinced by the tone of my voice.

"Good work," he says. "Meanwhile, you wanna explain why the perp in your open homicide is making house calls?"

"I wish I knew. Either he expected to find me there or—"

"He wanted to send a message."

"Like they say in the action movies, this time it's personal. Maybe Fauk wasn't happy with my prison visit. Maybe he found out and sent an errand boy to my place."

"Do you really believe that?"

"I don't know. I want Bridger to compare the knife to the one used on Simone Walker."

"Sure," he says. "Let's alienate Dr. Green for no good reason."

"I'll give you one. She tipped Lauterbach off about the supposed connection between his case and mine. That right there is enough for me."

He thinks it over. "I'll make the call. When should I expect you?"

"Three hours or so. But I won't be coming straight to the office."

"Understood. I'm treating the attack on Charlotte as part of the Walker case, and assigning Aguilar to work it for the time being. I don't have to tell you this guy cooked his goose. He can't go after one of us without reaping the whirlwind."

"Ten-four."

The lieutenant's pep talk doesn't reassure me much, but it gets me thinking. I exit the interstate and drive around until I find a Starbucks. I raise the flap on my briefcase, withdraw the laptop, and log on to the wireless network. My email inbox is flooded with the usual junk, but at the bottom of the list, sent at 7:00 a.m. sharp, there's a new message from Simone Walker.

> HI DETECTIVE,
>
> FOR AN OLDER WOMAN, YOUR WIFES SO HOT.
> YOU SHOULD WATCH HER THO. WHEN I DROPPED
> IN THERE WAS A YOUNGER MAN. ;-)
> I CUT HIM FOR YOU THO. SEE YOU SOON.
> LOVE, SIMONE

I read it over twice, ignoring the reaction the words provoke, then forward the email to Quincy Hanford's address, telling him to find out what he can.

A white Crime Scene Unit vehicle sits in my driveway. I park on the street and rush up the walk. Eric Castro slips through the front door, pausing in surprise.

"Detective—"

"Where is she? Inside?"

He nods wordlessly and I slip past.

She's in the living room, cradled in a wingback chair with the portable phone in hand. Based on the tail end of her sentence, probably talking to her sister Ann. She looks up, sees me.

"He's here," she says into the phone.

She rises as I move forward, opening her arms for me, pulling me close. Her body presses into me and I hold on as tight as I can, feeling her breathing, her warmth, inhaling the scent of her hair.

"Oh, Roland," she says.

When I loose my hold, she pulls back slightly, giving me a crooked smile.

"That's quite a shiner," I say, trying to make light of the swollen lid, the purple flesh around the eye.

"It's fine. It's nothing. It doesn't even hurt."

"Sure, it doesn't. You're very brave, you know that? And the guy who did this, he might as well have cut his own throat. He just signed his death warrant."

"Don't even talk like that." She pulls away. "It's not funny."

"It's not meant to be."

"If I wanted him dead, I could have done it myself."

"You're right," I say, the words coming out harsher than I intend. "Forgive and forget. When I find him, I'll tell him to mind his manners from now on."

"Roland," she says, cutting her eyes sideways.

For the first time I notice the audience. Carter slouches on the opposite chair, his gauzed forearm hanging over the side, and behind him, silhouetted in the doorway, a crime scene tech stands frozen, waiting for the action to pause before passing through the room. I motion him along, then sink onto the couch, pulling Charlotte down beside me.

"How's that arm?" I ask Carter.

He lifts the bandage for inspection. "I'll take this any day over getting shot."

"We did all right," Charlotte says, giving my hand a reassuring squeeze.

I can imagine them a few moments earlier, knowing my arrival was imminent, deciding between them to put a brave face on things. But all I can think of is my wife screaming as a knife-wielding psychopath beats down the door. I put my arm around her and remember the wounds on Simone Walker's back. He'd have done the same to Charlotte, even worse, if Carter hadn't arrived when he did. They can sit here with their awkward smiles and congratulate themselves on the outcome, and I can let out a hundred sighs of relief, telling myself everything worked out in the end. But only by the thinnest margin. If Carter had been slower, if her attacker had gotten through the door, would Charlotte have been able to shoot? Or would I have come home to find her cold and lifeless on the tile floor, another victim of the man it was my job to stop?

"Don't," she says. "I know what you're thinking, but don't."

I bury my face in her hair. "I can't help it."

"I should probably go," Carter says, rising to his feet.

Before he leaves, I shake his good hand and thank him again. "You saved her life."

"She saved mine, too."

The resentment I've built up the past couple of months, the frustration with his influence over Charlotte, ebbs away as he walks through the door. I watch him go and for the first time in a year I finally see him for what he is, just a young man willing to risk himself to do what's right. Whatever our differences are, I admire that. He'll never ossify with rust, never cut the corners. He'll never wake up across the room from his crooked doppelganger, uncertain which side of the line he's really on.

"I should probably go," I say. "Get on top of this thing."

A faint smile. "Yes, you should."

I sink back beside her, wrap my arm around her shoulder.

"There's so much to do," I say.

But I don't leave for a long time, afraid to put too much distance between us, afraid of what might happen if I'm not here. After a while she starts to tremble. And then the tears flow and I hold her tight.

"You're not staying here," Ann says. "No way."

Charlotte's sister drags her downstairs by the wrist, a hastily packed overnight bag clutched in the other hand. Within ten minutes of her arrival, she's taken charge of the situation, declaring the house unsafe and insisting Charlotte go home with her. She gives me a tongue-lashing for not having installed a security system, and I take it gladly, relieved that someone is finally putting the blame where it belongs.

"She's right," I say. "We can't take the chance that he'll come back."

"There's a police car out front. I hardly think he'd be that stupid."

Ann drops the bag near the door without releasing Charlotte's hand. "We're not arguing, sis. You're coming with me, end of discussion. Once your husband takes care of the situation, you can do what you want. Until then, I'm not letting you out of my sight."

"What about Carter and Gina?"

"What about them?" Ann says. "There's a police car out front."

I've never cared much for Ann, calling her the ugly duckling behind her back, but at this moment I could kiss her.

"Go with your sister. I'll come see you when I finish some things."

I follow them out, slipping Charlotte's overnight bag into the back. Ann guides her to the passenger seat, making sure she's settled, then closes the door. Coming around, she leans in close to me.

"You'd better not," she says.

"Better not what?"

"Come over. How do you think this guy found out where you live?"

"I don't know."

She shakes her head. "How would you do it?"

"I'd look him up, but we're unlisted."

"How *else* would you do it?" she asks. "Think about it. You work with a lot of bad people. Well, I've represented a few. It seems obvious to me."

"What does, Ann? Just spit it out."

"Did you ever think maybe he followed you? You were at the scene, your name is in all the newspaper reports, and he obviously knows how to email you. Would it be so hard to tail you around?"

I smile. "You think I wouldn't notice?"

"I think there's plenty you don't notice," she says. "So indulge me, all right? Let me take care of my sister and you focus on your case."

They pull out onto the street and Charlotte lifts her fingers in a hesitant wave. As the car rolls away I feel a bond drawing taut and, as her figure behind the glass grows small, finally snapping. It's terrible, her going away, but somehow right that she should be taken from me. I turn back toward the house, cold and deliberate, a dark intention forming at the back of my mind, a cancerous notion metastasizing, infiltrating blood and bone.

Hanford calls my cell, telling me his baited hook is ready to send. "You'll be able to find him with this?"

He laughs, unable to contain his excitement. "I think so. All he has to do is run the Mail software. When our message hits the preview screen, we'll get a location—it might be precise, it might be vague. But we'll also get a picture. He'll basically send us his identity."

"What about the message I sent earlier? Can you tell where it came from?"

"He switched up on us. The location was different, and I'm working on the provider to see if I can pinpoint it. He might have just used an open network. A coffee shop Wi-Fi signal, maybe even somebody's house. He could pull up to the curb just like he did with Dr. Hill."

"Couldn't he do that again, with our email?"

"Sure," he says. "The difference is, we'll see his face. Also, he'll be opening the software to compose a message. In the time it takes him to do that, we might be able to get there. You never know."

"So let's send our message and see what happens."

CHAPTER 20

Bridger greets me with an unaccustomed smile, approaching through the lab in a white coat, eyes sparkling behind his rimless glasses. He has one hand behind his back.

"That's not a knife," he says, channeling Crocodile Dundee. "*That's* a knife."

He brings the hidden hand around to reveal a bowie knife bagged in plastic. I take the knife, hold it up to the light, and whistle. "It's not what I expected."

"That is not a cheap throwaway, March. It's more like a trophy. The scales are made of stag, and the blade's all wavy like that because it's Damascus steel. And take a look at this . . ." He motions for the knife and points to a small line of text stamped into the blade near the hilt. "Eric Castro pointed that out when he brought the knife over."

I squint at the stamping.

It reads: 29 OF 50.

"A limited edition," he says. "Tell me that's not going to be easy to trace."

"If I get a hit on those prints, it'll save me the trouble. But yeah, I'm thinking it shouldn't be too hard." I can feel my mouth twisting into an involuntary smile. "He pretty much handed himself over on a silver platter."

"I would assume this is his ritual weapon. As much care as he took to clean up the Simone Walker scene, I'm surprised he would hold on to the knife."

"*Is* it the knife? You're sure about that?"

"If you'll follow me," he says, heading back into the depths of the lab. We pause before a pair of microscopes and a bank of sterile-looking computer screens.

"The blade had been wiped down, but the crime lab pulled apart the handle and scraped some dried blood. They sent some results over, which I've just been verifying."

With Bridger the answers never come easily. He considers these encounters to be teachable moments, forcing me to peer through microscopes and examine inscrutable charts on a variety of monitors, lecturing me all the while on blood type, blood cells, and the intricacies of nuclear and mitochondrial DNA. I nod my way through, waiting for the plain English explanation of his findings.

"You already know the prints on the handle aren't Simone Walker's," he says.

"I *didn't* know that. But why would they be?"

He ignores the question. "Do you talk to your crime lab people at all? I got the information from them."

"Why would the prints on the knife belong to the victim?"

"They wouldn't ordinarily," he says. "But somebody in your fingerprint division floated the theory that the fingerprints belonged to a woman—something about the ridge density. So they were checked against Walker's prints and didn't match. You don't know about this?"

"The man we took that knife from was trying to murder my wife with it. Pardon me for being a little preoccupied. Anyway, in case you haven't heard, our fingerprint detail is under a cloud at the moment."

"Maybe that's why they're turning this stuff around so fast. Trying to look efficient."

An impatient nod. "Yes, yes, yes. Now, what about blood, Alan?"

"Look for yourself," he says, pointing to a white-cased microscope with two black viewers jutting out at me.

"I already did. Can you please tell me?"

He chuckles. "The state of science education in this country—"

"I'm begging you."

"Please don't beg, March. Here's the deal. We have blood from two separate sources. Based on the viscosity, I'm guessing one is older and the other is fresh . . . as recent as a day or two. The older sample matches Simone Walker, so in my opinion—and this is backed up by your own people—this *is* the weapon used in her murder."

"For certain?" I clench my fist and all but pump it in the air.

"I've double-checked Dr. Green's measurements and they're consistent with this blade. She did a great job on those estimations, by the way. I couldn't have given you better."

"So this is absolutely the murder weapon?"

"In my opinion, yes."

"And what about the fresher sample? If it belongs to the killer—"

He shakes his head. "The second sample is from a woman, too. Your DNA section ran it through CODIS and came back with nothing, so whoever she is, she's not in the database."

"Maybe the prints are hers, then." I can hear the disappointment in my own voice. A couple of days ago, finding a woman's blood on the knife and being told that the ridge density of the prints might suggest a female, my mind would have raced to Joy Hill. But Carter didn't wrestle the knife away from a fifty-something woman.

"You'll have to wait and see. In the meantime, I would start checking on where the knife came from. If it's some kind of custom piece, there are bound to be records of who bought it."

"Thanks," I say. "I'll get right on that."

★

Apart from the number, the only word on the blade is SCHARF. An Internet search from Bridger's desk pulls up a custom knife maker in California named Wade Scharf. The photos on his site look vaguely reminiscent of the murder weapon, but I can't find any exact matches. I dial the phone number on his contact page and reach his wife. She informs me in a creaky elderly voice that Wade is out in the shop. After I identify myself, she volunteers to fetch him.

"A homicide?" he asks, like he's unfamiliar with the term.

I describe the knife and answer a couple of his follow-ups.

"That sounds like one of my Old School Bowies. Does it have a coffin handle?"

"You're gonna have to tell me what that is."

"If you hold it with the point down, the handle swells toward the top and has diagonal steps on either side, like a coffin from the eighteen hundreds."

"Then yes, I think it does."

"All right. Let me get my paperwork." Over the line I can hear him opening and closing metal filing cabinets, digging through papers. "That was a limited edition I did four or five years ago. Some of them were snapped up as preorders and some went to dealers. There's a dealer in Houston I do a lot of business with, and I'm betting your knife is one of those." He hums to himself while scanning a list, rattling names off under his breath. "Yep, I'm right. The dealer's name is Sam Dearborn. Here's his number if you've got a pen handy."

I write Dearborn's number down and thank Scharf for his help.

"This doesn't sit too well with me," he says. "People collect my work, you know. The prices are sky high. I'd bet most of my blades are never used at all—certainly not for something like this."

"There's a first time for everything," I say.

Getting in touch with Sam Dearborn is a little harder. The number rings to a voicemail box informing me business hours end at five. I leave a message for him to call me back. Searching the computer again, I find Dearborn's website, which also lists a mobile number. I dial and wait.

"Dearborn Gun and Blade," he says.

I explain who I am and tell him Scharf pointed me in his direction. "You received some knives from a limited edition he did, some coffin-handled Old School Bowies. I'm trying to find out who bought number twenty-nine."

"I'm not sure I can help you with that."

"This is a murder investigation, Mr. Dearborn."

"Don't get me wrong. I *want* to help. But if I remember correctly, I had five of those and sold them at gun and knife shows. I move a lot of product through my booth that way. If they paid with a credit card, I might have a record, but a lot of guys will pay in cash. Not to mention, collectibles trade hands. I know a lot of people liquidating collections in this economy, so there's no guarantee the person I sold it to is who you're looking for. In fact, I'd go out on a limb and say he's not. My customers are a pretty select group."

"Can you check your records and get back to me? This is an urgent request."

"Of course," he says. "It might not be until tomorrow. I'm already gone for the day."

"Maybe you could go back to the office and take care of this? Time is of the essence."

He lets out a huff of consternation. "I *guess* so," he says. "Should I call you on this number?"

"That would be fine."

After driving back from the medical examiner's office, I zone out in my cubicle for a few minutes, eyes closed, resting my head in my hands. Then I call Charlotte again and make sure she's all right. She says she is, but adds that what happened is just beginning to sink in.

"I don't think I'll be able to sleep tonight."

"Don't even say that word. Sleep. I'm gonna come see you later. Tell Ann not to worry—I'll make sure I don't have a tail."

We laugh together, and then Bascombe comes up behind me.

"Gotta go," I tell her.

It takes ten minutes to bring the lieutenant up to speed on the case, and another ten to relate the highlights of my New Orleans trip. He's intrigued by the story Bourgeois told about the envelopes, annoyed that we conducted the interview while a drugged prostitute was tied up and bleeding down the hall, and uninterested in Gene Fontenot's protestations of innocence in the Fauk confession. I leave out his admission of guilt in the recent case.

"So what are you doing now?"

"Waiting," I say. "The crime lab's supposed to be getting back to me on the prints, and I've got the knife dealer checking his receipts from the gun shows."

"Have you briefed Aguilar?"

"I was just about to."

"Well, do it."

When I poke my head over his cubicle wall, there's no sign of Aguilar, but the photos from my house, this morning's crime scene, are spread in a semicircle. The forced back door, the splintered bathroom entry, washed-out flash photography of Carter's injuries, and of the bruising on Charlotte's face. The knife. I pull the last one from the stack. If Carter was right about the man wearing gloves, then the prints on the handle probably belong to someone else. If the expert's speculation is right, they're bound to be from the same woman whose dried blood was under the grip scales. The coffin handle. I turn the photo so that the point aims down. The stag handles are bone-colored with rough furrows of brown. The prints would have come from the smooth parts on either side of the exposed tang.

"Detective."

I turn to find Eric Castro in the cubicle entrance, a report clutched in both hands like he's afraid of it getting away.

"You have the fingerprint results?"

He nods. "The criminal databases came back with nothing."

"Figures." I rub my eyes with the heel of my palm, suddenly tired.

"But . . ." he says. "When we ran them against the immigration database, we got a hit."

"Give me that."

I snatch the report away, scanning the page while Castro peers over my shoulder. The original check went through HPD to the Sheriff's Department and from there to DPS. I flip the page and find the immigration results, complete with Green Card photos of a fair-skinned, blue-eyed blonde in her twenties and a full set of prints.

"The name, the name—"

Castro points to a line near the top, then smiles. "How you're supposed to pronounce that, I don't know."

I say the words out loud: "*Agnieszka Oliszewski.*"

The Polish grad student who lived with Joy Hill, the one who had a relationship with Dr. Hill's husband. What were her prints doing on the handle of the knife? What was her blood doing under the scales?

Aguilar stands on one side of the red door, hand on the butt of his pistol, and I take the other. My second knock goes unanswered, so I try the bell. The chime sounds inside. I listen for movement, my ear close to the door.

"Police," I say, pounding a third time.

The house is on Sheridan a block off of W. Holcombe, the opposite side of Kirby from where Dr. Hill lives. Quaint single-family homes, mostly postwar construction evoking classic styles, with the occasional duplex conversion. Agnieszka Oliszewski's name is on the lease for the bottom unit of the two-story duplex, with the top unit still for rent. The original brick is clotted with recent white paint, the fake shutters black as oil. In the yard, a Realtor's clear plastic display box contains a few damp flyers with interior photos and a monthly rent that suggests Oliszewski's financial situation improved after she left Hill's house.

I bend down, conscious of a twinge in my leg, and take a peek through the brass mail slot. Some bills and a couple of red Netflix envelopes lie in a pile on the carpet.

"Maybe she's not home," I say.

We exchange a look.

We take the stairs up to the vacant unit and give the door a try, despite the key box hanging from the knob. This time Aguilar stoops down, pushing the mail slot open with his finger. He shakes his head.

"Empty," he says. "No furniture or nothing."

"Let's go around back."

Before we left downtown, Aguilar looked up the address online, pulling up a Google satellite map of the property. Scouting the lay of the land. Some kind of outbuilding—a shed, a one-car garage—screened the yard on one side, leaving just a sliver of green grass before the neighbor's fence encroached. We follow the driveway around, a melting glacier of concrete chips overrun by a sea of grass and weeds. The outbuilding, a wood-framed single stall garage, leans slightly with a mold-black line of water damage reaching about a foot high. I peer through the grimy glass window and see nothing but grease stains on the slab and a jumble of rusted rakes and shovels in one corner.

"Check this out," Aguilar says.

Just inside the fence that separates the driveway and the yard, a pale blue Vespa scooter rests on its kickstand, the tan leather seat speckled with flecks of dried mud. Pinned under the front tire, a blue tarp meant to protect the machine from weather twists gently across the grass.

I reach over the fence to unlatch the gate.

"What's that sound?" I ask.

A low, rumbling murmur, like a distant engine or maybe a washing machine cycle.

Following the noise, we move over the lawn toward a screened porch where the second level overhangs the rear entrance. A flimsy old structure of wood frame and wire mesh. The screen door springs squeak softly as I pull. Inside, situated against the exterior wall of the house, there's a teak-slatted octagonal hot tub. The cover rests slightly askew. I can hear the water bubbling like a slow boil.

Without a word we step to either side of the tub. On my signal, Aguilar dons a pair of gloves and draws the cover open another foot or two.

I get my first hint of the smell. The wet heat on my face.

The water churns dark and polluted, and a body bobs toward me, the skin veiny and translucent but pinkish purple, a lock of yellow-white hair swirling from the head.

A freckled shoulder, the spinal ridge, and the same half-crescent punctures I remember from Simone Walker's corpse.

I step back as the body rolls in the water.

Her mouth is set in a snarl of pain, the glassy blue eyes glistening. Between her breasts, the sawing, twisting gouge where the bowie knife entered.

Portable lights illuminate the yard as the Crime Scene Unit conducts its grim inventory, a fingertip search of the surrounding area, a catalog of every inch from the birdbath near the back fence to the sun-faded gnome lying facedown in one of the flower beds. The investigators from the ME's office have given the okay for Agnieszka Oliszewski's body to be removed, leaving the stretcher team to figure out how best to do it. Meanwhile two fatigue-clad techs from the HPD crime lab prepare for the task of draining the hot tub. Every ounce of water must be sifted for evidence and the tub's inner walls scrubbed. A still photographer is on hand to snap pictures as needed. A separate videographer gets everything on tape.

With no local politics to distract him, Hedges arrives on scene for a briefing. I lead him down the driveway to the back fence for a look at the scene, then around to the red door in front for a walk through the apartment.

"The lack of blood around the hot tub suggests she wasn't killed there," I say.

The floorboards creak under our weight. We pause at the threshold of Oliszewski's bedroom just as the lights are being switched off. A technician with a black light moves carefully around the bed, revealing a freshly glowing cast-off pattern with every wave of the hand.

"He *butchered* her," Hedges says under his breath.

"When we checked in here, the mattress had bloodstains on it, but the sheets had been stripped off and he washed down the walls. I think he used the sheets to carry her body out back, dumped her in the hot tub, then pulled them out."

"Have you found them?"

I shake my head. "He cleaned up after himself at the Walker scene, too."

"Any signs of forced entry?"

"He used her key. When she arrived home, she pulled her scooter through the gate but never got a chance to put the tarp over it. I think he approached her then. There are marks on her neck that look like some kind of cord or wire. If he came up behind her and choked her out, he could've dragged to the door and let himself inside."

"Did anyone see anything?"

"I canvassed the block myself, and Aguilar went a block over to check the residents with backyards fronting the property. Nobody saw the attack, but one of the neighbors across the street remembers her leaving the house around noon yesterday. We don't know when she came back, so that's a window of about twenty-nine hours from the last sighting to the time we discovered her. She was in the water for at least twelve hours, probably longer—though I can't get anyone to confirm that at this point—so my guess is, he attacked her early yesterday evening and was out of here by midnight."

"Midnight," he repeats.

"He broke into my place at four thirty in the morning, and I doubt he took that chance without scouting around first."

"Here's what I don't understand," he says, leading me back down the hall into Oliszewski's tastefully decorated living room. "This should have satisfied him, right? He gets his thrill from murdering the girl. So when he's finished, why go to your place at all? What would prompt him to do something like that? Did something go wrong here to set him off?"

"That's a good question," I say. "I don't know."

"See if you can find out." He pats me on the shoulder. "I take it Charlotte's doing all right? I feel bad keeping you on this when you should be with your wife."

"She might feel safer if I catch the guy."

"Sure," he says, heading for the exit.

For a moment there, the captain seemed like himself again. At the door, though, he pauses to straighten his tie, and I can see the lights of news cameras out on the street. Hedges makes a beeline for them.

Still, he raised a valid point. Why wasn't killing one woman enough? What drove him to kick down my door just a few hours later?

Bascombe comes through the entrance, glancing over his shoulder in the captain's direction. He frowns at the furniture, symmetrically arranged around the perimeter of an ivory rug, then draws close to me with a conspiratorial nod.

"He's really pushing for that promotion," I say.

"Seems like. Are we close on this thing or what?"

I bring him up to speed as quickly as possible, showing him the bedroom just as the lights are flipped back on. We walk as far as the back door, where Bascombe watches the coroner's people withdrawing the nude body from the now-tranquil water, then return to where we started. In one corner of the living room, a headless dress form stands, half draped in fabric. There are more swatches on the worktable, next to a white sewing machine. From the looks of it, Oliszewski wasn't just working in the dress shop for kicks. She had ambitions in that direction, ambitions that now will never be realized.

"The captain's right," Bascombe says. "It doesn't make a lot of sense him leaving here and heading to your place."

"He did, though. The blood on the knife recovered in my bedroom is what led us here in the first place."

"The question is, why?"

Eric Castro enters from the bedroom, though I hadn't noticed him there before. He holds an evidence envelope in one hand.

"Take a look at this," he says.

Bascombe intercepts the bag, inspecting the contents, then hands it to me.

"Maybe *that's* what provoked him."

Inside the bag, one of my business cards rests, a slight crease running down the center. A splash of dried blood hides part of my name. I flip it over and see my mobile number written in ballpoint ink.

"Where did you find this?" I ask Castro.

"It was on her nightstand. Tucked under the base of the lamp."

"When did you give it to her?" Bascombe asks.

"I didn't."

I look at the card again.

"But I think I might know who did."

PART 3

LET JUSTICE
ROLL DOWN

TUESDAY, DECEMBER 15 – SUNDAY, DECEMBER 20

We may bust you. But we won't judge you.

—MARTIN AMIS, *NIGHT TRAIN*

CHAPTER 21

TUESDAY, DECEMBER 15 — 8:30 A.M.

Early morning briefing. On side-by-side whiteboards, a projection screen, and a jumble of printed and handwritten pages, everything we know about Agnieszka Oliszewski spreads before me. All the detectives present at last night's scene sit bleary-eyed around the table, joined by a couple of CSU supervisors and Quincy Hanford, who summarizes in far too much detail the contents of Oliszewski's hard drive. Since the computer was a heavy desktop model, our killer decided to leave it—either that, or the discovery of my business card interrupted his flow.

"Let's move on," Bascombe says, presiding from the front of the room. "Unless you have anything tangible?"

Hanford starts distributing some stapled sheets. "I output the contacts on her computer so we'd have a starting point for the interviews."

"Excellent." He turns to me. "Now, what about the timeline?"

"We've painstakingly reconstructed her movements over the past forty-eight hours. She clocked out of the Times Boulevard boutique where she works at about six on Saturday, went for drinks with co-workers, went home. She left the next day around noon—a neighbor witnessed this—and a couple of hours later visited Dr. Joy Hill."

"Really?" Bascombe says.

I nod. "Dr. Hill is coming in to give a statement."

"Okay. Can you get Bridger on the line for a preliminary report?"

I punch some buttons on the speakerphone. Bridger must have been expecting us. When he picks up, he's ready to go.

"Just as in Simone Walker's case," he says, "the fatal blow came first—a single stab wound to the heart—followed by the six-puncture semicircular mutilations that cover her torso. The knife recovered at Detective March's house appears to be the murder weapon. That's no surprise, considering her blood and prints were on it."

Bascombe leans over the speakerphone, resting one big hand on either side. "Her prints on the handle . . . what do you make of that?"

"Maybe she got the knife away from him at some point."

I shake my head. I've been thinking about the question for hours, and there's only one thing that makes sense to me.

"At the Walker scene, he came up behind her, held his hand over her mouth, and brought the knife down. With Oliszewski he choked her out first. So he could have reenacted the same process, only this time he puts the knife in her hand and guides it in. So she's the one stabbing herself and not him."

"Could be," Bridger says. "You'll need a psychiatrist to comment on the significance of that."

Bascombe rolls his eyes. "What we need is a buyer's name on that knife."

"I've got another call in to Sam Dearborn, the dealer. He was supposed to get back to me yesterday. I guess I'll have to pay him a visit."

As the briefing breaks up, Jerry Lorenz pokes his head in. He scans the room, waiting for a few departing detectives to pass through the door. He raises his eyebrows at me.

"That professor showed up," he says. "I stuck her in Interview Two."

"Dr. Hill?" Bascombe asks. "Did you really have to drag her down here?"

"I got tired of making house calls. Since the election's over, I figured I could bring her in. Did I do wrong?"

He gives me a hard look, then dismisses me with a jerk of the head.

"Can I smoke in here?"

The gravelly voice has lost all its charm. Dr. Joy Hill slouches in her chair, an elbow hitched on the seat back, one leg dangling over the other. She waves a red pack of Dunhills at me. I shake my head. She rolls her eyes—*what is the world coming to?*—and tucks the cigarettes back into her purse.

"When I heard about Agnieszka, I was devastated."

"Really?"

"Why wouldn't I be?"

"I thought you'd be thrilled. Agnieszka seduced your husband, after all."

"Detective," she laughs. "*Anyone* could have managed that. And I already told you there were no hard feelings. If there had been, she wouldn't have come to me Sunday."

"Why did she visit you?"

"She'd gone to lunch with some girlfriends, and one of them brought up Simone's death. It was the first she'd heard, and the news really shook her up. Over the phone she started asking me all sorts of questions—what had happened, what did the police think—and thanks to your unannounced visit that morning, I told her you probably suspected me. That confused her and I said, 'Look, just come over and we'll talk.' So she did."

"How long was she there?"

"Not long. Ten or fifteen minutes, tops. The conversation was awkward. Agnieszka seemed preoccupied, so she'd ask questions, but when I answered it was like she wasn't listening. I told her about the man who said Simone was pregnant with his child, thinking that would get her attention. All she did was blink."

"Maybe she knew about that already."

She shakes her head. "I didn't get the impression they'd kept in touch. Agnieszka knew Simone casually, and recommended her when I was looking for a tenant. But they weren't girlfriends or anything."

"But she seemed very upset about Simone's death?"

Another nod. "She pushed past me and went out to the pool. She knelt by the edge of the water. She started to cry. I decided to leave her alone for a while, thinking she just needed to say her goodbyes. But her mood passed pretty quick. When I poked my head out, she was already on the phone."

"Did you hear what was said?"

"Not much." She lifts her head slightly, like she's hearing the conversation now. " 'I should have stayed.' She said that. And then she was quiet awhile, listening. She said 'I was a fool to believe that,' or maybe 'It was foolish to believe that.' With her accent it's hard to tell sometimes."

"I assume you don't know who she was talking to."

"No idea," she says. "You'll just have to trace the call."

After thanking Dr. Hill for her cooperation and escorting her out, I walk a billing statement from Agnieszka's phone down to the same non-sworn officer who helped me with Simone's phone records, asking her to find out who the girl called on Saturday afternoon.

"Leave it with me," she says, adding my scrap of paper to the growing pile beside her keyboard. "I'll get to it ASAP."

From the opposite side of a barred glass door, Sam Dearborn of Dearborn Gun and Blade inspects my badge a bit too long to be polite, then cranks the key, unbolting the lock with a dull *thunk*. Bells chime overhead as I enter. He's a portly black-haired man with a goatee and dark hair on his forearms, who wears a gold Rolex, a gold neck chain, and a thin copper bracelet around his wrist. He smells of hair spray and musky cologne.

"You didn't call me back, so here I am."

"Come on in," he says, beckoning me deeper into his shop. "You want some coffee? I was just making a pot."

"What I want is the name of your buyer."

"Ah." He raises a finger, then goes around a glass counter where a stack of papers and receipts is spread out. "Hold on just a second and I'll find what you need. I was just looking."

"You said you'd get this for me last night."

"Yeah," he says, running a thick finger down a column of figures without looking up. "Sorry about that. I had the best of intentions, but something came up. I wasn't in the office when you called."

I'm tempted to let him have it, but I'd rather save the energy. The quicker I can get a name, the quicker I can get out of here.

"Just look it up, okay?"

Through the back office door I can hear a coffee machine burbling, the smell wafting through the air. The small shop reminds me of my uncle's, the same glass cases, the same racks along the back walls for long arms. But instead of blued, workmanlike weapons—tools of metal and wood—Dearborn presides over an Aladdin's Cave of collectibles: ornate flame-bladed knives with exotic handles, even a few impractical-looking swords, along with high-end custom handguns and coveted black tactical rifles. There are no price tags on display, but I imagine most anything in the shop would be too expensive for actual use. He told me as much over the phone. His clientele collects weapons; they don't use them.

"Yep," Dearborn says, tapping his finger on the glass. "I was afraid of this."

"Of what?" I ask. "Was it a cash transaction?"

"That's not it." He shakes his head thoughtfully, then hands me a credit card slip. "The knife you're looking for was part of a lot I sold to a local collector. I know for a fact he's been divesting himself of some nice pieces, because I bought some things off him just last month."

I study the receipt. The customer's name is printed DAVID R. BAYARD, with an address I recognize as a downtown office building.

"Tell me about this guy," I say.

"Dave's some kind of oil consultant. I don't know exactly what he does, but he travels a lot to Africa and Scandinavia, places like that.

Brings back some interesting stuff, too. I've been doing business with him maybe ten years. He collects blades. I've tried to get him into firearms, but he's not interested."

"You said he's been selling things?"

"I bought a couple off him for less than he paid, including a couple of Scharfs—but not the one you're looking for. And I know for a fact he gave some things to another dealer on consignment for sale on the Internet. I can give you that guy's card." He goes into the back office and returns with a pair of cards, one for Bayard and another for the consignment seller. "You sure you don't want any coffee?"

"I'll be in touch if I need anything else. And next time a homicide detective asks for a favor, don't let anything distract you."

"My apologies," he says. "If it makes any difference, there was a woman involved."

"It doesn't." The door jingles as I exit.

Outside, I can still smell Dearborn's cologne on my clothes.

From a distance, the skyscrapers of downtown Houston look like so many glass needles aimed at the clouds. Reflecting the sky above and one another, they seem weightless and ethereal. Down on the street, though, walking the long stretch of sidewalk from the brainchild of one famous architect to the next, passing one, two, three abstract sculptures nestled in among the corporate logos, I feel like an ant in a redwood forest, awed by the imbalance of scale.

I badge my way through security in the lobby of Bayard's building, riding a mirrored elevator up to the twenty-third floor to the offices of something called ENERGY SOLUTIONS GROUP. Waiting in the lobby for Bayard, I browse through the corporate literature, learning that whatever these people do—the particulars are vague—they do it synergistically and on a global scale, innovating on behalf of a bright tomorrow.

A smartly dressed and unattractive woman in her early thirties clicks across the glossy floor, showing off chalk stripes and a lot of eye shadow. She blinks her very white, very black-rimmed eyes at me several times, like maybe I'll disappear if she keeps it up.

"You're here to see David?" she says finally. "I'm his personal assistant."

I rise from my chair and introduce myself.

"I'm afraid he's not in the office."

"Where can I reach him, then?"

"I don't know that you can."

Behind her, a flax-haired middle-aged man in shirt-sleeves walks up, adjusting his metal-framed glasses like they haven't refocused from whatever fine print he was reading a few moments before. His button-down collar bulges out at the sides. He introduces himself as ESG's corporate attorney.

"I already told this gentleman that Mr. Bayard isn't here," the assistant says.

"Detective, you have to understand—"

"If Bayard isn't here," I say, "then where can I find him?"

He clears his throat. "I'm afraid Dave is still in Nigeria. Lagos."

"Since when?"

"Since . . ." His eyes search the ceiling. "Last week. Monday the seventh."

The Monday after Simone's murder.

"And how do you get in touch with him?" I ask.

"We don't. Excuse me, Detective, but . . . Could you come into my office please?"

The lawyer guides me down a hallway into a small room with a breathtaking view of the opposite skyscraper, inviting me to sit in one of his guest chairs. He pulls the door shut behind us. There's a low hum in the room, probably ventilation or electricity, but gazing over the cityscape, the sound reinforces the feeling of flight.

We sit across from each other. He studies the lines in his palm.

"The thing is," he says, "I'm afraid that ESG recently ended its relationship with Dave. This hasn't been made public yet, which is why your questions are a bit awkward for us. We're not intentionally giving you the runaround, it's just—"

"I need to speak to Mr. Bayard in connection with a murder investigation."

A pause. "I can appreciate that. Unfortunately, I'm not sure we can be of much help. We haven't been in touch with Dave for a number of days, not since the termination."

"So let me get this straight. The man's somewhere in Africa—"

"Lagos," he says. "That's in Nigeria."

"You said that already." Something clicks in my mind. He's not the first person to mention Nigeria to me. "He's in Africa," I say, "and that's when you decide to fire him?"

"To be frank, I'm not sure how much latitude I have in discussing the matter. I think I can say that this situation goes back several months. There was a reorganization, which Dave chose to interpret as a demotion. There may have been some financial trouble at home."

"Not surprising these days," I say. "So you canned him for being unhappy?"

"We *canned* him for moonlighting on a side venture with one of ESG's competitors. The Nigeria trip was planned months in advance, and the feeling was that it might be best to take action while he was in the field. There were security concerns—and that's as much as I can say about the matter."

"Security as in the threat of violence?"

"No, no," he says. "Nothing like that. But Dave had access to a great deal of sensitive information. We needed to ensure he couldn't destroy anything. Or share it."

"Had there been any violence in the past?" I ask. "The man does collect weapons, you know that?"

His eyes narrow. "I wasn't aware of that. But no, there's never been anything like that with Dave. He's very professional, very good at what he does. But he's also a somewhat aggressive, somewhat unlikeable sort. His role here had evolved into too much of a front office position, whereas Dave's more of an in-the-field type."

If Bayard really is in Nigeria, the odds of him using his prized collectible bowie knife in an attempted double event over the weekend seem remote. But I still need to talk to the man. And I need to recollect why Nigeria is so fresh on my brain.

"Is there a number in Lagos where he can be reached?"

The lawyer reaches for the phone. Stops. "Can I be honest with you? Dave might still be in Nigeria, and he might have come home. We really have no way of knowing. For our kind of work, Lagos is pretty much the center of Africa. It's very cosmopolitan and there are plenty of . . . opportunities. All I can tell you for certain is that the return ticket has him coming back next week, and that hasn't been changed. Now, that doesn't mean he *hasn't* left Lagos. He may have worked something out with a competitor; he may have slunk home with his tail between his legs. He could be anywhere."

"Be that as it may, I have to speak to the man. How can I contact him?"

"Hold on." He picks up the phone and dials an internal extension, presumably the tight-lipped secretary's. After a little back and forth, he writes something down on a pad and slides it across the desk.

"That's Dave's home address and phone. You can speak to his wife, and maybe she'll know how to contact him. Then again, maybe not. My understanding is that it's a troubled marriage."

"*This* is his wife?" I say. "*This* is his address?"

Now I remember.

"Why? Is there something strange about that?"

The name he's written on the pad reads KIM BAYARD. The address is around the corner from Dr. Joy Hill's house in West U. The yards of the two houses are separated only by the privacy wall. When I did the neighborhood canvass, I spoke to this woman. It was she who sent me down the street to Emmet Mainz's house.

And now her husband, who is either in Nigeria or not, turns out to be the purchaser of the knife used to kill both Simone Walker and Agnieszka Oliszewski? Which means the killer I've been looking for could be the next-door neighbor.

CHAPTER 22

TUESDAY, DECEMBER 15 – 3:00 P.M.

Before I approach Bayard's wife, before there's any possibility that he'll be tipped off to how close I am, I want to know everything about him: his background, his movements over the last two weeks, the extent and status of his knife collection.

I divide the task with Aguilar, who volunteers to camp out at Dearborn Gun and Blade until he can put together a list of local collectors and consignment sellers.

"Work your way through, and if Knife 29 changed hands, let me know."

He heads to Dearborn's shop, leaving me to phone ICE—Immigration & Customs Enforcement—with an urgent request to flag David Bayard's passport and let me know whether he's reentered the country. No doubt the information is available at the stroke of a key, but the helpful bureaucrat on the other end of the line insists on a proper request, after which he'll get back to me with the information. Once I've jumped through that hoop, I'm left to hunt and peck my way through the online databases in search of Bayard.

Dave Bayard turned fifty-two this year. He's lived in the West University house behind Dr. Hill's for nineteen years, ever since his marriage to his second wife Kim. He has a son from a previous marriage, now a student at Texas A&M. His employment with Energy Solutions Group goes back to 2000, and before that he worked for Enron. Whatever financial stresses have assailed him recently, his credit record is superb.

In the past ten years he's been arrested twice for assault. Police arrived at the house in early 2002 after a 9-1-1 call from the son. Bayard, intoxicated, had manhandled his wife, who chose not to press charges. A second incident fourteen months later ended the same way. In that report, Bayard apparently told the responding officers he was undergoing therapy related to anger issues. After that, he either cleaned up his act or his son grew tired of ratting him out. The criminal record goes silent.

Several media pieces online refer to Bayard, citations in *Offshore* and *Pipeline & Gas*, all from the late '90s, and a column-length profile in another energy sector publication that has since folded. Clicking through the links, I discover a *Chronicle* piece from a decade ago in which Bayard is quoted on the subject of Donald Fauk's murder conviction.

This is unthinkable, he says. *For a generation of mavericks who looked up to Donald as an icon, his fall from grace comes as a real blow.*

I stare at the words on the screen.

Simone Walker's killer used a knife sold to Bayard. Her killer also arranged the scene to bear an uncanny resemblance to Nicole Fauk's. And now Bayard turns out to have regarded Donald Fauk as an icon? This has to be the man I'm after.

"Detective?"

I glance over my shoulder at the beaming smile of my non-sworn researcher, who clutches a sheaf of paper in her red-nailed hand.

"Your phone records," she says, handing them over. "The one I highlighted is the call you're after. It's a Dallas number."

"Whose?"

"Jack Hill." She smiles wider. "That's Dr. Joy Hill's ex-husband."

I snatch the phone handset and start dialing the number. As it rings, I mouth the word *thanks*. She gazes down on me with satisfaction, then floats away.

"Angie's dead? Are you being serious?"

"I'm sorry to break the news like this, Mr. Hill."

"And you're investigating . . ." He sounds disoriented, baffled. "I'm gonna need a second to process this. She was so . . . young."

"When I spoke to your wife—excuse me, your ex-wife—she said Agnieszka made a phone call while she was at the site of Simone's murder. According to the phone records, she called you. Could you tell me what that conversation was about, Mr. Hill?"

"I . . . You'll have to forgive me. I can't, I can't quite get my head around it. She's gone? What happened exactly? Was it the same person who killed the new girl?"

"Sir, if you'll please answer my question. Tell me about your phone call with Agnieszka."

"All right," he says. "If it was Joy that put you in the picture, then I assume you're aware that I had a special relationship with Angie. That didn't last long. You sound like an older fella, so maybe you can relate when I tell you . . . a man can hardly say no when someone so young, so breathtaking wants to be with him. But I could tell what she was looking for was a daddy, not a boyfriend, and if I'd wanted to be a daddy, well . . . you see what I mean."

"So the affair was brief, but you kept in touch?"

"Oh, sure. Angie needed a lot of help sorting her life out. The immigration stuff, getting on her feet. She wanted to be a clothing designer, and I helped her out with that, too. Financially. She reminded me a lot of Joy, to be honest. Very sophisticated as far as academic matters go, but without much skill for real life. Women like that—it's almost like for their minds to keep growing, their hearts have to remain fourteen forever."

"Why did she call you Sunday? As far as I can tell, you're the last person to speak to her alive."

I hold back the fact that his ex-wife overheard part of the conversation. If he attributes similar words to Oliszewski, then I'll have independent confirmation. If he doesn't, I'll know how to press him.

"Someone told her about the new girl getting herself killed, so Angie was in a state. She was a little angry with me, because there'd been some trouble back when we were both living in the house. The way I'd settled things didn't sit right with her. Bad as it sounds, Angie held me a bit responsible."

"Why would she do that?"

"Angie felt . . ." A sigh, like the air being let out of a balloon. "She believed she was being watched. When I put in that pool, all I was shooting for was to increase the property value. Joy doesn't swim and frankly my only use for it was to dress up the backyard for when we were entertaining. Angie, though, she lived out there. Her family back in Poland wasn't well off, and to her a swimming pool was decadent luxury. She was convinced one of the neighbors was peeping on her."

The hair on the back of my neck goes electric.

"I figured she was exaggerating. Maybe she'd seen somebody through the fence and drawn the wrong conclusion, movement in a window or whatever. If you've seen the yard—of course you have—it's pretty private. But she insisted somebody was watching her from an attic window next-door."

"At which house?"

"The Bayards' house."

Bingo.

"You said she didn't like your solution. What was it?"

He chuckles. "I called a landscaper and had some new trees put in. I mean, the yard was practically a jungle as it was, so I figured it couldn't hurt."

"Did you confront Dave Bayard?"

He pauses. "No, I don't guess I did. Naturally I was aware of his issues. His boy had called the police on him before, and that wife of his had the brittle smile of an abused woman. She made an effort to keep it a secret, though. Out of fear, pride, whatever. To be honest with you,

I didn't relish the thought of getting involved in all that. What was I gonna do, show up on the man's doorstep and accuse him?"

"You took the practical approach," I say, trying to reassure him. "If the problem is somebody looking through the window, obstruct the view and the problem's solved."

"Exactly. The maximum result with the minimum headache. Angie didn't see that, though. She wanted pistols at dawn. But once you get entangled in the lives of your neighbors, there's no going back." A grim laugh. "If I had known how soon I'd be moving out, maybe I would have played things differently. Probably not."

"So when she called you Saturday, what was she angry about? You said she blamed you."

"Maybe not blame, but . . . the trees were gone. She hadn't been back, so she didn't know. The idiot who planted them sunk 'em in the ground without taking the bags off, so the roots were all netted up and couldn't take hold. They just withered up. Joy complained about it to me—by that time I was out of there—and I told her to call the man and get them replaced. Instead I think she had them hauled off and got the money back. So Angie was mad because the trees weren't there. Her peeping Tom would've had a clear view of the new girl, she said, and that's probably why she was dead . . ." His voice trails off. "She really was angry. She'd trusted me to take care of it, and in her view I'd failed her."

"She was a fool to believe in you," I say.

"What?"

"She told you that?"

"Yes," he says. " 'I was foolish to trust you,' words to that effect." Close enough.

"The thing is," he says, "Angie's view of Dave Senior might have been colored by David Junior."

"By who?"

"The son. David Bayard Jr. The kid's pretty sharp, a professional student, and he and his dad are like fire and water. She met David in the neighborhood and he told her all kinds of stories about his dad, which just fueled her suspicions."

"What kind of stories?"

"Just stupid nonsense."

"Can you elaborate on that?"

"He claimed his father used to beat him. With his stepmother looking on. He said that his father had threatened to kill him, and that Bayard actually *had* killed someone over in Africa. Stuff like that."

"And you dismissed it?"

"Of course I dismissed it. Bayard might drink a little too much and slap his wife around—I'm saying *might*, because I have no idea—but the man had a high-powered job, two sets of golf clubs, and a pretty good recipe for throat-scorching chili. I never had kids, but I can imagine situations where you'd have to threaten a teenage boy within an inch of his life—not to mention, David Junior . . . he was just trying to get into her pants, that's all."

"He had a thing for Agnieszka?"

"Who wouldn't? If you'd met her, Detective, trust me: you'd want to impress her, too. She was the kind of girl who makes you want to come off better than you really are."

His voice goes soft, and I can tell he's picturing her in his mind, remembering what it was like to be in her presence.

"If you're serious about Dave Bayard as a suspect," he says, "you should talk to the son. The wife will keep the family secrets, but David will spill his guts just to even the score."

The way he makes the pronouncement, I can tell Jack Hill never felt the back of a father's hand, or stood by helpless as others did. No sympathy for a victim of abuse, or the impact such abuse can have on personality. If the son is dead set against the father, perhaps there are reasons other than spite. Perhaps he knows the true nature of the man who spawned him and has chosen in his own weak way to fight.

If Dave Bayard killed Simone before winging it to Africa, only to have his trip cut short by the termination, he could have returned in time to see Agnieszka out at the pool. Even though Hill never confronted him, it's a good bet he realized she had spotted him watching her. Which meant she could pass his name along to police. Is that why he had to kill her? Finding my card on her nightstand, he might have assumed she'd already done the damage. So he'd paid a rushed visit to my place, only to lose his prized knife.

There's just one problem. The emails. If Bayard was in Lagos, how did he manage to send an email from outside Dr. Hill's house? Until I hear back from ICE, I really can't say.

Candace Walker calls to tell me she's obtained a release and scheduled her daughter's funeral for tomorrow. The desolation in her voice touches me. The sound of a woman who never anticipated having to bury her own child.

"I thought you might want to be there," she says.

"I'll do my best," I say. "There have been some developments in the case, though, that could prevent me."

"Developments? I thought Jason was released."

"He's not our chief suspect, ma'am. As a matter of fact, we've pretty much ruled him out since his hospitalization."

"His what?"

I realize she hasn't heard of Jason Young's head injuries—but then, how would she? The lead investigator on her daughter's case hasn't kept her very well informed. As I stumble through an explanation, I make a mental note to follow up on Young's condition. For all I know, he could be dead. So much has happened since my Saturday night visit to the emergency room: my visits to Huntsville and New Orleans, the fresh homicide, the attack on Charlotte, the connection to David Bayard. The case has moved so quickly, so fast, despite my sense that time ebbs along slower than ever. I need to sleep.

"So he's in the hospital?" she asks, struggling to take in the news. "And you're certain he didn't hurt her?"

"The last I heard he was out of surgery, but he hasn't regained consciousness. And I'm fairly confident he was not involved in your daughter's death."

"Should I . . . should I wait, then? For the funeral? He'd want to be there."

"I'm not sure what to tell you, ma'am. I believe his injuries were quite serious. From what I gather, he might never wake up."

"All right, then. I just want to do whatever's right."

"Of course." I listen to the sound of her breathing. "Candace, tell me something. Did Simone ever say anything about being watched? Did she think someone might be observing her, a peeping Tom or something like that?"

"Not that she ever told me. Why do you ask?"

"Just wondering," I say. "I'll see you tomorrow, all right? Unless something comes up, I'll make a point of being there. And I will keep you informed if we have any developments."

Saying so makes me feel better, but Candace Walker gives no sign of being reassured by the words. She rings off with the same uncertain tone she had at the beginning. Lost in a world of the familiar where nothing makes sense anymore. I've been there. I know.

With some help from the computer I track down an address and telephone number for David Bayard Jr., who has an apartment in College Station, about ninety miles northwest of Houston. I leave a message for him to call me, giving him my cell number. If the semester at the University of Houston, where Dr. Hill teaches, is winding down, then A&M is probably in the same situation, meaning David Jr. might already be back in Houston for the Christmas break. I'd like to get his story before approaching his stepmother or his father.

Aguilar calls in from Dearborn's with an interesting tidbit.

"I got a list of everything Bayard tried to move through the consignment dealer," he says, "and the dealer told me why the collection was being liquidated. According to him, Bayard's wife put her foot down. She wanted all the knives out of the house, or she'd walk. That was his story, anyway."

"From what I'm hearing about the wife, I don't see her issuing ultimatums. Any sign of Knife 29 on the list?"

"Nope. The dealer said he'd remember one of the bowies. March, these things sell for over two grand, you realize that? For a knife?"

I thank him for the effort and promise to return the favor sometime.

Glancing at the clock, I see it's past six. Apart from my early morning field trips to Dearborn's and the offices of ESG, I've spent the better part of the day in the office. Easing out of my chair, I shake the numbness from my legs. I could clock out, head home, and go straight to bed. Eight hours of sleep would do me a world of good right now, and I've pushed the ball far enough forward that I could steal them without guilt.

The lights inside Bascombe's office are dim. The captain's door is shut, the blinds drawn.

I decide to go for it. I'll swing by Bridger's place to check on Charlotte, then get my head down for some much needed, hopefully dreamless sleep.

Grabbing my jacket off the back of the chair, I remove my side arm from the desk drawer and holster it. I head for the exit with my chin tucked, not glancing around for fear of making eye contact with anyone who could fault me for leaving. I'm safely through the door and into the hallway before I hear my name called.

"March!"

Stephen Wilcox bounds toward me from the far end of the corridor, his pale cheeks flushed, his blond eyebrows knit together, one of them cockeyed from a childhood scar. I'm half tempted to slip through the doors of an arriving elevator. The look on his face promises nothing good. I stand my ground.

"What's the matter, Stephen?"

"Can I have a word with you?" he hisses, taking my arm in his hand and pushing me across the elevator's threshold. He waits for the doors to shut. "The days of me covering for you are long over, compadre. I'm not going to lie for you anymore."

"Okay. You wanna tell me what this is about?"

"It's about Fauk, what do you think? They're gonna put it all together, March, and when they do, they'll figure out you were there . . . even if I *don't* volunteer the information. So there's no upside for you if I don't, and plenty of downside for me. I'm just warning you that it's coming. Not that I owe you even that much."

"Stephen," I say, "I have no idea what you're talking about."

He pauses. The elevator doors open. I follow him into the ground floor lobby.

"This morning," he says, "somebody slipped a shiv into Donald Fauk."

I stop in my tracks. "You're kidding."

"In the breakfast line," he says. "Fauk's standing there, and somebody comes up and starts stabbing him. Some kind of metal rod, sharp on one end and wrapped in tape. Six or seven wounds, I don't know exactly. He was rushed to the hospital. They had to re-inflate one of his lungs."

"Is he gonna make it?"

Wilcox throws his hands up. "How do I know? The point is, you went there. You go to Huntsville, and forty-eight hours later, somebody tries to rub him off the board. Do you have any idea how that looks? With your reputation?"

"Calm down," I say. "I had nothing to do with it."

"That's not how it'll look. And if I don't come forward, if they find out I knew in advance what you were doing, do you know what they'll do to me?"

I can feel a twitch in my eye, which I try to smooth with my fingertips. He really believes this. He really thinks I'm capable of putting a hit on someone, of solving the problem of Fauk's appeal by putting a word in someone's ear, setting murder in motion with the snick of a homemade shank.

"Get real," I tell him. "If you think I had anything to do with this, you're insane."

"Cause and effect," he says. "You go there, he gets stabbed."

"Pure coincidence—"

"*Coincidence!* Right. I've got to tell them, March. I have no choice. I hope you can see that. If I don't, I'll look just as bad as you."

I take a step back to let a uniformed sergeant slip by. He moves between us like a blind man, purposefully taking no notice.

"You're making a scene," I tell Wilcox. "Look, do what you have to do. I'm not going to argue with you. I went to the pen to see an informant. There were corrections personnel in the room. I've got nothing to hide."

I turn my back on him and head for the parking garage. I don't check my six until I've cleared his field of vision. Wilcox is a lost cause. He can't see past his own suspicions and I'm tired of taking responsibility for them.

Down in the lot, I toss my briefcase onto the passenger seat and slide behind the wheel. I snap my seat belt into place, then turn the key. The engine roars to life.

Fauk has been stabbed. He's in critical condition.

In my head I go over my conversation with Coleman, checking it for inconsistencies, for any line I might have uttered that could have been taken in the wrong way. Peter O'Toole asking his knights who's gonna rid him of Richard Burton's troublesome priest. But there was nothing like that. Besides, Coleman's not the kind of inmate to shank someone, and he doesn't have the juice to have it done by proxy.

I put the car in drive. I put it back in park. I sigh.

My eyes burn, the lids heavy with exhaustion. Eleven days. That's how long I've been running on this thing, pulled from one break to the next, taking aim at suspect after suspect without much more than hunches to go on until now. There was a time when I cleared cases fast, when nothing slipped past me, when I could work the endless hours without them ever catching up. Not anymore.

Twenty minutes ago all I wanted was a night off. Now I'm afraid to let up for even an hour, afraid my suspect, the first person I can link to the murders through concrete physical evidence, will slip through my fingers if I don't keep them clenched.

My phone vibrates in my pocket.

It could be Wilcox ready for another. Bascombe wanting to grill me about Fauk. Charlotte ready to leave Ann's and come home.

I check the screen. None of the above.

"Hello."

"I heard about Charlotte. I'm really sorry. And this new homicide . . . It looks like you were wrong about the serial killer."

"What do you want, Brad?"

"I think we should talk."

"About?"

"For one thing, I heard what happened today. Donald Fauk. The timing is pretty incriminating."

"Brad," I say.

"Yes?"

"Nothing," I say. "Goodbye."

The phone buzzes again. I toss it next to my briefcase on the seat.

That's another conversation I need to play back in my head: the call from Templeton when he discovered Simone Walker had been murdered at Joy Hill's house. If he'd cooked up his serial killer theory with Lauterbach long before, why lay on all the innuendo about Hill? He'd all but labeled her a suspect, and I was gullible enough to follow his lead.

He's right. We should talk. I need answers about his role in the investigation. And I want to know what was inside the fat envelopes Fauk mailed to him. He took so much trouble to avoid censorship. I need to know why.

I pick up the phone and call him back.

CHAPTER 23

Templeton chooses the rendezvous point, a window table at the Epicure Café on West Gray, a couple of blocks from his house. I arrive as a party of moviegoers push through the exit, heading a few doors down to the bright marquee of the River Oaks Theatre. Templeton waves. He licks some kind of pastry off his fingertips. As I approach, he extends his hand, which I ignore and not just for sanitary reasons. Maybe he's ready to mend fences, but I'm not.

At the table beside ours, a hirsute man in a brown cardigan flips through the newspaper, tortoiseshell reading glasses across the bridge of his nose. The paper isn't the *Chronicle*; it's the *New York Times*. Pretentious.

"I didn't order you anything," Templeton says.

He pushes his plate to one side, drawing a foamy cappuccino closer. He's placed an open notepad on the table. I can't make out the upside-down writing without leaning toward him, and I'm too proud to do that.

"You lied to me, Brad. About Joy Hill."

He does a quick breathing exercise to show me how serene he is, releasing a long, cleansing breath. "Everything I told you about that woman was true."

"You said she was putting moves on Simone Walker, and that resisting those moves was probably what got Simone killed—" He starts to protest, but I cut him off with a swipe of the hand. "Maybe not in so many words, but you strongly implied as much. And all the while, you'd cooked up this alternate theory. You never believed for a moment in Hill's guilt."

He smiles. "I'm not the detective."

"Here's the thing. You knew—or thought you knew—that Walker's killing was part of a larger series, and you didn't say a word about it. Not only that, you intentionally put me on a false trail. I want to know why."

"When we met at the Black Lab, I had no idea your case would have anything to do with Fauk. You're the one who told me, remember?"

"You and Lauterbach have been working together for months."

"I only met him in September. At your cousin's conference. I already told you this. When I tried talking to you about it, you wouldn't answer my calls. You didn't bother until you wanted something from me."

Everybody lies to the police. In interview rooms, I've gotten hardened murderers to open up by playing on their fear of losing control of how the facts will be spun. With the writer, there's no technique required. He likes talking. He likes to nuance the details.

"Here's the thing, March. I don't trust you. If I held information back, it's because I wasn't sure exactly what you'd do with it. I'm not interested in helping with a cover-up. I admitted already that I've been in touch with Donald off and on. When I was writing *The Kingwood Killing*, he must have thought I was going to prove his innocence. When that didn't happen, he made sure I knew how disappointed he was. But he kept in contact, and eventually some of the things he said started to make sense."

"Like what?"

"For one thing, he made me wonder if I'd gotten Detective Fitzpatrick's involvement wrong. The way I presented him in the book, he's basically a buffoon past his sell-by date, trying to unload the Fauk case so he can retire. But he and Donald were pretty close at that point, and Donald says the serial killer angle was solid. They just focused on the wrong villain. Fitzpatrick's only mistake was fixating on the Railroad Killer."

"You really believe that?"

He glances through the window at a passing couple. "It seems to fit."

"And what about Fauk's confession?"

"When I look at the transcript of the confession, it's obvious the man's not right. All that stuff about having to murder his wife so that he could meet someone new and father that little girl. Like it was destiny. That's more than just a proud father talking."

"A proud father."

"They've stopped visiting him," Templeton says. "The wife and daughter. He's out of his mind with anxiety. Feels rejected. It's no wonder he wants to get out."

I smirk. "Are you aware of the channels Fauk's been using to communicate with you? He sends his letters via released inmates and pays them off for their trouble. Why do you think he'd go to all that trouble?"

"Maybe he's paranoid. You people have given him good reason to be."

"There's something in those letters he wanted to make sure I never see. Not just me but anybody in law enforcement. He's afraid the censors will be reading over his shoulder. Now what could possibly be in those documents, Brad? You're the only person who can answer that."

"Nothing," he says.

"Then you won't mind if I have a look."

"I would mind, March. Very much. I feel that you'd use the information to undermine the course of justice. For all I know, you're the reason Donald's in the hospital right now. Maybe getting the letters from me could be your next step. Cleaning up the loose ends."

"You sound like Wilcox," I say. "If you honestly think I'm capable of any of that, then you haven't read your own book." I lean over the table. "Of course, I know something you don't. I haven't been getting all my information from one source."

He stares at me. He tries to wait me out. Finally he throws up his hands.

"Are you going to tell me or what?"

"You've read the appeal, I assume. One of the things they allege is that the crime lab has conveniently misplaced the DNA samples from the case, so that they can't be retested. If he was framed, the logic goes, then a new set of tests would bring back a different result. Everybody knows what a joke the DNA section has been, but they're alleging something worse: corruption."

"Makes sense. You can't tell me the missing evidence isn't suspicious."

"It's *very* suspicious," I say. "More than you realize. You see, lab results like that are often verified by independent labs. That's what happened in Fauk's case. And unlike the HPD crime lab, some of these independents have impeccable reputations."

"So the samples are in storage at an independent lab?"

"No, Brad, they're not. That's what's so strange. Two separate sets had to disappear, and there's no one who has the power to make that happen, not officially."

"A police cover-up—"

"You're not listening. The whole point of an independent lab is to produce independent confirmation. The chief of police himself can get on the phone and tell these guys to make some evidence disappear, and it won't make a bit of difference to them. Their reputation is based on that firewall between the police departments and their work."

For the first time, his confidence seems shaken. "So what are you suggesting?"

"It's simple. Fauk's been campaigning for a while. You admitted as much. Maybe he decided that with his wife and daughter cutting him off, he couldn't do the time anymore. Your mistake was in thinking you were the only person he's been lobbying. Those envelopes I told you about? You're not the only one receiving them. Donald Fauk has a lot of money. I think he's used some of it to make that evidence go away."

"Did he pay off the psychiatrist to backdate a diagnosis? Did he pay Eugene Fontenot to rough him up in the holding cell?"

"Fontenot's under investigation now," I say. "It wouldn't surprise me if some of the allegations against him had come to light thanks to Fauk's deep pockets. He's not a spotless lamb by any stretch, but when Fontenot fell, I believe Fauk's legal team was poised to take advantage."

"So he paid to suppress the evidence, he paid to make Fontenot look guilty, and I suppose you think he paid me, too?"

"That's the irony, Brad. He didn't have to. He just put the worm in your ear and let it go to work, same as you did with Lauterbach."

He takes a sip of his cappuccino and looks surprised that it's gone cold. Whether my words have struck deeply or not, I have no way of guessing. The most I can read in his guarded expression is a note of concern.

"I made myself some notes," he says, consulting his pad for the first time. "Since you insist on treating this as some kind of conspiracy, I figured there were a couple of facts you needed to know. Maybe I'm wasting my time, but here goes."

He takes another sip. Clears his throat.

"This whole thing started after that conference your cousin organized. There were questions afterward, and somebody asked whether there were any serial killers currently operating. I had just received some information, one of those letters from Donald you're so worked up about. He cited two murders with similar circumstances to his wife's death: that housewife in the Woodlands, Tegan McGill, and another woman named Mary Sallier. So this guy in the audience asks about current killers, and I throw the names out there as an example of a possible connection that's never been followed up.

"When I do that, Lauterbach gets a funny look. The Mary Sallier case was his, he says, and he thinks there's a link to a more recent homicide, too, a physical trainer who was discovered in a gymnasium pool. Everybody in the room is kind of stunned. Out of nowhere, it's like this serial killer just took shape, and none of us could quite believe it. We got through the rest of the Q&A and afterward spent more than an hour comparing notes. Lauterbach got so excited . . . and meanwhile I felt sick to my stomach.

"Your cousin Tammy, she was just glowing. Dean Corll is her thing, obviously, but that little club of hers is equal opportunity. The idea of a new serial killer emerging from her Q&A session . . . she was ecstatic. And sharp, too. She knows the subject, and knows the kind of questions to ask. She drilled us both until we pretty much had to admit there was something to this thing.

"Up to that moment, I never took Donald's rambling seriously. All the sudden, I realized that what he was saying made sense. Now, you can sit there and say that Fauk hired himself a serial killer to commit crimes that would match the one he was convicted on, but even you have to admit that strains credibility to the breaking point."

I nod slowly. "There might be connections, I don't know. But that doesn't mean Fauk didn't kill his wife." Now I sound like Bascombe, conceding when I'd said I wouldn't. "I went through Lauterbach's case files and I can tell you this with absolute certainty: Nicole Fauk's murder is different, and so are the two I'm working."

"You can tell yourself that." He rises. "But who are you really trying to convince?"

He throws a few dollars on the table and heads to the nearest door.

"I want to see those letters," I say.

But he's out on the sidewalk. The door swings shut.

If Cavallo were here, she'd defend him. With an experience like the one he just described, how could Templeton have come to any other conclusion? Lauterbach, enthused by what he thought was a major breakthrough, would have pushed him over the edge. Whatever doubts he might harbor about Fauk, here was a cop with special training in serial murder independently validating the connections Fauk had handed him.

I can imagine Fauk, sitting in his cell a couple of hours north, stunned beyond belief at how successful his gambit had been. There's no way he could have predicted the two men meeting at the crime conference, or the catalyzing question from the audience. This was a perfect storm, and even Donald Fauk can't control the weather.

Now he lies in a hospital bed. Fated, perhaps, to be his deathbed. For all the strings he managed to pull on the outside, life behind bars outmaneuvered him. And now everything is out of his control, just as it's out of mine.

The fan revolves in lazy circuits overhead, and I toss back and forth on the empty mattress, warm despite the air on my skin. On the night-stand, glowing red from the digital clock, my SIG Sauer lies on its side, a round in the chamber, in case of a repeat visit from Dave Bayard. I don't know for a fact it was him who broke into the house. I don't know for a fact he kicked the bathroom door into splinters and would have sunk Knife #29 into my wife's soft flesh. But in my sleep-addled mind, I've attached his name to the menacing silhouette.

I wish he would come back. I wish he would make my job that simple.

He could at least open up Simone Walker's laptop and send me a message. I'm getting lonely here, and nothing would please me more than a candid photo of my unsuspecting suspect. If he's back in the States—I'm sure he is—and holed up in the family home, then our early morning search warrant execution must have spooked him. He sent an email and we showed up on his doorstep or thereabouts. Too close for comfort. He couldn't resist sending the second one, but he took the precaution of doing so from a public Wi-Fi network. Now even that must strike him as too risky.

My laptop rests at the foot of the bed. After sitting up for an hour, checking email every few minutes on the off chance he'd overcome his shyness, I gave up and decided to get some sleep.

But now I can't sleep. The fan turns, my skin grows uncomfortably warm, sticky to the point of feverishness, and I turn the case over in my mind. And when I do sleep, when I slip into a restless, slit-eyed state that could pass for sleep, something Jack Hill said comes back to me, how Bayard's son claimed he'd killed before. I see a machete-wielding shadow cutting its way through African jungles, and racing ahead, just out of the blade's reach, the alternating faces of Wayne Bourgeois, the man I chased through the cemetery, and of my cousin Moody. The knifing shadow is sometimes Bayard and sometimes myself.

Wake up. No more of this. Give me sleep, dreamless sleep.

I close my eyes. When I open them, someone's on top of me, pinning my arms under the weight of her legs. Tammy and her pillow, torturing and laughing, laughing and torturing. When I really awaken, there's a pillow against my face. But it's Charlotte's and my only attacker is me.

I crawl out of bed sometime around three and pad down the stairs, taking a bottle of water from the fridge. I sit in an armchair in front of the glowing TV, holding the bottle against my temple and then taking another swig.

I'm alone.

Alone in the house and alone on the case. In the past, even at my low points, there was always someone I could rely on. Once it was Wilcox. After that, for a short time, it was Theresa Cavallo. But they're not with me now. If anything, they're on the other side. And while Aguilar is as good a cop as any to take a statement or run through a checklist, he's unimaginative, and as partners we keep pretty much to ourselves.

When you're alone, there's no one else to tell you the things you don't want to hear.

So I tell myself.

I'm not satisfied with Templeton's version of events, and I know I'll get nothing better out of Lauterbach. But according to the writer, someone else was there. Asking all the right questions. Overjoyed to be part of the process. She may have tried to suffocate me as a child, and the way she's turned my cousin into a self-serving cause célèbre might disgust me, but the fact is, Tammy was there. And if I want the full story, she's the only one to ask.

I switch the television off and return the water to the fridge. Upstairs, I fall onto the bed, pushing my face into the pillow, and fall asleep.

CHAPTER 24

In my black funeral suit I could pass for a reject from *Reservoir Dogs*. All I need are the shades. After wearing my father-in-law's wardrobe for so long—not my own yet, not in my mind—the fabric feels stiff, the squared shoulders like a set of football pads. In his dark jeans and windbreaker, Aguilar blends better with the other mourners, a small group of no more than a dozen, most of whom are dressed down despite the occasion. The morning fog has burned off, promising light gray skies. I get a few looks from other people as we slip inside the funeral home. They're probably mistaking me for an undertaker.

Beneath a wash of artificial light, the white casket gleams, half open in a foam of colorless flowers, the distant face of Simone Walker pale as the rest. The monochromatic tableau lends an inappropriate beauty to the scene. Her mother, Candace, sits between two larger women, co-workers judging by their single-minded devotion to her grief, which doesn't touch them personally. A few rows behind, Joy Hill maintains her icy composure, eyes fixed on the coffin as if she's afraid to look away.

A prerecorded organ dirge fills what would otherwise be an awkward silence, harmonizing the whispers of a few young women near the back with the occasional sob from Candace Walker's direction. Aguilar slips into the rear pew, unzipping his jacket. I advance down the center aisle to pay my respects. The jigsaw of stained glass in the arrow-slit windows casts colored rays across the empty seats.

I nod at Dr. Hill. She takes no notice.

Each of the women beside Candace grips one of her hands tight. Her lip trembles and a line of fresh tears travels over the swell of her cheekbone into the depression of her cheek. She looses a hand to wipe it away, then presses her wet fingers into mine.

"Thank you for coming," she says. "I know it means so much to her."

No stranger to grieving mothers, I whisper a few words of sympathy and pull away.

At the casket, I gaze on Simone's face. Its startling placidity and all the layers of makeup leave me with the uncomfortable feeling that regardless of my tireless efforts, I've never really *seen* her before now, and wouldn't recognize her if she walked up to me on the street.

I know her as symbol: the Victim. When we die, if there's to be any recompense, it's left to strangers to make. I know her only as a corpse, a medium for her killer to communicate through, a repository of evidence.

As I return down the aisle, the back door opens and Sean Epps slips through. He hides a shiner behind his sunglasses and looks like someone stuffed his right cheek with cotton. He files down a pew toward the front, settling himself with a creak that draws every eye. None of the women seem to recognize him. Dr. Hill would, but again she doesn't glance over.

"Did you get a look at him?" Aguilar whispers. "I wonder what the other guy looks like."

"Yeah," I say, thinking of Jason Young.

The minister emerges from a door up front. He keeps a brief vigil at the casket, says a few hushed words to Candace. He takes his place behind the lectern and opens in prayer. The eulogy that follows is so full of platitudes and borrowed anecdotes that it's soon clear he knew Simone no better than I did.

Aguilar leans over. "Catholic funerals are better than this."

"I don't think she minds."

The man tells a story of Simone's childhood, a time she'd found her mommy upset about something and told her not to cry. He sentimentalizes the tale, making it sound like something that transpired between June Cleaver and a baroque cherub, and ends by gazing misty-eyed in Candace's direction, saying, "Even as a little girl, she brought so much joy to her mother. She dried so many tears."

Candace sobs, prompting her minders to close in.

The double doors open again, this time to reveal a tentative-looking man in his mid-to-late twenties, unkempt, with thick black eyebrows and a dense twist of hair. He looks around, keeping his hands buried in the pockets of his knit pullover. Seeing me and Aguilar, he creeps across the carpeted aisle and slides into the pew in front of us.

I lean forward, whispering over his shoulder. "David Bayard?"

He turns slightly, nodding his head.

"Did you know Simone?"

He seesaws his hand, then lowers it quickly, self-conscious in the funeral setting. "Not really," he whispers. "Only by sight."

Several of the young women across the aisle glance over. David freezes.

"We'll talk afterward," I say, giving his shoulder a reassuring pat. "Thanks for coming."

When I sit back, Aguilar gives an imperceptible shake of the head. Whether it's directed at me or at the Bayard kid, I can't tell.

We don't accompany the mourners to the graveside. In the parking lot, I guide David Bayard Jr. toward our car. As a college student, I'd pictured him younger. As a scion of West University, I'd pictured him better turned out. Jack Hill's description of him: a professional student.

I'd pictured a young slacker, but there's a calm intelligence in David Junior's eyes, a self-possession overshadowed by his nerves.

Fortunately, what Jack Hill said about his willingness to talk proves entirely accurate. I'd sensed as much over the phone when he returned my call early this morning. Anxious to talk. Ready to tell me everything he knows. The anger flaring in his even voice at the first mention of his father's name. Silence at the news of Agnieszka Oliszewski's vicious murder, which was news to him.

"Sit tight for a second," I tell him.

He leans against the car, hands in pockets, shoulders hunched up like he's freezing in the mid-fifties weather. Aguilar walks a few paces away to make a call. I motion for him to stick near David, then jog across the parking lot to where Sean Epps is getting into his car.

"Mr. Epps, hold on a second."

He pulls the door shut and starts the engine.

I catch up, rapping my knuckles on the glass. After a pause, the window buzzes down.

"Cut the motor," I say. "Step back out here."

"I'm sorry, man. I really gotta get going." He keeps his jaw tight, speaking through clenched teeth.

"I already asked you nicely, Mr. Epps. Don't escalate the situation."

He kills the engine but leaves the keys dangling. I step back so he can climb out of the car.

"Remove your glasses, please."

He complies.

"You know what you look like?" I ask. "A man who got in a scrap with a jealous husband. You wanna tell me what happened to you?"

He shakes his head.

"Is that your final answer?"

He thinks. He nods.

"Because I saw a guy not too long ago that looks just like this. Beat up pretty bad. You wouldn't know anything about that, would you?"

He shakes his head. He waits. "No," he says.

"Tell you what. I'm gonna have you do something for me." I pat my pockets down, removing some plastic gloves. I peel them apart and shake one out until the palm opens up a bit. "I want you to take this glove and breathe into it. Go ahead."

"What?"

"Take it."

He pinches the edge between two fingers, holding the glove away from him.

"Breathe in it," I say. "Like this." I take a deep breath and blow.

"What for?"

"For a man in a hurry, you sure do drag your feet. Now go ahead and blow. Keep blowing until the fingers inflate."

He exhales into the limp glove, then hands it back. I cinch the opening with my thumb and forefinger.

"Now, is there anything you want to tell me about Jason Young?" I ask. "Once I bring this to lab and run the tests, it'll be too late for you to tell your side of the story."

He looks at the glove. He looks at me. He leans against the car and makes a moaning sound, covering his mouth with his hands.

"Tell me what happened," I say.

"I don't know how he found me." He touches his swollen cheek. "The phone bills, I guess. He must have gone back through her calls and figured it out. All I know is, this guy wants me to show him a property, this house on Bissonnet that's been on the market forever."

"You get there and what? He's waiting?"

Epps nods. "I let him through the gate, and as soon as I close it, he's on me."

"He punched you with his fists?"

He slides down the car, resting on his haunches, his hands half covering his mouth, like he wants to keep the words from coming out. "There were some bricks. Some loose bricks stacked inside the fence. I grabbed one. I had to defend myself."

"So you hit him?"

"We struggled for a while, and then he just stopped fighting. He stopped fighting and let me beat him. And I couldn't stop beating him."

"And afterward?"

"I dragged him out to the curb." His face convulses in a series of dry sobs. Then a preternatural calmness overtakes him. "I ruined everything, didn't I? I ruined my whole life."

"Stand up, Mr. Epps."

He gets to his feet, bracing himself with one hand against the car.

"When you leave here, I want you to call the police. Understand? I want you to call and make a statement. Ask to speak to whoever's in charge of the investigation, and then tell him everything you told me. If you do that voluntarily, it'll work in your favor. If you don't—if I check back and you haven't done it—then I'll drag you in myself and frog-march you in front of the judge, and so help me he'll dig a deep hole and bury you somewhere forever."

"No," he says. "I'll do it."

"This is a favor I'm doing you. You owe me for this."

He covers his dazed expression with the sunglasses, then slides clumsily behind the wheel, bumping his head on the doorframe.

"Hand me your phone," I say.

He goes through his pockets, producing the plastic brick of a smartphone he'd brought to the interview room. I punch the numbers in myself, then hand it back to him.

"As soon as my back is turned, you call."

"I will," he says.

I head back across the parking lot, not giving him a second glance. My stride is long, my muscles tingling with the old excitement.

I noticed the injuries. I made the connection. I got the confession.

Like a beat cop of old, operating on nothing but ego and sleight of hand. I was a wave of moral authority sweeping away everything in my path.

At my approach, Aguilar perks up, sensing the change in mood. He glances over my shoulder and back at me.

"What's he doing?" I ask.

"He's on the phone."

I ball the glove in my fist, then toss it away. Aguilar looks at the glove, then back at me. Baffled. I choose not to explain myself.

"You've finished the semester?" I ask David.

He looks down at the pavement and shrugs. "My last final was yesterday."

"What are you studying?"

"I'm supposed to be working on a dissertation." He smiles. "But it keeps getting away from me."

Aguilar steps away for another phone call, still eyeing Sean Epps from across the lot. He exchanges a few words, then snaps the phone shut and gives me a look. Enough of the small talk. Time to get down to business.

"Your father returned to the United States on Thursday, the tenth of December. Is that right?" I have the response from ICE in my briefcase, so I already know the answer. "He leaves the country on Sunday the sixth, the day after Simone Walker was murdered, and he comes back four days later. That's four hours from here to New York and another sixteen hours to Nigeria with a stop-off at Heathrow, so let's say twenty hours total one way. Then he turns around and comes right back. Does that seem strange to you?"

"I don't know," he says with a shrug. "I don't keep track of him."

"But you know he's back?"

"I saw him this morning at breakfast. He said it was going to be a tight Christmas this year. He got fired from his job."

"Did he say anything about Simone? Or Agnieszka?"

He shakes his head. "He didn't say a word to me. My father kind of talks to the room, if you know what I mean. He went into his office for some kind of conference call. He's trying to get a new company to hire him."

"But you've talked to him about Agnieszka before, right?"

He cocks his head. "She told me he was looking at her, if that's what you're getting at."

"What did you do when she told you?"

"What did I do?" He blinks. "I didn't *do* anything. I told her to be careful of him. I told her he's a bad person. She wanted to complain, to call the police. I didn't think that would be a good idea." He pauses. "He's killed people, you know?"

He says it with a doubtful lilt in his voice, like he's not sure we'll believe him.

"You told her that?"

"*He* told me. It happened over there. In Africa. He said some guys tried to force him into the back of a car, and he stabbed them." He stops. Wipes his hand over his mouth. "I know it sounds crazy, but I didn't doubt him for a minute. He has all these knives. He has a stone to sharpen them, and he'll sit upstairs and you can hear the scraping sound. If it sounds crazy, well . . . *he's* crazy. He likes to hurt people."

"Did he ever threaten to hurt you?"

"He did hurt me. He did *this* to me."

David draws his left hand from his pocket and holds it up, fingers splayed. The ring finger juts crookedly, with a fat notch of skin missing near the knuckle, the surface covered in shiny scar tissue. A similar scar runs down the side of his middle finger, like someone flayed the skin with a sharp blade. I take him gently by the wrist, pulling the hand closer. He trembles at the touch.

"How did he do this?" I ask, my voice shaking.

He swallows.

"How did he do it?"

David snatches his hand back, hiding it away. "There's a game he likes to play."

"With a knife."

He nods. "You have to spread your hand out. You stab the knife between each finger. Really fast. I couldn't do it. I tried to go too fast and this happened."

"He made you do it?"

"And then he laughed. He can do it very fast. According to him, you have to be a real man to do it that fast."

Aguilar beckons me over with a nod. I touch David on the shoulder, trying to reassure him, but he shrinks away ever so slightly. We walk a few paces off, far enough so he can't overhear.

"That was Bascombe on the phone," he says. "We have our warrant to search the house. We're good to search for knives, records related to them, evidence connected to either victim—including Simone's laptop and cellular phone—a pretty broad scope. Ordway and Lorenz are down the road from the house, keeping an eye on the place. They haven't seen Bayard, which means he's probably holed up in there."

I call to David: "Is your mother at home?"

"She's always at home. She doesn't work."

"Okay." I lower my voice. "With what he just told us about the knife game, I think we're good to go."

"All right." He glances at David, then back at me. He flips his phone open. "It's been a long road, March, but I think you've got this one down. Should I do the honors, or do you want to?"

I take the phone and start to dial. Then I close it.

"You know what," I say. "Let's do this ourselves. I want to be there when they take the door. I want to get a look at this guy and see the house for myself. Agnieszka told Jack Hill there was an attic window he used to watch her from. I want to check out that view."

"Your call. What about Junior over there?"

"We'll drop him off downtown, keep him handy while we interrogate the old man. He might be useful, after all."

David resists the idea of leaving his car and coming with us, but after some assurances he finally relents. While Aguilar drives, I turn sideways in the passenger seat to keep an eye on him. He looks at the floor, looks out the window, and eventually cracks an uncertain smile.

"Are you going to arrest him?" he asks.

"What would you think if we did?"

"I don't know," he says. "I guess *somebody* should."

CHAPTER 25

The original structure must have been demolished to make way for the Bayard house, a looming brick box sitting on the lot like a big passenger squeezed into a coach airline seat. The walls crowd the sidewalk on the front and side, and a porte cochere juts over the wide drive.

With a couple of patrol units on the curb, I send Ordway and Lorenz down the driveway, giving them a minute to get positioned in back. Then I lead Aguilar and a couple of uniforms to the front entrance, including Nguyen, the officer who worked the perimeter the night Simone Walker's body was discovered.

I punch the doorbell button while Nguyen uses the butt of his ASP baton as a knocker.

Kim Bayard opens up with a broad and puzzled smile, eyes roving from one man to the next in increasing perplexity. I hand her a copy of the search warrant and ask for her husband. I call into the house over her shoulder.

"Mr. Bayard? Dave Bayard? It's the Houston Police Department."

"I don't understand," she says.

Nguyen maneuvers her back and starts explaining the warrant. She listens, polite and attentive, the same way she'd listen to the mechanic outlining repairs to her car. Aguilar and I ease our way through the door and across an ocean of blond hardwoods, pausing at the foot of a circular stairway hemmed with more wrought iron. At the top of the stairs, Dave Bayard stands with one hand on the railing.

"What's going on?" he says.

My first glimpse of the killer.

Bayard dresses like a high school math teacher. Medium height with a broad muscled chest concealed under a sleeveless v-neck sweater and a checked shirt. The crease in his gray wool slacks sharp as a knife. His salt-and-pepper hair, clipped short and receding on the sides, creates a thin promontory over his high forehead. His skin brown, his hands large and rough.

The blue light of a telephone earpiece twinkles in his right ear. He touches it and speaks in an undertone: "Some people are here. I'm gonna have to call you back."

I wait until he's halfway down to mention the search warrant. His eyes narrow. He pauses. The annoyance of a moment before ebbs out, replaced by a rush of anxiety.

"Please join us," I say.

He continues down the stairs, watching every step. Afraid of slipping.

When he reaches the bottom, I lay a heavy hand on his shoulder, all but claiming him. Like his son, he exudes a quiet, calculating intelligence, watching everything, taking in the smallest details. But there's something else, an explosive physicality. Like the corporate lawyer said, a man made for the field rather than the front office.

"What can I do for you, officers?" he asks.

"We have a warrant to search these premises," I say. "We are investigating the murders of Simone Walker and Agnieszka Oliszewski."

At the mention of their names, Kim Bayard yelps audibly, covering her mouth with a ringed hand. Bayard's mouth turns down, either at my words or his wife's reaction.

"Don't worry, babe," he says, jaw clenched. "It's only natural with the one girl getting killed in our backyard. Isn't that right, officers? You have to be thorough, don't you?"

Like his clothes, his voice contradicts his body language. He sounds calm, but looks like he's ready to run. Or fight.

I exchange a look with Aguilar. "Your wife has a copy of the warrant. We'd like you to accompany us as we search. If anything is removed from the property, we'll provide you with an inventory before we go."

"I see." He glances at the warrant in his wife's hand. "And you have to do it right this minute? I was actually on a pretty important call."

I don't dignify the question with an answer. I motion Nguyen toward the back of the house to let the others inside.

"I think . . ." Bayard rubs his chin, uncertain. "Maybe I should call my attorney."

"You're welcome to," I say. "But we won't be taking a statement here. We just need to search the property. Like you said, a woman was murdered, practically in your backyard. We really do need to be thorough."

I can see him processing his risk level, going over in his mind everything he stands to lose. His jaw relaxes. He lets out a deep breath.

"Kim," he says. "Just to be on the safe side. I think you'd better call."

I move my hand to his elbow, asserting more control. "Now, if you don't mind, sir, we have a search to conduct."

My first impulse is to head to the attic. Look for the window with a view of Dr. Hill's pool. But a proper search must be systematic, deliberate. We must divide the house into quadrants, assign every officer with a task, ensuring that nothing is missed and every discovery is properly witnessed and documented. I keep Bayard by my side, judging his reaction as we move from one part of the house to the next.

He makes an effort to appear affable, probably thinking that's how innocent people react, friendly and helpful.

He's wrong, of course.

No one is more inconvenienced, more outraged by the invasion of privacy than the man who has nothing to hide. Knowing what a waste our efforts are—he's done nothing, after all—an innocent man grows increasingly irritated and impatient. Of course, everyone has something to hide, and when you're innocent and those little secrets are revealed anyway, you feel the injustice keenly.

Only the guilty look relieved when their misdemeanors are uncovered. They hope finding the smaller offenses will blind us to their felonies.

His windows of his upstairs office look out onto the backyard. But the swimming pool where Simone Walker died is entirely screened from view by the hedge and Bayard's own four-car garage, which sides diagonally across part of the yard. For a desk he uses a long antique table with a green marbled leather top and brass corners. On closer inspection it appears to be a high-dollar reproduction.

Aguilar makes him unlock each of the drawers in turn while I scan the floor-to-ceiling bookcases that line the room on three sides. The bottom rows are occupied by oversized coffee-table books, mainly art and photography, with hardbacks on the middle rows and smaller volumes above eye level. There's even a ladder that runs along a brass rail.

One section of shelving holds not books but a series of locking glass cases. Inside, a series of knives are displayed under pinpoint lights. Seeing my interest, Bayard actually moves to the wall and twists a dimmer dial, bringing up the luster of the blades. He appears at my side, smiling, not even trying to conceal his pride.

"Are you a collector, as well?" he asks.

"No," I say. "It's just that my victim, she was gutted with a knife like one of these."

A condescending smile. "I doubt it was like one of *these*."

I'm tempted to wipe that smile off his face by rattling off the details: SCHARF. OLD SCHOOL BOWIE, #29 OF 50. But I'm not here to clue him in on our case. Besides, he already knows. He dropped his prized weapon on my bedroom floor.

"March."

I turn to find Aguilar at an open desk drawer. In his gloved hand he holds a small, thick paperback book.

The Kingwood Killing by Brad Templeton.

"I'm a reader," Bayard says, laughing nervously. "What can I say?"

I take the book in my own gloved hands, flipping through its pages. The glossy photo insert appears pristine. There are no markings inside. I'm about to hand it back for bagging when I notice something on the flyleaf. A handwritten inscription in ink.

FOR DAVID,
THANKS FOR YOUR INTEREST!
ALL THE BEST,
BRAD TEMPLETON

"I knew him," Bayard is saying. "The Donald. Donald Fauk. Unbelievable story." He pauses. "*You're* not . . . Are you the same Detective March—?" He reaches for the book.

I hand it to Aguilar, who seals the paperback in a plastic evidence bag.

"You're *taking* that?" Bayard says. "I don't get it."

"Have you been consulting the book recently?" I ask. "It's in your desk drawer."

"What? No, of course not. I don't even know what it's doing there."

"But it is your book? You're not denying that."

"Yeah." His big shoulders slump in defeat. "It's mine."

A narrow staircase leads up to the attic, hidden behind a locked door. We ascend single file: Aguilar, Bayard, me, Nguyen. Through another door, we enter a small finished room with a cork floor, a small tufted couch, an older television set with a dusty VCR player attached.

"This was originally going to be a media room," Bayard says, "but when David Junior moved out I just decided to convert his room. It's bigger."

Along the wall, a row of empty bottles are stacked, their labels soaked off. I count eight of them. At the end of the line there's a metal gasoline container, the type you'd find in a garage next to a lawn mower. I lift it with a gloved hand. Next to empty.

"What's the deal with all this?" I ask. "You making Molotov cocktails?"

"Hardly," he says. "I don't know what these are doing here."

"We need to photograph these, then take them," I say to Aguilar. "Check them for prints. Mr. Bayard, if you've been manufacturing explosives—"

"I told you I don't know what they're doing here."

"Then who does?"

He says nothing.

"And what's through here?" I ask, indicating a small door on the far side of the room, half blocked by the couch.

"Nothing. Just storage. The eaves were too low to make finishing it out worthwhile."

"Let's take a look."

We drag the couch out of the way. Reaching inside, I flip on a row of bald bulbs nestled inside the exposed framing. There are some cardboard boxes stacked near the door. Beyond them, nothing but plywood flooring over joists.

"Where's the window?" I ask.

"The window?"

"There's a window overlooking the neighbor's pool."

He rubs his chin again. "Oh. It's just decorative. You'd have to walk across the joists that way to reach it." He points past the boxes into the darkness. "The finished room kind of boxes it in, so you have to go around. There's no light, though."

I pull my Fenix light. "Not a problem."

Leaving Bayard with Nguyen, I start across the joists with Aguilar balancing behind me, taking it slow so we don't lose our footing. I don't fancy the idea of plunging through a high ceiling, landing two floors down or getting impaled on a chandelier.

"You think it's booby-trapped?" Aguilar whispers.

"Because of the bottles?" I smile. "Guess we'll find out. You wanna go first?"

"Be my guest."

We keep the wall of the finished room on our right, turning the corner after a minute of slow progress. Ahead, I spot a faint slit of light and start toward it.

The window is closer than it appears. A length of blackout cloth hides most of the light. With the aid of my flashlight I make out a loose piece of plywood situated at the window to serve as a makeshift floor. On top, there's a metal folding chair. Under the chair, a wooden cigar box with the lid ajar. As I get closer I see something concealed behind a flap of blackout cloth, perched on the windowsill.

"What is that?" Aguilar says.

I reach the plywood and move across. I draw the curtain back. Standing on the ledge, a pair of black binoculars, expensive ones, with a red dot Leica logo.

From the window I can see over the hedge and into Dr. Hill's back-yard. The pool glistens in the cloudy daylight. A woman sunbathing by the water would be easy to observe. I lift the binoculars with two fingers, raising them just in front of my eyes. I can make out the detail of the slate surrounding the pool, the latticework of the metal chairs. From here, using these binoculars, he could have studied every inch of her at leisure.

Aguilar clears his throat. "Look at this."

I put the binoculars down. On the edge of the platform, there's another bottle. This one is three quarters full, with some wadding stuffed down the neck. I run my light all around it, looking for trip-wires. Nothing.

"I've seen some weird things in my time," Aguilar says, "but this . . ."

"Let's take a look in that cigar box."

I prop it open with a pen. There's a bag of weed inside, some rolling papers, and a fat white envelope with something sticking out. I turn the edge of the envelope. A stack of photographs. Digital shots output on an inkjet printer. Aguilar shines a light with his free hand. I ease the deck of photos out, flipping through them one by one.

"That's the Polish girl," he says.

Oliszewski in a flower-print bikini stretched on a recliner by the pool. On her back. On her stomach. On her stomach again, undoing her top with a twisted hand.

"And Simone."

One shot after another: Simone in a variety of swimsuits, in the water and out. Sitting under the pergola. Talking on the phone. Looking at the screen of her laptop. And then I flip the photo and Aguilar jumps.

"No way."

Simone stripped to the waist, lying facedown on the slate, her legs in the water, the bloody wounds chewing up her back. It's a grainy, nighttime photo, snapped from a few feet above the body. I flip to the next one. Night again, but bright this time. Illuminated by the crime scene lights. The photo, taken from the window, shows three dark silhouettes around the pool. A tall man, a shorter one, a plump woman in a white jumpsuit. Bascombe. Me. Dr. Green.

"Okay," I say, putting the photos back. "Get in there and make the arrest. Have Nguyen put him in the car for transport. I want all of this photographed *in situ*."

"You coming?" he asks.

"In a minute."

As he creaks across the joists, I return to the window, gazing down on a scene Bayard must know by heart. The voyeur, aloof and untouchable, seeing everything. Present with the women when they thought they were alone.

He would have come up here, rolled a joint, and enjoyed the show, taking photos, printing the most meaningful, the most intimate.

His secret place, his nest.

And when Agnieszka spotted him and Hill had the strategically placed trees planted, what did Bayard think? He must have been enraged. Maybe frightened. But the Polish girl left and the trees came down. The new tenant, Simone, had no idea she was being observed.

Looking through the same window, standing in the same place, I imagine what he must have felt. The photos play back in my head.

I need to remember this. I need to capture it. The voyeuristic glee. The sense of intimacy with these strangers, feeling as close to them as a lover. Did he know their names? Had he met them in ordinary life? Did he experience an illicit thrill when he encountered them, reveling in his secret knowledge?

He must have sent the first email from here. Not on the curb in front of Dr. Hill's house. From this spot he could access the neighboring wireless network just fine. Our sudden arrival on scene must have spooked him, forcing him to change up.

We have enough to make the arrest. We have enough for a conviction. But I want more. I want to put the crowbar in and crack him open. I want him to look in my eyes and admit what he did. He stabbed both women over and over. He broke into my house, he went after my wife, and tried to do to her what he'd done to them.

"March." Aguilar's voice.

I cross the joists and reenter the finished room. Bayard stands at the center of the room, arms pulled back, wrists cuffed. His face bloated and red, eyes moist. Nguyen guides him to the top of the stairs.

"I don't understand," Bayard says. "What are you people doing?"

Aguilar follows. I bring up the rear.

"This is insane," Bayard calls back. "You're making a mistake."

"Are you ready to make a statement, sir?"

"You want my statement? *You want my statement?*" He stumbles, but Nguyen rights him. They reach the landing and Bayard turns. "*Here's* my statement, Officer: I want my lawyer."

"You disappoint me, Dave. You really do."

Bayard's lawyer is a slender woman in pearls and a red pantsuit, unflappable even in the face of the photographs recovered in her client's attic. They've already been processed by the crime scene unit, along with the Molotov, but I hand each one over in its evidence bag, making her look through official plastic.

"That's the kind of man you're representing," I say.

She doesn't respond, just moves through the photos. "There's one victim depicted here. What about the other?"

"The first pictures were of her."

She shakes her head. "In those, she's still alive. I'm talking about the other crime scene. There are no photos of that. All this proves is that someone likes to snap photos from the window. That doesn't make him a killer."

I hand her the most incriminating shot. "This one was taken standing over the body."

"That's debatable."

"When we find the camera that took those pictures," I say, "we might recover photos from the Oliszewski scene, too."

"You might. Then again you might not."

"Either way, we're going to want to talk to your client."

"He's not prepared to make a statement at this time. You took your shot. You can process him and put him in a cell. We'll go before the judge first thing."

She gathers her things and heads for the conference room door.

"By the way," she says. "I'm also representing Mr. Bayard's son. You have him here as well, don't you? Are you planning to charge him, too?"

Bascombe, who's been watching from the corner the whole time, opens his mouth for the first time. "The son is cooperating with our investigation."

"Not anymore he's not."

She lets the door slam behind her. I exchange a look with the lieutenant.

"What do you think?"

"What do you mean, what do I think? It's down. Good work. The ADA's gonna want to sit down with you and go over everything." He checks his watch. "Let's plan on first thing tomorrow morning."

"I wanted to take a crack at him."

"I know," he says. "But we've got more than enough."

"Nothing beats a confession."

304

He shakes his head. "That guy's not gonna talk, March. I could see it right off. You need to be thinking about the forensics. Those photos, the binoculars, the improvised explosive—we need results on all of that. We need to check his prints against the ones on the outside table, too. And you didn't find the missing laptop, so we need to know where else he might have hidden it. There's plenty to do on this thing yet."

He leaves me to box the evidence from the table. I put everything away, then fit the lid on, carrying it all back to my desk. Ordway lingers in the aisle between cubicles, trying to scare up some company for a celebration.

"Libation time, gentlemen," he keeps saying, but the rest of us ignore him.

I call Charlotte.

"Where are you?"

"Home at last," she says. "I'm gonna take a nice, long bath. Are you working late?"

"Not anymore. My suspect is behind bars. My lieutenant is pleased with my work. My colleagues are organizing a pathetic after-hours bar crawl . . ." I say this last bit a little louder, prompting a jeer from Ordway. "So I think I'm gonna call it a day."

On my way home I stop at the grocery store and buy a vaseful of white flowers, pausing a moment to remember Simone Walker's funeral earlier this morning. I've done right by her, as right as I can. The man who killed her is in jail and I'm going to see to it he remains there. The memory of looking through that window, my thwarted effort to get into his brain and use the resulting insight to drag out a confession, leaves me uncomfortable.

Standing at his window, looking at his photos, I've seen Simone the way he saw her. And I can't help feeling guilty about that. Tainted. Sharing in something so dark, trying to understand it even for a moment, to stand in those shoes. See through those eyes.

The fragrance of flowers fills the car, making my nose itch. Making me want to sneeze. When I get to the house, Carter and Gina are just leaving. Dinner with Murray Abernathy, they say. After tucking Gina into the passenger seat, Carter pulls me aside.

"I'm staying at the outreach center," he says. "I think you were right. I've got to make the best of the situation."

I say goodbye and go in. Up the stairs, bearing my coming-home present in both hands, I pause at the battered bathroom door, reproaching myself for not having had it fixed already. Over the threshold, she sits glistening in the tub, a hand on her shoulder, her hair pinned up. She smiles at the sight of me.

"Roland," she says. "You brought me flowers."

CHAPTER 26

Another case goes into the black. Two bodies accounted for and a killer
behind bars. But the work doesn't stop there. The ADA takes another
run through the evidence, frowning at the gaping hole where Bayard's
confession goes as if she's never heard of a conviction without one, then
with the usual admonition to dot and cross, pronounces her tentative
satisfaction. I exit the meeting with a checklist of things to follow up on,
mostly aimed at covering unlikely challenges from the defense. There's
plenty of forensics still out too, so it falls to me to make the inevitable
series of badgering phone calls.

Bascombe checks out as soon as the meeting breaks up, but the
ADA lingers, rearranging the paper in her legal briefcase.

"We have a friend in common." She smiles. "Charlie Bodeen."

"You know Charlie," I say, stating the obvious.

"He took me under his wing from day one, pretty much taught me
everything I know about prosecuting a case—all the stuff they don't
cover in law school. He told me about your situation. The Fauk appeal,

I mean. There's been a lot of talk about it in my shop, I'll tell you that. Especially now. With Fauk in the hospital."

"I see." I shift in my chair, trying to remember whether she was in on the district attorney's confab, whether she saw Roger Lauterbach's slide show. "And does this talk include the fact that I went up to Huntsville last Sunday morning?"

She nods. "But Charlie says you're not involved."

"That's nice to hear. Last time I saw him, he didn't look too happy with me."

"Well," she says, "his exact words were, 'Even March wouldn't be that stupid.' But he was very emphatic."

"That's more like it."

She's working up to something, only I can't tell what. A couple of detectives flash by the conference room door on their way to the coffee concession. She glances over her shoulder, waiting for them to get clear.

"Look, March, I don't know whether you've been keeping with the Sheriff Department's serial killer investigation—"

So she *was* there.

"—but there's been an interesting development. Remember Raúl Guzman, the original suspect in the Fauk murder? The Sheriff's Department was looking at him for their serial killings, they told this story about him taking a construction crew to Lake Charles and getting rousted by the local police for trespassing."

"The girl by the swimming pool. I remember."

"It turns out there's a little problem with the identification. The Raúl Guzman who got mixed up with the Louisiana police is not the same Raúl Guzman interviewed in the Fauk case. They're both in construction, they're both around the same age, but only one of them has a record—and guess what? The original Guzman? He's doing federal time at the pen in Beaumont on a smuggling beef. He's three years into a ten-year jolt, which lets him off the hook for at least a couple of those murders."

"And Lauterbach knows this? He said he'd interviewed the man personally, so I don't see how a mistake like that would slip past him."

"It did," she says, "and now the sun's not shining as bright on his theory as it was a week ago. Bringing in a serial killer case with a suspect pretty much in cuffs is one thing. But putting the public on notice, announcing a Swimming Pool Killer and then not being able to catch the guy? That's another story. Not to mention, the number of victims keeps getting whittled down. You heard about Tegan McGill's parents? No? Well, they got wind of what the Sheriff's Department is up to, and they've had a civil case going against her husband forever. Now they're threatening to sue the county for helping him get away with murder. It's a regular circus back at our place."

I'm tempted to open up to this woman, to tell her what I know from Templeton about the origin of the serial killer hypothesis in Fauk's letters, to clue her in about the independent lab's missing samples. But I can't substantiate the first claim and the second is already in good hands. And whatever else he might be, Lauterbach is still a cop. As much as I want his house of cards to fall, it won't be me who does the demolition. Not behind his back, anyway.

"What's on your mind, Detective? You look like you're about to say something."

"No," I say. "It's nothing. I was just thinking . . ." My voice trails off.

"Thinking what—?"

I hold my hand up for silence.

The idea snuck up on me while I wasn't looking. A connection so obvious I should have seen it right off. Am I missing something? I check the fittings and touch the wires together. And they spark.

Of course, of course, of course.

"I think . . ."

"Yes?" she says.

"I think I know what happened to Donald Fauk."

Her face lights up. "Lay it on me, then."

"I'm sorry." I give her a bashful smile, scooting my chair back. "I'm not going to say anything until I'm sure. Nothing to a prosecutor, anyway."

★

The Mitsubishi rolls across the gravel parking lot. Brad Templeton slides out of the driver's seat. He casts a nervous eye over the sweaty Mexicans enjoying Tecate and enchiladas for lunch. He frowns at the ice house's corrugated facade, perhaps a little too authentic for his liking. Passing through the diffused sunlight into the shade of the open patio, he pauses to let his vision adjust. Tejano music blares from a stereo atop a stack of milk crates. He winces visibly at the sound.

I motion him to the table, patting its knife-scarred surface to entice him over.

"How do you even find places like this?" he asks.

"When I was in uniform, I used to *live* in places like this." My weathered briefcase slouches against the table leg. I reach under the flap and produce my newly purchased copy of *The Girl Who Forgave Her Killer*. I slide the book across the table. "You never did sign one of these for me."

"Are you serious?"

I reach into my jacket—a gray Donegal tweed, according to Charlotte, whose father seems to have had a thing for tweed—and produce a metal ballpoint. He rolls his eyes a little, then reaches into his own coat pocket for a fat Mont Blanc fountain pen, which makes a scratching sound across the page. I inspect the inscription, then close the book with a smile.

"I'm going to give you something," I say. "A chance to redeem yourself."

He frowns. "I'm listening."

"I told you about the way Fauk was smuggling those letters out. But I may have been wrong about the reason why. I thought he was trying to avoid the censors. Maybe corrections was the least of his worries. Prisons leak like a sieve, and I think he had a secret that needed keeping. That secret's what put him in the hospital."

"Go on."

"It was one of Fauk's letters that connected Tegan McGill and Mary Sallier, right? And when you mentioned this, Lauterbach added

Ramona Sanchez to the list. Here's my question: how did Fauk put those names together?"

He shrugs. "Maybe he hired a private investigator."

"There are easier ways when you're in the penitentiary. People talk."

"Meaning?"

"Think about it. Did somebody talk to Fauk? Or did somebody talk to somebody who then spilled everything to Fauk? Assuming Lauterbach is correct about the Sanchez murder tying in, then you'd be looking for an inmate who went inside sometime between her death in April and whenever Fauk posted that letter in September."

"Wait a second," he says. "You're telling me the real killer is already in jail, and he decided to open up to Fauk about it?"

"Last Sunday I went up to Huntsville to have a talk with Coleman, a guy who's helped me out in the past. He put me onto the smuggled letters, but apart from that, he didn't have much to trade with. So I asked him to come up with more. The thing is, he's not the sharpest tool in the shed. I think he must've asked the wrong person some questions, or tipped off somebody who could put the pieces together."

"But even you didn't know about Fauk connecting the cases, not until I told you."

"No," I say, "but all an interested party would have to do is check up on the details of Fauk's appeal. My visit to Coleman must have been the catalyst. The bad guy got wind of it, and as far as he was concerned, Fauk was shopping him in exchange for some kind of prosecutorial consideration."

"So he decides to take care of business."

"Exactly."

He weighs the idea. He slumps forward, elbows on the table. "In which case, Fauk's been playing me right from the start."

"That we already knew. And at the risk of repeating myself, the man confessed."

"People make false confessions all the time."

"Yeah," I say, "but they don't volunteer them."

"All right, all right. So why are you coming to me with this?"

The million dollar question. "You owe Lauterbach a name. If you find out how Fauk made the connection between McGill and Sallier, you can help him out of the bind he's gotten himself into. He's so far out on a limb right now that without one, he's gonna be picking up the sheriff's dry cleaning for the foreseeable future."

"Which would be icing on the cake for you."

"You think so?" I shake my head. "You really don't know me, then."

He pauses. "Fair enough. But you may be overestimating my relationship. If Fauk's gonna talk, it won't be to me. Now you, on the other hand—"

"I don't have any jurisdiction up at Huntsville," I say, "and with the appeal going, I can't exactly waltz into Fauk's hospital room and start asking questions."

"If you're right and Fauk's been selling me a bill of goods, I don't see what I can do. Now, are we going to eat or what?"

"Bad news," I say, checking my watch. "I'm going to have to take a rain check."

"You're not even buying me lunch."

"With taxpayer's money? You'd be picking up the tab either way." I grab the book and slip it into my briefcase. "There is one more thing." I withdraw a photo of the inscription Templeton wrote on the flyleaf of Bayard's copy of *The Kingwood Killing*. "You remember this?"

He studies the image. "This is the reprint. They did a new one when *The Girl Who Forgave Her Killer* came out. I'm guessing I signed this at Murder by the Book when they hosted the reading. Or wait . . ." He puts the photo down and leans back, checking the ceiling like his memories are kept up there. "You know what? I bet this was at your cousin's shindig. The reprints were out then, and I was still using my old pen." He pats the Mont Blanc through his coat. "I splurged on this one before the big night at MBTB."

"So you remember signing it for him?"

"Not really, but that's my best guess."

"This guy," I say, tapping the image with my finger. "He's the one who killed Simone Walker and Agnieszka Oliszewski. I guess he's a big fan of your work."

It's a low blow, but considering his unwillingness to right his own wrong, it's more than justified. I'm halfway to the patio before he calls out.

"March, wait."

I pause. He snatches the photo and comes after me. "Are you absolutely sure about this?"

"He's in custody now," I say. "The homicides are down."

"And this is the guy who broke into your place and attacked Charlotte?"

I nod.

"You should have a chat with your cousin, then. If this guy is who I'm thinking, she seemed to know him. When I left, she was still there talking to him."

"About what?" I ask.

He looks at the photo. "I'm not a hundred percent, but . . ."

"But what?"

He has to drag the words out, each one a thick link on a heavy iron chain. They rattle down on me with the force of lead.

"*I'm pretty sure they were talking about you.*"

The last time I saw Tammy Putnam face-to-face, my uncle tried to weld us back together with his hand. After the last stroke, he'd lost the power of speech. All he had was one stiff and spotted appendage to nudge through the air.

His meaning was clear, but I just stood there.

My daughter, Jessica, was only a couple of years gone, and I still nursed a savage rage. Bridger once said about me that I was all or nothing, with no capacity for moderation. He said it through a cloud of cigarette smoke after I'd admonished him to quit. He was right. When I hate, I keep nothing in reserve.

Her house in Katy sits on a cul-de-sac lined with basketball hoops, molded plastic tricycles, and a couple of starter cars for teenage kids. In contrast to the lived-in look of the neighboring properties, Tammy's staid two-story gives off the sterile vibe of a model home. On one side of the yard, a painted-wood Joseph and Mary flank a light-up manger, and on the other a winking, red-nosed Rudolph is poised for flight. But there's no cheer to the decorations. No reverence, either. They're just brightly colored surfaces with nothing behind them but emptiness.

I park in the driveway. The front door is slightly ajar, as if she expects me to let myself in. I ring the doorbell. Nothing. I push the door a few inches farther, peering inside.

Tammy stands there in a glittering red short-sleeved jacket, a cheap sequined wrapper for the squarish lump of her body. She holds her hands toward me, her knuckles concealed behind a row of mismatched cocktail rings.

"Roland," she says. "You actually showed up. Come on in."

I follow her through an arched doorway into the dining room, recognizing the table and chairs that used to belong to my uncle and aunt. On the table, lined up like soldiers on parade in four rows of three, a series of glossy red bags with rope handles, stuffed to the gills with green tissue.

"You caught me at a bad time," she says. "I'm hosting a jewelry party tonight, and these are the favors." She leans over the table to adjust the perfectly aligned bags. "It's the perfect time of year with all the last-minute shoppers. I just hope I have enough treats here."

"I have some questions for you," I say.

"Questions?" She wheels on me. "Questions for me. I can hardly believe it. You have no idea how long I've been waiting. But I knew this day would come."

"I want you to tell me about someone," I say. "A man named Dave Bayard."

"Bayard?" She touches her chin in thought. "*Bayard, Bayard, Bayard.*"

"He was at your conference. The one where Brad Templeton spoke. Brad signed a book for him."

She snaps her fingers. "Oh, *Bayard*. Right. I know exactly who you mean. What an interesting evening that was! You should have been there, Roland, you really should have. I've never witnessed anything like it. The conference was *such* a success. Everybody thought so."

"I'd like you to tell me everything you talked about with him."

"We talked about *everything*. We talked for *hours*. You can't expect me to remember it all. And anyway, why are you suddenly interested in my work? You've done your best to ignore me up until now."

She walks me through the kitchen, immaculate and bare, then into an open plan living room as tall as it is wide, where two tapestry-covered wingback chairs and a plush, overstuffed sofa squat below a pendulous brass chandelier. I reach into my breast pocket for my slim digital recorder, the one I use for interviews.

"Oh," she says, slumping onto the couch. "You're going to record this?"

"Start at the beginning and tell me everything about Bayard."

"Everything?" She clears her throat. "Well." She raises her voice for the tape. "As you know, I'm the founder of an organization devoted to the victims of murder here in Houston."

"Talk in your normal voice," I tell her.

"We hold regular meetings for our membership, but a couple of months ago we hosted our first event for the general public. It was an unqualified success, with so many new faces in the audience, so much fresh enthusiasm. I invited Mr. Templeton to talk about his books. We've been working together on his latest: a new history of the Dean Corll case. I'm an expert on Dean's crimes, naturally, so Mr. Templeton thought—"

"Dean," I say. "You're on a first name basis?"

"Mr. Templeton thought it would be a good idea to pick my brain. You might have a hard time believing this, Roland, but there are people out there who take what I do very seriously, and he's one of them. One of the *many*, Roland. My website has an international audience."

"So Bayard showed up at your conference? Had you ever seen him before?"

She shakes her head. "He must have seen one of the flyers we put up, or maybe read about it online. He sat in the back through all the sessions, but I could tell he was riveted. Hanging on every word. And he wrote a lot of things down. At first I thought maybe he was a reporter. But no." She frowns at the memory of disappointment. "Still, he's the one who made the Q&A session such a success. He asked so many good questions."

"What kind of questions?"

"The detective speaker, Mr. Lauterbach, went over all the things a modern investigation would do differently hunting a serial killer like Dean. It was *so* fascinating. David wanted to know whether they really were hunting any serial killers, right this minute. The detective said he couldn't comment, but then Mr. Templeton said there were a couple of cases *he'd* been looking at, some murders that seemed to be connected. And the detective got this shocked look on his face, because one of those cases was his—and he'd made a connection too, but to a third murder. They started going back and forth. The rest of us went along for the ride."

This is more or less the scene Templeton described.

"He wanted to know everything: why the killer would kill, why he would leave the bodies in the swimming pools, everything. Motive questions. Method questions. He was eating it all up. We all were. He'd never heard about the Fauk case before—Mr. Templeton talked about the case during his slide show—and he asked a lot of questions about that."

"Brad did a slide show, too?"

She nods. "It wasn't as fancy as the detective's, just the pictures from his books."

"His books? Do you have a copy of *The Kingwood Killing*?"

She goes to the bookcase on the far wall, her sequins shimmering. "I have that one and the new one. He signed them both for me, too."

I flip through *The Kingwood Killing*, turning the glossy image from the Nicole Fauk crime scene around so she can see. "Was that one of his slides?"

She nods. "It's bloodcurdling, isn't it? The way he bleeds them and dumps the bodies."

The present tense isn't lost on me, but I ignore the implication. Turning the book back around, I gaze at the black-and-white photo.

All this time, the pristine condition of Bayard's book has been gnawing away at me. It should have been annotated and dog-eared, a physical artifact of his homicidal obsession. Instead, the pages were clean, apparently unread. Now it makes sense.

The book wasn't the focus. The book was never the focus. The image drove him, and he didn't need the book for that. Templeton had projected Nicole Fauk's murder onto the big screen; he'd narrated the details, leaving nothing to the imagination, stamping the image indelibly into Bayard's memory. He could have drawn on it anytime. Staging the scene to resemble Fauk's was just another dodge, just another improvisation to make his crime blend in with those of the serial killer the detective and the author had just hypothesized into existence.

Only the killer is real. He just happens to be behind bars up at Huntsville, spinning stories in front of The Donald.

"Afterward," she says, "when everybody else had left, me and David stayed behind to listen as the two of them went back and forth. It was fascinating, Roland, the way they built up the profile. Like there were four of us to begin with, and by the time they were done there were five. Like another person was with us in the room."

"The killer, you mean."

She nods.

"Did Bayard tell you *why* he was so interested?"

Her face lights up. "He was so sweet. I'm a little surprised he hasn't come back for the regular meetings. I really took a shine to him, too. But I couldn't help it. My maternal instinct kicks in. He reminded me of my own boys. The two of us stayed after Mr. Templeton and the detective left, and he just poured out his whole life to me in a gush. And he wanted to know all about me, too."

"About you," I say. "And did my name come up?"

She frowns. "So I'm not allowed to mention you, is that how it is? Not even in private conversation? I've always made a point in my writing not to mention you by name, not after the way you freaked out—"

"Did he want to know about me?"

"He did ask a question or two. It's only natural since you investigated both of the cases in Mr. Templeton's books, and since I'm your sister—"

"You're not my sister."

"—he naturally wanted to know. Don't worry. I didn't say anything negative. I told him you were very successful, that you were married to a beautiful woman. A lawyer, no less. A wealthy heiress." Bitterness in her voice. "How for all your achievements in life, you still live in the old neighborhood, you're still so down-to-earth—"

"Tammy, stop it."

"Well," she says. "I have to lie to people or they wouldn't understand."

The anger inside me. A kettle on the boil. I try to suppress it, to keep the lid halfway on. I can't storm out. I can't hit back. There's something in all this I'm not seeing.

My maternal instinct. My own boys.

"How old is Bayard?" I ask.

"Roland, I don't know exactly." An annoyed shake of the head. "He must have been in grad school. He said he was studying criminal justice, that's why he came. He was doing a paper on serial killers."

"You're talking about David Junior," I say.

"Who are *you* talking about?"

My head fills with white noise.

I stop the recorder. I put it into my pocket. I rise from the chair. I retrace my steps to the front door.

"Roland, wait," she says, looming behind me, snatching at my arm.

She stops me at the Christmas tree, her grip surprisingly strong. Her nails dig into my arm, gripping my sleeve in her fist. She jerks again with enough force to turn me toward her.

"You can't just walk out on me like this. We still have some issues to confront. You need to face up to what happened." She shakes me like she did when I was a kid. "Listen to me, Roland. I know this is hard for you to accept, but it's time to let go of your guilt. It's not your fault Moody died the way he did. It's not your fault Dean killed him. There's nothing you could have done, but what you need to do now—what he needs you to do for him—is accept what happened. Stop fighting the truth. You *know* what happened."

I try to pull my arm free, but she holds tight. I jerk harder, dragging her forward, until a ripping sound shocks us both into silence. She drops her hand. The left sleeve of Lyndon Pellier's Donegal tweed jacket hangs free from the shoulder, my shirt visible through the weft of veiny threads.

"Oh, Roland," she says, stepping backward. "Your nice jacket. I'm so sorry."

I move toward her. "You're right about one thing: I *do* know what happened. And, Tammy, I'm not the one fighting the truth. I face it head on every day. I look it in the face and I don't blink. The truth is Moody wasn't murdered by some depraved pedophile. I know that and your father knew it, too. Dean Corll didn't kill him. Nobody did."

"That's not true, Roland. You have to face the truth."

"I know what happened, Tammy. Listen to me." I take her glittering sleeve in my own hand now, shedding sequins on the floor. "I know what happened because I saw what happened. I saw it with my own eyes. He stole a gun from your dad's shop. He left me on the sidewalk and went with them. He got into the car, Tammy. It was a green Ford—an LTD, I think. They all left together, Moody and those boys he'd been running with, and they were going to Dallas and who knows where after that."

"No," she says. "You're wrong."

"I'm not wrong. I saw it."

"You were just a kid, Roland. You don't know what you saw. He didn't go with those boys. Daddy already warned him off them. That gun was to protect himself. He was afraid of the Candy Man, and that's where he was heading when you saw him. He was on his new bike and the bike disappeared—"

"It didn't disappear," I say. "I took it."

She shrinks back. *"What?"*

"They never found the bike because I took it. I hid it in the space between two of the storage buildings. Moody said I could have it, but I was afraid your dad wouldn't let me. So I kept it there. When I went back to ride it later, somebody had stolen it. That's why the bike was gone. Simple as that."

Her face drains. "You never told me."

"It's hard to talk when you're being smothered," I say. "I told your dad. Later. Once the search was over. Moody told me to wait so he couldn't be found."

"Daddy never said anything like this to me."

"That's between you and him. I told him, and I assume he did some checking, but your brother was long gone. A few years later, when I was working with him in the shop, he told me not to worry about it."

"What does that mean?"

"I don't know. I guess he'd given up and moved on."

She rests her hand against the front table, clinking two of the hand-painted cottages into each other. "Why?"

"Why what?"

"*Why would he run away?*" she sobs, her throat raw with emotion.

"I don't know, Tammy," I say, moving my hand to the doorknob. "I was eleven years old. To be honest, I always assumed it was because of you."

I regret the words the moment they're out. I regret them more when she slumps against the wall, pulling the cotton ground out from under the nearest cottage, sending it crashing to the floor. I could spare a fellow cop like Lauterbach the indignity of a stab in the back, deserving as he is, but for my half sister, for the daughter of the people who raised me, there is no such mercy.

The air outside is thick. There's even a hint of the accustomed Houston warmth. I walk to the car, my ripped sleeve drooping with every step. At the car door I start to pull the jacket off, then change my mind and leave it. I strap myself in, turn the key in the ignition, and back into the cul-de-sac, narrowly missing a red-framed bike lying on the pavement.

I pause. I shift into park. I undo my seat belt. The door pops open and I stand.

Tammy stands in the open doorway, bracing herself against the frame. Her shirt twinkles, forlorn in the gray light. I strip Lyndon Pellier's torn jacket off, first one arm and then the other, balling the fabric and tossing it onto the backseat. My gun exposed. My cuffs and badge. My true and only nature revealed.

I glare at my cousin and she glares back.

I get in the car and I drive.

CHAPTER **27**

I am stumped. I am confused. I am staring at a computer screen on the sixth floor of police headquarters. I am in my cubicle. I am clicking through the records. I am trying to make up my mind whether David Bayard Jr. is a victimizer or a victim. I am wondering whether this is a useful distinction anymore.

When I debriefed Aguilar on the results of my interview with Tammy, he studied his shoes a little while and went, "Huh." Now he's on his way across town, running late for his daughter's Christmas recital. "It'll keep," he said. It'll have to. The lawyer representing both of the Bayards has the right idea. For her clients, anyway. Not for me. They won't be making statements to the police at this time. They won't be cooperating with the investigation.

There's not much in the system about David. No adult record, and if there was any record of juvenile offenses, it's been expunged. Which is why I'm cold-calling after normal business hours, hoping to get lucky with past associates.

The College Station landlord says he never had a problem with the man personally—the rent was always on time—but David hasn't lived there for over a year, and when he left, there was a charge assessed for damages to the property.

"Cleanup mainly," he says, "and the cost of repainting. He'd written all over the walls. Taped and tacked stuff up everywhere. It was like some kind of psycho pad. I like 'em quiet, but there's such a thing as too quiet, you know?"

"You never had an issue with him," I say. "But did anyone else?"

He pauses.

"This is important, sir."

"There's a tenant of mine you should talk to," he says. "She lived right across the hall from him. I'm not saying anything one way or another, 'cause how do I know? But talk to Kristie and see what she has to say."

Kristie turns out to be a sweet-voiced economics major with one semester to go before graduation. She confirms that David lived across the hall from her until last year, but says as long as she knew him, he'd never been enrolled as a student. She assumed he dropped out. If he had a job, she wasn't aware of it. People assumed he was living off his parents.

"He can get really intense. Really . . . obsessive. People kind of stayed clear of him, you know? And that's just not my way. When I see somebody ostracized like that, I always try to reach out. Not everybody knows how to make friends, but they still want to have friends, right?"

"Were you and David friends?"

A pause. "I thought so."

"But something happened."

She takes a deep breath. Lets it out. "Something did happen. We were talking in the hallway one time, and he had something he wanted to show me in his apartment. I'd never been inside and I was kind of curious, so I went in. He shut the door behind us, and this little voice in my head was going, *Something's not right.*"

"What did the apartment look like? The landlord called it a 'psycho pad.' "

"Pretty much." She takes another breath. "There were pictures he'd taken. The bedroom window overlooked the pool, and when we'd lay out in the summer, people would say they could see him watching from the window. I thought they were just being mean, but there were a lot of pictures. All the girls in the building, all the ones who laid out. He had pictures of me, too."

"How did he explain that?"

"The pictures are what he wanted to show me. He wanted to know if I thought they were good. I said I didn't think so, that it was illegal, but he said if you're displaying yourself in public, then it's not. That's what he called it: *displaying yourself.*" She gives a nervous laugh. "I mean, I'm standing there looking at these pictures of myself, and I'm trying to be polite, but I just want to get out of there, you know? And he's not letting me. He put his hand on me—he has something wrong with his hand—he'd put it on me and then he'd push. Not hard. Just this little push. Backing me up a step or two. I told him to stop, and he acted like it was a game. He kept doing it. He'd touch me and I'd push his hand away. But he was backing me into the bedroom.

"I told him to let me go. He ignored me. Then I heard people passing in the hallway and I started calling out to them. That's what spooked him. He started laughing again and saying he was just joking with me. I got out of there and I never talked to him again. I had extra locks put on the door. Even then, I think he'd watch me through the peephole, keeping track of my coming and going."

"Did you report this to the police?" I ask, hoping there might be a paper trail.

"I should have," she says. "I did tell some of the guys in the building, and they had a 'talk' with David, which I think was more than a talk."

"And that's why he moved out."

"I guess."

I thank her for the help.

"There's one more thing," she says. "And maybe I shouldn't say. It might have nothing to do with him."

"I think you'd better tell me."

"Somebody tried to set my car on fire. Some guys in the apartment saw him doing it, pouring something over the car. They chased him off and came and got me. The car had gasoline all over it."

"Was it David who did this?" I ask, remembering the Molotov cocktail.

"They couldn't say. But I think it must have been him."

After the call, I let out a long breath.

When Agnieszka spotted a watcher in the neighbor's attic, she had assumed it was the man of the house, David Bayard Sr., but she was wrong. From Kristie's story, it sounds like he was showing all the warning signs back in College Station: watching the sunbathers by the pool, taking illicit photos like the ones recovered in the Bayard attic, perhaps even stalking the girl he'd culled from the herd. And that pushing thing. Pressing his scarred hand against her skin. I can imagine him doing it, spreading the fingers out, eyes fixed on the gaps of flesh between his fingers.

One, two, three. Four, five, six.

I've been had. While I was tracking the father's movements, I took the son's on faith. I assumed he was a student, assumed his schedule would correspond with the academic calendar. The fact is, I don't know where he lives. I don't know his comings and goings. I brought him in not as a suspect but a witness, and let him walk right out without a charge.

I flip through my notes back to my first contact with Kim Bayard. She'd told me her husband was out of the country, but made no mention of her stepson, even though he clearly had access to the house. Either she didn't know about the nest up in the attic, or she was intentionally concealing the fact. When we took her husband away, she could have protested, could have put the blame on David, but she didn't. I can understand a father—even an abusive one—covering for his son. But why would she?

I didn't get Kim Bayard on tape that first day, but she sent me to Emmet Mainz. I fast-forward through the Mainz talk, listening for any mention of the Bayards' son. There's nothing.

I reach for the phone.

"Yes?"

"Mr. Mainz," I say. "This is Roland March. If you have a minute, I'd like to talk."

"A minute?" He chuckles over the line. "Detective, I have all night."

"Good. I'll see you in a quarter of an hour."

In the car, I call Charlotte to let her know I'll be home late.

She accepts the news with a sigh. "The lot in life for the policeman's wife."

"That rhymes," I say. "And I'm sorry."

"Don't be. I'm used to it."

"I'm not apologizing for being late. There's something else I want you to do for me. You'll think I'm crazy and overcautious, but I'd feel better if you'd pack a bag and go to Ann's again tonight."

"But, Roland," she says. "The guy's behind bars. Did he get out on bail already? Even if he has, the locksmiths were here today, and I took the initiative and called the security alarm company, too."

Things *I* should have done. Things I meant to.

"He's not out yet," I say. "But between you and me, I think I screwed this one up. I arrested the father, and I should have bagged the son."

"And he's not in custody?"

"No, he's not."

She sighs again, resigned. "All right, then. But I don't feel right leaving Carter and Gina here. They could be in danger, right? I'm going to see if Ann can put them up. Otherwise, I'm going to put them in a hotel."

"Carter's a big boy," I say.

"And Gina's pregnant. So either I get my way, or I stay put."

"You're the boss."

I start to hang up, but she stops me. "Oh, Roland, we got another message from the tailor, too. You need to go pick up the rest of Daddy's suits. They're done."

"Good," I say, "because one of them's going in the trash bin."

"What?"

"My cousin Tammy ripped the sleeve off."

"Really," she says. "You saw Tammy."

"And I didn't use my pepper spray. In therapy they'd call that a breakthrough."

In the corridor outside Emmet Mainz's conservatory, I notice a new letter to the editor framed on the wall. Pausing, I see the printed copy side by side with his signed original. This time he made it into the *Times Literary Supplement*, disputing the facts in some fifty-year-old literary controversy.

"Congratulations," I say.

His rheumy eyes sparkle behind the heavy round glasses. He gives me a coy smile.

The baby grand gleams in the lamplight. He resumes his customary seat at the piano, leaving me to choose which of the chairs I prefer. I decide to stand, leaning into the crook of the piano, running my hand over the cool black wood.

"When I was here before, I didn't know what I was looking for. Which means I didn't know the right questions to ask."

"And now you do?"

"I hope so. It was Kim Bayard who first mentioned you. I assume you know that family at least as well as you do the Hills."

His long fingers glide over the ivory keys without applying any pressure. He pulls them away, setting his hand in his lap.

"Not particularly," he sniffs. "The husband, I'm afraid, is a bit of a Philistine, one of those boy-men who makes a lot of money and spends it on the same things he wanted when he was fifteen. Cars. Gadgets. Stuff. For all I know, women, too. The temporal delights, and by no means the most delightful of them."

"I'm not sure I know what you mean."

"Really?" He laughs. "I am speaking English, aren't I?"

"Are you?"

He laughs again, clearly considering this kind of banter more of a delight than cars, gadgets, and women.

"The Bayard I'm interested in is the son. David Junior. What do you know about him?"

"Ah," he says. "David Junior. I know that you wouldn't want him feeding your dog while you're out of town. I tried that once, and it was a disaster."

I glance over my shoulder. "You have a dog?"

"Not anymore." He notes my expression. "It's not *his* fault, though. He didn't kill the dog. But he did *something*. That poor creature was miserable when I got back, and that was the last time I left a key for David Junior."

Animal torture. *Check.*

"How old was he when this happened?"

Mainz touches his forehead. "How old? A teenager, I suppose. Maybe fifteen, but don't quote me on that. Before he went away to school. They sent him to boarding school, did you know that? Who sends children to boarding school anymore?"

People whose child has a behavior problem. People raising a sociopath.

"Do you know why he was sent away?"

He shakes his head. "What I do know is that Bayard *père* used to travel a lot, even more than he does now. Maybe he was too much of a handful for Kim on her own. He's not her son, you know? But that is pure speculation. You'd have to ask her about that."

"That's why I'm here."

He pauses. "Whatever do you mean?"

"I'd like you to give her a call and invite her over. Preferably without mentioning my being here."

The significance of my suggestion dawns on him. To his credit, Mainz agrees to help.

"I don't know if it'll do any good," he says, "but I'll give it a try."

He rises from his bench and moves lightly across the room, bending down behind the corner of the couch. He straightens with an old-fashioned phone in hand, a long cord unspooling as he returns. The black plastic gives a little ring when he sets it on the piano.

"Do you have the number, or should I look it up?"

I dig through my notes, sliding the number in front of him. He dials with a slender digit, punching the numbers with crisp precision. "It's ringing."

The conversation takes thirty seconds, and when he hangs up, there's a grin on his lips.

"She'll be right over."

Mainz goes to the door alone, greeting her in a high-pitched, stagey voice, tut-tutting at her inaudible remarks. As they come down the hallway, he pauses to prepare her for the shock.

"Now, don't be angry with me," he says. "I have a little surprise."

When Kim Bayard sees me on the sofa, she stops in her tracks.

"You're the one who searched the house and took Dave away."

"Roland March," I say, rising to extend my hand.

"I shouldn't be talking to you."

"You don't have to if you don't want to. It's just that I have some questions and you're the only person who can answer them."

Mainz guides her to a chair, easing her down, then positions himself to one side. "If he tries anything fresh, don't worry. I'll be right here."

I hadn't expected him to stay. It's a little unorthodox, conducting an interview with an audience. But it's his house and I can hardly ask him to leave. His presence might go a long way to helping her open up. So I smile at the little man. I smile at Kim. I take the recorder from my breast pocket, then open the Filofax on my lap to consult my notes. She shakes her head.

"I don't want you writing anything down," she says. "I'll answer your questions, assuming I can, but only off the record. I won't testify against my husband, but if I can help him by clearing up your confusion, I'm willing to do that. *Off* the record."

I close the Filofax, sandwiching the running recorder between the pages. I set it on the couch beside me, hoping either that she didn't notice the little device or, seeing me remove it from inside my jacket, mistook the shiny metal case for a pen.

"We were just talking about your son," I say. "Where exactly does he live?"

"You know that big high-rise on Kirby? He has a little place there. His father pays the rent. His father pays for everything."

"I see. And he's not a student at A&M anymore, is he?"

She shrugs. "He's supposed to be working on a dissertation, but he had some kind of trouble over there and came back."

"David has a problem with his hand. An injury. He told me his father did that to him."

"He did?" She shakes her head in mock admiration. "You know, he told one of the counselors at St. Thomas that he had a little sister who wasn't allowed to go out. He said we kept her in an upstairs closet because she was deformed. They obviously didn't believe that, but in this day and age, you have to be sure, don't you? It was humiliating."

"What happened to his hand, then?"

"He did that himself," she says. "My husband collects knives. When David was in high school, I heard a scream from upstairs, and when I found him I thought he'd chopped his finger off. There were all these little holes in his father's desk, and blood everywhere, and I couldn't get him to hold still long enough to see what was wrong.

"What happened was, he was stabbing the knife between his fingers, seeing how fast he could do it. He'd seen Dave showing off in front of some guests. But the knife turned in his grip and cut into him. It took a big chunk out of one finger and sliced up the other. I wanted to get rid of all the knives, but Dave wouldn't listen. That's when he had the glass cases installed, to keep David away from the weapons."

"Mrs. Bayard," I say. "Are you aware that the knife used to kill Simone Walker and Agnieszka Oliszewski was one of your husband's?"

She blinks. Freezes.

"What I can't figure out is, if your husband didn't kill them, how did the killer get the knife?"

Silence.

"Can you think of an explanation?"

"Well," she says. "David sold some of his collection recently."

"This wasn't one of those knives. But now that you mention it, I was wondering why he sold them? Did he need the money, or did you put your foot down again and this time he listened?"

"I'm not sure," she says to the floor. "I don't know why he did it."

"I think you do."

She covers her mouth with her hand.

"It's essential that you tell me the truth."

The hand drops. "I think . . . I think one of the knives went missing."

"Missing."

She nods. "But that was long before the murders. That was more than a month ago."

"David took the knife," I say. "And his father responded by selling off some more. Like he was trying to cover it up. Like he thought David would do something bad with that knife."

"No," she says, shaking her head. "You don't understand at all. My husband is the only person who can get through to him. If he was going to do anything—anything *serious*—Dave would've stopped it from happening. He's always . . ."

"Always what? Always stopped things from happening?"

She nods.

"Only he couldn't this time. He was leaving for Africa. His job was in jeopardy. He had other things on this mind. David comes and goes as he pleases, doesn't he? The things we found in the attic, they belong to him."

She sinks into the chair, nodding wanly. Surrender. Mainz, sensing the shift, pulls a chair up beside her, putting his hand over hers.

"He has a room in the attic," Kim says. "He used to live up there, and when he came back from College Station, he moved back in. But I made Dave tell him to go. He moved everything to the high-rise."

"Not everything," I say. "This was recent, wasn't it? You're making it sound like your stepson has been living in the high-rise a long time, but that was a recent development."

"Afterward," she says.

"After what?"

"After Dave came back from Lagos."

"After the first murder, you mean."

Nothing.

"Why, then? Why kick him out after Simone's death? You knew, didn't you?"

She crosses one leg over the other, bouncing it nervously at the knee. She gnaws at her fingernails, staring off to her left.

"Let go of it," I say. "This isn't yours to carry."

Her eyes dart toward me, then away.

"Kim, it's time to tell the truth. I've brought more people through this than you can ever imagine, and I know all the signs. You can't live with what you're holding, believe me. If you don't get clear of him, he'll drag you down, too."

"I don't know anything," she says. "I can't prove anything."

"You don't have to. Just tell me what you do know."

"Unwanted touching," she says.

"Come again?"

"That's why he was asked to leave the first school. He was only nine. He didn't mean anything by it. But the others, they all acted so shocked, like nothing had ever happened like this before. Like there was something wrong with us, with me and Dave. I told them he was a normal boy. I told them he was just . . . curious."

She covers her mouth again, closes her eyes. The tears come. I expect Mainz to lean over and comfort her, but instead he shrinks back, his mouth curled downward in disgust. He strokes the fabric of his trousers, wiping his hand up and down the crease.

"There were doctors," she says. "There were diagnoses and prescriptions. It got so complicated that I couldn't remember what the problem was supposed to be in the first place. He grew so docile. So withdrawn. But it never seemed to stop. All we were doing was masking the symptoms. Underneath it all, he was so bad. He would do things to himself. Hurt himself. And if it wasn't knives, it was fire. I always had to watch him. I was afraid of what would happen the moment I looked away."

"Did he ever hurt anyone else?"

"No," she says. "Not that I know of. Not really. When he left home for college, I thought, *finally we can start living our lives again. Finally I* could start living. Dave was gone so much, he expected me to be the one to . . ."

She glances at Mainz, noticing the distance between them for the first time. Her cheeks flush.

"It's easy to assign blame," she says, "but I did the best I could. He wasn't mine."

I give her a nod of encouragement.

When a witness opens up against her better judgment, against her own self-interest, I'm the most understanding person in the world. But Mainz can't help himself. The deeper into my world he's drawn, the more uncomfortable he grows, all his urbanity and wit evaporating on the hot skillet of reality. The recognition dawning that all these years, he's lived a few doors down from an unfathomable evil, a darkness beyond his comprehension.

As his sympathy fades, mine burns brighter and brighter.

Talk to me, it says. *Open your heart to me. Confide all your secrets and sins. I am your confessor. You don't need to hide anything from me. There is nothing I have not heard, nothing I have not seen.*

"Mrs. Bayard," I say. "Your stepson was stalking a woman in College Station a year ago. I've talked to her. He followed exactly the same pattern then as now. Watching her. Taking photographs of her. He even got her alone and started touching her. He did it like this." I hold my hand up, fingers spread. "He just pushed. Gently at first, with his fingers wide like that."

"Why are you telling me this?"

"The man who killed Simone Walker, he did the same thing. He put his hands on her, and he stabbed her like this." I grasp an imaginary ice pick in my free hand, bringing it down like a piston, again and again. "The same six wounds, over and over. In a half-moon pattern. That's what he did to Agnieszka, too. That's how he treated them."

Her burning eyes follow every movement, seeing the scene in her mind. She knows what he did. She knows her own guilt. She wants to unburden herself.

"Tell me what happened," I say. "Tell me everything."

She opens her mouth to speak.

A chime sounds inside her purse. She freezes. She takes the ringing phone out, holding it at arm's length.

"It's him," she says. "David."

"Where is he now?"

"I don't know. Should I answer?"

I nod.

She puts the phone to her ear—"Hello? Hello?"—then lowers it to her lap: "He hung up."

"Mrs. Bayard—"

"No," she says. "I can't. I shouldn't even be here."

She wrenches herself out of the chair.

"If he does know, then you aren't safe. You realize that."

"I shouldn't have come here."

She stamps across the floor, breezing past me with a sob. Mainz stands. I motion him not to follow. We stare at each other, listening to her footsteps disappear down the corridor. The front door creaks open and crashes shut.

"Well," Mainz says, dropping back into his seat.

I switch off the recorder and return it to my pocket. I gather the rest of my things. We share a last awkward moment, not certain what to say to each other.

"Good night, Emmet," I say. "And thanks for your help."

He makes no move to escort me, so I let myself out.

CHAPTER 28

There's no sign of her outside. She roared away in her car, heading in the opposite direction from her house. I slip behind the wheel, pondering my next move. She's convinced of her husband's innocence. I'm not. But I am convinced of her stepson's guilt.

I stood there in the funeral home parking lot and didn't see it. I urged him on in hushed, sympathetic tones. I felt sorry for him. It's not the first time a suspect's played me.

This one hurts.

My phone rings and it's Hanford on the line. His voice charged with excitement.

"I apologize up front," he says. "I got my eye off the ball. There's been a development, though. A big development."

"Go ahead."

"Have you checked your email recently?"

My pulse quickens. "Not in a couple of hours."

"Well, he did it. He used Simone Walker's laptop. There's probably a message waiting for you right now—"

"What about your email to him? Did it work?"

A pause. "*Yes.*"

"You got a photo?"

"*Yes.*"

"And a location?"

"Yes, yes, yes," he says. "I can't believe it really worked. I didn't even have to trace the IP addresses, because I recognize the location from the picture. He was at Brasil, the coffee shop on Westheimer. It was still light out when the picture was snapped. His hand is covering part of his face—but it's a very distinctive hand." He stops to catch his breath. "I'm sorry, though, about the delay, and I know you've already got someone else in custody—"

"Don't worry about that. How old is the photo? If it was still light outside . . ."

"There was a lag in the message going out, and a lag in me checking. I realize time was of the essence, but—"

"Never mind. We need to get people to that coffee shop right away."

"I took the liberty of alerting some units. I sent a copy of the photo to Dispatch. I figured that's what you'd want."

"You figured right. I'm on my way."

I put the shifter in drive and hit the gas. A car rushes past on the street—I didn't see it—forcing me to mash down on the brake. Up ahead, the driver flicks on his headlights. No wonder I missed him. I take a deep breath, check the mirrors, and get going.

I take Kirby all the way to the right turn on Westheimer, making a mental note to get a warrant for David's high-rise apartment. I turn on Dunlavy, parking behind a line of patrol cruisers on the curb. Nguyen is there, and just inside the patio I run into Sergeant Nixon himself, the shift supervisor. He smirks at me, palms up.

"Here for your coffee fix, Detective? Or are you having a late dinner with the missus?"

"None of the above. I take it he's not here?"

He shakes his head. "But look around if you want."

About half of the tables are packed and things seem busy at the bar. The pack of loners who infest such places during daytime, earbuds inserted, faces lit up by the glow of computer screens, has considerably thinned out. The patrons eye us with interest, sitting mostly in groups. Out on the town. Surprised at the sudden arrival of the police.

A couple of uniforms stroll through the tables, double-checking faces. I do likewise, determined to make the effort.

Nix is right, though. David has left the building.

I go back outside to my car, the uniforms coalescing in my wake. I grab my briefcase from the passenger seat, open the laptop right there on my hood. The Outlook software chugs along, filling my inbox with recent arrivals.

"You mind if I release these units?" Nix asks. "I guess I'll write this one up as a wild goose chase."

The banter irritates me. "That's the nature of the game, except when it isn't."

He chuckles. "If the law enforcement thing doesn't work out, you might have a bright future in the exciting world of fortune cookie writing."

The message from Simone Walker's email address is there, just as Hanford said. I glide the cursor over her name. I click. The pretense from before is dropped: he hasn't bothered to pretend the message is from Simone. The strange chattiness is absent, too. There's just a single veiled threat:

I GUESS THINGS ARE ABOUT TO HEAT UP

As the cruisers pull away, Nix returns to my side. With no subordinates to impress, he adopts a sober expression. We've known each other a long time. He leans over to squint at the screen, nodding as he reads the line of text. Then his eyes cut over and he recognizes the name.

"You been getting a lot of those?" he asks.

"Enough."

"And the guy in the picture, he's the one?"

I nod.

"All right, then," he says, clapping my shoulder. "You look out for yourself, okay? Don't do anything stupid."

"Don't worry, I won't. And listen: I'm gonna need some more muscle from your shift. We're not letting go of this guy. I need to round up my partner and my lieutenant, then we can all drop in on him at home. He's got a place in that high-rise on Kirby."

"Tell me where and when," he says. "I'll bring the chips and dip."

I get back in the car, situating the open laptop on the passenger seat. The photo of Bayard is waiting in my inbox, too. He sits at a patio table with his chin cradled in the scarred hand. The image is fuzzy but unmistakably him. He stares just below the camera. His eyes are lucid and hard. Again, the pretense is gone, all the glancing away, all the awkwardness and evasion. Without the mask, I see him for the first time as he truly is.

Calculating. Intelligent. And all too normal. The serial killer whose existence I denied. The unifying intelligence behind the seemingly unconnected acts.

No, that's not right.

I'm giving him too much credit. The connections were obvious. The crimes, actual and attempted, were clumsily executed. Only the cleanup showed the genius of evil. The rest was simple depravity.

The story Kristie told me, the girl from across the hall, provides a template for speculation. I can imagine how Simone's murder must have gone down. She would have been surprised by his presence, perhaps. Or maybe she invited him in. Their relationship would have been like the one he'd developed with Kristie. She would have pitied him.

When he put his hands on her, when he began his pushing game, she might have sensed what was coming. But probably not. She'd have seen him as a big child—"emotionally stunted," in Kristie's words— nothing she couldn't handle. *Stop*, she would have told him, and she'd turned her back on him. And in a flash he rushed up, knife in hand, closing his fingers over her lips as he inflicted the fatal wound. Then, crouched over her dead body, he'd begun the ritual stabbing. Clumsily again. Learning.

There must have been some contact before. She might have had emails from him. She might have had his name and number programmed in her phone. He'd known all along he'd have to take them.

With Agnieszka, everything must have been different. That was a rush job.

He'd watched her out by the pool, complaining to Jack Hill over the phone. He'd failed with Agnieszka before, but he wouldn't this time. She had the power to connect him directly to the crime. So when she left, he followed. He learned where she lived, then positioned himself for an ambush when she arrived home. There was no question of coaxing her—she was on her guard—which explains why he resorted to the ligature, choking her first, and then stabbing her. Putting the blade in her hand before plunging it home.

That was personal, and it makes sense: she was the first real target. With Kristie, he was just feeling his way, discovering for the first time what was truly inside him. Watching Agnieszka, the fantasy must have taken root in him. He saw what he would do to her. He could stare the act in the face and recognize himself. But then she short-circuited the process and the obstructing trees went up. Only later, when the new tenant arrived, could he execute his plan.

Simone was his first. I'm certain of that. An experienced predator wouldn't hunt so close to home. In time he'd gain a kind of trade craft, teaching himself how to commit his crimes while avoiding detection.

Now he will never have the chance. I can at least comfort myself with that.

Yes, things are going to heat up for you, David.

Just not the way you were expecting.

"Gina's here with me," Charlotte says, "but I couldn't get Carter to listen. He said you'd understand. He said he wasn't going to be a bystander."

"Great. I'll call him."

"What about you? Is everything all right?"

"Everything's fine."

Aguilar taps on the window, motioning me to hurry up. He's not too happy about being called out. Through the windshield I can see Bascombe slipping a vest over his head while Captain Hedges, already in body armor, rests the butt of a decorative shotgun on his hip, probably practicing for the cameras he expects after the fact. It wasn't my idea to drag him out to the high-rise—and judging from the lieutenant's tight features, it wasn't his, either.

"Charlotte, I gotta go."

"Be careful," she says.

The tactical team, stacked up alongside their van, is ready to go. I get out of the car and vest up, press-checking my side arm one more time. So many officers, so many guns, it might seem like overkill to bring in a single knife-wielding nut job. But overkill is our specialty, the firstest with the mostest, overwhelming force applied to an enemy's weakest point, nipping all opposition in the bud before it can materialize. Textbook blue.

I just wish I knew for certain Bayard was waiting in there. We haven't done our strategic homework. We haven't had time.

"If he's home, he knows we're coming."

"Let's get in there, then," Aguilar says.

We meet a concierge in the lobby, then travel up the elevators in groups, forming up in the hallway down from David's apartment. When everyone's ready, Hedges makes the call, trailing personally behind the tac team, leaving the rest of us to follow in his wake. At the door, the rammer sidesteps politely so the next man in line can insert the concierge's key. We pause a few moments, breathing hard, keeping the muzzles of our shotguns and pistols and MP5 submachine guns aimed discreetly at the ground.

The lights are off inside the apartment. Our flashlights cut through the darkness, left and right, until someone gets the idea to flip the switch. A dozen policemen fan out through five hundred square feet, figuring out pretty quick that David isn't here.

"The view of downtown is impressive," I say.

Hedges glares at me.

There's a stack of mover's boxes in the bedroom, some clothes in the closet. Not much else. From the bathroom, Aguilar calls out. I push my way past the tac squad. The bottom of the tub is scorched. In the middle of the burn, a melted laptop computer. A charred brick that used to be Simone Walker's cell phone.

"He's covering his tracks," Aguilar says.

"It's too late for that."

In the kitchen, tucked into the refrigerator door, another wine bottle filled with gasoline.

"So this is a bust," Hedges says. "We'll need to leave a team here, stake the place out. Bascombe, will you see to that?"

The lieutenant nods. After making a show of conferring with the rest of us, making sure the scene is secured, Hedges punches out. He lets us all know what a good job we're doing and to keep it up. As he squeezes my shoulder and repeats the sentiment under his breath, I realize he's been campaigning so long behind the scenes that now he's wooing us, too.

As soon as he's gone, I exchange a look with Bascombe.

"The promotion," he says. "It's not gonna be him and he knows it."

"You sure? He was trying pretty hard just now."

"Exactly." He shakes his head in disgust. "If he switches it off now, it's obvious to everyone what he's been up to. So he's gotta keep it up for a while."

"It's already obvious to everyone," I say.

"And if he realized that, how do you think he'd feel?"

I look at my lieutenant with new eyes. He's not commiserating with me. He's sending a message. The captain went crazy on us, but he's a good man. His head will be screwed back on in no time.

"Some people," he says, "if they saw the emperor strutting around with no clothes, all they'd do is laugh. You and me, we're not like that."

"I hear you, sir. No, we're not."

He puts one of his big hands on my shoulder blade, resting it there a moment, then he goes to work rounding up all the stray officers.

Down the elevator and back on the pavement, Nix leans against the wheel well of a cruiser, arms crossed.

"You're batting zero for two this evening, March."

"At least I'm still swinging, right?"

Behind the wheel again, making my way north toward home. Carter Robb picks up the phone and gets an earful from me about not being a bystander. I don't like my words being used against me.

"You should've listened to what Charlotte said. There's a dangerous man out there, and he knows where we live. Until he's in custody, I'd just as soon not have you playing the cowboy over there. He already cut you once."

"Like I said, I've had worse. And if he does show up, somebody needs to be here to welcome him, right?"

"You mean you? What happened to turning the other cheek?"

"Jesus preached love," he says, "not stupidity. You're twisting that verse out of context."

"You can lecture me on the fine points later. Right now I'd appreciate it if you'd get in your car and go. Ann would be more than happy to have you over there. Just don't try any public prayer or she'll call the ACLU. Hey, better yet, maybe you can convert her. If anybody needs it—"

"Roland," he says. "You wanna cut it out. When you start up like this, I do have to turn the other cheek. But I don't have to like it."

"Then do what I say. I'm serious, son. This is no joke."

I cross under the Southwest Freeway, retracing my route from an hour before. I roll to a stop at the light on Richmond. A guy in a Santa suit stands on the corner with a restaurant sandwich board over his shoulders.

"I'm not afraid," Carter tells me. "And anyway, we do have one thing in common. I'm not gonna stand by and let bad things happen. How did you put it? I'm one of the braves."

The edge in his voice is enough to cut. Hearing that term on his lips. The two of us are always locking horns, always picking up on the same unfinished conversation.

"Sure you are," I say. "You don't have to prove it, either. You already have. Now get over there, all right? While you're standing on principle,

Charlotte and Gina are all on their own, with nothing but a chain-smoking pathologist to protect them. Bridger's got no cardio. Are you really gonna put your trust in him?"

He laughs, but it's not the easygoing humor of earlier days. We were on a roll for a while when they first moved in, glossing over our differences, and I'm afraid we'll never get that back. For one thing, he's always pulling stuff like this, second-guessing when it's clear I know better. Barking back at the alpha dog.

"Carter," I say. "Please do this."

A pause. "I'll tell you something. Maybe you were right the other night, when we were driving back from dinner. All that stuff about evil and free will. I've been thinking a lot about what you said. That's what I do when we have our little talks: think a lot. I get the feeling you don't. I think you forget as soon as they're done. But what you said stuck with me, and I feel like I gave you talking points instead of what I really think."

"Carter—"

"What I really think," he says, "is that I don't know why there's evil in the world. I believe God is loving, and I believe nothing can happen without his say-so. But there's more to him than those two things. He has reasons for what he does, and for what he allows."

"I'm sure he does."

"Impenetrable reasons," he says. "For evil and suffering. All I know is, those things don't mean to him what they mean to us. Not that he doesn't care, but for him, just staying alive isn't the highest good. There are things more important than living, more important than being happy, more important than never feeling pain."

In the rearview mirror, a pair of headlights dip. I glance back. I'm passing the Huntington on my right, approaching the intersection of San Felipe. The car behind me looks familiar.

"Let's continue this another time," I say.

"Like always. Listen, I'm staying."

"I've gotta go, Carter. I'll talk to you later."

He's already off the line. I look in my mirror again to be sure. I only got a flash of it before, when I had to slam on the brakes to keep from getting hit. On the curb in front of Mainz's house, just down the street from the Bayards'. Is it the same car? I think so. I slow down a little, hoping to close the distance. The driver adjusts for my speed. I accelerate quickly, not wanting to let on I've spotted him.

Nix said 0 for 2, and I'm reluctant to make it 0 for 3.

But I remember Ann's throwaway question: *Would it be so hard to tail you around?* Yeah, it would. At least that's what I've always assumed. Why should it be any harder for Bayard to follow me, though, than it was for me and Aguilar to tail Jason Young. Surveillance works not because it's impossible to detect but because most people aren't even looking for it.

A memory flashes. This happened before. I was pulling out with Carter in the passenger seat, and a car whizzed around me, like it had to veer to keep from hitting me. Just like what happened in front of Mainz's house. That's no coincidence. It was David Bayard. Trying to work up the nerve for a confrontation.

I call Bascombe, keeping an eye on the lights in my rearview.

"Are you positive?" he says.

"I'm not a hundred percent. I think it's the same car, and if it is, then it makes sense it would be him. That's probably how he found my house in the first place. I led him there."

"So what do you want to do?"

"I want to bushwhack him."

A pause. "Keep him busy, and I'll call you right back."

The gas station Bascombe chooses occupies the block between Shepherd and Durham, across from a fried chicken joint and a barbed-wired used car lot. All I have to do is turn into the parking lot and roll up to one of the gas pumps, like I'm filling my tank before heading home. Bascombe will be there in his black Ford Expedition. Some officers from the tac team in an unmarked van. Aguilar too, in his pickup. An ad hoc welcoming committee assembled from the leftovers of our last gig, sketchily briefed by phone, armed with my description of the car. I've called the plates in and had them run. The car is registered to David Bayard Sr.

His father pays for everything.

He tags along a few car lengths behind me, still taking pains not to be seen. That's a good sign. The ambush will catch him by surprise.

No traffic. Just a few cars on the road. We move from the orbit of one streetlight to another, getting closer and closer to the end of the road.

If I kept traveling along this route, I'd reach the church where I rousted Jason Young the morning after Simone Walker's murder. It's too bad we couldn't arrest Bayard there.

Poetic justice.

But driving into a gas station full of cars is one thing. He won't suspect a trap. A church parking lot at ten o'clock would look a little suspicious.

I cross the intersection and see the gas station up ahead. I drift over into the left-hand lane to make the turn. In my rearview I see him moving over.

I hit my blinker. He doesn't signal.

Bascombe's car is right near the entrance, parked in the rightmost space in front of the convenience store. We'll both have to pass him to reach the pumps. The tac van is in the same position on the opposite side of the store. Once he's in, Bayard can't get out without going through them. When Bascombe and the van reverse into the lane, he'll be boxed in. Cops in front of him and behind him, the store on his right and the pumps on his left.

Aguilar sits with his engine running by the air dispenser on the far side of the gas pumps, ready to cut either way if needed.

I make the turn, coasting past Bascombe's bumper. Bayard's car follows, closing the distance a little. I pull toward the pump, rolling to a stop. Any moment the tac van will reverse into position. I loosen my seat belt and pop open the door. I pop the thumb break on my holster.

David rolls by me slowly. I glance over. He comes to a stop, window down.

He looks at me with the same hard eyes from the photograph, a different man than the one I interviewed before. There's a cruel smile on his lips. An orange glow flickers against the side of his face. But I don't have time to observe much else.

He raises his hand. There's a bottle in his fist. Sloshing liquid. A tongue of flame hanging from the neck.

A Molotov.

His arm cocks back and releases.

THINGS ARE ABOUT TO HEAT UP.

Maybe he intends to throw it, but the distance is wrong. I stand there, flat-footed. My hand moving toward the butt of my gun. He doesn't lob the bottle. He christens the car with it, breaking the bomb against the roof like a magnum of champagne against the hull of a ship.

Tires screech.

A film of gas ignites across the top of the car. A wall of flame rushing toward me with a fatal hiss.

Then I'm on my knees. I'm crawling. I'm dragging myself between the pumps. The fuel pumps. Full to bursting with gasoline. The roar behind me, filling my ears, and in my fevered mind a mushroom cloud on the horizon, a timer ticking down to nothing.

I scramble to my feet.

Shouting, lots of shouting. Across the column of flame that envelops my car, I see David's car hemmed in by the tac van, a half dozen muzzles ringing him round. A half dozen voices yelling for him to get out.

I draw my gun. I rush toward them.

A shell-shocked station attendant appears from inside, Bascombe on his heels. Both of them wielding fire extinguishers. They step up to my car, releasing torrents of white fog.

"Get out with your hands up!"

"Hands where I can see 'em! Hands where I can see 'em!"

David ignores the stream of commands. His silhouette is visible behind the glass. He's rolled the driver's window up. His engine idles.

The last lick of flame goes out. The fog envelops my scorched car. I level my pistol at David Bayard's head, shouting with the rest of them.

He shifts behind the glass.

"Watch his hands!"

A ball of orange flame engulfs the car's interior. Bright as the sun behind safety glass. We jump back involuntarily. I see a head, a hand thrashing behind the windshield.

Bascombe bashes in the driver's window with the butt of his extinguisher, releasing a puff of fire. He sprays into the opening, reaching inside to unlock the door.

I holster my gun and take the other extinguisher from the attendant, following my lieutenant's lead. The smell of gasoline is sickeningly strong.

We empty the extinguishers into the car. I pull the door open. I reach with my free hand and grab at Bayard's clothing, pulling him out onto the pavement.

The writhing husk is unrecognizable. Red and black and bubbling. Twitching on the ground. Charred from the waist up, parts of him almost melted. I can't look.

"March. *March!*"

Bascombe's hand on my arm.

"Get yourself together. We need an ambo. Now!"

I stare at him, uncomprehending.

"He's still breathing, man. Call an ambulance!"

"I'm on it, boss." Aguilar. Over my shoulder.

I drop the extinguisher. I walk to my flame-blackened car. The top and passenger side are scorched. I pull the door open and strangely my briefcase lies unharmed on the passenger seat. Like nothing happened. I push it to the floor mat, making room, then lower myself down. The sight replaying in my mind. Immolation. He burned himself up rather than surrender.

One, two, three. Four, five, six.

I'm sitting in the passenger seat with my feet on the pavement, inhaling the odor of fuel and flesh. I rest my face in my hands, but all I can see is his face, his hands. I pull them away, and my palms are full of tears.

CHAPTER 29

If you play with fire . . .

Morning briefing. Then a debrief on last night's incident—me and Aguilar, the head of the tactical team, Bascombe and Hedges. Everybody's gonna write on it and, without dictating the course of events, the lieutenant wants to be sure we're all on the same page. That nobody questions what went down: a well-organized police operation that accounted for everything that could be accounted for. The wild card being the suspect's reaction.

Next to me, Aguilar takes careful notes. At least it looks that way. On his page, the same line repeated over and over. Cartoon illustrations in the margin.

You're gonna get burned.

A quip from an action hero, something he wishes he'd said on scene, when it could have earned him respect from the tac boys, and not thought of at the water cooler the next morning, along with everyone else.

If you play with fire . . .

Back at my desk, there's a voicemail from Gene Fontenot. There are four, in fact, left over the course of the last week. He hasn't tried my cell, though. Maybe leaving messages is what he needs to do. Maybe the last thing he wants is for me to pick up.

Monday AM: "You sure shot out of here fast. You ever heard of leaving a note?" *Delete.*

Monday PM: "Hey, I just heard about Charlotte. I hope she's all—" *Delete.*

Thursday AM: "Is it true what I hear, that you arrested your—" *Delete.*

Friday AM: "You are not gonna believe what just happened, man. Another notch on your belt, and you didn't even know it. Call me when you get this, you dog."

I cradle the phone on my shoulder, fingers poised over the keypad, reluctant to make the call. But I'm a desk jockey today, stuck in the office, killing time before my appointment with the head shrink. It's just procedure. Another hoop to jump through. The fact that I never discharged my weapon doesn't seem to matter. My reaction gave Bascombe "cause for concern."

Like it didn't concern me, too.

"You're not gonna believe this," Gene says.

"So I hear."

"Are you sitting down?"

"All day."

"Remember that ex-con you chased through the cemetery?"

"Of course," I say. "Wayne Bourgeois."

"Guess what? They found him."

"That's good." I know I must sound disinterested, but how much enthusiasm can I be expected to muster? I saw a man burned to a crisp last night by his own scarred hand, and saw him gurneyed, still breathing, into an ambulance. But Bourgeois did assault that young prostitute, so I'm glad he'll get the justice that's coming to him. I say as much to Gene.

He laughs. "Justice? He got it already, March. And it was you that dealt the card."

"You wanna explain yourself?"

"When I say they found him, that's exactly what I mean: *they*. Not us, not NOPD. We did our usual perfunctory search and made the obvious conclusion. The athletic young perp had managed to escape the clutches of the wheezing, middle-aged cop—"

"You're one to talk, you cripple."

"Hey, I'm with you a hundred percent. So anyway, a couple of days pass and Bourgeois doesn't turn up. I figured he was back in your neck of the woods by now. But we got a call this morning from one of the caretakers out at the cemetery. Said he'd found something mighty disturbing: one of the bodies wasn't in its crypt."

My eye starts to twitch.

"No," he continues, "Bourgeois never made it out. To me, you seemed like a tortoise out there running, but that boy looked over his shoulder and saw the hound of hell. He poured on the speed, lost his footing, and went on down. Crushed his head open on the edge of a marble step."

I remember the sound from that night. A distant yelp of pain.

"He was breathing long enough to crawl between two of the crypts, probably trying to hide himself from you, and right there's where he bled out. Our search must have walked right past him, and nobody shined a light between the gap."

"He's dead," I say.

"As a doornail. You saved us the cost of a trial, and if it was up to me, I'd cut you a check right now out of gratitude. But that's not how we do things down here. Anyway, I thought you'd get a kick out of that."

"Right," I say. "Thanks."

"Hey, March . . ."

"Yeah?"

"The kid did slip, right? You didn't help him along or anything?"

"Next time I'm in New Orleans," I say, putting the receiver down, "I'll be sure to get a hotel room."

Dead. A snap of the fingers. Just like that. One moment he's on his feet. He's actually winning the race. And then he falls and his head cracks open like an egg and he's down for the count, down forever after. Down, down, and down. No trial or conviction. No sentence to be carried out. A summary execution, a hit carried out by fate.

Evil and suffering. Inflicted on the evil one, on the source of suffering. They don't mean to him what they mean to us. There are things more important than living. Sometimes the blow falls like lightning from heaven. How are you supposed to argue with that?

And other times a killer, a man with no good reason to live, douses himself in gasoline, lights himself up out of nothing but spite, nothing more than the desire to deny his enemies the satisfaction of taking him. A certain death. Only he's still breathing. The blow hasn't fallen, the fatal hand is stayed, and the charred and blistered object of my hunt lies anesthetized in a coma, out of surgery and about to go back in, a victim once more, despite the blood on his hands.

How are you supposed to argue with that, either?

You're gonna get burned.

One of the keys to a long career in law enforcement is learning how to tell police psychologists what they need to hear without sounding deceptive. The only alternative is good mental health, which to me has always seemed too unrealistic a goal.

My chat with the psychologist goes reasonably well. It doesn't hurt that at the scene of a suspect's near fatal injury, an injury which I did not cause and only narrowly avoided myself, I made an involuntary show of remorse and disgust.

Bascombe might worry that I've cracked, but the head shrink gives me the impression I might be the last emotionally functioning human in the Homicide Division.

She's wrong, of course.

"Is there something you want to tell me about last night?"

"Like what?"

"Like Carter waited up and you never came home."

"Oh," I say. "Right. There was a development."

"You could have called."

"Yes," I say. "Right. I'm sorry about that."

"Where were you?"

"I was . . . thinking."

That's one way to put it. Another way would be sleeping in the reclined driver's seat of a half-scorched car, nauseous from fumes real and remembered, rolling over occasionally to glance out over the dashboard at the building that used to be the Paragon.

"Roland," she says. "Are you all right? You don't sound all right."

"I have a clean bill of health. It's official."

A pause. "I can't talk to you when you're being this way."

"What way? I'm not trying to be a 'way' at all. I should have called, I'm sorry. Something strange happened. You'll hear about it soon enough. The guy who broke into the house? He lit himself on fire. We had him cornered and he decided he wasn't going quietly."

"That's terrible. Is he—?"

"He's alive," I say. "Whatever that means under the circumstances. He was unrecognizable afterward. Like melted wax."

She draws in a breath. "Don't tell me any more."

"That's the reason I couldn't call. I had to be alone. I had to process." A good therapeutic word. "I'm not sure it's so terrible, though. Didn't he get what he deserved?"

"Roland," she says. "Are you going to be late again tonight?"

"No. I'm riding the desk. Working the phones. Following up on some loose ends for the ADA. We got a fingerprint match to the table at the scene. We might get more, now that it doesn't matter. I'll leave when my shift ends, just like always. Everything back to normal."

"I'll be waiting," she says. "And there's something else. Remember what Charlie Bodeen told you? About the future of the firm? It's official. You've been so distracted I didn't want to burden you with anything."

So I'm not the only one keeping quiet.

She waits for me to say something. I don't.

351

"The good news," she says, a thin coat of cheer on her voice, "the good news is, I'm starting a new job."

"A new job."

"I got an offer from one of the big firms."

"The 'unsavory BigLaw types'?"

"They're not that bad," she says, not realizing I'm quoting her words back to her. "They've been shedding associates like so much dead weight, but they still made me an offer." Pride in her voice. "A good one too, Roland. It would be quite a step up."

"That's great," I say.

"Only I'd have to go into the office. It wouldn't be the contract work. I wouldn't be working from home anymore. And there might be some travel involved, too."

"Good. That's really good. I'm happy for you."

"Are you?" She listens to the silence. "Because if you're not, I don't have to accept. I just thought . . . with you working so much, keeping such crazy hours, you wouldn't miss me if I had to pop out of town every so often. Or work a late night myself."

"I'd miss you," I say. "But it's good. I approve."

"I'm glad," she says. "We can talk about it tonight. I've been waiting to tell you, but I couldn't wait any longer or you'd have heard it from somebody else."

"I understand." A thought occurs to me. "There's one stop I need to make after work. It won't take long."

"Okay." She draws the word out, wondering if I'll elaborate.

I don't. "I'll see you."

"I love you, too," she says, hanging up.

I sit at my desk, staring at the computer screen, reflecting on the difference between what I said and what she heard. Like she wasn't hearing, or was hearing too much.

The man behind the desk is Hedges, the old version, wearing one of the boxy gray suits that disappeared around the time the promotion bug bit him. His bent Aviators hang from the breast pocket like he's just come in from the field, though it's so gray outside he might only have forgotten them there from the last time he wore the suit.

Bascombe sits at his right hand—or to be more precise, on the credenza over his right shoulder. The lieutenant looks happy, which is to say he looks mean. Satisfied to be playing bad cop to the captain's good. Back to normal. God in his heaven and the earth in its proper orbit.

"The DA's office just got a proffer from Bayard's attorney," Hedges says. "Apparently the father is ready to go on record against the son."

"That's convenient."

He nods. "Be that as it may, they want our input. Given the trajectory of your investigation, I assume you now consider the arrest of Bayard Sr. premature? It was the son who killed those girls, not the father."

"As far as I can tell, that's true. But the father bears some responsibility. At minimum he tried to cover up the son's tracks. He can't just walk free by pointing the finger."

"No," he says, "but if he's willing to plead on that, you're not going to lose sleep, right?"

"That's your question or the DA's?" I ask. Then: "Never mind. I don't care whose it is. I'll do whatever you want. It's not my call. Either it goes to the jury or they work out a deal. My bit is done. The real killer sentenced himself."

"You don't sound happy about that. Most people around here feel otherwise. Saved us the trouble of going to court."

Fontenot's sentiment exactly, talking about Wayne Bourgeois.

I glance down, feeling the weight of both pairs of eyes on me. I went home before coming in, changed out of my reeking clothes. But I still smell the scent of fuel on me.

Whether it's really there or not.

"He saved us the trouble," I say. "But I wish I could have interrogated him. Found out what made him tick. For a while there, he was going back and forth with me. I think I could've gotten him to talk."

Hedges sighs. He leans forward, elbows on his desk.

"It's not knowing that gets you, right? I understand where you're coming from. But there's one thing you're missing. Maybe you can't put a label on him. Maybe it's not enough to say he was insane or evil or a product of a bad environment. But in this case, there's one thing you do know. He's guilty. There's no doubt about that. And if you have that much, March, I'm not sure any of the rest really matters. To the sociologists maybe, but not to cops."

"You're right about that," I say. Hoping to believe it one day.

I'm outside the office, listening as the closed blinds rattle against the door, and it occurs to me I made it through the whole meeting without the lieutenant interjecting once. He must be thrilled to have the old boss back. So satisfied he didn't feel the need to add a single word.

I park near Rice Stadium and walk the rest of the way to the Medical Center. It's good to be outside, good to be walking, good to be alone. A few joggers dodge around me on the path that runs along University. A few cars zip by on the street, slowing down for the traffic stacked up at the intersection with Main.

Notes to self: *Get a Christmas tree. Buy some gifts. Rejoin the normal world.*

I pick my way through the Medical Center maze, approaching Ben Taub from the wrong direction. I pause in front of the Baylor College of Medicine, sit on the lip of the fountain, wondering if this is such a good idea after all.

According to my watch, it's half past six. Charlotte will be waiting, full of news to share, ready to catch up, to have her husband back. It's less than a week since Bayard broke into the house and nearly killed her, but she's coping better than me. Not that I'd have any way of knowing, since my solution to the trauma has been to pack her up to Ann's.

Note to self: *Spend a day with Charlotte. Do whatever she wants. Remember what it's like to be a couple again.*

I get up, brush my pants off, and continue the journey, taking the long way round. Inside the hospital, I search for the gift shop, not sure that I've ever actually seen it before. It's closed. I check my watch again. Now or never. Put up or shut up.

"What are you doing here?"

I turn. Kim Bayard stands there, clutching her purse like she's afraid I'll snatch it. Her husband, out on bail, comes up behind her, puts a restraining hand on each of her shoulders. He sees me and stops.

"Is something wrong?" he asks. "Is there a problem?"

Fear in his eyes. Fear of what I could do to him. Fear of what I have done.

"It's probably better if we don't talk," I say. "Your lawyer would tell you the same thing."

"What right do you have coming here?" She spits the words out, shocking her husband as much as she does me. *"What you people did to him is monstrous! It's inhuman!"*

He grips her tight, afraid she'll slip the leash.

I step back, palms up, too tired to argue who did what to whom.

When I'm far enough off that the curious bystanders start to lose interest, I wheel around in search of an elevator. Monstrous and inhuman. She uses the words like they mean something, like she'd recognize the things they describe. There's a recording I could play back for her . . . but there's no point now. She knows what she's been harboring. She knows where the guilt lies. Her guilt is what's crying out, and not at me.

I know a little something about guilt. I can cut her some slack.

I ride the elevator. I get off. I find a nurses' station and get some much-needed guidance, then ride the elevator again. The room I'm looking for is at the end of a long corridor. I pass one half-open door after another, names written on whiteboards, the glow of televisions over rumpled bed sheets. I pause at one of the doors and knock.

Reverend Blunt pulls the door open, his finger jammed between the pages of a book to mark the place he left off.

"Detective?" he says.

"Do you mind if I—?"

"No, no," he says, moving back.

The room is lit by a table lamp. Pinpoint lights blink on the machinery that flanks the bed. Blunt returns to his chair, setting the book down. He stands awkwardly by the rail, leaning forward slightly, hand knotted, as if he's presenting the patient for my approval.

"Still unconscious," I say.

"He could wake up anytime according to the doctors. Or not. The family's been in and out, his mother especially. I told them I'd stay tonight so they could make some long-term arrangements. They're hoping to remain in town until he's better, but his dad has to go back to work Monday morning."

I approach as far as the foot of the bed, pausing there, letting my eyes travel up the immobile form of Jason Young.

"He's in a coma, but not on life support. Like I said, he could wake up at any time. There could be . . . paralysis." He lowers his voice in case Young can hear. "That's something they don't seem sure about, the extent of the damage."

I listen to all this and nod. Not sure why I've come.

"We got him," I say.

He tilts his head in confusion.

"We got the guy who killed Simone. He's right here, in this hospital. He burnt himself to a crisp."

"Where is he?" he asks. "What floor? Maybe I should pay a visit. In a pastoral capacity."

"I'm not sure you'd be allowed to," I say, which seems to satisfy his sense of duty. "Anyway, I guess it won't make a difference to Jason one way or the other."

"You're wrong about that. He'll be glad."

"Well . . ."

"Speaking of which, have you heard? The man who did this to Jason, he turned himself in. Called the police department and confessed. It wasn't a bar fight at all—you were wrong about that. He was attacked by the man who'd been having an affair with his wife. I guess his conscience got the better of him. Though it's hard to imagine a man like that having one."

"It's not that hard," I say.

He goes silent, maybe sensing I know more than I'm letting on.

I grip the foot rail. Cold to the touch.

"I said some things to you," he begins, "the last time we met—"

"It's fine, Reverend. There's no need to apologize. I can't think of anything you said that wasn't justified under the circumstances. I'm just sorry he ended up this way."

"You're just doing your job, I'm sure. The Bible talks about that, you know." He reaches to the chair for his book. "The magistrate, I mean. The civil authority. 'He beareth not the sword in vain.' "

"Romans thirteen," I say, surprising him. It's a conversation I've had before, with Carter.

He cracks open the book. " 'He is the minister of God to thee for good.' "

"If he wakes up, Reverend, I'd appreciate a call."

"Let me pray for you," he says, setting the book aside and moving toward me.

He puts a hand on my forearm and raises the other high, like he's about to swear an oath in court. He utters a few lines in an incantatory monotone, speaking of my being lifted up and granted wisdom and kept safe on the mean streets. When he finishes, the man in black hugs me, his silver belt buckle dinging the foot rail.

Out in the hallway, the high-pitched gasoline reek strong in my nostrils, I run my hand down the wall for guidance. Past the nurses' station and into the elevator. Then home, home at last, into the arms of a woman who can say as much as I can about suffering and loss.

CHAPTER 30

SUNDAY, DECEMBER 20 – 10:29 A.M.

The man onstage wears a black robe. He stands behind a table of bread and wine. I watch through the winking flame of the advent candles, seated next to Charlotte near the front. I glance over my shoulder at the dimly lit congregation, hundreds of faces glowing from the spotlights onstage. His eager voice gives the ancient, dusty words an electric charge. Even a reluctant observer can't help being a little moved.

Smiling toward us, his easy manner cutting against the grain of the formal liturgy, he speaks the lines written before me in the program, which Charlotte tilts for my benefit.

"Let us proclaim the mystery of faith."

She joins the people seated around us in responding:

CHRIST HAS DIED.
CHRIST IS RISEN.
CHRIST WILL COME AGAIN.

A tremor goes through me. Recognition, maybe. Nostalgia. My strict and beautiful aunt lining us up in the family pew, Moody and I in our short-sleeved shirts and clip-on ties. Mouthing the words at the right times, or at least a rough approximation of them.

Behind us and to the left, Carter and Gina are holding hands. Young parents-to-be. Earlier in the service, when the strangers all around suddenly came to life, shaking hands and greeting each other, a small throng gathered around the couple, who'd just revealed their news. They'd swarmed me too, and all but killed the fatted calf, happy to see Charlotte's prodigal husband in attendance, however awkwardly.

This is what she'd wanted. This above all things.

So I obliged, even to the point of donning another of her father's tailored tweeds and letting her straighten my tie until the dimple was just right.

On the far side of the auditorium, a piano plays. There's a cello, a violin, even a flute. The congregation sings and the mood is very different than I remember from childhood. More joy than morbid introspection.

The worshipers in front of us rise by row, filing toward the aisle and then forward. Up front, the waiting elders and deacons dispense first the bread—"The body of Christ broken for you"—then the wine—"The blood of Christ shed for you."

As one row clears, the next rises. The people just in front of us get up, putting hymnals and programs down on their seats before going forward.

Charlotte leans closer. "I'll stay here with you."

"It's okay." I squeeze her bare knee. "You go ahead."

She glances at the Robbs, then takes my hand, only dropping it when it's her turn to go.

I watch as she edges toward the waiting sacrament. Carter and Gina follow behind her. Alone in my now-empty row, feeling more concealed than conspicuous, I see my wife cup her hands together to receive the bread. She places it in her mouth. She moves to the short line of people awaiting the wine, reaches the front, then accepts the little plastic thimble from the man in the black robe, drinking it down, her eyes fixed on the backlit cross above the stage.

She returns with a glow that has nothing to do with the reflection of stage lights, scooting her chair closer to me, taking my hand in hers. She says nothing. She doesn't have to.

In the time it takes for the whole congregation to go forward, commune, and cycle back to their seats, several verses are sung. I watch them all, the men and women, old and young, white and black and brown, perhaps with nothing in common but this. It's enough to make me forget the television hucksters and the paranoid conspiracists and the smiling, feel-good hypocrites, enough that I can almost see why Charlotte takes comfort in being here.

The minister ends the service with a benediction, his hands elevated. The gesture brings back Curtis Blunt's strange prayer over me. If he could see me now, in church for the first time in ages on the heels of his incantation, would he claim credit? I smile at the thought.

Afterward, lunch at the Black Labrador, where Carter casts a few loaded glances in my direction, uncertain what my presence this morning might mean. They all know about the fire that consumed David Bayard, about the flames that nearly caught me. Maybe he's telling himself that a near-death experience brought me round. Maybe he's thinking there are no atheists in foxholes.

What he doesn't know—what none of them do—is that a week ago today I chased a man to his death. If he did, if he knew that Bayard's melted face and the crushed skull of Wayne Bourgeois have coalesced in my mind as a kind of bogeyman, hidden behind the curtain of sleep, he might make something of that, just as the psychologist would if I were foolish enough to share. But I won't, and personally I don't know what to make of it. I don't know what to think of a policeman more haunted by the fate of the guilty than their victims.

"You're quiet," Charlotte says. "What are you thinking?"

What I didn't tell my uncle, what I've never told anyone, is that the day my cousin Moody stole that gun and ran away, the boys he was with threw me in the trunk. They did it as a joke, Moody egging them on, and after running me around the block a few times, letting me stew in the sweaty darkness, he'd pulled me out again, pushing me down on the curb next to his abandoned bicycle. When he reached out, I shrank away.

Come to me, kid. Don't be scared.

He had the gun in his waistband. The others looked on. I didn't know what was happening and I still don't.

You can go here and you can go there, but you can't go away.

But I didn't understand. Moody smiled an old man's smile.

You just tell him I said that, okay?

When I did tell my uncle, finally working up the nerve, he made me repeat the words back to him several times over. He never told me what they meant. Only that it was a song.

"Roland," Charlotte says. "What are you thinking?"

They all pause over their plates, silverware suspended, waiting. And waiting.

"I was just thinking there's something I need to do." I check my watch. "If you can spare me for the afternoon."

"O-kay," Charlotte says, probing.

"I'm gonna drive up to Huntsville again. There's a guy in the hospital I'm gonna try and talk to. A loose end to wrap up."

Her knife and fork clink to the plate.

"Don't worry," I say. "I'll come home. No side trips to New Orleans this time."

Carter takes a bite of fish, chewing, staring at the knots and grain in the rustic table. Gina slides her hand across to Charlotte's, clasping it in a show of sympathy. I pretend not to notice.

There are more hoops than usual to jump through, more assurances to give. Not to mention the patient's consent, which is given only grudgingly. After an hour and a half, after alternating expressions of impatience and inexorability—*I will wait, but I will not be denied*—I am escorted into the presence of Donald Fauk.

Seven years have passed since I last saw him face-to-face, and in that time he's aged more than I would have expected. A wizened, almost emaciated man, distilled by time and trauma into a bitter essence. Eyes lit up with a malevolent gleam.

"You," he says in a voice dry as parchment. Then to the corrections stiff: "Don't leave me alone with him. He'll try and kill me if you leave us alone."

The guard shrugs, retreating to the corner, nodding me toward a chair placed some distance from Fauk's bedside. According to the doctor, he'll make a full and complete recovery. Anything else would be too much to hope for.

I unbutton my jacket and settle onto the chair, crossing my legs with studied nonchalance, getting comfortable for the show. Fauk seems amused by this. He licks his lips. The deep lines in his skin take me by surprise. He doesn't look quite the way I remember him.

"It's been a while," I say. "I hardly recognize you."

"If you're here for another confession, you can pack it up right now. Unless you've brought your thumbscrews along. Have you brought them, March?"

"Don't worry. I'm not here for a confession. And if I was, I wouldn't beat it out of you. I wouldn't have to. We both know that."

He says nothing.

"I've been talking to a mutual friend of ours," I say. "Your pen pal, Brad. I also had a run-in with one of your messenger boys, a con named Wayne Bourgeois."

"So?"

"So I have a pretty good idea what's been going on. I see your strategy, and I see where it's gone off the rails." He snorts. "Like I said, I'm not here to get a confession. The reason I came is to give you some advice. I'm in a position to help, Donald. I possess a certain expertise."

"You're gonna help me? What am I supposed to do, say thanks?"

"You don't have to thank me. I owe you. You were decent to me when my daughter was killed. You didn't have to be, but you were. And I think that was genuine. That was the real you. You didn't have to, but you did the right thing. That told me something about you, Donald, something I wouldn't have expected."

He sneers. "And what was that?"

"You're a lot like me. No, I'm serious. I haven't done what you have, I'm not saying that. But you're a father. You love your kid the way I loved mine. Now mine is gone and because of all this"—I wave my hand in the air, encompassing the room, the walls outside, the prison complex—"you can't see yours. I got to thinking about that, Donald. I did some checking. It's been a long time, hasn't it, since you've gotten a visit?"

He turns his head away, gazing toward the barred window.

"I know what it's like, believe me. That's one thing I can understand. The longing that can't be satisfied. The sense that the cord between you, the cord binding you, is all but broken. We understand each other, don't we? We always did. And that's why I know that the man you're protecting, the one who did this to you, he's *not* like you."

"I'm not protecting anyone."

"Protection is exactly what it is," I say. "What else would you call it? By my count he's killed three women, but maybe it's more than that. He's smart, too. Smart enough that we never caught him, not for his real crimes."

"That's not saying much."

"Maybe not. We can be slow on the uptake. I can be slow. Which is why I need your help again, and why I'm prepared to help you, too."

He keeps his face bladed toward the window, saying nothing.

"You're playing this all wrong, Donald. I spoke with your doctor, and he says you'll be fit as a fiddle and ready to return to the general population. Maybe you're thinking your money will be enough to buy some protection, but it didn't help the first time around."

"I don't know what you're talking about."

"Here's your problem: Brad Templeton has some documents in his possession—which means I have some documents in my possession—that tend to implicate you. If you looked guilty before you got shivved, believe me, you're gonna look like a full-blown cooperator by the time you get back. I'm going to see to that personally."

I pause to find out whether he'll call my bluff. He doesn't.

"Maybe you're thinking your appeal is going to work. If so, you're more naive than I gave you credit for. We've got it pretty much figured out at this point. The disappearing evidence, the alternate suspect, everything. The DA can't wait for this to go to court, assuming it ever does. He's looking forward to a reelection-quality performance."

Again I pause and again he says nothing.

"What can I say, Donald? You're in a tight spot."

Nothing.

"Except for one thing . . ." I wait.

And wait.

Finally he cranks his head around, looking at me with blank eyes. "Fine. I'll bite. Except for what?"

"Except for this. You used it wrong, but you *do* have a card up your sleeve. And I'd be happy to help you play it. Let's be realistic, though. You murdered your wife. You confessed to that fact, and the confession is good. The court's already ruled it that way, and no appeals judge is going to overturn that—"

"My attorneys think otherwise—"

"They're paid to think otherwise. I'm giving you the straight truth. On some level you know that. You're letting hope get the better of you. Pursue this thing if you want and see where it gets you. At the end of the line, we'll be sitting right here, and I'll be saying I told you so. Assuming the next improvised knife doesn't do more than collapse a lung, in which case I'll be sure to put some flowers on your grave. You like them in a wreath or a vase? You seem like more of a wreath guy to me. Anyway, the flowers won't make up for being dead."

"I'm touched."

"You will be, and not by me. What I'm suggesting is, there's another way for this to end. No judge in Texas is going to set a murderer like you free. But you might get some time knocked off your sentence, and there are some considerations that can be made. You can be relocated, for example. You can get certain privileges."

"In return for what? Being a rat?"

"In return for staying alive. And in addition to what the DA might do for you, I have my own incentive to kick in."

He rubs a hand over his weathered chin. "Are you going to tell me what it is, or do I have to guess?"

"Your second wife. Your daughter. I'll find them and I'll do my best to get them here."

"That's it?" He laughs. "You think I can't do that myself? You think I can't send people of my own?"

"I'm sure you can, but it's not the same. Coming from me, your wife might actually listen. Coming from me, you might see that daughter of yours again. If that's not worth it to you, then I'll go. I'm sorry to have wasted your time. But if I were in your shoes, with death on one side of the scale and life on the other, with a chance of seeing the people I love most in the world . . . well, I know which way I'd go."

I've made my pitch for better or worse. I rise to my feet. I turn to go.

"Wait," he says.

I pause.

"What exactly would you want from me?"

"Not much," I say. "Just a name. The rest we could manage ourselves. We're not so bright all the time, but when we get our teeth into somebody we don't let go. All I need to know from you is whose leg I should be biting."

I look at the guard, nodding my head toward the door. He walks before me, reaching for the knob.

"Just a name?" Fauk says. "That's all?"

I draw a pen from my pocket and turn. "You don't even have to speak it out loud. Just write it down for me on a piece of paper and I'm out of here. Your name won't come into it, the letters you sent to Templeton will stay in his file cabinet, and when it comes time for you to go in front of the parole board, I won't be there to stand in the way."

He reaches for the pen. He takes a notepad from the bedside table. Glancing at the guard, he scratches the ballpoint across the paper. He takes the top sheet off, folds it, and hands the sheet and pen back to me. I put both of them in my pocket, patting the front of my jacket to show they're safe.

"You're not conning me, right? You will talk to her? All I want is for them to come back. To visit again. It's not right I can't see my daughter, March. You'll tell her that and make sure she comes."

"I will."

"You swear to God?"

I smile. "Would that make a difference to you?"

He holds my gaze, then snorts again. "You're something, you know that? I don't know what it is about you. If you say you'll do it, I guess I have to trust that."

"I guess you will."

The guard opens the door for me, then follows me out. In the hallway, Roger Lauterbach leans against the wall, arms crossed, his thumb and forefinger stroking his Fu Manchu mustache. As I walk, he pushes away from the wall, falling into pace beside me.

"Whelp," he says. "Did I just waste my afternoon or what?"

"I wondered if you'd come."

I reach into my pocket for the folded sheet. I open it and stare at the name. I refold the paper and hand it to him.

"Follow this up and you'll find out if the trip was worth making."

He glances inside. "I know this name. He was a person of interest in one of the murders—Mary Sallier, I think."

"Seriously? Then I think Fauk just made your case."

He gazes down at the writing, the paper trembling in his hand. Then he folds it and slips the note into his jeans pocket. "All right, then."

We emerge into the sunlight together, a charged silence between us, heading for the parking lot and the concentric ring of perimeter fences. When the time comes to part ways, Lauterbach lingers, rubbing the pavement with the toe of his boot.

"I suppose this is where I apologize."

"For what? Doing your job?"

"No," he says. "For misjudging you. I got my impression from the wrong sources, and maybe I didn't give you a chance to correct it."

"Don't get your hopes up," I tell him. "You just happened to catch me on a good day." I nod toward the note in his pocket. "Let me know how it pans out."

I head for my car.

"Will do," he calls after me. "Tell me one thing. What did you have to promise him to get this name?"

"Nothing I won't deliver."

He nods.

"And, Roger? Tell the sheriff I'm sorry about his conference table."

It's past dark when I get home. I slip my new key in the dead bolt, letting myself inside. The lights are on inside, but everything's still and silent. I call out. Nothing. I climb the stairs and pass through the bedroom door to find the side-table lamp on, the covers turned back. But no Charlotte.

The bathroom door is ajar, the wood still fractured from the week-old blows. A soft light filters through. I pause to listen, but only silence.

I peel my father-in-law's jacket off and toss it aside. Unconstricted. I unsnap my holster, twist the weight of the gun away. Drop my cuffs, my tiny flashlight. All the ballast weighing me down. And finally my badge. I untuck my shirt, undo a few buttons, and pull it over my head. I drop it on the floor, then undo my belt, letting my pants drop, stepping clear.

I feel weightless. Free.

I imagine her, sliding in the water. Lifting a hand perhaps, drops falling from her outstretched arm. I think of her hair pinned up, her skin flushed from the heat of the tub. Eyes closed and a smile on her lips. I picture her in the water, no one but her.

No thought of knives or pools. No thought of patterns cut into skin. Or flesh consumed by fire.

I stand naked outside the door. I press my hand against the fractured wood and listen for the sound of her breathing. I imagine her turning in the water, moving to face me.

I push the door wider. The tile cold on my feet.

But in the soft light, the room stands empty.

ABOUT THE AUTHOR

J. Mark Bertrand has an MFA in Creative Writing from the University of Houston. After one hurricane too many, he left Houston and relocated with his wife, Laurie, to the plains of South Dakota. Find out more about Mark and the ROLAND MARCH series at *jmarkbertrand.com*.